Just Thelma

Just Thelma

By
Roger Storkamp

Just Thelma
©Roger Storkamp 2005

Just Thelma is a work of fiction. All incidents and dialogue,
and all names and characters are products of the
author's imaginations and are not to be construed as real.

ISBN: 1-932993-24-X (Print)
ISBN 13: 978-1-932993-24-0
ISBN: 1-932993-25-8 (E-Book)

Library of Congress Number
LCCN: 2005933617

Edit and Interior Design by Mystique Design & Editorial
Cover Design by Star Publish

A Star Publish Book
http://starpublish.com
Nevada, U.S.A. and St. Croix, U.S.V.I.

Published in 2005 by Star Publish

Printed in the United States of America

I wish to acknowledge those who assisted in the creation of this fictional narrative, both directly or indirectly. Jeannie Cooper recognized early on a germ of poignancy in the characters and their plights, and she spent countless hours cajoling (for lack of a better term) language improvement line by line. Dennis Flicker, friend since grade school, gave his seal of approval and encouraged me to publish. Sun City Writer's Club of Las Vegas and Critiquer's Cavern through MSN internet offered patient assistance with many rewrites, each an improvement over the other. Also, I wish to acknowledge my hometown community, Pierz, Minnesota, from which I gleaned background material for the fictional town of Bovine, Minnesota and its inhabitants.

Roger Storkamp

1995

When a man with grizzled whiskers sauntered into Emma's Café, stopped near my table and stared down at me, I realized my homecoming was a bad idea.

"Davie Smith." He addressed me like I was still a child. "I'll be damned." He plopped down across from me, kicked back the chairs on either side of us and gestured toward two men who were filling three coffee cups at the self-serve counter. "Boys, sit down. Today, we're takin' our coffee break with Bovine's favorite author."

I felt like a stray dog about to be petted—or kicked.

"What brings you back after all them years?"

"Just checking on some old acquaintances." I struggled to recognize the face hidden behind the beard.

"Grins and me is old acquaintances." He cocked his head toward the older of the other two men, but his eyes remained fixed on me.

The man with the identifiable nick-name nodded, then squinted. "You didn't forget who me and Joe was?"

"I meant neighbors." If either of them lived near the farm where I grew up, their faces would be more familiar than my vague recollection of them.

"Neighbors like Thelma Rastner and her kooky brother? Those two codgers still live down the road a piece from your old place."

"As a matter of fact, I am here to see Freddie Tate." Joe's mention of Thelma and Iggy Rastner had jogged my memory. The Rastner family adopted Freddie when he was an infant, and Thelma raised him after her mother died. The day before I left town thirty years ago, I argued with Freddie here at Emma's Café. We'd have fought if Freddie's wife and five-year-old son hadn't been with him. My relationship with Freddie might be the unfinished business my therapist wanted me to repair. My muscles tensed as I recalled her note scratched on yellow lined paper following an apology for missing our appointment.

Take some time to explore your roots. Revisiting key events from an earlier time in your life might help build your confidence and develop your sense of self worth. Focus on relationships that ended without proper closure.

Returning to Minnesota to pursue proper closure wasn't my style. I seldom even said goodbye when my phone conversations ended. My childhood experiences were unpleasant, and I was loathe to relive them. However, after a triad of successful novels and as many unsuccessful marriages, my life was at a standstill. I could neither write another story nor chance a fourth relationship.

Repelled by her suggestion, yet desperate enough to try anything, I left the key to my Chicago apartment with my editor and tried to make light of what could be a serious matter. "If I don't come back in two weeks, contact the Minnesota Highway Patrol."

He snickered, "It's more like I'll be hearing from them, David, if you travel through the Minnesota hinterlands without a bodyguard."

The tinge of resentment aroused by his comment alerted my defenses, but I chuckled to express agreement. What I discovered at the café in Bovine that morning was no laughing matter.

"Ain't you heard?" Joe scooped sugar into his cup. "Freddie killed hisself and his wife. Long time ago."

Shock and anger erupted inside like the aneurysm my doctor predicted if my stress level weren't reduced. My disgust for Joe peaked when he described the effects of a shotgun blast on the human body while he poured cream into his coffee.

When Joe took a long slurp, the younger man said, "Freddie woulda blowed his kid away too, but Teddy was at school." He glanced toward Joe then Grins. "Ain't that right?" Our eyes met. "I knowed Teddy. Me and him was in kindergarten when it happened."

Joe swiped a shirt sleeve across his beard and moustache. "If you want the full scoop, talk to Thelma and Iggy. They still live at the home place." He winked. "Just like they was married." A smile emerged between dark bristles. "But, Freddie didn't do the job there. He blew his head off in Henry Tate's old barn." He gestured toward Grins. "Me and him drove out there after work.

8

God-awful mess." He shook his head and grimaced. "Got the wife in the kitchen while she was eatin' lunch."

I wanted to yell back that her name was Doris, but my voice faltered. Throughout my high school years, I bussed dishes at Emma's Café, and she waited on tables. I visualized the pained expression etched on her face years later when she apologized for her husband threatening me. I hadn't seen or heard from them since.

With dirt-encrusted fingernails, Joe penetrated his thick beard and scratched his chin as if in serious reflection. He asked, "Didn't you and Freddie go to the same country school?"

I shook my head. "Freddie finished the eighth grade the year before I started." I felt the muscles in my face relax. I smiled. It was an incongruous reaction to our discussion, but a safe haven from my past emerged.

Two columns of children faced each other on a playground in front of a white schoolhouse. I was a five-year-old who escaped the confines of my back yard to join the kids during recess.

Children's voices chanted, "Red Rover, Red Rover, send that little kid over."

The girl next to me shook her hand free from mine and said, "Red Rover is calling you." The others shouted, "Run, Davie."

They directed me to charge through the line of the opposing team who waited, hands linked. Trying to impress them with my best speed, I ran directly toward the tallest boy at the end of the line. I broke through and he dropped to the ground.

"Wow, for a little kid you sure are tough. You knocked me over." He extended his hand. "Help me up and you can be on my team." Freddie had imitated an adult imitating a child by falling down to please me.

That was the Freddie Tate I wanted to remember, but Joe continued to assault my selective memory.

"Say, weren't you with us that night we toppled Rastner's outhouse?"

"Oh, no. I'd have been too young to hang with you guys."

"Too young, hell. You were old enough to work here at the café when me and Grins dropped out of the 'leventh grade. As a matter of fact, you informed us that Freddie's family kept their outside privy. That was before him and Doris got hitched." He furled his brow. "Remember how that little witch giggled when we told her what we done?"

Joe had penetrated my defenses.

"I remember 'cause you said they probably used it for more important bowel movements." His eyes shifted to the younger man. "Davie actually said *bowel movements*."

I began to hate him.

Joe returned his attention to me. "It tickled the shit outta me and Grins." His deep throaty laugh developed into a hack. Spittle sprayed across the table, and he wiped his eyes with his sleeve. "I meant to say, it tickled me and Grins 'til we almost had bowel movements." He made a fist and flung it inches from Grins' face. "Ain't that right?"

His appropriately named buddy rubbed his chin. "Yeah, Joe, that's right."

My self-image as champion of Freddie's honor was shattered by my own youthful indiscretions.

Joe added to my guilt by reviewing the details of our caper. "We drove past the farm a couple times with our headlights out 'fore we parked behind some hedges along the ditch." His eyes rolled toward the ceiling as if a picture of the Rastner farm were displayed there. "Studied the situation a bit and then rushed the outhouse from behind." He pointed, nearly touching Grins' nose. "When we toppled it, this clown almost fell into the hole." Laughing, he slapped his buddy alongside his head and knocked off his cap. Grins merely smiled and put it back.

"But, the funniest part was Freddie sticking his head out through the hole and yelling that he was locked inside. It got a bit scary when Iggy busted out of house and blasted his shotgun into the air."

Joe leaned back, pointed an imaginary rifle over my head and faked its recoil. "Probably the same gun Freddie used to blow hisself and his wife away." He pursed his lips and released a gust of foul breath into the approximate area where the end of the barrel would have been.

He stood and pointed his make-believe gun at my head.

"Bam." He laughed and aimed it at each of his two buddies. "Bam. Bam."

I reacted with a stony wall of contemptuous silence.

Wordlessly declaring victory, he extended his hand, but my fingers remained gripped to my coffee cup. He rerouted his arm and adjusted his John Deere cap. "I'd like to hang around and jaw with you, but some people gotta work." He pulled a brochure from his shirt pocket, unfolded it and tossed it in front me.

"Out behind Cunningham Implement, we've set up a game of Bovine Bingo. Stop by. The heifer might shit on your lucky number." He stuck his thumbs under his belt, hitched his pants over his protruding stomach and walked to the counter, his grinning and groveling yes-men close behind. They paid the cashier, armed themselves with toothpicks and sauntered out the door.

I glanced at the paper on the table, and a graphic depiction of a cow, teeth displayed in a sardonic grin, leered back at me. She stood on a grid drawn on the ground and defecated onto a single square. Dollar signs splattered in all directions. I felt insulted and humiliated, my emotions as drained as my empty cup.

I took a deep breath, stood and walked to the pay phone next to a bulletin board peppered with notices of farm auctions. From a phone book that spewed open like an accordion, I found the number I wanted. I readied a dime for when the connection was completed. When I heard a raspy yet vaguely familiar voice on the other end of the line, "Rastner Residence," I dropped the coin into the slot.

Thelma Rastner, 1995

CHAPTER ONE
A NEW BABY IN THE HOUSE
(Fall, 1932)

When the Model "A" Ford turned off the gravel road and stopped in front of her house, Liz Rastner realized that her family would soon learn what she and her sister had decided.

"Aunt Martha's here," she announced to her teenaged daughter, Thelma. "We had better...."

Liz watched the car brake, then lunge forward. Martha's husband, Henry, had popped the clutch and continued to hold the steering wheel like the reins of skittish horses. He made no effort to help Martha out of the car. Didn't he realize how sick she was? Did he understand that his wife was leaving her baby to live with her sister? Liz decided to avoid him.

"Go help Aunt Martha and Freddie to the house. I'll wait here."

"Okay, Ma." Thelma skipped through the kitchen doorway into the front porch and peered out one window and then the other. She grabbed the hem of her apron and wiped the flour from her hands.

Liz followed her daughter and tugged at the straps of Thelma's apron. "Take this off."

"My apron, Ma?"

"Yes, let Aunt Martha see the nice dress you made."

Thelma hung her apron across the pump at the wash stand and brushed wisps of brown hair from her eyes. She rushed outside, down the walk and through the gate. Liz followed as far as the front step where she checked to see if Svez and their boys were unloading cornstalks, but the silage chopper sat idle next to the silo. She was glad. Maybe Henry and Martha would be gone before they got back. She reckoned Svez would accept her decision to take Freddie, but he hadn't agreed to it. When they talked about Martha dying and wondered what would happen to her baby, Liz hinted that she might take him.

He told her, "You can't just pass a baby from one woman to another like it was a stray calf." Filling silo and getting the farm ready for winter kept everyone busy, and she didn't have an opportunity to convince him that there was no other option. Maybe the doctor was wrong, and she'd just keep Freddie until Martha got better.

Liz ignored the commotion of the dogs, chickens and geese as her daughter waved to her uncle and ran to the passenger side of the car. Henry wouldn't even face Martha. Was he mad that Freddie was coming to live with her family? Didn't he realize his wife was dying? When Liz saw her sister struggle to stand with the baby in her arms, she walked a short distance from the house but resisted the urge to rush out and help. She watched Thelma take her aunt's hand, put an arm around her waist and half-carry her across the yard.

Their faces now cheek-to-cheek, a repeat of family traits Liz and her boys escaped, small gray eyes shielded by caterpillar-like brows and wide noses underlined with thin lips. Too homely to marry anyway, Liz and Martha's father said of the daughter who remained home to care for his dying wife and then to run his household. Until he found a young bride and had no more use for her. Henry Tate, left with two boys to raise, was in no position to be fussy.

Liz shook off her anger with her father and reached out to her sister who collapsed into her arms yet held tight to her baby. Their eyes met and gradually Martha relaxed her hold on her son. With one arm clutching Freddie and the other wrapped around Martha, Liz led her sister into her house.

****

Thelma hesitated, glancing toward the trail beyond the barn that led to cornfield where her father and brothers might appear with their teams of horses. She shuddered as her gaze settled on Henry, his eyes shaded with the brim of his felt hat. She took two steps backward, turned and ran to catch up with her mother, aunt and baby cousin.

****

16

Henry didn't release the steering wheel until Martha's brat of a niece stopped staring at him. He envied his brother-in-law for having a strong daughter and a healthy wife. Svez don't ever got to eat cold leftovers after slaving out in the field all day. And he's got four grown boys to do most of his work. He fought back a thought that had been haunting him. That little fieldwork during haying season ain't what made Martha sick. Doctor said cancer runs in some families. How was he to know she was pregnant? Her smart-ass sister better not blame him.

Henry wiped at the moisture that collected on the windshield from steam escaping the radiator, but it was on the outside. He got out and leaned against the hood to capture some of the heat radiating off the engine. He studied the length of his shadow and then checked the level of the sun above the horizon. Days were sure getting short. Frost last night put an end to the growing season. He pinched the peak of his hat, lifted it above the suntan line on his forehead and brushed back a shag of hair the color of year-old cobs. Gotta get the corn into the silo 'fore the snow flies.

He spied the chopper, its snake-like neck reaching up and into the rusted dome on the top of the silo, and he listened for the chug and whirl of the gasoline engine. He couldn't hear over the noise of dogs barking, chickens cackling and a gander extending his neck and trumpeting at him. In a distant hill behind the barn, he spied Svez and one of his boys, probably Iggy, loading corn stalks. That boy weren't quite right, but Svez got a lotta work outta him. Ain't fair, him getting his work done while Martha's using up daylight visiting with her sister.

He glanced toward the house and hoped to see his wife come out. Shielding his eyes from the low-lying sun reflecting off the chrome of the radiator, he saw a figure ambling across the yard. Svez' bachelor brother, Arnie, lumbered toward the barn. Bet Liz just tightened his truss 'cause he walked like he had a corncob up his ass. He didn't never go into the house 'cept for that and to eat or sleep. Why had Svez put up with that old bastard all them years.

"The Missus gotta talk to her sister." Henry rehearsed aloud what he might say when he saw Arnie stop and squint at him with his one good eye. He muttered, "Just keep movin' on. Me and you don't got nuthin' to talk 'bout. Bad 'nuff makin' conversation when the wife drags me here for Sunday dinner." He watched Arnie fidget with the visor on his cap and then rub his hands on the sides of his buckskin jacket already shiny as glass from manure, milk splatter and calf slobber. Henry sent a spray of tobacco juice toward a gander that

17

annoyed him and muttered, "Can't tell the difference if it's summer or winter by that jacket he got on all the time. They's goin' to bury him in it."

Henry glanced toward the field and then the house. "I gotta get out of here." Suddenly, he regretted allowing his wife to leave their son with Liz. He wanted more children, that was one reason he married Martha. He also needed help with raising his other two boys who were barely school-age when their ma died.

"Now she's gonna die on me too." He slapped his hand against the hood of his car. He and the boys could raise that kid after she was gone. He could find another old maid who'd be needing a husband. Afraid someone might have heard him he scanned the yard and barn. The louvers in the cupola flapped, and he suspected Arnie was watching him.

****

Martha worked her way along the kitchen wall back into the porch while her sister prepared a laundry basket to serve as a crib for her baby. She reached for the handle of the pump next to the washstand to gain her balance and glanced out the window just as Henry hit the car. Liz rushed to her side and caught her as she started to teeter. Alone, they're eyes locked and they held each other and they wept.

Martha pushed herself free and stared out into the yard. "He told me he approved, but I know he don't like it. Said if I died, he'd find another wife to raise Freddie, but I don't want that." She touched one of her emaciated breasts. "I got no milk."

Liz put both arms around her. "It's okay. We'll just love Freddie, and when you get better…."

"That ain't gonna happen," Martha sobbed. "I gotta go." She glanced toward her husband and then back into the kitchen. "If Thelma will…."

"Did you call me?" Thelma carried Freddie into the porch, his blanket dragging nearly to the floor. Liz covered him.

"Yes, please." Martha touched a tear that had tracked a line etched in her face. "I need help." Liz reached for Freddie, held him against her shoulder and patted his back. Martha wanted to hug him one more time, but she was afraid she'd change her mind about leaving him. She released one hand from the washstand near the outside door and touched the blanket covering her baby's head. She put both arms around her niece's neck.

"I can't do this alone."

18

Her legs buckled as Thelma helped her back to the car, lowered her to the seat and lifted her feet onto the floorboard. She thanked Thelma with her eyes and braced herself for a painful ride to her husband's farm. Thelma ran back to the house and stood alongside her mother. Liz waved with her free hand. Martha lifted her arm and let it fall back onto her lap. She had kept her promise to Henry that her errand wouldn't take long. She waited for him to get back into the car. She needed to go home.

****

Liz stopped waving and, reaching out to Thelma, pulled her close. She held her arms around what was now her two youngest children. She watched Henry get into the car, slam the door and start the engine. He held the steering wheel with both hands and faced straight ahead. She grimaced when the car lunged forward, and Martha clung to the dashboard. Henry maneuvered out the driveway and onto the dirt road. She wanted her sister to turn and wave, but she couldn't see through the cloud of dust.

Arnie's head poked through the hayloft door and then melted back into the dark interior. A team of horses trotted from the field toward the barn. Svez leaned on a pitchfork atop the wagon loaded with corn stalks, and Iggy snapped the horses' reins.

"The rest of the boys won't be far behind." Liz peeked into the blanket. "They'll be wanting their supper soon, and we got a lot of work ahead now that there's a new baby in the house."

Iggy kicked at a chicken that crossed his path as he strolled toward the house. He yelled, "Whatcha got, Ma?"

CHAPTER TWO
THELMA

"You guys better let that baby alone." Thelma whispered her threat, brandished the broom handle and shoved the bristle-end toward her four brothers clustered around the crib she had lugged down from the attic. "Ma, they've had breakfast. Make them go outside so Freddie can sleep."

"When he wakes up, he'll be hungry." Liz didn't scold the boys. "Don't forget to skim off some of the cream from his milk and add a teaspoon of syrup after you warm it." She opened the medicine cabinet above the kitchen sink, moved a shaving mug and held a bottle of Watkins hair oil up to the light from the window. She put it back, grabbed a same-size bottle half-full of a brown liquid and mumbled, "Martha will probably need this." She turned back toward Thelma. "His little tummy can't handle much food just yet."

"What about these guys?" Thelma glared at them and, with a swish of her broom, knocked all their caps onto the floor.

"Take off his diaper soon as he poops." Liz lifted the metal plate from the top of the cook-stove and stoked the fire. Sparks flew and flames briefly surged. "The boys won't hang around when that happens."

"You hear that?" Thelma hooked George's cap with the broom handle, scooped it from the floor and pinned it to the ceiling. "When Freddie poops, you guys gotta leave."

"Keep his diaper off for a while so he don't get a rash." Liz pointed toward the sink. "Be sure Iggy dumps the slop pail, and not just outside the porch." She fumbled with the handle to the

Frigidaire, opened it and peered inside. "Make the guys sandwiches for lunch and heat up leftovers for supper. If you need me, send George because Henry don't got a phone." She glanced toward their telephone, a wooden box Svez had nailed to the wall above his desk, shook her head and removed the shawl that was draped across the top of it.

"George put it there." Thelma stuck out her tongue at her oldest brother. "Said it looks like Father Reinhardt's sister, Stella. She holds her nose up just like that mouth piece."

"She don't blink her eyes, neither, like them two bells," George said as he grabbed for his cap and missed.

Herman and Ralph scooped theirs from the floor and held them to their chests like they were in church, but Thelma stomped on Iggy's before he could get to it. She felt a surge of anger as her mother walked out and closed the door behind her. George grabbed his cap off the broom-handle, hooked it to the back of his head and pulled the visor low over his brow.

"Heard Freddie peed all over you yesterday when you took off his diaper." He squinted down at his sister. "I'm gonna hang 'round just to see that." He stuck his face into the crib.

"Freddie peed on Thelma. Freddie peed on Thelma." Iggy danced around her.

"Good grief. Act your age." His age gave her an idea. "Okay, let's set some rules." She raised her index finger. "Only one of Freddie's brothers at a time can be in the house." She liked to refer to Freddie as one of the family. "George is oldest so he gets to be first." She started sweeping the floor, each swipe a step closer to her brothers as they backed away. "The rest of you, scat."

"How long 'fore I can come back in?" Herman peered at her through a screen of black hair. "I'm next oldest."

"Twenty one minutes 'cause that's how old George is." Thelma set down the broom and picked up a pencil and a Co-op weight-slip from her father's desk. "I'll mark it down on this scrap of paper." She pointed the pencil toward Herman. "Then, you can have twenty minutes, and Ralph can have nineteen minutes."

"That ain't fair." Iggy counted on his fingers. "George gets four more minutes than me just 'cause he's oldest." He pursed his lips. "You're the youngest, but you get to stay with Freddie all the time."

"Look at Iggy," Ralph faced his older brothers and winked. "His mouth looks like a hen's ass after she's laid an egg."

"Eggs don't come out from a chicken's ass," Iggy said as he covered his mouth with his hand.

The door opened and a crispy oak leaf whisked across the kitchen floor. "I'm the oldest, in case no one around here noticed." Svez seemed to fill the doorway as he walked through and plopped onto his chair at the head of the table. "I'll give you guys sixty of 'em to get that first load of corn back from the field, chopped and into the silo." He gestured toward the stove with his cup.

"You ain't sixty, Pa." Thelma grabbed Iggy's cap from the floor, tucked it under her apron and filled her father's coffee cup.

"No, but that's how long I 'spect to take for breakfast." He splashed the black liquid into a saucer, raised it to his lips and slurped. "Get out there and harness up both teams of horses. Arnie's probably got his wagon half loaded already."

Only Iggy hesitated. He stared back into the crib, wiped his nose with his sleeve and moved closer to Thelma.

"Well, whatcha waiting for?" Svez demanded.

"Thelma's got my cap."

She pulled his cap from under her apron and ran around the table. The second time they passed, their father kicked a chair into their path, and Iggy ran into it. He began to pant but, biting his lips, his breath gurgled and whistled through his nose. Thelma mussed his hair and stuck his cap on his head, visor facing back. He frowned, then grinned and finally laughed with his Pa and Thelma until Freddie stirred. She started toward his crib.

"Let Iggy get the baby. Soon's you get my breakfast, me and him can follow the boys with the second team."

"But, Pa, you said sixty minutes." Iggy turned his cap forward without lifting it. "That's a whole hour." He faced the clock and backed into Freddie's crib.

"You only get seventeen minutes with him." Thelma took the scrap of paper from her apron pocket and scratched off George's name.

"We ain't going by age no more." He reached into the crib, hesitated and pulled his hand back. "I least get 'til Pa's done eating." He gazed at Freddie. "Which end do I pick up first?"

"Go sit at the table." Thelma pointed, and he obeyed. "I'll bring him to you soon as I get Pa's bacon into the pan."

When Thelma lifted Freddie, she sniffed and set him back down. She took off his diaper and wiped his bottom with a wet cloth. She picked him up, naked below the stained band that covered his navel, and laid him on a towel in front of her brother.

"He's a boy baby just like Podue's a boy dog." He pointed to Freddie's tiny penis.

"Podue?" Svez asked.

23

Iggy rolled his eyes up toward Thelma.

"Yesterday, Harry Gross said he found a puppy in our mail box when he opened it." Thelma returned to the stove and cracked four eggs into the sizzling skillet. "He brought the puppy to the house and joked that there was postage due, so me and Iggy named him Podue." She set the pan with eggs still bubbling in bacon grease in front of her father and pushed Iggy's hand away from Freddie's penis. "I think Larry Collins put him in there as a prank, but Iggy wants to keep him."

Svez grabbed the pan by its handle and scraped bacon and half cooked eggs onto his plate with his fork. "I 'spose we can use another dog around here."

Thelma and Iggy jerked their hands back as a small stream arched from between Freddie's legs. Thelma ran to the sink, Iggy put his hand in his pocket and Svez laughed.

CHAPTER THREE
IGGY'S PROBLEM

Iggy crouched under the eves of the house and peered through a small crack between the shingles on the porch. His Pa had sent him up there to chase out squirrels that nested in the rafters, and he found this tiny opening. Through it, he saw the pump, the basin on the washstand and if he squinted he could see the hole in the floor where the mice came in. Mice weren't so smart. Pa set his traps by their hole. Thelma weren't so smart either, to chase him outside when she wanted to take her bath in the porch when the kitchen got too hot from canning. Iggy wiped his mouth with his sleeve. He chuckled when his sister glanced through both windows but not up toward his peephole. She returned to the sink and loosened the towel that covered her naked body. She let it drop to the floor. He silently exhaled as he waited for her next move, something different that she'd been doing since Freddie came to live with them. She cupped one of her breasts and pulled on the nipple like a baby was sucking on it. She don't got no milk, and that won't do the new baby no good if there ain't nothing for him to drink.

He tried not to think of how babies were made, and longed for the time when that thought hadn't been important to him, back when he and his sister could swim naked in the creek behind their barn. His mind wandered to his friend, Larry Collins. He closed his eyes and thought about one of their games of cops and robbers when he hid in the branches of the oak tree alongside the creek.

"Robbers don't hide in trees." Larry had spotted him right away. "They hide behind rocks and things. Only kids or stupid crooks hide in trees."

"I didn't want you to find me." He scrambled to the ground.

"Well, I found you. It was too easy."

"When I hide good, you quit looking." Iggy kicked a stone into the water. "I don't like it when you run home 'cause you can't find me."

Larry shrugged. "Sometimes, I get tired of playing that dumb game."

"Then, let's do something else when the game's not fun no more."

"It's not fun already. Let's swim." Larry swooped his arms as if he was either flying or swimming and ducked out from under his opened shirt when it ballooned in the wind. He opened the button on his pants, spun around letting them twist down around his ankles and kicked them into the air.

Iggy slowly unhitched the straps on his bib, let his overalls drop and stepped out of them. While unbuttoning his shirt, he felt Larry's stare.

"You don't got hair like me." Larry puffed up his chest and put his hands on his hips.

Iggy brushed a few strands from his face.

"Not up there, stupid. Down here." Larry lowered one hand over his penis and pinched thin strands of pubic hair with his other. "I got hair down there, and you don't got none."

Iggy covered himself with both hands and wished he hadn't undressed.

"Let me see." Larry shoved Iggy's hands aside. "I thought so. Nothing." He pulled back the hand covering his penis. "Wanna see what else I can do?"

That day down by the creek, Iggy wanted Larry to stop, but he was too astounded to speak. He wished he hadn't shown Larry his pubic hair when it began to grow. He had expected Larry to ask him if he had jacked off yet, or even make Iggy prove it while he watched. But Larry never made him do that.

As he crouched between the roof and the rafters to watch his sister explore her body, thoughts of playing games with Larry Collins faded. Touching his crotch, he glanced around to assure himself that Pa and his brothers were still in the barn. He remembered the time when Pa caught him doing that to himself, and he made Iggy feel bad by laughing and shouting something to Arnie. Even Arnie who seldom laughed chuckled, and Iggy cringed. The next day, his mother, not his father, told him to confess his sin to Father Reinhardt. That was a couple of years ago, and Iggy still hadn't told the priest.

But, he did tell Larry Collins one day while sitting on the bank of the creek. "You know, that thing you told me to do." Iggy pointed to his crotch, then shoved both hands into his pockets.

"What thing?"

"That time we went swimming."

"We gone swimming a lot." Larry pulled a blade of grass and slid it in and out through pursed lips.

Iggy's face reddened. "That time I showed you I had hair too."

"Yeah, what about it?"

"Ma wants me to confess to Father Reinhardt 'bout what I did."

"Reinhardt don't need to be told nothing." Larry stood, pulled the frayed stem from his mouth and grinned through teeth stained green. "Better yet, just tell him that you jacked off."

Iggy giggled, but he knew he could never say that in church, and he was sure Larry never said that to the priest either. He agreed that it was none of Father Reinhardt's business, but Larry's mother wasn't making her son go to confession. Iggy couldn't decide if he should tell Larry that he lied to his mother about confessing what he did. He knew Larry would enjoy that, but he didn't feel good about his dishonesty, and he didn't want Larry to tease him. If Father Reinhardt agreed with his mother that it was a sin and he must stop doing it, he would have another problem.

Last week, Thelma got to stay home with Freddie but his mother made him go with her to Saturday evening Devotions at St. Alphonse Church. As they knelt side-by-side in the vestibule, she nudged him.

"The line is short at the confessional. Go tell the priest all your sins."

"Aw, Ma, I don't wanna do that. Not now."

"Go. I'm trying to say my Novena."

Iggy got up and stood behind three other people waiting at the confessional. He felt his mother's eyes on him, yet every time he peeked around the pillar she had her head down with her hands covering her face. When it was his turn, he tip-toed in and fumbled with the curtain that hid him from Ma. He didn't wanna tell the priest what Larry told him to say, so he just confessed the things Ma usually scolded him for, like getting mad at his brothers, teasing Thelma and not going to Church on Sunday. He made up a number for the times he committed each of these offenses and ended by saying, "That's all Father." He learned this procedure when he and Thelma had gone to Catechism class. He was sure the priest suspected there was more, but he just repeated the memorized line, "That's all, Father."

When they left the church his mother asked, "Did you tell the priest your sins?"

"Yeah, Ma. I told him." He put his hands in his pockets, turned and stared up at the steeple.

"Did you tell him the one we talked about?" She touched his shoulder.

He nodded, faced the ground and wondered if she suspected he had done that sin more than just that one time Pa caught him.

"Did you say your penance?"

He nodded. Next time he was forced to go to confession, he'd tell the priest about this lie. He hated whispering secrets, listening to little bits of advice and being told to say *Our Father* and *Hail Mary*. He didn't know all the words to these prayers, and when the priest recited them in church he didn't understand what they meant.

At their car, she said, "Why don't you drive. And, let's stop at Emma's Café for ice cream." She slid onto the passenger seat and clutched her purse. "You did good tonight."

When they got to the café, Iggy rushed in and sat at a booth near the front window. The waitress brought two dishes of ice cream, and he gobbled his. He felt his mother's eyes on him.

"You don't go to Ida's, do you? You know, to do chores and stuff."

His face felt flush, and he heard his breath as it passed though his nose and mouth, something he usually got scolded for. "No, Ma. Ralph helps her when George and Herman are busy. She ain't never asked me to help."

He knew something was not right about going to Ida's, because whenever his brothers teased him about her in front of Thelma she always yelled at them to shut up. He knew why his friend went there, but Larry never said anything about helping with chores.

"Pa thought you might." Her eyes fixed onto his. "I don't want you to go there."

"Even if she asks for me to help? Her pa's dead, and George said her brother's too crazy to do any work."

"She never asks. The boys just go there."

Iggy watched a man get up from his booth, pay at the counter and leave. Two boys who sat with him got up and followed. He licked his spoon and held it like a lollipop as he stared at them through the window. They jumped onto the front seat next to the man.

"Do you ever hang around with Ozzie?" She touched the empty spoon in his hand and guided it back onto the table.

He lifted his dish, slurped out the chocolate colored liquid and mumbled, "Who, Ma?"

"That man that just left. Pa asked me if you ever hung around with him."

"I don't know who he is. I never come to town, 'cept with you, or Pa." He wiped his mouth with his sleeve and brushed a shock of black hair that fell over his eyes.

"You're just like your brothers."

"That's not what Thelma says." He grinned and a trickle of chocolate appeared from the corner of his mouth. "I think I'm just like 'em."

"She's probably right. You're different, but you look like them with your wild black hair always hanging down your forehead. You should get Thelma to cut them shorter. I hope you don't ever grow a mustache like them guys. They just wanna look like Pa. George started it, and now Herman and even Ralph is trying to grow one." She shook her head and shuddered. "With your dark eyes it'd make you look like the devil."

"I wanna look like a vampire. Larry said I'd make a good one. Will you make me a black cape sometime, Ma? Larry said all vampires wear black capes." He held up both hands, shaped them into claws and bared his teeth.

"Please, don't do that. It makes you look silly."

"That's how vampires look. Larry got this paperback, and we read that part."

"Well, don't make those gurgling noises when you breathe. I'm sure vampires don't do that."

"What noises, Ma?"

"Never mind. It's just something you do when you're excited. Try not to do that."

"Okay."

"Do you like Father Reinhardt?"

"He's alright, I guess. At least he don't get mad like Father Busch used to."

"Father Busch was just getting senile."

"Senile?"

"Just old. He wasn't in his right mind any more. Father Reinhardt's much nicer, don't you think?"

Iggy nodded. "But he scares me."

"Don't worry about that. You just tell him all your sins, and he'll help you be a better person. You did tell him everything, didn't you?"

"Yeah, Ma. Can I have your ice cream?"

"Of course. But, I'm afraid you'll have to drink it."

"I'll lap it like Podue." He showed her his tongue.

"Don't you dare."

He sucked it back into his mouth as she reached with her thumb and finger like she intended to pinch it. He enjoyed his mother's teasing.

But memories of ice cream, vampires and Father Reinhardt disappeared when Thelma moved from his line of sight. He knew her next move and, anticipating it, bit his lip to keep from crying out. Thelma returned to the mirror, held her flowered nightgown over her head and let it glide past her shoulders and over her breasts. It stopped just below her knees. He had watched her sew the nightgown from old flour sacks and wondered if she slept naked under the thin cloth. Since learning her secret, he visualized her nakedness under the smooth cotton material and imagined how soft it would feel against his skin. He hoped the little noises that, despite his tightly pinched lips, escaped through his nose sounded like the squirrels looking for their nests. He panicked when he saw her raise her head and glance up. She had heard. Did she see him?

He slowly edged his way down from the rafters and plopped onto the dry grass behind the house, his legs too shaky to run and hide. Visualizing Thelma running after him in her nightgown excited him, until he realized how mad she'd be if she knew he'd been spying on her. He didn't feel safe again until he saw light through the window in her bedroom. He wished his friend was with him. He had told Larry about some of his sexual urges, but never included Thelma when sharing his fantasies.

Once, after giving Iggy a detailed account of Ida's shapely body, Larry added, "…not all humpty-dumpy like your sister."

Iggy chuckled when he thought of Thelma all broken into pieces like the egg in the nursery rhyme. He disagreed with Larry's opinion about her body, but couldn't tell him without revealing his worst secret.

After that time Pa and Arnie laughed at him, Pa said, "You'll never see any of the animals doing that. That's not what it's 'sposed to be for."

But, *what it's 'sposed to be for* is what he wanted to do with his sister, and that frightened him. Animals from the same litter tried to do that, but Pa and Arnie always kept them apart. Iggy never understood why.

CHAPTER FOUR
ARNIE AND SVEZ

With his elbows pointing outward and his chin resting on the top rail of the hog pen, Arnie studied a dozen shoats as they shoved and grunted at the feeding trough, competing for the slop he had poured. One particularly aggressive young boar alternately ate and snapped at the others, and they gave him the space he demanded. Arnie hit him on the head with the pail and watched his reaction. Selecting a few of the others at random, he repeated the process until he felt satisfied.

"Which one do you think?" Svez approached the fence and being taller, stooped to rest his chin alongside Arnie.

Arnie paused, then nodded in the direction of the boar he considered right for breeding. A direct answer might damage his imagined thread of authority over a younger brother on whom Arnie depended for his existence. He continued to stare into the hog pen and waited for Svez's agreement. The bachelor brother made most of the breeding decisions on the farm.

Time had eroded each of their unique physical differences. Aging only slightly loosened the skin on Arnie's more rotund face, while excess flesh sagged around Svez's once taut cheeks and neck. Arnie usually shaved near the end of the week, even though he stayed home Saturday nights and seldom went to church on Sundays. Svez shaved often and kept his small mustache well-trimmed. Arnie's hair had turned from auburn to snow-white while Svez's changed from black to medium gray. Both men wore Oshkosh overalls, Arnie's jacket was buckskin, Svez's denim.

Arnie rolled his tongue over his upper gums and blew a flake of tobacco that had lodged in the space between his two front teeth. "That one." He expected Svez's approval. The end of his finger extended from a gnarly knuckle and pointed at an angle missing its intended target. "The one with the spot over his left eye." As Arnie stated his choice, the eye in the center of the spot briefly met his. Then, the animal continued to vigorously chomp into a mixture of ground oats and kitchen scraps. "He's too busy eatin' to pay any attention to gettin' hit with the pail. I think he's the one who chewed the ear off that solid one." An all-pink pig, smaller and missing half an ear, had been squeezed out by two larger animals as they stuck their front feet into the trough. Failing to nose his way back, he wandered to the end of the line. With his good ear erect, he entered the trough with all four feet and ate his way forward and backward, his snout reaching the corners neglected by the larger pigs.

"He's too smart." Arnie frowned, and slanted lines etched toward his drooping eyelid. "Hard to keep a boar like that penned up." He stretched his forehead as smooth as the jacket he rubbed with the palms of his hands. "Gotta keep one that just eats and fucks."

"Remember to separate that runt from the rest after he's castrated." Svez lifted his chin from the rail but continued to lean forward as if denying his full height. "Gotta get some weight on 'fore we butcher him." He put his hands on his hips, momentarily stretched and then resumed his normal posture. "I'll get the boys to move the one with the spotted eye to the barn so they don't castrate him by mistake. Jake'll be good for one more breeding, and then this one can take over."

Arnie felt sad for the old boar. Since childhood he named most of the animals, especially those kept for breeding. Jake earned his name after a guy from Iowa with that name came to their farm and offered only seventy-five cents each for a litter of piglets. Arnie baptized the sire of that litter in honor of Jake, the hog-buyer.

"You got a name for this one?" Svez asked.

Taking a momentary break from his usual hesitant and reclusive manner, Arnie produced a tight half-smile, turned his head and looked up from the rail. "How 'bout Reinhardt?"

"Oh no. Liz would kill both of us. You don't gotta go to church with her like me and the boys. I'll just bust out laughing when that damn priest gets into his pulpit and tries to scare us with hell and damnation." Svez paused and turned his head toward the house. "Every Sunday lately." He shook his head. "Wants me and the boys to go to church every Sunday." He shrugged. "You gotta think up a different name."

Arnie thought about naming the boar after Svez' oldest son who talked about getting drunk all the time, but he said, "How 'bout Buddy?"

"Good idea. That'll nail George good with all his talk about Buddy's backroom. That hole-in-the-wall ain't much better than this hog pen." Svez glanced down. "And when Herman and Ralph get the notion, they'll be nosing up to the bar with George just like them pigs."

Arnie reflected on the boar with the missing ear and thought about Svez's youngest son trying to squeeze in with his brothers. Would Iggy figure out a way to fit?

"That baby...?" Arnie didn't finish his question but waited for the furrows to deepen across his brother's forehead.

Svez continued to stare at the hog trough. "Liz's sister's baby. Freddie."

Arnie remained quiet.

Svez straightened and faced Arnie. "He's here to stay."

Arnie grimaced. He already assumed that Freddie was staying. He just wanted to hear his brother admit it. His hernia, not the new baby, bothered him, and he needed to get his truss tightened. He left Svez standing at the hog pen and walked to the house.

Although separated by a span of ten years, the two brothers had been close since they were children. They worked on their father's farm until he died and their oldest brother claimed his hereditary rights to the family homestead. Svez and Liz were free to marry and move to their own farm.

Arnie, then a forty-three year old bachelor asked, "What about me?"

Liz said to her husband, "Let's take Arnie with us to our new home." That arrangement lasted more than twenty years.

****

Liz was darning socks in the front room when Thelma stopped snapping beans in the kitchen and yelled, "Ma, Arnie's standing in the porch in his underwear."

"He probably needs help with his truss." She had begged Arnie to have the necessary operation to repair his hernia, but he refused. Instead, he found an ad for a truss in the Sears and Roebuck catalogue, his source for all items not available at Cunningham's Implement or York's Mercantile in Bovine. Arnie, who seldom bought anything in town and never went to a doctor, asked Liz to order the truss for him. She warned him that the cute nurse shown in the ad didn't come with the contraption. She teased him that it looked like something from the women's clothing section. She reminded him that his rheumatism and arthritis would make it difficult for him to reach the straps in back. But, she couldn't change his mind.

When the truss arrived, Arnie managed to get it on but couldn't apply the necessary pressure to hold his hernia in place. When he mentioned this to Liz, she realized it embarrassed him to ask for help, so she offered to take the place of the nurse that didn't come with their order. From then on, Arnie came to the house, waited for Liz to help him, grunted approval and headed back to the barn. At night and in the morning, he managed to remove and replace the unit or, as Liz suspected, slept with it on.

"Thelma, I think it's time...." Liz saw an expression of fearful anticipation and changed her mind. She must shield her daughter from this task. Reaching into the crib setting near the kitchen stove, she scooped up a sleeping Freddie and yelled to Iggy who idled about the front room and his parents' bedroom searching for Christmas presents. That year, Liz started buying and wrapping presents early, right after Thanksgiving, and she couldn't keep Iggy away from them.

"Arnie needs help. See what you can do for him."

Iggy responded, "Ma, I can't do that. You gotta do it."

"I'm holding the baby. Besides, this is a man's thing. Poor Arnie's embarrassed every time I help him. This will be your new chore from now on." Since talking to Martha's doctor, Liz had been slowly delegating more and more tasks to other family members, mostly to Thelma. Iggy's groan that began in the front room continued through the kitchen and ended in the porch. She heard Arnie mutter, "Just pull on the strap," obviously unconcerned about who helped him. Through the kitchen doorway, she watched Iggy tug, and then, without comment or permission, he ran outside, apparently forgetting about the Christmas gifts.

Still holding Freddie, Liz waited until Arnie hooked the straps on his Oshkosh overalls and then wandered into the porch. "I hope Iggy did you right with the strap. I'm sorry I had my hands full, and," she lied, "Iggy wants to be more useful around here."

Arnie gazed at the child in Liz's arms.

"My sister's baby." Liz waited for his reaction and it surprised her.

"I saw Svez when he was a baby, only he had dark hair. Ma said I had yellow hair like Martha's baby. But now it's white."

34

Liz considered the differences between Freddie and her boys when they were babies. All four of them had dark hair, narrow faces with thin lips and small pointed noses. Freddie had a round face and a small flat nose, similar to how Thelma looked as a baby.

"I guess all children are different, Arnie, but this one's special." Liz wanted to continue their conversation, hoping it would encourage him to accept her sister's baby.

"Ma said I was her special child." He reached and pulled back the blanket that half-covered Freddie's face. "Not special no more." As he walked out of the porch, she heard him mumble, "Not special, just different."

Liz followed him with her eyes all the way to the barn. *I bet you were her special child. All my children are special.*

Iggy appeared from behind the large oak tree in their front yard and wandered back into the house. "Ma, I don't wanna do that for Arnie no more. Let Thelma do it." He walked into the front room and started to inspect Christmas gifts again. He picked up each present, shook it and held it up to the light. Since no names were attached yet, he guessed and then asked if he was right.

Liz watched him and thought maybe he was a little more special than the others. Like Arnie? What did Arnie mean, *not special, just different*? Is that how he survived all those years? She remembered her mother-to-son talk after Svez caught him masturbating. Would Iggy turn to Ida? She knew her older boys went there and gave that ridiculous excuse about her chores. Could Father Reinhardt save him from that? From abusing himself?

"Please don't make that noise with your mouth. It makes you sound like Podue."

"I like puppies. Pa says George, Herman and Ralph are tomcats. I don't wanna be one of them."

"I'm sorry I compared you to a puppy. And, your brothers aren't tomcats either."

Iggy held up another present and asked, "Is this one for me? I think I know what's inside. Is it mine?" Not waiting for an answer, he grabbed another box and shook it.

Could her son learn something from Arnie? Could he gain strength from his differences, even power? Or had he already figured that out?

"Helping Arnie with his truss is your job from now on. You guys all have to pitch in and do more of the work around here."

"This one feels like a shotgun. Is it mine?"

CHAPTER FIVE
LIZ AND MARTHA
(Winter, 1932)

Liz sat with Freddie on her lap and forced herself to smile Christmas morning while Thelma opened her present. "It's your first store-bought dress. I hope you like it."

"Thanks, Ma." She stood and held it to her shoulders with both hands. "I love it." She carefully draped it into the open box and sat back on the floor. "I'm gonna save it for church on Sundays."

Liz looked at Iggy who clutched his unopened present and squirmed on the couch next to her. She was proud of him for waiting until Thelma finished. He had been the only one of her children who objected to her rule of youngest first when opening Christmas presents. He tore away the bright outer wrapper and the rounds of newspaper under it.

"A shotgun! I knew it." He aimed it at the ceiling and yelled, "Pow! I got me a goose. Thelma can fix it for dinner."

"Me and Ma already got a goose roasting in the oven." Thelma reached under the tree and selected Ralph's present. "Some chickens, too." She handed it to him where he sat between George and Herman on one of the kitchen chairs she and Iggy had lined up between the couch and the tree.

"That weren't a goose you shot." George, who sat closest, reached toward Iggy. "You just shot our poor little Christmas-tree angel."

Iggy gave up his gun and tilted his head toward the top of the tree. "Hey, Ma. Where's the angel?"

"You shot him, Iggy." Ralph grabbed his present from Thelma's hands. "But, that's okay. He didn't wanna be stuck on that dumb tree anyhow. How'd you like to have pine needles stuck up your ass every Christmas?"

Herman said, "Shut up, Ralph, and open your present."

Iggy continued to face the bare treetop. "I didn't..."

Liz saw the dismayed look on her son's face and wished she could protect him from his brothers' cruel teasing, but she realized that soon she would be unable to protect him from anything. Pity momentarily overcame her fear.

"You didn't shoot the angel. He's not up there because he's busy and won't be back 'til after Christmas."

"Hope he ain't out buying more presents." Svez stuck his foot out and slid the largest decorated box toward the captain's chair where he sat. He wedged his reading glasses onto his nose, studied the nametag and looked disappointed. "From the looks of this pile, you sure can't tell we had a bad harvest." He shook his head, glanced over his glasses at his wife and shoved it back under the tree. "Might be buying hay 'fore winter's over."

"I used egg money I'd been saving for a rainy day. I wanted this Christmas to be special." She turned toward Ralph who was fondling his unopened gift. "Besides, these are all the things you'll be needing."

"Needing?" Svez's eyes met hers. "For what?"

She ignored him. "Ralph, go ahead, you're next."

"Yeah, Ralph, get the lead out." George faked another shot at the tree and gave the gun back to Iggy. "I gotta get to Buddy's soon as we're done here."

Svez said, "Emma's Café is closed, and that includes Buddy's illegal beer joint in back. Folks would sic the Revenuers on him if he sold beer on Christmas."

"George gets in through a side door." Herman learned toward the tree, grabbed his present and leered at Thelma. "Buddy lets all his good customers in that way when the café is closed."

Ralph removed the wrapping from his present but set the box on the floor unopened. He faced George and then his father. "Buddy let me in one time. My moustache makes me look as old as George." Ralph pulled on a few scraggly hairs sprouting under his nose. He reached into his pocket, took out a jackknife and cut the strings from around the box in front of him.

"You keep talking smart and I'll pull them out with a tweezers when you're sleeping." Herman tore a corner of the colorful wrapping loose and peeked inside his package.

"You guys better stop talking dumb." Thelma squinted toward the tree. "Where'd you put the angel, Mama? I took him out of the box like all the other ornaments. Why ain't he up on the tree?"

Liz noticed that Thelma called her Mama, not Ma like usual, and the boys didn't even tease her about it. She put the nipple from the bottle into Freddie's mouth and wished her breasts had magically filled with milk.

"The angel took Martha to heaven, and hasn't come back yet." She knew her family didn't believe her. She also knew the angel would never again grace the top of future Christmas trees. He would lay side-by-side with Martha forever. She liked the image of a Christmas tree angel, pine needles and all, leading Martha to heaven.

"Your Ma don't need that angel no more." Svez stood and walked over to her and the baby. "She gotta new one. A live one at that."

Liz beamed.

When all the presents had been opened, and her family fussed with a collection of shirts, pants, tools, sling shots, one shotgun, books and a couple of baby rattles, Liz said, "Thank you for the nice shawl. I'm sure all of you pitched in to help Thelma knit it."

"I helped Thelma wind the yarn from the skein."

"I'm sure you did, Iggy, but I'm afraid Christmas wore me out. I'm gonna rest before we eat." She pointed at the single unopened present. "You boys take this out to the barn and give it to Arnie while Thelma prepares dinner." She pushed herself up with one hand on the arm of the couch and faced her daughter. "You don't mind getting everything ready, do you?"

"Course not." Thelma carefully re-folded her new dress and announced, "Dinner won't be ready for a couple of hours, and I don't want you guys pestering the cook." She stood and put her hands on her hips. "That's me, in case you don't know."

"Here, take Freddie with you into the kitchen where it's nice and warm." Liz placed the baby in Thelma's outstretched arms and pretended not to see her stick her tongue out at George. Through the archway between the kitchen and the front room, she watched Thelma carefully place Freddie in his crib near the stove. Herman grabbed Arnie's present from under the tree and ran out the door, Ralph chasing after him. George followed as far as the kitchen, paused and turned back.

"Thanks, Ma."

Liz glanced toward the top of the tree and waited for the storm door to slam shut, but all she heard was a gentle click. She then walked into her bedroom and softly closed the door behind her. She lay on her bed but couldn't sleep. Her emotions were drained, and only a nagging sadness remained. She realized she expected too much from Thelma, but she needed to prepare her daughter for…. The words failed her. Some girls her age were already married with families to take care of.

She turned her attention to Martha whose presence she felt and spoke quietly but directly to her. "I didn't marry 'til I was twenty-one and you were even older. You were Thelma's age when Ma died, and I wasn't there to help you. All those years, you stayed with Pa even after the boys left. And then, him taking that new wife. We all knew she's the reason you married Henry. In your thirties, what other prospects did you have? Poor thing, you were forced to marry an old man with horrible sons." She felt a surge of anger. "That's what made you sick."

Someplace between dozing and dreaming, she remembered Martha's sad voice from her hospital bed. "There are certain things I want to do before I rest in the arms of Jesus."

Henry cowered in the corner of the room and muttered, "She ain't dyin'. Don't need to do nuthin' in nobody's arms."

"I don't want to die in the hospital." She turned her head toward her husband. "Take me home, Henry."

He glanced down at his wife as she struggled to sit up and then said to Liz, "Find her clothes. I'll get the car."

"You'll have to check her out first. Down in the business office." Liz opened the small closet door across from Martha's bed.

"I 'spose they want money, too." He stormed out of the room.

"He gets mad at me 'cause I can't make him and the boys meals anymore. I don't think he likes our baby either. Yesterday, when the nurse brought Freddie to me, he left the room and didn't come back. Today, he told me he had more important things to do than watch me try to feed my kid." She looked down at her breasts, and a tear fell on her hospital gown.

Liz set her clothes on the foot of the bed and brushed strands of hair from her sister's face. "You can't help it that you got sick. And, you were carrying a baby, your first. I know that's not easy. Henry's got to understand that."

"He ain't a bad man. He works hard and wants what's best for his two boys. He took me in when I had no place to go. I couldn't stay with Pa and his new wife, it wouldn't have been right."

Henry stomped into the room and said, "Get her ready. We're gettin' out of here." He jammed some papers into his coat pocket and put on his hat. "Guess a fella can't pay for doctorin' with a few chickens and a smoked ham like Pa did when Ma went to the hospital. They charged me more'n the rent that north forty cost me."

While a nurse helped Martha get dressed, Liz and Henry stood in the hallway and the doctor explained her condition. "The pregnancy might have slowed her cancer somewhat, nature's way of favoring the unborn child inside. Her baby is doing just fine, but don't be surprised if her condition gets worse quite rapidly." He crossed his arms around the clipboard he held against his chest. "I'm sorry, but we can't do anything for her here that you can't do at home. Just make her as comfortable as possible. Is there anyone who can help take care of the infant?"

"I'm her sister." Liz watched Henry push the toe of his work shoe back and forth on the floor, his eyes glued to the track it made. "I can take Freddie for a while." She stared at the name printed on the white coat behind the clipboard. "Are you sure it's cancer? Martha's only thirty-five. Isn't that kind of young for that to happen?"

"Sometimes it just runs in certain families. If you're her sister, you might want to see your doctor for a checkup."

Not sure if she had been dreaming or if she was still at the hospital, Liz asked, "What good did doctors do for poor Martha? I'm afraid they can't help me either."

She got out of bed, dipped a washrag into the basin on her dressing table and dabbed her face. Maybe her loss of energy was a false alarm, and she didn't have Martha's illness. Dying of cancer didn't frighten her as much as leaving her family to fend for themselves. Would Svez remarry like Pa did and force Thelma out, or would he keep his only daughter at home never to have her own family? She told herself she wasn't going to die, opened her bedroom door and listened to the conversation in the kitchen.

She stood in the archway and asked, "Why's everybody squeezed to one end of the table?"

"We all moved down to make room for Freddie. I gave him my place 'cause I ain't the baby in the family no more." Thelma continued to carry platters of meat and potatoes from the stove. "I wanted to put him in my old high chair, but he's too little. We just pulled his crib to the table instead. I hope you don't mind."

"Of course, I don't. I see George is back." She sat at her usual place next to her husband and glanced at the new family member on her other side.

"Freddie didn't want me to leave, so I skipped Buddy's today." George touched the baby's nose and then sat down.

"I don't think you cooked a big enough goose, Thelma. Not if Freddie's going to eat with us." Herman grabbed the gizzard from the end of Iggy's fork.

"That's dumb." Iggy glared at Herman and stabbed his fork into slices of white meat on the platter. "He ain't got no teeth."

"His Pa ain't got no teeth either, but he eats okay." Ralph grabbed a drumstick, laid it on his plate and held his knife protectively above it.

41

"Yeah, but he's got special-made ones that he keeps in his pocket till eating time." Thelma glanced into the crib and sat beside it.

Ralph held the drumstick like a Billy club. "He's 'bout the same size as a goose." He ripped off a strip of meat with his teeth. "Maybe we should pass him around the table."

"Ralph!" Liz scolded.

"Sorry, Ma. I meant just to look at, not eat."

"Maybe he is a goose." Herman sucked fat off his fingers. "Did you ever see that stuff he keeps in his diaper?"

"I'd sooner clean his underwear than yours, Herman." Thelma touched the mashed potatoes, reached into the crib and let Freddie suck on her little finger.

"Herman's underwear weren't bad 'till I started him chewing tobacco." George grabbed the gravy bowl, covered his meat and potatoes to the edge of his plate and handed it across the table to Thelma. "Here. Give Freddie something to go with them spuds?"

Svez said, "That's enough dumb talk. Your Ma ain't liking it."

"I liked what George said about Freddie not wanting him to go to Buddy's." Liz reached into Freddie's crib and wiped the trace of potatoes from the side of his mouth. When she looked up, she saw Arnie standing at the end of the table. "Eat with us, Arnie. It's Christmas. I don't want you to eat in your room today." She pointed toward the crib. "Look, we got a dinner guest."

Arnie glanced toward the crib and made a coughing sound in his throat. Everyone faced him as he held his plate and waited for the food to be passed. With his free hand he spooned a large helping of potatoes and smothered it with gravy. He steadied his plate with both hands and said to Thelma who carried a platter of chicken from the stove. "Gimme a couple of them legs." But instead of turning to leave, he set his plate on the table and sat down.

Surrounded by her entire family, Liz whispered, "Thank you, Arnie."

****

Thelma realized Iggy needed to talk when he wandered over to the kitchen sink, grabbed the towel and wiped the plate she had washed and rinsed. She teased him. "I thought you'd be out shooting rabbits with your new shotgun. You aren't sick are you? Helping me with the dishes?" She brushed a soapy hand across his forehead. "Here, let me check for a fever."

"Hey, you're gettin' soap in my eyes." He wiped his face with the towel, walked around the kitchen table twice and returned to the sink.

"Was it bad to look at her?" When Thelma didn't answer, he went on. "I don't think I'd wanna look at the body. Did you have to touch it?"

Thelma closed her eyes and returned to the day her aunt died. Henry's oldest son, Herbert, had driven into their yard in his father's Ford. Ma cried, "Oh, dear Jesus! It's happened," and she ran out to him. Thelma waited until the car drove off and then joined Liz who stood and stared toward the barn. Without looking at Thelma, she said, "Aunt Martha passed away this morning. Run and tell Pa. We have to leave right away. Iggy can watch Freddie."

"Do I have to go, too? I hate going into Uncle Henry's dark and smelly house." She rushed to the barn without waiting for an answer.

On the way to Henry's farm, her mother explained what had to be done. "Aunt Martha's gone, certainly to heaven after her hard life here. But, there are things that need to be done to the body she left behind. The priest will do what's important, but we have to get her ready before he can see her."

Thelma imagined Aunt Martha's body lying on the bed, or worse, on the floor. Surely, Henry would have at least put her on the couch. The rest of her mother's instructions were a blur.

They found Henry sitting at the kitchen table drinking coffee, and he spoke to them in short bursts. "Good, you're here. She died in bed, early this morning. I sent Herbert to get you. My phone don't work no more. The boys are doin' the chores. I stayed in the house. She's in bed, in the front room. Couldn't go upstairs to the bedroom no more."

Thelma wished he'd stop talking. She wanted to follow her mother into the front room, but was afraid of what she might see. Henry suddenly became quiet, pressed his lips together and made grotesque movements with his mouth. She thought of Iggy who made faces to tease her.

"Damn false teeth." Henry pressed his thumb against the roof of his mouth, and a trickle of dark liquid ran down his chin.

She heard her mother call from the front room, "I could use some help in here."

"I gotta git to the barn. Go help yer Ma." Henry leaned over the sink, released a string of tobacco juice and left the kitchen.

The memory of it made Thelma gag as she stared into the soapy dishwater. Why did Aunt Martha let the men chew tobacco in the house? Ma never allowed that. Her mind refused to go back into the room where her mother had stood over Martha's naked body.

"Thelma?" Iggy twisted the towel and sounded frightened.

She didn't answer but continued to wash the plates and rinse them in the basin. She placed them on the drain board for him to dry, but he just stood and held the towel with both hands. He wadded it into a ball, laid it on the washstand and started walking toward the door.

"Yeah, it was hard to look at Aunt Martha lying cold and all blue in the face. I did have to touch her, but Ma did most of the work."

"Work? What work needed doing?" He stopped and gaped at Thelma. "Was she dressed?"

"She died in her night gown, but Ma had to take it off, so we could wash her and put on her burial dress." Thelma knew he didn't even like to see dead animals. When her father and Arnie butchered a cow or a pig, he hid in the barn until the meat was cut up into small pieces and ready for the smokehouse. When her mother chopped heads off chickens or geese, he looked the other way until they stopped flopping and bleeding.

"Did you have to help dress her?" He returned to the sink, picked up the towel and wiped his forehead.

"Ma made me lift Aunt Martha's head while she combed her hair." She was glad he stopped asking questions. The experience still frightened her, and she didn't want him to dwell on their Aunt's nakedness.

For a few minutes he just stood next to her knotting the towel. He put it back and said, "I don't think I could've done it." He walked into the front room and returned with his shotgun. He dug through the desk against the back wall of the kitchen and grabbed some twelve-gauge shotgun shells. "I gotta go shoot me some rabbits."

"Thought you didn't like to touch dead things."

"Rabbits is okay, if I get to shoot them." He went through the porch and slammed the storm door behind him.

Thelma picked up the towel and continued to dry the dishes. "I didn't think I could do it either, but I did."

44

CHAPTER SIX
SHIFTING ROLES IN THE FAMILY
(Summer, 1933)

Svez felt dumbfounded when Liz stopped the car beside the empty hay wagon where he had been waiting for Iggy to bring the team of horses.

She rolled down the window. "I'm going to see Father Reinhardt because I want to put Freddie's baptismal records in the family Bible."

"You're going to do what?" He jabbed the pitchfork into the ground and grabbed the car door as if he might yank it open.

"Freddie lives with us now, and I want to know that everything's done right. I promised Martha we'd treat him like one of our own, and Father Reinhardt will tell us how to make it proper."

"Course he belongs with us. You and your sister settled that last fall. I agreed, and even Henry went along with it. She touched his hand, and he pulled it back. "Reinhardt ain't got nothing to say 'bout that. It's our business, not his."

"I'll be back this afternoon." She let out the clutch and slowly inched forward as he walked alongside. "Thelma will take care of Freddie and make lunch for you and the boys."

"What if I need you when you're gone?"

"Well, you better get used to it." She sped out the driveway.

He yanked the pitchfork loose, tossed it onto the wagon and grabbed the hitch as Iggy guided the horses back toward him.

On the way to the field, Iggy snapped the reins as his brothers waved and cheered from the top of their load heading toward the barn. "They beat us, Pa."

"That's 'cause there's three of them, and only two of us." That didn't explain why they hadn't even started loading, but Svez blamed that on Liz and her foolish notion. And, what did she mean, *better get used to it?* He had stopped at the barn to talk to Arnie about it and then grabbed a second cup of coffee in the house. That was why the boys got ahead of them. He didn't admit that to Iggy.

He was still thinking about Liz's strange behavior while he stood on the wagon and caught the hay as Iggy tossed it up to him. Got to get used to what? There had been babies in the house before. He reflected and totaled five running the names through his mind. He wanted Liz to believe he had accepted Freddie just like their real son. That damn priest can't fix something that don't need fixin'. On top the load, he sniffed the air like an animal checking for danger when a pitchfork sailed up with the forkful of hay.

Iggy squinted against the sun, small bits of leaves and dust floating in the air. "Oops. That weren't just hay that time."

Svez gasped, "I gotta get back to the house. Get up here and drive the horses. I need my hands to stop the bleeding."

"What bleeding?

"You got me in the leg. Now get up here."

"I can ride 'em." He jumped on the back of one of the mares and slapped the other's rump to get the team moving.

Svez fell back into the hay as the wagon jerked forward, and Iggy forced the horses to a trot faster than normal for draft animals. When they got to the yard, Iggy jumped off and brought the team to a full stop near the barn. At the water trough, the horses drank while Iggy sloshed his face to clear away the sweat and dirt.

With one hand thrust behind the bib of his overalls clasped to the wound on his inner thigh and his other hand grasping the fork handle its tines anchored deep in the hay, Svez lowered himself down the side of the wagon.

He yelled, "Liz," forgetting, possibly wanting to forget, that his wife was away. "Elizabeth." He still refused to admit she wasn't home, as he leaned forward and limped toward the house. He felt embarrassed when he saw Thelma walk toward him. "Get your Ma."

"She went to town. Won't be back 'til this afternoon. What's wrong? Are you hurt?"

"Iggy tossed the hay, pitchfork and all, while I was on top the load." He had to look up at his daughter, and his stooped posture humbled him. "I just knew that as soon as your Ma left to see

46

Reinhardt, I'd need her. The horses are riled, and them clouds is full of rain. Ain't gonna hold back much longer."

"Iggy's getting the horses settled down, and I can help you."

He brooded. Baptismal records weren't reason enough to make a special trip to town. When old Father Busch was still pastor, women didn't run to him for every little thing. Matter of fact, Busch didn't hardly see no one. Housekeeper did everything, 'cept say mass on Sunday. Maybe she shoulda done that for him, too. Then he might still be here and Reinhardt stuck back in that school for priests where he couldn't mess in people's business.

"The fork got me in the leg." He purposely left Iggy's part out. "I knew something like this would happen just when your Ma's off to see that priest. I shoulda let Arnie have his way." He chuckled at the idea of a boar pig named Reinhardt.

****

Her father's reaction confused Thelma, and she was unsure how or if she should help him. What would her mother do? "I can help you. I'm almost sixteen, and Ma says I should start acting like a full grown woman." She saw blood seep through his overalls. "Come sit by the sink."

He went directly to his captain's chair in the front room. Whenever he sat there, her mother kept the family away to give him some alone time. Thelma stood in the kitchen, not sure if she should follow.

"Bring some soap and water and some of that iodine from the Watkins man. Find an old sock or towel in the rag bag to stop the bleeding."

Thelma froze. How bad was he hurt, and could she bear to look at it?

"Hurry."

Her reaction to obey overcame her fear. When she stood beside him with the washbasin and towel in one hand and small bottle of a red liquid in the other, she panicked. His pants had to come off. Flushed with fear and embarrassment, she assured herself that she could do whatever her mother would have done.

"Take off your overalls."

She played her mother's role in a skit like the ones the students presented in country school, but no teacher was there to give directions. She was thrust onto a stage with her father and no audience. He stood and unhitched one of the straps from the bib but couldn't reach the other. She hesitated until she saw how helpless he looked. She set down her improvised medical supplies and with both hands released the second hook gently easing the loosely fitting overalls down to his shoes. The blood had oozed and dried between his fingers that seemed to be glued to his inner thigh, and Thelma gasped when she realized he had thrust his hand through the inside of his boxer shorts.

"Good thing I weren't wearing long johns." He sat down hard, his feet still tangled in his pants. "They'd have to come off too."

She nodded, but couldn't help but feel her father was already naked.

"When I pull my hand away, put that towel on the cut to keep it from bleeding." He slid his hand back through his shorts and held it awkwardly in the air.

Thelma pressed the towel on the wound, then lifted it. The sight made her feel weak.

"It's stopped," she whispered and waited for more instructions but got none. She dipped the towel into the basin of water and, careful not to reopen the cut, dabbed at the dried blood. A bulge began to appear on his shorts, and she averted her eyes, fixing her gaze on his reddened hand protectively raised above her. It mesmerized her. She lifted his other hand from the arm of his chair and placed it on the rag.

"Hold this tight to your leg so the bleeding don't start up again." She reached up, gently touched his blood-stained hand and guided it into the basin of warm water. She washed each of his fingers and felt his hand become limp.

The image of the hand reddened with blood slowly melted into the memory of an earlier time when her sow, Tess, was giving birth. The first two piglets quickly squiggled out, but Tess seemed angry and snapped at them. Thelma shuddered when her father placed them out of the sow's reach and explained that they sometimes kill their babies. She had been used to the harsh realities of life on the farm, but not for what happened next. Her father rolled up his sleeve and reached into the birth canal. Her shock turned to delight as he drew out a squirming piglet, apparently angry about being yanked from its warm and cozy home. He handed it to her, and she felt warm liquid pass from his hand to hers. That same feeling returned as she held and caressed and washed her father's hand. She felt she was washing the blood off her little piglet, and she relished in the warm liquid as it oozed through their entwined fingers. He lifted her hand from the water and laid it on the rise in his boxer shorts.

Her hand found the slit, and she felt another source of wetness. She had hesitated to take the pulsating piglet, and now her reluctance embarrassed her. She felt his hand gently but firmly hold hers to the warm, wet, pulsating creature. She accepted the gift, hesitantly at first and then willingly, as she enclosed it between her fingers. Together they gently stroked it. She wanted to show her willingness to accept this rite of passage, but his eyes averted hers, and his whole body quivered as he leaned back and groaned.

When she realized what had happened, she noticed one of his hands back in the basin and the other suspended above her as if to protect her or, she shuddered, to slap her. She stared at her hands resting on his lap, cupped together as if offering or receiving a gift. She was not sure if she should show or expect appreciation. Her father gave no sign of either as he gazed toward the ceiling.

The rag covering the wound had fallen away. The cut looked ugly, but it was clean. Her hands needed washing, and she placed them in the reddened and somewhat warmed water. She waited for a response. She got none.

She covered the wound and wrapped yarn around his leg to hold it firmly in place. Again, she looked for some acknowledgement of their intimacy, but he just stared into space and breathed deeply. Years ago in a birthing pen, he had soothed her fears. Was it now her turn to comfort him? Is this what her mother meant about acting like a woman?

"Everything's okay. You can put your pants back on." He stood, reached for the straps to his overalls and pulled them over his shoulders. "Ma can check if I done good when she gets home."

She watched him limp across the yard toward Iggy who was still standing near the water trough with the horses. She noticed Freddie had tossed his toy over the side of his playpen.

"Freddie. You're a naughty boy. What am I gonna do with you?" She picked him up and held him so tight he couldn't move, but he didn't cry. *Mama, am I grown up now? It don't feel good.*

CHAPTER SEVEN
LIZ'S REVELATION

"Stella." Father Reinhardt had finished his daily reading from the Breviary and was ready for his morning coffee. He closed his prayer book and smiled when he heard a tingling sound that announced his sister advancing toward his office. He became a child again, scolded for tracking mud on her clean kitchen floor. A picture of his mother began to emerge from a depth of consciousness. Normally, these childhood memories were vague, only enhanced by the pictures and various stories his sister told him. This, however, was an actual vision of his mother talking to Stella.

Although blurred, he distinctly remembered her saying, "He's an eight-year-old boy. What do you expect?" He recalled how his sister's scolding melted into a hug and a visit to the cookie jar. Tracking mud into the house wasn't his crime this time, but would there be a cookie jar after the scolding?

Stella extended the hand she was not wiping on her apron and flapped a small bell up and down. Following the quick back and forth motion of her head, her salt and pepper hair momentarily flared and resettled into equal halves divided precisely at a part in the middle.

"I'm sorry, Stella." He stood, reached for the bell and placed it on his desk." I'll keep it in front of me so I won't forget to use it."

"Bring it with you to the dining room tonight. You do remember Frank and Gloria Lorenz are dining with you?"

He knew Stella encouraged his relationship with this couple, and he wondered if it was because they owned the bank, or because she considered their Spanish Catholicism more interesting then the usual German variety found in Bovine.

"Why don't you join us for dinner? They're really quite nice people."

"No, it isn't proper for the priest's housekeeper to dine with the guests. You just remember to use this bell when you want to be served. I'll have the pot roast ready around six. They're scheduled to arrive at five."

"Stella, you're not just my housekeeper. I hate to have people think that I'm excluding or hiding my own sister."

"Everyone in town knows that I am here, I can tell you that." A light blotch of red appeared on shallow cheeks. "Don't forget, I kept this house for Father Busch until he…." She made the sign of the cross.

Shamus glanced down at his appointment book, but he knew his eyes betrayed the smile that he kept from his lips, and it vexed her. Stretching to her full height, she reached the approximate level of his shoulder, his mother's hazel eyes glaring at him.

"Father Busch served St. Alphonse Parish when it was just a missionary post, and Bovine was still called Skunk Hollow. I was with that holy man for twenty years, while you were hidden away in that monastery." She took a step back. "Now, God has brought us together, and I won't let you discredit Father Bush." She shook her finger. "He was a holy man."

"Of course. I'm aware of Reverent Busch's holiness, especially after his reincarnation of the patron saint he emulated all those years."

She peered at him past her finger, no longer shaking but still pointing, crossed herself a second time and lowered her head. "That was terrible, Shamus, what happened. I knew his mind was leaving him when he asked me to call him St. Alphonse. That would have been sacrilegious, but I agreed to address him as Saintly Father. It seemed to satisfy him, yet he insisted the entire congregation be informed of his transformation."

"Did he really announce from the pulpit that Bishop Schweibach committed adultery?"

"I'm afraid he did mention it during one of the bishop's visits. First, he accused church council members of all kinds of sins and described punishments that would have made Dante blush."

"But adultery? Technically, that's not possible because the bishop's not married."

"Well the folks of this parish didn't make that fine distinction, or Bishop Schweibach didn't feel they had. He stopped Saintly

52

Father in the middle of his sermon and suggested immediate retirement at St. Benedict's home for old priests. If you remember, your first official task as pastor was to read the letter he sent apologizing for Father Busch's remarks."

"He didn't deny the adultery charge."

Stella crossed herself a third time. "Shame on you for making fun of Father Busch and Bishop Schweibach. Isn't it a sin to disrespect a bishop? Or, are priests dispensed from obeying God's second commandment?" Her eyes rolled toward the ceiling. "Or was that His fourth?"

"I'm not sure. I better ask Bishop Schweibach the next time I see him. Besides, I want to show him the card you gave me when I was ordained. The one that says, *NOW, I AM A PRIEST. IN CASE OF AN EMERGENCY, PLEASE CALL A BISHOP.*"

"Don't you dare. That was supposed to be funny. You better not keep that in your wallet."

"Of course, I keep it on me at all times, just in case of an emergency. It's got your name on the back." He watched lines of anger form on his sister's face as she abruptly turned and left the room. He summoned her back with the bell.

She returned and gave her imitation of a British butler, "You rang, sir?"

Assured that he had been forgiven, he said, "I'll be meeting with Mrs. Sylvester Rastner this morning. She should be here any minute. Please offer her some coffee and show her in."

Her lips formed into a tight circle, and he knew she was mentally gathering tidbits of information about his visitor, but he didn't give her an opportunity to share any of her interesting details. He sat down and began thumbing through papers in a folder.

"She said something about baptismal records, so I'll meet with her here in my office rather than the parlor."

"Of course, not the parlor. I'll bring her directly to your office when she gets here." She reached across his desk and retrieved the bell. "I'll put this by the chair in the parlor. Don't forget to use it." She flashed him a grin, turned and left.

Shamus seldom used his front room because Stella reserved it for special visitors. She encouraged him to associate with couples like the Lorenz's, or the Cunningham's who owned the John Deere dealership in Bovine. When his uncle from back East gave Shamus his used Cunningham Motor Car, Stella arranged for Victor Cunningham and the local newspaper editor to meet at the railroad station in Harrington when it arrived. A story with pictures of the two Cunninghams, the car and the man, appeared in the newspaper, and it embarrassed Shamus. Stella and Victor were ecstatic.

When Bishop Schweibach assigned Shamus his first parish he confided, "Your sister refused to leave St. Alphonse, and she might feel responsible for keeping you from a parish in a larger town such as Harrington."

Shamus thought St. Alphonse was frightening enough, and he was glad his sister wanted to stay.

"My argument about more opportunities to socialize didn't appeal to her." The bishop sipped some wine and brushed at the drop that landed on his cassock. "She reminded me that her vocation was a calling to the service of God's priests, not the community. Claimed she had worked hard to establish a proper distance between herself and the people of this town and, she didn't want to go through the process again." He filled his glass and gestured with the decanter, but Shamus shook his head. "I do prefer priests having their sisters as housekeepers, however, that's not the main reason for my decision." He sat back in his chair and folded his hands. "Quite frankly, it's time you got involved with parish work, and St. Alphonse is an excellent place to begin. You'll find it very different from being the chaplain at the St. John's Abby. Gracious, you've been a part of that seminary since you were ordained there."

Stella's cough interrupted Shamus' reverie. He looked up and saw her standing in his doorway with a woman behind her. He stood and glanced back at his appointment book to be sure he spoke the correct name.

"Mrs. Rastner, please come in. Has Stella offered you coffee?" He shifted his eyes to Stella, and she turned and disappeared back down the hall. "Stella's bringing coffee. I find it refreshing after I finish my morning prayers."

Because he was new to parish work, he took extra precautions when receiving a female into his home. He instructed Stella to remain visible but not obtrusive. He never used a woman's first name, except possibly Frank Lorenz's wife, Gloria, because she insisted on it, but certainly not a farmer's wife who he barely recognized in the congregation on Sundays. He worked with these country folks, willingly accepted the assignment, but discovered that they only came to him on occasions of birth, marriage, and death. He wondered which of these events brought Mrs. Rastner to his office.

His questions about the health of the Rastner family members were acknowledged with nod and a few mumbled answers. He felt relieved when Stella returned. Perhaps her presence might make his guest more comfortable.

****

Liz stared at the shiny coffeepot, two tiny containers for cream and sugar, and two delicate porcelain cups with saucers on an ornate silver tray that Stella placed on the desk in front of her. Stella's comment, "Shall I pour the coffee, Father?" unnerved her. She couldn't imagine calling either of her brothers, father.

"We'll be just fine. I'll ring if we need anything else." He glanced where he set the bell, now missing, and grinned. With an exaggerated movement of her head, Stella marked the direction that her body would follow and abruptly left the room.

Liz feared that she might be listening from the hallway, but when Father Reinhardt got up from his desk and shut the door, she felt embarrassed. He returned, poured coffee into two cups on saucers and handed one to her. She accepted it, but when she noticed her hand shake she immediately placed it back on the tray. She shook her head when asked if she used sugar or cream, and kept her hands folded on her lap. Shamus sat at his desk across from her and fingered a black prayer book.

"All priests spend about an hour each day reading the Divine Office. It's a wonderful book of prayers, and I like to sip coffee while I reflect each day's message."

She watched the large man delicately raise the tiny cup to his lips but felt too shaky to do likewise. She wished she was back at home with her family.

"Today's reading dealt with circumstances in our lives that create sadness. Yesterday's was about joy." He held the cup against his lips but didn't sip at it. "I find that with God's grace, joy and sadness are quite similar, both necessary ingredients for a healthy Christian life."

She realized he was trying to make her feel at ease, but she needed a direct invitation to speak.

"I hope the reason for your visit is one of the joy variety?" He sipped and placed the cup back on its saucer. "Perhaps this meeting is not about joy, but certainly happiness derived from sadness." His smile slowly turned into a frown. "Tell me about it."

This command cloaked in gentle tones unnerved her. Father Reinhardt assumed a totally different posture in the pulpit where she felt waves of fear pass through the congregation when they heard his commands for moral behavior, the very thing that kept

Svez away from him. Even she, who felt more comfortable with him than she ever felt with Father Busch, had trouble making the adjustment from Reinhardt the pastor to this Reinhardt, her spiritual adviser.

Unable to bear the silence, she blurted out, "It's about Freddie." She watched his frown turn into a scowl. She quickly added, "Freddie is, was, my sister's boy. I promised to take care of him before she died." She weighed her words carefully, not wanting to appear insensitive or unrefined. Was *dead* an acceptable word or should she refer to her sister as passing on? Certainly she wanted to erase the priest's inquisitive expression. She felt relieved when he nodded and his smile returned.

"I am aware of your act of charity. Your sister would be very pleased."

She felt confused and distracted. She watched him fold his hands, as if in prayer. He put his head down and touched his lips to the tips of his fingers, but his eyes remained fixed on her.

"Tell Father what is troubling you."

This direct command worked. The figure across the desk from her ceased to be a person and took on the dimensions of a religious symbol qualified to interpret God's plan for man, in this case God's plan for her.

"I'm afraid I can't fulfill my promise to my sister." She paused, not for effect, but to regain her composure, as she fought off sobs developing deep within her chest.

He extended one hand toward her as if preparing to offer a blessing and said, "Sometimes God can see qualities and strengths in us that we are not aware of in ourselves. Remember that God will never give us a challenge that He knows we cannot handle. With His help and—"

"It's God who's keeping me from my promise, not helping me with it." Her sobs surfaced in a mixture of anger and sorrow.

"That's blasphemy." He grasped the edge of his desk. "How can you possibly blame God for your failure?"

His reaction frightened her and between sobs she whispered hoarsely, "Father, I'm dying."

The priest closed his eyes and took a deep breath, and Liz ran out the door, past Stella and down the hall. She turned and saw the door to his office close and Stella was nowhere in sight. She didn't stop again until she got to the car.

Blasphemy! She understood the consequences of that unforgivable sin. Her fear turned to panic. Dying was painful, but the threat of everlasting damnation made it unbearable.

Suddenly, she needed Svez. She sat behind the steering wheel and felt enveloped in the seat where his body had formed a deep depression in the cushion. She inhaled his scent, pungent tobacco and acrid sweat. Finding a pair of his work gloves, she held them to her face and wiped her tears. A Scapula of the Sacred Heart dangled back and forth under a button on the dashboard, but it couldn't give her as much comfort as the gloves she brushed against her cheek.

When she saw Father Reinhardt's hazy figure through the screen door, she panicked. Overwhelmed by thoughts of her family, her house, and the animals on the farm, she jammed her foot against the starter and engine came alive. Father Reinhardt slowly grew smaller and smaller until he and the parish house and the church and the entire town disappeared.

"Father, I'm dying," his accusation, blasphemy and her desire to be with Svez, whose glove had found its way onto her hand, were whirling madly about in her mind. Blurred pictures began to assemble and reassemble on the windshield. Angels and saints, the recipients of many of her prayers, were choosing to show themselves. An image of Martha appeared, and she spoke to it.

"My dear sister, what are you trying to tell me? I see in your eyes the sadness and fear. I know that you're beyond those earthly things, yet I feel your concern for me, and for your son. Why has God...?"

She suddenly realized that wisps of steam had created these images. She forgot to put water in the radiator. Svez had cautioned her about the leaky hose, and her carelessness jolted her back to reality. Her mind had played tricks on her. She shut off the engine and let the car coast to the bottom of the hill near a small pond. However, the fading images still frightened her. The steam would continue, she knew, until the car cooled enough for her to add water and drive the last two miles. She needed the comfort and safety of home. She allowed her mind to create the faces of her family in the waves of steam advancing and retreating in front of her, and a final burst resembled the image of a cross dripping slowly downward. The engine had cooled enough to add water. She found an empty can in the trunk, filled it from the pond and poured it into the radiator. She continued her journey home where everything would be in order.

CHAPTER EIGHT
DEATH IN THE FAMILY

Liz studied her family seated at the supper table, and she felt her emotions rise and fall in waves of fear followed by anger. She decided her children were nearly full-grown and could get along without her, but she worried about Freddie. Thelma would be there to take care of him, but she'd have her hands full feeding and caring for Svez and the boys. And Iggy. What would become of him?

Her anger crested, and she challenged God's plan for her. Why did He decide to take her when there were so many others who aren't needed? She had been a good mother and a faithful Christian. She didn't deserve to be punished. God ain't fair. She remembered the shocked expression on Father Reinhardt's face and his charge of blasphemy. She became fearful for her salvation.

She whispered, "Jesus, Mary, Joseph, save me." She glanced around the table, but no one seemed to hear her.

Mary, mother of God, would intercede. All the Novenas she had made throughout her life should count for something. Reassured by her faith, she felt certain that God wouldn't abandon her. The same kind of determination that helped her survive the rigors of farm life would get her through this crisis. She refused to die. God would help her destroy this demon that attacked her body.

Her fear receded, but she felt her face flush from her anger. She remembered when her father raised his fist and cursed God because things went wrong on his farm. Was she becoming just like him? She remembered the razor-strap and the howls from her brothers when he punished them with it. She refused to cry when he hit her, but she shed tears when he died. May God have mercy on both their souls.

Relieved that her husband and not her father sat next to her, she whispered, "Svez," but through the din of conversation he didn't answer her call for help. When they were first married, Liz felt she had been passed from one man to another at the altar, but she soon realized Svez was different. He expected a lot from her, but never demanded anything. He even listened to her advice when making major decisions.

Another wave of fear passed through her, and suddenly she felt guilt. She had made a very important decision without consulting him, and she wouldn't be around to take responsibility for it. Why didn't she ask permission to take Freddie into their home? At least, tell him what she intended to do?

In her mind, she heard him laugh and say, "You want another baby? Why not? There's always room for one more."

She wished she had asked him. She glanced at him hoping for some sign of approval but he appeared distant, even unapproachable. Yet, she found comfort in his presence and in her knowledge that he had always been a good father to the children. He gave Arnie a home when their parents died and treated him like one of their family for more than twenty years. He would do the same for Freddie.

She glanced at Arnie's empty chair and then across to Iggy. Those two weren't so different, always got what they wanted. When she scanned the men surrounding her and her daughter, she realized they all got whatever they wanted. That uncharitable thought increased her feelings of guilt.

She knew her husband was angry with her for seeking help from the priest and that it was wrong to lie about her reasons for doing it. Some important matters like her being pregnant and, she shuddered, dying should be first shared with him. Maybe he already knew. He always claimed to have a sixth sense that told him if any of the animals were sick or in some kind of trouble, even before he got up in the morning. They just sort of talked to him.

She glanced at him without lifting her head and whispered, "We're your animals, too."

"Huh?" His eyes seemed fixed to the food left on his plate.

She felt another wave of emotion, went to the stove to replenish the meat and potatoes, and wiped her eyes with her apron. She listened to her family discuss an incident that deeply troubled her, but she hadn't yet sorted through the details.

"I hear Iggy almost put Pa outta commission with a pitchfork. He shoulda had some of this sticky stuff on his hands." George poured the last of the syrup onto his bread, grinned at Iggy and handed him the empty bottle.

Iggy held it over his plate and stared at the few drips that landed on his sausage.

Herman poked Ralph. "The news must have gotten to Buddy's if George heard about it."

"George didn't hear it at the bar 'cause he weren't there today." Ralph grinned at Thelma. "Besides, he just goes there to sleep." His eyes roved from Herman to George. "We knowed you slept there one night, and Pa had to fetch you the next morning."

"That's right, and when you guys dry out behind the ears, you can join me."

Thelma said, "Well, at least you'll have company."

"What makes you think I was alone? Mildred from the bank came to spend the night with me." Herman and Ralph laughed, Iggy giggled, and Svez grimaced.

Liz remembered the incident. Buddy had called and woke Svez and her in the middle of the night. She heard Svez tell him that George paid enough rent to sleep there 'til morning when he'd fetch him on his way to the Co-op. She laughed when he yelled at the rubbernecks on their party line to go back to bed 'cause the show was over. She knew he had solved the problem, and waited anxiously for him to come back to bed and tell her about it. Their bed was that sacred place where they shared each other and discussed problems that came up during the day. She felt blessed to be included in her husband's business; not many other wives she knew were that lucky. Who will he talk to about important matters when she was gone? Another wave of denial swept through her. Please, dear Jesus.

Iggy held the syrup bottle to the light and peered into it. He stuck his finger inside, put it into his mouth and made a popping sound as he pulled it out. "It were an accident, what happened today." He wiped his hand on his shirt. "Thelma fixed Pa's leg, real good." Thelma jumped up and went into the front room. Svez said nothing, but his face flushed, and he redirected the conversation.

"That's 'enough stuff 'bout Buddy's. Talk 'bout something nice for a change."

Her husband's annoyance with the boys' teasing surprised Liz, and Iggy's comment brought back the unsettling matter of the accident. Earlier, when she asked to see the wound, Svez said, "It's nothing. You can check it tonight."

Thelma returned to the kitchen holding Freddie who appeared to be sleeping. "Pa hurt his leg like I told you, Ma, and I helped him fix it. I did so good that Pa and Iggy went right back to work in the field."

"Was Freddie fussy?" Liz stooped to pick up the end of the blanket that trailed onto the floor.

"No, Ma. He never fusses." Liz took him from Thelma and placed him in his playpen. Her intuition warned her that something had happened while she was away, but she buried her fear in a secret compartment in her mind.

George said, "Thelma, them was peaches I saw you canning yesterday. Why don't Iggy run down to the cellar to get some?"

"Ma, tell George they're for next winter. There won't be any left if we start breaking them open already."

Liz didn't respond. She just stood and stared into the playpen.

"Iggy, get some of them peaches." George spoke with the authority of an oldest child.

Iggy said, "Soon's I finish supper."

Thelma looked at her mother and then said to Iggy, "Ya gotta tap the lids. We need to open them first that didn't seal proper."

"Is Arnie eating in his room again?" Svez glanced up and asked.

The sound of his voice pulled Liz back from behind her walled-in hiding place. "I think having the baby in the house is making him edgy. Maybe he feels there won't be room for him now that Freddie's with us."

She had planned to share this feeling with him in bed, but an engulfing cloud kept her from discussing her concern for her brother-in-law.

"I'll talk to him tonight in the barn."

All conversation stopped when Arnie entered the room, paused as if he were about to say something, but merely passed through the kitchen and out the porch on his way to the barn.

Thelma said, "He didn't bring his cup and plate down with him."

"He never does." Liz returned to the table. "You gotta fetch them."

"He gets mad at me when I mess with his stuff, and I know he's got a lot of dirty dishes in his room, some with bits of his supper still on them. Always tells me he ain't done yet. Likes to save something for late at night when he gets hungry."

George said, "You better get them, 'fore an army of mice clean them for you. Counted 'bout twenty of them little critters crawl out of Iggy's bed this morning and head to Arnie's room."

"Talking 'bout mice in my bed don't bother me none. I can just keep eating."

Herman said, "Naw, them ain't mice that Iggy keeps in his bed. Them's the squirrels he kicked out of the rafters above the porch." His eyes fixed on Thelma. "Still goes up there every night to see they don't come back."

Iggy jumped up and sulked out to the porch. He came back and said, "I gotta get them peaches for George."

Liz asked, "What's come over you? Just settle down."

"Them ain't mice or squirrels, Herman. Them's little piggies sticking their heads out from under Iggy's covers." Ralph lifted his foot and touched the tip of his shoe. "This little piggy went to market, this little piggy stayed home." His eyes followed Iggy until he disappeared through the open trap door to the basement and then fixed on Thelma. "Remember when you pretended his toes were little piggies and you squeezed them 'til he got off giggling?"

Thelma jumped away from the table, walked to the stove with her plate, but immediately came back with it still empty.

"Now what's the matter with you? Has everyone gone crazy?" Liz tossed her hands into the air.

"Pa hurt his leg today, and I helped him fix it real good, Ma."

Liz said, "I know...." Svez stood, but she stopped him before he left the kitchen. "Sit back down. We got some things to talk about, as a family."

Svez mumbled, "Gotta get the chores..." but he plopped onto his chair.

****

As Father Reinhardt turned his car into the driveway, he saw an older man in a buckskin jacket stand rigidly near the gate that separated the house from the barnyard. That must be the brother. Stella had said Svez was quite tall. The man faced the car until it came to a full stop, and then he continued across the yard. When Shamus rolled down the window, cleared his throat and said, "Good afternoon," the man turned his head, rubbed his palms on the sides of his jacket and hurried toward the barn.

"It must be this darn car," he muttered to himself. "Times like this I wish I had my Ford back." The rich aroma of leather and cigar smoke blended with the earthy smells of the farm and created an inharmonious blend much like the confusion and uncertainty he felt. He checked for dogs and measured the distance to the open door of the white farmhouse. The bare ground where chickens and geese scratched and pecked at tiny insects contrasted with the grass and shrubs surrounding the house inside the fenced area. He scanned the area again, but other than the two dogs that followed the man into the barn, none were visible.

As he approached the house, he saw people sitting at a table and heard the murmur of conversation. This would be his opportunity to talk to both husband and wife, and maybe repair the injury he may have inflicted on Mrs. Rastner earlier that day. Her disclosure and quick departure left him sitting at his desk, unable to offer words of comfort, unable to offer any words at all to this distressed member of his flock. By the time he explained the situation to Stella, and agreed to say a short prayer for Mrs. Rastner's soul, she had escaped. He now wished he had followed her to the parking lot instead of listening to his sister.

He had failed her and now, away from his element at the rectory, he felt like an outsider, as out of place as his ostentatious car. Yet, he was determined to do the right thing for this family. They were his parishioners, and he had been charged with the responsibility of taking Christ's message of peace to them. He braced himself for the strong odors from the food popular with country folks and the sparse interiors of their homes. He entered the porch and held his hat in front of him with both hands.

"Knock. Knock." He announced his presence and leaned forward, peering into the kitchen. Everyone stopped talking and faced him. He felt awkward standing in their doorway with the sun on his back, dressed in black and wearing a cape rather than a coat. He opened his mouth to start a conversation about families breaking bread together, an idea he rehearsed while walking to the house, when a creak from the back corner of their kitchen distracted him. On the floor, he saw a door open like the lid to a coffin, and through the hole a ghost-like figure rose carrying what looked like a golden tabernacle emanating rays of brilliant light. The apparition, probably blinded by the sunlight, must have seen him standing in the doorway, because it let out a high pitched scream. He produced a sound two octaves lower.

"A vampire, just like me and Larry read about." The boy stopped screaming and held the jar of peaches protectively in front of him.

Mrs. Rastner glanced at him and said, "Hush, now." Then she looked at their visitor. "Are you all right, Father? Would you like a drink?"

Shamus spied a pail with a dipper hooked on its rim, the probable source of drinking water, and declined. The man at the head of the table glanced toward his wife and then stood. With shoulders hunched forward, he craned his neck and peered at Shamus over his glasses. He resembled someone needing forgiveness and begging for mercy. He stepped back and gestured to the young men at the table who immediately got up and hurried out of the house. He pointed to the chair closest to him.

"Please, Father, take George's chair." He extended his hand. "We've never actually met. I'm Svez Rastner."

He accepted Svez's hand, sat next to him across for Mrs. Rastner. His gaze moved back and forth between them. "I'm sorry if I interrupted your boys' dinner." Svez just shrugged.

Mrs. Rastner said, "They have their chores to do. Can I get you anything, Father?"

"No, thank you." He sniffed quietly, trying to identify an odor, and then blurted out, "Kraut?"

"Would you like some sauerkraut, Father?" Mrs. Rastner gestured toward the stove. "It's from an old family recipe."

He realized this as an opportunity to reach out to Mrs. Rastner. "I haven't had sauerkraut in years. Yes, I would like to try a little, please."

"Thelma, fix Father a plate." Mrs. Rastner spoke to the young girl who had been clearing the dishes from the table.

From the corner of his eye, he saw her take a plate from the stack, give it a quick swipe with her apron and fill it with a glob of sauerkraut, strings dripping from the ladle. A burst of strong aroma filled the air.

"Would you like some potatoes too?" Mrs. Rastner asked. "You might need them. The kraut is pretty strong to eat by itself."

"Yes, thank you. I'm sure, that will be necessary." He laced his fingers together but resisted cracking his knuckles. "I truly am sorry for bothering you folks at dinner time."

The boy across from him stood behind his chair and whispered to his sister, "This ain't dinner, it's supper, and I 'spect we don't get to eat them peaches."

Shamus looked at the plate in front of him and decided to get to the point of his visit. "I feel duty bound to make myself available to families of St. Alphonse Parish who are experiencing troubles God has chosen to send their way."

Iggy clutched the unopened jar of peaches, and his breathing became audible. He retreated to the porch where he stood as if he were being punished.

"Trouble? We don't got no trouble, that I know of." Svez grimaced as he glanced at Thelma and then back at the priest. "What kind of trouble do you mean?"

In an almost child-like voice, Thelma said, "Father, after you've eaten why don't you come out to the barn to see my baby pigs?"

"I should like to see all the animals and," as an after thought, "bless them while I'm here."

Liz said, "Thelma, you haven't raised pigs for some years now. What's gotten into you?" She took a deep breath and said, "Iggy, go tell the boys to come back to the house. Better bring Arnie along, too. I've got something to tell everyone."

CHAPTER NINE
DEATH WILL BE WHAT IT WILL BE
(Winter, 1933)

Svez took several deep breaths and continued to lay along side his wife's body. Her brief struggle had awakened him, and he wondered if she heard the promises that he made before she fell into her deep sleep. He had studied her face while her breathing became fainter and fainter until it finally stopped. For a moment, he pondered her last utterance, Thelma. He then sat up and reached for his pants crumpled on the floor beside the bed. He stepped into them, struggled with a single strap that he pulled over his nightshirt and hooked it to the wrong side of the bib. He was reaching for the other strap that dangled inside his pant leg when Thelma rushed into the room.

She shrieked, "Mama."

"Ma's gone."

Thelma crawled over the foot of the bed and, on hands and knees, stared into her mother's face. "She ain't dead, Pa. She can't be."

"I better get the boys up." He stood beside the bed and studied his bare feet, unable to decide if he should first put on his shoes. He turned to his daughter who lay on the bed with one arm across Liz's body and her face buried in his pillow. She used to sneak into their bed when she was a child, frightened or cold. He felt weak and wished he could lay back down with them and pretend nothing had happened.

Thelma turned her face toward her mother. "I failed you, Mama. I can't remember what I'm supposed to do." She began to sob.

Iggy brushed past Svez, gawked at Thelma and began to cry. "Ma's dead, Iggy."

Iggy peered at the lifeless figure lying next to Thelma and whimpered. "She's still got her nightgown on." He appeared to be confused, like he was trying to put the pieces of a puzzle together.

"She died in her sleep, didn't she, Pa?" Thelma got up, wiped away her tears and put her arm around her brother. He stopped crying.

Svez stooped and pulled a shoe over his bare foot. "She asked for you before she died." He picked up a sock, but tossed it back on the floor and stared at his other shoe. He saw Iggy's chest heave, and air whistled through his nose and mouth. "And for you, too, Iggy."

George, Herman and Ralph appeared in the doorway. Thelma and Iggy began to sob again. George put his arms around them. Herman and Ralph tip-toed to the bed and peered at their mother's face.

Svez stepped into his other shoe and wished he had put on his socks first. He glanced around the room and felt his family stare back at him.

"I was just going to wake you boys."

He wanted his two younger children to stop crying. The sounds of their grief made his chest tighten and his eyes water. He looked at Freddie's crib. He had built it when George was a baby, and Liz made him put runners under it so she could stick her foot from under the covers and rock it when the baby fussed. He remembered a Fourth of July many years ago when his entire family crowded around their bed. Thelma was sleeping in the crib, and the boys burst in yelling about going to the parade.

"Gotta get the chores done first." Svez smiled. "Then the parade."

"The parade, Pa?" George released his hold on Thelma and Iggy, backed away and bumped into Freddie's crib. Herman and Ralph glanced at their father, then back at their mother. They hesitated, turned and walked out of the room single file but stopped outside the door. Everyone looked at George who leaned over the crib and tried to steady it. Freddie rolled over, grabbed the side-slats and pulled himself up. He lost his balance and plopped back down. With his thumb in his mouth, he blinked and faced his family who was staring back at him.

Svez took the baby from his crib and placed him on the pillow next to Liz. Freddie touched her nose, closed eyes and colorless mouth. His lips twitched and contorted slightly as if he were ready to beak into a cry or a laugh, but he did neither. He turned toward Thelma and appeared to search for a clue about what he should be feeling. He began to whimper. Svez seldom heard or saw Freddie show any emotion, and he felt a mixture of tenderness and pity. He remembered how much Liz wanted to raise this boy and feared leaving him.

That night last summer, after Father Reinhardt left, she had told him, "The rest of you'll get along, but what about Martha's son? Our son?"

He had assured her they would love and care for Freddie, but now that she was gone, he felt frightened for the child. And for himself. He remembered the one important instruction she had given him.

Struggling to remain calm, he blurted out, "Father Reinhardt."

Almost in unison, Herman and Ralph repeated, "Father Reinhardt," backed farther into the front room and then darted toward the kitchen. George still clung to the crib as if it might start rocking again and stared at the lifeless form on the bed. When the storm door slammed, he turned and left the bedroom.

Svez stood beside the bed and felt helpless as he watched Thelma gather some of Liz's clothes from their closet and dresser.

Between sobs, Thelma said to him, "I gotta get Ma ready for Father Reinhardt. He can't see her like this. She told me what she wanted to wear when she meets with God, and how I should get her ready." She faced her mother. "I can do this, Mama. You'll look good when Father Reinhardt gets here to anoint you with oil and pray for your soul like he did for Aunt Martha."

"Guess you know what to do. I'll call the priest." He realized that Liz had given all the important instructions to Thelma, not to him, and he felt sad.

As he stood next to the phone on the kitchen wall with the receiver held tight to his ear, he thought about what he would say if Father Reinhardt's sister answered. He was glad when he heard a man's voice. While he explained what happened, he watched Thelma stoke the coals in the stove and pump water into a kettle. After a cup of coffee, his nerves would settle down. When he finally slumped onto his chair at the table, he realized Liz's bath water steamed on the stove, not his coffee, and he felt too ashamed to mention this oversight to Thelma. He just sat there with his hands covering his face.

He knew Liz was dying ever since that night Father Reinhardt came to visit them, but he denied the sight of her frail body, even though he saw her undress as they got ready for bed each night. He didn't feel the effects of her loss of energy or notice any change in the daily routine, because Thelma's efforts increased, and the family's needs were met without interruption. Thelma made their meals, cleaned and mended their clothes, and took care of Freddie. She tended to the chickens and butchered them for their meals. Had Liz and Thelma been a team of horses, he would never have missed the shift in the workload from one to the other. His job dealt solely with tending the land and caring for the animals. Paying attention to family members never occurred to him, as Liz always took care of their needs, and they seldom interfered with the other's role. He never heard Thelma complain, so maybe she didn't realize the shift in the workload either.

****

Iggy tried to follow Thelma but he felt his feet locked in place near the foot of the bed. He watched Freddie touch their mother's face, pinch her nose and pry at her eye lids, and hoped Ma would lift her head and say boo like she used to. She wouldn't do that, he knew, and Freddie should stop. But he didn't. Instead, he crawled on top of Ma, sat on her chest and plopped up and down. Iggy closed his eyes. When he opened them, he saw Freddie lay on his tummy, his face buried in the pillow and his foot caught in the strap of her night gown. Her breast was uncovered. He squeezed his eyes back shut and wished he was upstairs in bed having a bad dream. He felt awful and wanted Thelma to cover Ma's breast and take Freddie away.

He stared at the crumpled quilt half off the bed, and imagined his mother struggling for her life. Years ago when a nightmare woke him, he peeked into this room and saw his father pounce on her until she made a face like she was crying. He wanted Pa to get off, but he was unable to scream no matter how hard he tried. When he figured out what they had been doing, other frightening images plagued him. His seed squirted into Ma, being squeezed into a little ball and then pushed out, a squishy bloody mass. It made him sick. He didn't like the idea that his parents made babies the same way the animals did.

Suddenly, he felt Arnie standing behind him, his breath adding to the musty odors of the room and the turmoil in his stomach. He tried to swallow the saliva collecting in his mouth and gagged.

Arnie said, "Ya shouldn't be watchin' your Ma when she's 'bout to feed the baby. It ain't right for a boy your age to see that."

70

"Ma's dead." A hiccup, barely audible.

Arnie took one step closer, stared at Liz, and hurried out of the room.

Iggy grimaced when he heard Pa say, "She's dead, Arnie," a long silence and then the storm door slammed.

When Thelma returned with towels and a basin of water, Iggy leaned his back against the wall and watched. She stood Freddie next to his crib where he clung to the slats until the bed rocked, and he plopped onto the floor. He reached up but played with his fingers instead. Thelma covered Liz's body to her neck with the bed sheet.

She looked at Iggy and said, "You can stay until I have to undress her."

He watched Thelma touch the wet cloth to their mother's forehead like she was checking for a fever.

"Mama, I can do this. I hated to touch Aunt Martha, but touching you is easy. I love you. That makes it easy."

Iggy liked Thelma calling their mother Mama. Maybe, she would hear and wake up.

"I need your help, Mama, with the things you want me to do." She stroked her mother's face with both hands. "Please don't ever leave me." She kissed her gently on the lips.

Iggy gasped. He remembered a fairy tale about a kiss waking a dead person, but he lost this glimmer of hope when he realized Thelma was staring at him.

"You gotta leave now, Iggy. I'm gonna wash and dress her. You can kiss her first, if you want to."

Iggy wanted to, but he turned and sulked toward the kitchen where he sat on Ma's chair next to Pa and waited for Thelma to make his breakfast.

****

Svez wished his son would sit at his own place, but he was unable to tell him to. He meandered over to the sink and checked the coffeepot from last night. He grunted an approval and set it on the stove, still hot from the fire Thelma made.

He sat back down and told Iggy, "Grab a couple of cups and pour us some of last night's coffee. We can sugar it up good 'nuf 'til Thelma gets done with Ma."

Iggy obeyed, and they sat quietly at the table until Thelma brought Freddie into the kitchen and put him in his playpen.

"I'm sorry, Pa. I should've made fresh coffee. I'll do it now, while we wait for Father Reinhardt." She peered into the coffeepot and made a face. To Iggy, she said, "Put another piece of wood in the stove while I clean and fill this."

Iggy jumped up and went to the wood box.

Svez just stared at the grounds at the bottom of his cup. Soon, the crackling of the fire and the percolating of the coffee filled the kitchen with familiar sounds and aromas.

When Father Reinhardt arrived, Svez rose, shook the priest's hand and said in a low soft voice, "Elizabeth left us."

Unable to say more, he sank back into his chair and stared straight ahead. Ever since that night Father Reinhardt came to the farm, Svez felt competition with him for Liz's trust and confidence. A renewed wave of that rivalry swelled as Thelma led the priest into their bedroom. Iggy, his head lowered, trailed behind them.

Svez knew that Liz thought priests were God's representatives on earth, given special spiritual powers to reach beyond the grave. He wasn't ready to grant that much importance to any priest, especially Father Reinhardt, but he respected his wife's beliefs.

However, he couldn't deny that Liz needed this man now more than she ever needed him. His gloom dropped to a level of near despair. A rage he never experienced before surfaced, and he didn't know where to direct it. Although annoyed and irritated with this priest, to unleash his anger at him for trying to help Liz was unthinkable. He never blamed God for his problems, but this time he asked questions, aware that even the pope couldn't answer.

"Why me, God? Why Liz?" He paused, but heard only Father Reinhardt's voice chanting words in that strange language.

When the voice stopped, he heard Thelma and then Iggy say, "Amen."

He whispered, "Amen," and he turned his anger against himself. *My God, did I do something to deserve this?* He never believed that God punished people for doing bad things, but he couldn't hide from the possibility that he may have brought this on himself. Maybe he didn't treat Liz proper, but he had no notion of what he could've done different. Maybe gone to church more often. That would have pleased her. An incident that happened when he still drank hard liquor flashed through his mind, but she had forgiven him.

Thelma! He immediately forced back that recent memory.

He spoke to Freddie who stood and smiled at him. "Your Ma loved you." He stood and bent over the playpen. "Wanted me to love you, too." He lifted Freddie and pressed his face against the stubble of his beard. When the baby squirmed but didn't cry, Svez stood him on the floor. Freddie grabbed onto his pant leg, teetered a bit, and waddled off into the bedroom. Svez followed as far as the open door. He watched Thelma scoop Freddie up with her free hand, her other hand only momentarily left Iggy's shoulder. Huddled together, they faced Father Reinhardt who put oil on a cotton wad and dabbed it on Liz's face and hands.

He gave the cotton to Thelma. She touched her mother's forehead, already shiny with oil.

"Goodbye, Mama."

Iggy took it, quickly dabbed his mother's arm and gave it back to Thelma who held it to Freddie's outstretched hand.

"She's your Ma, too, Freddie." She helped him pinch the cotton between his thumb and finger, and they touched their mother's face with it. Freddie dropped the cotton, put his fingers in his mouth and cut a face.

Svez realized that was Freddie's only serious reaction to anything that happened that morning.

Father Reinhardt touched the heads of the Rastner children, gave a customary blessing and, glancing up, acknowledged Svez' presence with a nod.

"Why don't you children spend a few quiet moments with your mother while I talk to your father."

Together, they walked through the kitchen and out to the porch.

"I'll come around this evening to say the rosary at seven o'clock." Father Reinhardt checked his watch and then glanced through the door toward the barn. "Liz belonged to the Christian Mothers so they'll come as a group. I'm sure some of them will offer to stay and join in the wake if you wish." He paused, his eyes averting Svez's. "We can make the necessary arrangements at that time. It's customary to hold the funeral on the second or third day, which would take us to Thursday or Friday. Either day is fine with me."

Svez didn't answer.

"Is Friday okay?"

Svez nodded.

"Good. It's all set then. I'll see you tonight."

****

Arnie took off his gloves and breathed into cupped hands to warm them. He had taken the ladder to the loft and crawled across the mounds of hay to the cupola, the highest vantage point on the farm other than the windmill, which he refused to climb. He put his gloves back on when he heard a car door slam, and twisted the louvered vent to allow a more favorable view of the house and yard. To his surprise, Father Reinhardt wasn't in the car, but walking toward the barn. Arnie slid off his perch, a brace holding the cupola to the roof, and landed on the soft hay that reached nearly to the peak. On hands and knees, he crawled to the end of the barn where he crept down the ladder to the floor of the haymow. He listened at the open trap door to the ground floor for familiar sounds of cattle disturbed from their sleep, but he heard none. He crawled down the ladder and saw only one standing, her shit splattering in the gutter. The boys hadn't started milking but were huddled around the feed bin. He climbed over the rails and into a pen where a cow was licking her newborn calf. There was a flash from the bright morning sun when Father Reinhardt opened the door and walked into the barn. Arnie saw him hesitate with the sun on his back. Either he waited for his eyes to adjust to the dark, or he couldn't stand the smells from the cows waking and relieving themselves. Maybe he'd just leave. Arnie was disappointed when the priest closed the door behind him and put his hand to his forehead as if he were saluting.

"Hello. It's sure dark in here." He glanced around and walked to the feed bin where the boys stood. "Jesus was born in a barn something like this. I believe he still favors those who tend to his animals."

First George, and then the other two nodded. Ralph began to cry, then Herman broke down. Soon all three of them sobbed uncontrollably.

"I know that you miss your mother already," more nods and more sobs, "but she is in the care of God now, and we have to look out for each other." After a pause he added, "And God's animals."

"Yeah! Yeah!" They seemed to say in unison.

Ralph said, "This morning the brown Guernsey dropped a healthy calf. Arnie said we can make this Ma's calf, and he promised not to butcher her, even after she stops calving. She'll be ours forever." A fit of crying overcame him, and his two brothers put their arms around him.

"Is Arnie here now? I should talk to him."

George turned toward the pen where Arnie stood and said, "I think he's with Ma's calf. Over there."

Arnie watched Father Reinhardt walk down a row of cows, heads locked in stanchions and nosing through bits of silage searching for the last morsel of ground oats. He hoped the rotting smell of the silage mixed with the sweet smell of milk oozing from the cow's distended udders would make the priest gag. He waited until Father Reinhardt was close before he squeezed a teat, and the thick yellow milk of a cow that had just calved drenched his hand. He turned toward the calf already licked clean, rubbed its nose with his milk-saturated hand and put his thumb into its mouth. He picked it up, placed it near the cow's udder and exchanged his thumb with one of her teats. The calf sucked noisily.

"That's a fine looking calf you have there, Arnie. The boys told me you'll take special care of that one."

Arnie mumbled, "I take care of all the animals. If it wasn't for me none of the calves would make it to their first breeding." Then with a glimmer of trust and confidence, "I got the secret of getting the heifer to take the bull. I know how to get her to let her milk go after she drops her calf. I can...." He never revealed his third secret, but just patted the cow on the rump and crossed over to the others waiting to be milked.

"Take good care of the animals God has entrusted to you."

From the corner of his eye, Arnie saw the priest make a blessing motion with his hand.

"And may God protect you."

Arnie snorted, grabbed his stool and milk pail, and sat under the first of a long row of cows.

CHAPTER TEN
A NEW ORDER

Thelma preferred Father Reinhardt's explanation, "Your mother is a new star in the sky," over the story the nuns used to tell her and Iggy during catechism class. She knew Iggy believed in angels. Her mother used to tell him that the angels cried when he disobeyed, and he would right away do what she told him to. If Aunt Martha became an angel like Ma said, certainly she must be one, too. Maybe the star Father Reinhardt told her about was only a window in heaven for her mother to look through and hear a daughter's evening prayers. The night of Liz's funeral, Thelma chose a star that she could see from her bedroom window.

"You looked real nice, Mama. I had you in your black dress like you wanted, and everyone came to see you." She sat up and pulled the tattered blanket over her shoulders. "They brought food and said the rosary and tried to make all of us feel better." She leaned forward and put her elbows on the windowsill. "I think Iggy'll miss you the most. He said he'd sleep on the couch in the front room forever, right next to where you were laid out. I'm sure he felt bad, because he was too scared to stay up alone with you. The rest of us took turns so you were never by yourself even for one minute. Pa said it would give each of us a chance to be with you for the last time, to sort of say good-bye without anyone watching. Iggy and I stayed up together, and when he fell asleep, I went right up to you and touched your hand and your face." She squeezed her eyelids shut. "I told you about that terrible thing I did the day Pa hurt his leg."

She wished there was a better name to describe what she had done to her father than the word her brothers used when they joked about doing it to themselves. Sometimes throughout the day, her memory of what she had done became too vivid, and dwelling on it embarrassed her. She had to force it out of her mind.

She opened her eyes and looked back out the window. "Am I forgiven? Is Pa forgiven?" She wanted her mother's forgiveness for her father as well as herself, but she took most of the blame for what happened. "I thought I was doing what a grown up woman would do. I'm really sorry." The star continued to twinkle, but she needed more. "Did you hear me say I was sorry?" With her chin on the windowsill, the warmth from her breath created a fog on the cold glass. "I wanted to tell you when we were still together, but I was afraid you might not understand. Please, don't be mad at me." As she wiped away the moisture and watched her mother's star disappear behind black lace. "Come back, Mama. I need to tell you that me and Pa both felt bad about what happened. I was just trying to be grown up like you told me, and Pa needed my help. I didn't want to be grown up that way."

"I was bad, I know, but it was a woman-thing, wasn't it, Mama?" She plopped on her pillow and pulled the blanket over her head. She sat back up and checked the sky, the blanket tight under her chin. "I did everything you told me to do. I cried real hard at first, but I think a woman can cry if she needs to. I love you and I want to talk to you real often. I know you'll help me be the best grown up woman in the whole world."

The star reappeared form behind the cloud, and a sense of confidence replaced Thelma's doubt and guilt. Leaves rustled in the wind and the rain gutter tapped against the eaves. She sensed her mother's approval. From somewhere inside the house, she heard someone sobbing. She sat up, put her feet on the floor and shivered. She reached for her socks and put them on. When she peeked into the boys' room, she saw them quietly asleep. At Arnie's door, she heard familiar gasps and raspy breaths. The disturbing sounds were coming from downstairs. In the front room, she found Iggy uncovered and shivering on the couch where he held his belated vigil with his mother. He wept in his sleep. Thelma covered him with the special quilt Ma made for him. She rubbed her fingers across the soft red-checkered squares and remembered the shirt that at least two of her brothers used to wear to church on Sundays. Iggy was lucky because his quilt had patches cut from his clothes and some that were handed down from his brothers. Of all the quilts her mother made for the boys, his was the best.

Thelma thought about the squares of cloth for her quilt still neatly bundled and setting in the bottom drawer of the buffet in the front room. Her mother had said, "Your quilt will be the best, Thelma. We have so many colorful dresses to choose from. But, we have to wait 'till you finish school so we can include a graduation dress."

That was four years ago, Mama.

Shortly after completing the eighth grade, Thelma took the initiative. One afternoon, while her mother was outside, she cut squares of cloth from her baptismal dress, from her first communion dress and from the new dress made especially for her graduation. She put them in a pile and took them out to the garden.

"What have you done?" Her mother's voice sounded angry, but her eyes were hidden behind the brim of her straw hat.

"I made squares for my quilt."

"Not your new graduation dress. That was to be worn to church." She continued to chomp weeds with her hoe. "Guess I'll have to find time to make you another one."

"I'm sorry. I thought...."

"That's all right. We can start the quilt real soon, maybe this fall when the gardening is done." She pointed to the squares in Thelma's hands but didn't touch them. "Put them in the bottom drawer of the buffet."

Thelma felt a tinge of envy and anger, as Iggy snuggled under his quilt. She quietly promised to finish the quilt Ma had neglected and said aloud, "As soon as I get time." Suddenly, she felt she connected with Ma. She was tempted to rush back to her window in case her mother wanted to hear more, but Iggy had quieted and sobs alternating with rapid gasps of air came from her father's bedroom. She peeked in and saw Freddie asleep in his crib. Her father wouldn't let her take him upstairs with her because it was too cold. He promised to call her if Freddie cried during the night. In the light of the moon, the outline of Svez's body beneath a single sheet rose and fell with each rasped breath. He faced the window, and she wondered if he had found her mother's star.

She whispered lightly, "Pa," and got no response. She picked the quilt from the floor and covered him and the side of the bed where her mother had slept. He pulled the quilt tight around himself, taking some of Liz's share with him. He mumbled, "Come to bed."

"Ma's gone, Pa. She ain't here no more." She listened to her father snore, the buzz saw she and her brothers thought was funny and her mother said was comforting. She sat on the edge of the bed and remembered some of the secrets that her mother had shared with her shortly after she had her first period.

"In bed, a husband and wife can talk about things and do things that could never happen in the daytime. Husbands listen to their wives and sometimes tell them how they feel."

Who's Pa gonna talk to now? Thelma sat on her mother's side of the bed and wanted to see her star, but her father lay next to the window, and she didn't want to face that way. Instead, she rested her head on the pillow where she sensed her mother's presence. *Pa's okay, Ma. Iggy was just cold, but I covered him with his quilt.* She felt a chill and reached for the bit of quilt her father hadn't pulled away. Unable to explain to her mother why she was lying next to her father in her nightgown, Thelma shivered, but was afraid to move.

Her father rolled on his back, releasing Liz's share of the quilt, and Thelma pulled it over herself. Scared and cold, she felt like a child again, stealing into bed with her mother and father. But, she knew she was no longer a child, and her mother was not there to protect her. She snuggled under the quilt, relished in its warmth and softness and fell asleep.

Thelma couldn't separate her dream from reality because the edges of each blurred one into the other. She dreamed of a hand reaching under her nightgown. In reality she felt her father's hand against the soft flesh of her inner thighs. In her dream, a hand gently encouraged her legs to spread. In reality, her father pressed his heavy weight on her body. She could neither accept nor reject these advances. In her dream, she felt a sudden thrust as the fantasy figure entered her body. In reality, she endured sharp pain. In dream and in reality, a hot sensation rose down deep inside.

The dream and reality merged when her father whispered her mother's name and rolled over. She felt desperate to escape, but she didn't want the light from her mother's star to touch her and the bed she was lying in.

****

Svez awoke early the next morning and went outside to urinate. The chilled morning air and the cool wet grass beneath his bare feet awakened him thoroughly. A frightening realization of what happened the previous night struck him. His nightmare was confirmed when he returned to the bedroom and saw his sixteen-year-old daughter snuggled in her mother's quilt. He grabbed his clothes and ran out the door. On the barn silhouetted in the predawn light, color began to emerge. Louvers in the cupola flapped and rotors on the windmill

80

screeched as the north wind scattered flakes of snow that pin-pricked against his face.

Both sexual encounters with his daughter confronted his conscience. That first time didn't matter, because it was an accident. Neither meant for it to happen, and no real harm was done. But this time, he couldn't wash away a guilt ten times worse than that which he felt the night Liz admitted to her family in front of Father Reinhardt that she was dying. The unbearable sadness they shared in bed that night began to well up again in his chest. He had cried with his wife, promised to stand by her and the family, and confessed some of the bad things he had done, excluding the one with their daughter. They talked about the time he had beaten Liz, and how it changed their lives.

At a board meeting the men of the township had gotten together to decide if a road should be built north of the east-west intersection past his farm. He needed one to reach the meadow where he could cut hay in the dry years. Without this access, the low land had little or no use for him. When the board voted to approve it, Svez and his neighbors celebrated.

The Clapboard Brothers fought against it because, they admitted, it would run too near the place where they made their moonshine. Svez knew about their still and didn't want the Revenuers to bust the brothers, but he and others needed access to their fields. The brothers showed no hard feelings and brought out a crock of their best hooch so all the men could pass the jug around and have a draw of whiskey. Svez wrestled with a demon soon after the second or third round. He made a few swipes at the phantom that was harassing him, and he enjoyed making everyone laugh. He couldn't remember the rest of the night.

He had passed out in the wagon, but the horses knew the way home, and the next day he realized this probably saved his life. When his eight-year-old son, George, brought the horses back to the yard, and Liz came out of the house to meet them, Svez sat in the wagon and stared at her badly bruised face and scratched arms.

"Did I...?"

"It weren't your fault. When I climbed onto the wagon wearing my white nightgown, you thought I was a ghost or something. You started swinging and yelling, and the horses bolted. I fell off the wagon but, luckily, I didn't get run over."

That night when they talked about Liz dying, Svez touched her face distorted with grief, and he remembered the bruises he had caused so long ago.

"I'm so sorry, Liz." His apology as he faced her in bed, although fifteen years late, was sincere. "I never meant to hurt you. I felt so ashamed when George brought me and the horses back to the yard."

"I forgave you right after it happened. You know that. Maybe you don't know how proud of you I am for keeping your promise to never touch liquor again."

He remembered her thanking him for all kinds of wonderful things he had done for her, most he never realized were that important, but he continued to see her bruised face. He struggled with his memory to produce her face at a more pleasant time. Instead, a vision of Liz's cold features as she lay in her coffin emerged, and he began to cry. Every emotional pain he ever repressed surfaced. He cried out of remorse and shame. He cried for all his losses.

Liz's words that sorrowful night in bed gave him encouragement for the solemn promise he now needed to make to himself in front of God. Facing the sky as if he were gauging the weather, he made his second vow, a sacred, silent promise directly to his daughter. He no longer had liquor to blame for his behavior, and he made no other excuses.

"I was totally to blame and, no matter how I am tempted, I cannot ever let that happen again."

CHAPTER ELEVEN
THELMA'S QUILT
(Fall, 1934)

Thelma decided to serve her family their Thanksgiving dinner in the parlor. Her mother had done this on certain occasions, and Thelma wanted this day to be special. Besides, her father invited Henry, Freddie's father, and she didn't want him to dribble tobacco juice into the kitchen sink while everyone was eating. He would have to leave the room or, better yet, take out his chew before he sat down.

She counted the plates and realized she had set one too many. After her mother died, Thelma continued to save a space at the table for her until one day her father reached across and pulled Freddie next to him. Everyone shifted slightly, and the void was filled. Today, her mother would be remembered. She shoved Freddie's highchair down one place setting.

She returned to the kitchen in time to see Iggy peek into the oven and yelp when he picked up and dropped a hot cover. He danced in front of the stove with his fingers in his mouth.

"Get out of there," Thelma scolded. "Dinner ain't ready yet."

"Just checking how everything tastes."

"Well, does it pass inspection?"

"I'm not sure. I better check them sweet potatoes." He swiped his finger through the pot steaming on the stove, licked the hot sticky goo and ducked Thelma's playful blow.

"Get out of my kitchen. Or, make yourself useful and put a chair at each place setting." She grimaced as he scraped chairs across the floor and banged them into the woodwork. "Be careful and leave Freddie's highchair where it is."

"Why we eating in the front room? We got company coming?"

"I told you to call it a parlor, not the front room." She shook her head. "Have you forgotten already?"

"Used to be the front room." He grasped the arms of his father's chair, held them like the reins of horses and steered out of the kitchen. He returned and grabbed Arnie's chair. "That's what Pa calls it."

"Well, today it's gonna be a dining room, and never you mind about company." She enjoyed his confusion and decided to keep Henry's invitation a secret. "Just be careful with Arnie's chair."

That chair, according to Thelma's mother, came with Arnie when he joined their family. Up to that time, it hadn't moved from the foot of his father's table even after the older brothers left home, and it was Arnie's turn at the honored position next to his father. Svez, the younger brother, sat there until their father died and he was free to marry. Even after Arnie started eating most of his meals up in his room, his place at the table was reserved.

"Hey, you set too many plates." Iggy stood in the archway between the two rooms and counted on his fingers, "Pa, Arnie, George, Herman, Ralph, you, me and Freddie. That's eight and you got ten plates."

"Oh, I forgot to tell you." Thelma fibbed. "Father Reinhardt and his sister are coming to dinner." Before he could react, she pointed to the teakettle on the stove. "Take that hot water to the basin in the porch and wash up good for dinner." To annoy him, she added, "And don't forget behind your ears." She followed him as far as the door, peeked into the porch and listened.

"Thelma's lost her mind. Father Reinhardt and his prissy sister's gonna eat with us." He faced each of his brothers one at a time. "She's set two extra plates."

"Naw. One of them's for Henry." George wiped his razor with his finger and flicked a glob of shaving cream speckled with black bristles at Iggy. "Pa made me drive to his place yesterday to invite him. He don't got no phone."

"Okay, but what about the second plate?" Iggy set the kettle on the washstand, wiped the soap from his shirt and scraped it into the slop pail.

"Maybe Ida's coming to thank me for helping her with the chores," Ralph chuckled, "and stuff."

Iggy didn't laugh with his brothers.

"Imagine Thelma's face if Ida sat next to her." Ralph slapped his knee, tears in his eyes. "She'd throw the plate away after Ida ate, not bothering to wash it."

Thelma stuck her head into the porch and yelled, "Will you guys knock it off. I know when you laugh like that it's something dirty what's tickled you. Besides, dinner's almost ready. When Uncle Henry gets here we can eat."

Soon the splashing and towel slapping stopped, and all four brothers traipsed through the kitchen sniffing at the aromas.

"Where's the table?" George glanced around the room.

"We's eating in the front room today." Iggy puffed up his chest.

"The parlor, Iggy." She tossed the towel over her shoulder and made a pushing gesture with both hands. "We're eating formal so get upstairs and dress for dinner. I got your Sunday clothes laid out on your beds."

Svez and Arnie sat at their respective ends of the table and appeared unfazed at the change in procedure. Thelma felt proud when her brothers, dressed in their Sunday best, joined them.

"We're ready. Where's the grub?" George yelled into the kitchen.

"Just hold your horses." Thelma stood in the archway, hands on her hips. "I'll bring you guys something to drink, and you can talk about the weather or something while we wait for Uncle Henry." She glared at Ralph. "No more smart talk about going to see Ida." She returned with the coffeepot and noticed Ralph, red-faced and staring at his plate.

When she heard a car drive into the yard, she opened the kitchen door and started filling the serving platters. Henry stomped into the porch, stood in the doorway and stared into the kitchen.

"We're eating in the parlor, Uncle Henry." She picked up a platter of chicken and glanced over her shoulder. "Go in and sit down while I bring in the food."

Henry's nostrils flared. "Parlors is fer dead people." He glanced around, put two fingers and a thumb into his mouth and removed a squishy mess of tobacco.

"Just put it in the slop pail under the sink and have a seat next to Uncle Arnie." She felt strange calling Arnie *uncle*, and it apparently annoyed him because he stood and picked up his plate as he did when things didn't suit him.

She set the chicken on the table, walked over to him and touched his arm. "Please, Arnie, eat with us today."

For a tense moment, Arnie and Henry stood motionless, their eyes fixed on each other until Svez said, "Here, Henry. Come sit next to me." He tapped George's shoulder. "Move down and make room for Henry." Arnie seemed to relax, and he sat down.

Thelma whispered, "Thank you, Arnie." When Freddie banged his spoon on the tray of his high chair, she said, "There goes the dinner bell," and everyone laughed except her father. She worried that the extra place setting annoyed him. Would he pull Freddie to his side and push Ma away from the family again? He didn't. Others glanced at the empty space but no one said anything.

When Thelma returned from the kitchen with dessert, George cleared his throat and said, "Why don't you sit at Ma's place from now on?"

She felt pleased and honored as her brothers and her father nodded in agreement.

The next day, exhausted from preparing, serving and cleaning up after the holiday dinner, Thelma took a break from cooking. She checked the apple pies baking in the oven. The men—she thought of them as men even though her father called them boys—hadn't said anything about their cold sandwiches for lunch, but they might complain about a supper of leftovers. She took the pies out of the oven and set them next to the fresh bread already cooling on the table. That should stop their complaints. They were preparing the farm for winter and wouldn't be in the house until evening chores were done. She had a few hours to herself.

The parlor felt oppressively quiet after the clamor yesterday, but slowly melted into a comfortable blend of wind driving the sleet against the north side of the house and the whisper of her voice as she sang her favorite church hymns. She knew different songs, but they were mostly polkas and other fast tempo dance tunes that didn't fit the solemn mood of this lonely, snowy afternoon. She gathered her mother's shawl around her shoulders. The kitchen would have been a warmer place to work, but she didn't want to smell the fresh bread and apple pies. From the lower drawer of the buffet, she removed her quilt, still in a bundle of neatly cut squares. She selected a shiny square of black cloth, glanced over her shoulder to see if anyone was watching and fingered it tenderly as she touched it to her nose and lips.

"I know I did wrong, Mama, but this is something from you. If heaven is so wonderful, the angels won't care that it's missing." She held the piece of cloth from Liz's funeral dress against her breast. "You don't need it as much as I do. No one who came to your wake ever noticed the hole in the back of your dress, not even the Christian Mothers who checked real careful to see that I had prepared you just right."

Ordinarily, Thelma would have enjoyed the thought of her mother surrounded by long deceased relatives fussing with her dress and trying to explain the missing material. Today, Thelma's mood was dark. She pressed the square from the dress against the sewing table, took a larger piece cut from her white baptismal dress and placed it near the black one. The sharp contrast pleased her.

"Mama, you're the centerpiece of my quilt." She rationalized that through her mother's death her quilt could come alive, and Thelma forgave her for putting it off. She framed the dark piece with the white one. "You baptized me and made me a Christian." Afraid that she offended her mother with her anger over the unfinished quilt, she said, "You taught me how to sew, and when I finish the quilt it'll be from you. I'll do all the things you couldn't finish because God took you away from me." She remembered the advice her teacher, Miss West, gave her. "And, I can still find time for me."

Thelma had her first pleasant thought that cold November afternoon, and she reveled in it. Her teacher had stressed that she look out for herself because she was the only girl among many brothers, each making demands on her. Thinking about her school experience, she searched the bundle for cuttings from her graduation dress. She remembered the look on her mother's face that day in the garden when she showed them to her.

The room darkened as the sun dropped below the trees in back of the house. She pulled the string on the single light bulb above her head and saw her reflection in the window.

"I'm sorry, Mama. I just had to cut it up. I was still a little girl then."

The dress reminded her of graduation day and the strange advice Miss West gave her that felt like an assignment due some time later in her life. After excusing the rest of the students for summer recess, Miss West walked to the back of the room where Thelma and Iggy sat and congratulated her eighth grade class of only two students.

She handed Iggy his diploma and explained that the school board agreed to let him graduate even if he didn't pass all his final exams. He began to cry. She held out his diploma with one hand and her handkerchief with the other. She excused him to join his friend, Larry Collins, who had been peeking through the window. Iggy grabbed his diploma, wiped his eyes with the back of his hand and ran outside. Miss West tucked her handkerchief back into her sleeve and sat at Iggy's desk.

Larry graduated the year before, and Thelma felt he came to taunt Iggy if he hadn't received a diploma. She felt proud of her brother and stuck out her tongue at Larry. She felt uncomfortable with her teacher so close and started to fidget with the frills on her dress.

"What a beautiful dress. It makes you look so grown up."

"Ma and me...I mean, my mother and I made it special for graduation. Iggy got a store-bought shirt and pants from York's in town." She paused, sensing that her teacher wasn't interested in those details, and the room, usually filled with noisy students, became eerily quiet.

Miss West smiled and said, "The very first day you came to school, I saw a spark of light that has since developed into a delicate flame. If you're not careful, it will flicker and may even go out. You must fight to keep it alive."

Confused, yet now comfortable with her teacher sitting next to her in the student section, she said, "I can do that."

"The demands of adult life can squelch a woman's spirit quite easily. There are lots of men in your family who might use that fire to their advantage, and it will extinguish if you are not on your guard."

Thelma nodded, confident that her teacher meant something different than a real fire but wasn't sure what. Like reading the books that were assigned, the real meaning had to be figured out.

"They'll mistake your enthusiasm for a need to please and expect you to wait on them. Your role as a woman is important, and you must be on guard to defend your dignity. Living with a house full of men, you must constantly remind yourself that you are someone special."

Back in that one-room country school, a thirteen-year-old Thelma felt confused. Now, at seventeen, she thought she understood what the flame inside her meant, and the possibility of loosing it frightened her. But George, Herman or Ralph weren't the problem. Except for some of their crude jokes, they always respected her privacy. It was that poor innocent Iggy, as Miss West sometimes called him, she had to guard against. She felt a surge of anger at him for snooping on her from the roof of the porch.

Like a thunderbolt, her anger turned white hot, and she screamed, "Pa is one of the men Miss West meant!" She felt this revelation explode like coffee boiling over in an open kettle. The strength of her voice disturbed the silence of the parlor, and it startled her. Cautiously, she began to release the feelings she had been harboring.

"You're a good person, Pa, the way you took Freddie and how you treat Arnie. You're kind to Iggy, and I know you're proud of George and Herman and Ralph. Freddie and I never have to be afraid of your anger because you don't get mad like a lot of other fathers." She paused and then shouted, "I trusted you." She found the key that released the anger she had buried and hoped would never surface.

"You violated me!" The words and their force frightened her, but she catapulted forward. "I was an innocent little girl playing house while my mother wasn't there to protect me. You allowed me," she paused to find a stronger word, "made me touch you in a way no daughter should touch her father. You should've stopped me. You're my father."

All the memories of what happened the day Svez was injured vanished when the taboo of the second incident with him in her mother's bed, hidden even deeper in her heart, broke loose. The dam burst. In her mind, she replayed his sexual penetration.

This time she screamed, "Stop, Pa! Stop!" He didn't stop, and Thelma again felt the pain and the humiliation. She sobbed and confronted him. "You made me feel dirty. Even if you didn't want it to happen—I had to make myself believe you didn't—it did happen. When I woke in Ma's bed, I blamed myself." She put her hands on her hips. "It wasn't my fault." She stared at the black cloth with its white boarder. "I tried to explain it to Mama, to make her understand that it was an accident. I don't think she understands. I don't understand."

Through a rush of tears, Thelma stared at the bay window covered with smears of frost making sweeping swirls around central vortexes. At another time, she would have interpreted them as angels or as her mother or as devils. She saw none of these. Her mind and her emotions were chaotic. All she saw were swirls of frost on a cold bay window in the parlor.

****

Svez found his voice after savoring the aroma of baked bread and apple pie. "Thelma, are you in the house?" He looked toward the front room and saw her staring at some sewing she was doing. She didn't seem to notice him. He left the house as quietly as he had entered. Trusting his sixth sense that trouble was brewing, he felt bewildered by a gnawing urge he thought he had conquered years ago. He wanted alcohol, felt he needed that drink to erase the pain he couldn't understand. He sought the refuge of the barn to sort out his feelings.

He didn't eat supper with his family. Instead, he spent the evening with the livestock wrestling demons. When he was sure everyone had gone to bed, he meandered back to the house and was surprised to see dirty dishes still on the table including empty pie plates. He took off his shoes and shoved them back into the porch. He expected to see Iggy asleep on the couch in the front room and Freddie nestled in his crib alongside his bed. The couch was vacated and the crib was missing. He went upstairs, checked the boys' room and saw Iggy sprawled out on his bed. He heard Thelma's voice and assumed she was consoling a fussy baby. He tiptoed back downstairs and crawled into bed.

CHAPTER TWELVE
FREDDIE
(Summer, 1937)

He sat on the platform near the top of the windmill and squinted at the sun. The rotation of the fan broke the light into manageable segments, explosions of sunlight immediately erased by the tack of the next blade. He covered one eye and when the other began to water and his vision blurred, he moved his hand to the other side of his face. The wind shifted, and the fan no longer filtered the light. With both eyes open, he spread his fingers and peered between them as he waved them back and forth. His hands appeared to magically grow additional fingers that fluttered and danced in the sunlight.

A pleasant cool breeze brushed across his face. He closed his eyes and watched tiny black dots chase back and forth across a blood-red background. Dream-like figures appeared and disappeared, creatures that lived in his world of fantasy. At night in bed, he saw these same images, but they were outlined in black against a gray background, and they frightened him. Today, they were not scary because they played in a field of bright and vivid colors. Was it a trick to fool him until nighttime when they would change into dark monsters? If he could tame them critters, they might never frighten him again. Thelma told him they were farm animals looking for a place to sleep. This made them seem less scary and seeing them in daylight even made them fun.

He opened his eyes and gazed on the horizon. This view pleased him because he could see so much at one time, and it was safely far away. The distant woods, crisscrossed roads and farm buildings looked like those in the coloring book Thelma had given him for his fifth birthday. He was always careful not to color outside the lines. He saw a giant finger gradually gather from nowhere in the sky, darken and point to a bright red tractor. When the tractor stopped at the end of the field, it drifted away. It reappeared, but now it came out of the tractor, formed a dark cloud and disappeared into the blue sky. Magically, the color of the ground behind the tractor changed from gold to black.

The wind shifted and the rotating blades swung open like a door. A vast cornfield appeared. Tassels swayed gently and created sheen of ever changing shades of green. They shimmered like the tinsel on Thelma's Christmas tree. When he heard Thelma call, her voice too loud and high pitched, he refused to answer. He didn't want to give up his hiding place. He liked time alone even more than playtime with his family. He did not want Thelma to find him. She would make him come down. He wanted to be away from the world below.

****

"Freddie." Thelma shielded her eyes and gazed around the yard. "Freddie! Where are you?" She paused and listened. "Answer me, Frederick."

After searching all his usual hiding places she visualized the unthinkable. The road. The Creek. Wanting to run both directions at once, she checked the gravel road past their farm, even though she told him never to play there. He usually obeyed. Relieved to find no broken body, no cars and no unsettled dust from recent traffic, an even more horrible image emerged; Freddie drowned in the creek and carried away by the current. She rationalized that the creek was low that time of the year, and two fences separated it from the yard. He was merely playing hide-and-seek, the only game he ever played with her and Iggy.

She tried a new strategy. "Ninety-nine, one hundred. Ready or not here I come." She listened carefully for the rustling sounds that sometimes gave away his hiding place. All she heard was the wind working the windmill and the water swishing as it pulsed through the pipes to the horse trough. Desperate, Thelma looked up at a wisp of clouds. *Ma, help me.* But her star wasn't available.

She wished Iggy was home. He'd know where to find him. Freddie never asked anyone to play with him, but he always got excited when Iggy suggested the game of hide-and-seek. When she had time to join them, Freddie and Iggy, hand in hand, would run off together. Her father could make Freddie laugh by pretending to steal his nose, pull things out of his ears and romp on the floor. George, Herman and Ralph sometimes made him giggle when they teased and played rough. When the games ended, Freddie always pulled back and never begged or even asked for more playtime. Sometimes, when she was busy, she'd forget about him until he wandered into the kitchen to eat. Today, he failed to come in for his afternoon snack.

Frightened and frustrated, she wandered into the barn and sat on the three-legged milk-stool her father used twice every day. Her brothers' chairs had only one leg, and they attached it to themselves with a leather strap. She thought they resembled beasts of burden hunched forward lugging pails of milk, a wooden tail protruding from their rears. She avoided going into the barn at milking time because they would swing the stool around, point the leg forward and ask, "Did you want something?" Once, George dared Iggy to walk outside the barn with his stool on backwards, and Liz caught him. The next day, Iggy told her about the scolding Pa gave him, and the boys agreed not to do that anymore.

Thelma had to put up with bawdy comments and rude behavior from the boys and men who outnumbered her and her few female cousins. When neighbors and relatives joined the Rastner men at harvest time, someone would tease her father in front of her.

"Svez, how come ya got so many sons?"

"It's too easy to make a girl," was his favorite answer. "I got the model right in front of me."

"It looks like you took the easy route when you made Thelma."

Thelma would cringe as she waited for his usual response.

"I thought I'd make one girl before the model wore out. While I could still recognize it."

Liz usually ignored Svez's crude humor, but it disgusted and angered Thelma. "Ma, make him stop talking like that," she would plead but seldom got support, so she buried her feelings. She noticed that men had different kinds of laughter depending on what they thought was funny. Her father's came out in short bursts that encouraged others to join him. It became especially loud when bawdy jokes were exchanged. When he released little puffs of air that curled into a tight giggle, Thelma figured he was embarrassed, frightened or angry. He never admitted any of these emotions, but reacted like something had amused him.

She distinctly remembered an afternoon when he walked into the house and saw Liz tenderly coddling an infant. He stood with his thumbs in the straps of his overalls and gave his not-so-funny kind of laugh. After an uncomfortable silence, he released one thumb and with his index finger pulled the blanket from the baby's face. He said one word, a question.

"Freddie?"

Ma nodded. He left the house and didn't return until suppertime.

Thelma heard him laugh that way another time when Freddie's pa came to visit while they were eating breakfast. She stood and said, "Hi, Uncle Henry," mostly because being called uncle seemed to annoy him. He sneered, sat down on her chair, grabbed her half-empty cup and held it out to be filled. She took the pot from the stove and dribbled some hot coffee over his fingers as she filled what had been her cup. He set it on the table, licked his finger with a tobacco-stained tongue and flashed her a toothless grin.

"Hey, Svez." He paused and slowly moved his gaze away from Thelma. "You got all dem boys. Why don't you let me have one for a while? Herbert's gone to work in town, and with just Clyde I'm a bit short handed."

"Boys ain't like a piece of field machinery." Her father produced his false laugh. "You just can't borrow one from relatives."

"You got to keep Freddie."

Svez looked somber. "He's just a baby."

"Babies grow up."

"I 'spose I can let Ralph help you a couple of days."

As Thelma sat on her father's stool, she pulled her dress over her knees and parted her legs, the normal position for holding a milk pail. Seeing the cream-colored flesh of her thighs, seldom exposed in broad daylight, frightened and titillated her. She remembered her terrible fear the one time her period came late. Had her father gotten her pregnant, her child would be a year younger than Freddie. Suddenly, the chair under her felt white-hot.

She jumped up and screamed, "Pa." Knotting her clinched fists into her lower abdomen, she ran from the barn and yelled, "Freddie! Frederick! Where are you?"

She listened for an answer, but she might as well have been calling the cats. She did call Freddie's dog, Podue, and he meandered from under the corncrib looking confused.

"Go find Freddie." She made an arcing gesture with her arm, and the dog followed the movement with his head. She knew how to order him to fetch the cows but had no idea how to tell him to find a lost five-year-old. He just looked bewildered and returned to his spot in the shade. Thelma sauntered back into the house and continually peered through windows hoping Freddie would get hungry enough to come in for a snack.

****

Arnie reined the horses and climbed down from a load of hay. "I 'spect he's atop the windmill," He suggested to Thelma as he unhitched his horses, removed their harnesses and let them trot off to the corral behind the barn. "Goes up there some times."

Thelma rushed to the tower, pulled her dress to her knees and reached for the lowest rung of the ladder. No way Freddie could have reached it. Had he cat-walked along the cross braces?

"Iggy gets him down, usually." He gestured toward the field-road. "Him and yer pa is just 'round the corner." He walked into the barn, closed the bottom half of the door and watched.

Thelma stepped down, ran toward the oncoming wagon and shouted, "Pa, Freddie's up there." Svez tilted his head the direction she pointed. "Arnie said Iggy's gotta get him down."

"I'll be damned." He glanced back at Iggy, then gestured with his head toward the small face peering down at him. "Go up and help him." He slid down from the load, wandered into the barn and dowsed his face in the cooling tank.

"Hurry, before he falls." Thelma sounded frantic.

"Soon's I get the horses unhitched." Iggy peered down at his sister and jumped to the ground. "There's no hurry." He slung the harnesses over the gate and slapped the horses' rumps. They trotted off. "Won't come down 'til he's ready, anyway."

Iggy understands more 'n any of them. Arnie walked to a ladder that stretched to the haymow and climbed up to the cupola. He peered out the vent and saw Iggy's head poke through the opening in the platform on top of the windmill and his arm reach out toward the boy. Freddie shoved his hand back.

Boys, yer little secret's out. Now whatcha gonna do? Arnie felt the breeze that drove the fan, heard the gears meshing and saw the arm of the cam driving the rod up and down. *I ain't never goin' to climb that damn thing. Folks on the ground kin see a body up there.* He felt safe in his cocoon as he watched the boys crawl down. Iggy led and Freddie followed. Iggy aimed Freddie toward the house and then disappeared into the barn.

Arnie waited until Freddie strolled into the porch before he crawled down to start his chores. He stood by the calf pen, listening to the boys' reaction to Freddie's accomplishment.

George, Herman and Ralph, noses up to the bellies of the cows they were milking, laughed and talked above the swoosh-swoosh of milk splashing into pails.

"Freddie just broke your record, Ralph." George grabbed his cow's tail as it slapped him in the face. He held it above his head and peeked out at his brother across the aisle.

"Yeah, I was seven 'fore I climbed that tower." Ralph stopped milking, stood and peered toward George over his heifer's back. "I guess Freddie ain't no baby no more."

Herman grabbed his cow's tail, tucked it between his leg and the half-full pail of milk and said, "Too bad Ma ain't here to give him his proper scolding."

Arnie held his breath when he heard Liz mentioned.

Herman paused, stood and then stooped as he massaged his cow's udder. The leg of his stool drooped toward the gutter. "Ain't that right?"

George and Ralph froze, hands clasped to their cows' teats. Neither said a word. Slowly the rhythm of milk spurting into milk began, first two beats, then four. Soon Herman sat back down, grabbed two teats and added to the harmony.

Arnie crawled out from the calf pen, wandered to the half-opened barn door and stared at the house. *The kid don't need Liz for scoldin' or for nuthin' else. He's got Thelma now.*

****

A year later when Thelma enrolled Freddie for the first grade, the experience turned out to be more unsettling for her than for him. After introducing him to Miss West, she helped him find his assigned desk. He raised and lowered the seat before climbing on to it. He slid his hands along the edges of the desk-top, across the surface scarred with initials carved by previous students and fingered the hinges. He lifted the lid, faced Thelma and grinned. She handed him tablet, color crayons and pencils, and he aligned them side by side in the compartment he had discovered. When an older student stopped to talk to him, he opened his desk and stared inside. She felt sad for him as she stood back and watched.

Miss West gestured for Thelma to return to the front of the room and sit beside her. "How have you been these past few years?" She capped her ink pen and placed it alongside the inkwell. "So often, I was tempted to stop at your place after school, but I just didn't feel right interfering that way. I know that you're doing a wonderful job of caring for those men in your family since your mother died. My mother died when I was in high school, but I wasn't left with responsibilities like you have. Goodness, you've been too busy to properly grieve your loss."

"I'm afraid I cried when it happened. I really didn't want to."

"Nonsense. Crying is a noble effort to clear out some of the hurt we sometimes gather inside ourselves." Her eyes rolled up toward the ceiling, and she shook her head. "If only men could express their pain. I wish my boys would cry rather than get angry and throw things."

Thelma agreed about the anger but couldn't imagine her brothers crying. Except maybe Iggy when he was teased and when Larry Collins was mean to him.

"How are Iggy and your other brothers accepting the loss of their mother?"

"Okay, I guess. It's been four years since she died."

"Now that I have another Rastner child in my custody, I will try hard to be more successful with him than I was with George, Herman and Ralph."

"Freddie's last name is Tate. Pa never wanted to change that. He didn't think it proper."

"Of course. He shall be Frederick Tate. I do insist on calling my students by their Christian names. Frederick will become comfortable with it very quickly. I hope you and your family continue to use his nickname. It's more intimate."

Thelma excused herself when a student asked to talk to her teacher and walked back to Freddie's desk. He opened the lid and showed her his tablet with crayons on one side and pencils on the other, all pointing forward.

"I have to go home to make lunch for the men, and I'll come back with yours." Walking to school that morning, he asked her not to kiss him on the forehead at school like she did at home. "You be good now for your new teacher, and she will help you if you need anything." She glanced back from the door, but Freddie's face was hidden behind his opened desk.

Miss West stood and faced Thelma. "New students don't have to stay. This is just get-acquainted day." Freddie touched each pencil and crayon in his desk, closed the lid and lifted the seat before he walked to the door. "Frederick, I want to see you tomorrow at nine o'clock sharp."

Freddie nearly disappeared into the folds of Thelma's dress. "Thank you, Miss West." He grabbed Thelma's hand and pulled her through the door.

Thelma felt proud that he remembered what she taught him to say. "You were very good today, Freddie. You were polite, and I think Miss West likes you."

They began their mile-long walk home, and Freddie pulled his hand from hers and stuck it into his pocket. "But why does she call me that name? My name is Freddie, not Fredik."

"Frederick," Thelma corrected. "Your full name is Frederick, but we call you Freddie because," she fumbled to find the correct reason, "because we love you." Freddie seemed to mull her words over in his mind, smiled and kicked a loose stone into the ditch. "Remember that time when you climbed up on the windmill, and I called and called for you. I finally said, 'Frederick, where are you?'"

"Didn't you love me when I climbed the wind mill?"

A pheasant flew out of the grass from where Freddie's stone landed. Thelma touched his shoulder and they stopped as the bird settled in a near-by cornfield.

"Of course I did. I was just frightened when I couldn't find you. I thought you were hiding from me."

"Is that what my teacher thinks?" He took Thelma's outstretched hand. "I was just putting things away in my new desk."

"Miss West loves you, and she knows you weren't trying to hide. She just likes to call students by their proper name." She remembered a similar discussion seventeen years earlier. "Miss West wouldn't call Iggy by his name either."

"What did she call him?"

"Ignatius. She called him Ignatius, and Iggy really liked it once he got used to it."

"Iggynis?" He squinted and his lips tightened.

She laughed, but encouraged him to keep trying until he pronounced it correctly. From his expression, she knew he planned to use his brother's full name.

"I see Ignatius." Freddie shook his hand free from her grip.

"That's enough practice for now. I don't think Iggy would like us playing with his school name."

"No, I see Ignatius, Iggy, down the road." He pointed.

Thelma saw a lone figure stroll out of their yard and head toward them. "How do you know it's Iggy that's coming to meet us?"

"Because, I can see him. He's coming to ask me about my new teacher." Freddie ran ahead, stopped and turned. "How do I say my new name again?"

"Fred-er-ick." Thelma barely had the name pronounced when he ran toward his big brother. By the time she caught up, they were already calling each other "Ignatius" this and "Frederick" that. Thelma knew Miss West had just earned Freddie's trust.

The next morning, Freddie ran out of the house before Thelma had time to give him his lunch. She had put two sandwiches and a candy bar into a lard can that Iggy had fitted with a wire handle and wooden cover. She stood on the front steps and yelled at him, but when he looked back she said, "Have fun." She would use his lunch as an excuse to stop at school and check on him. When she delivered it, he was sitting at his desk busy with his colors and tablet. He took the pail by the handle and set it under his desk.

"You can go home now."

Freddie's courage pleased Thelma, and she waited eagerly to hear about his day when he came home that afternoon. From the porch door, she watched George, Herman and Ralph stop him at their driveway.

"Hey, Freddie, let's play football," George yelled as he ran toward him.

"Where's the ball?" Freddie giggled. "We don't got one."

George scooped him up and ran toward the house.

Herman tried to grab him but got hit by a swinging lard can.

"Pass the ball to me." Ralph held out his arms.

"Catch." George tossed Freddie, and Ralph caught him just as Herman knocked George to the ground.

"Got 'em." Ralph ran to the house, yelled, "Touchdown," and set Freddie on the step in front of Thelma. She tussled his hair and told him to come in for milk and cookies. He sat at the kitchen table, ate his snack and worked on his homework until his brothers came in from the barn.

He turned the paper face down on the table and said, "No one can see it 'til Svez and Arnie get here."

Thelma wondered about Miss West's reaction when she heard Freddie call their father by his first name.

Surrounded by his entire family who had gathered for the evening meal, Freddie showed his paper. "My teacher told me to draw a picture of my family." He pointed to stick people of various colors and said, "Here are George and Herman and Ralph." At the end of each of their extended arms were five short lines for fingers. "This is Svez with the pitch fork." As if practicing for his presentation the next day, Freddie carefully pronounced their father's difficult name. "Arnie's milking a cow." A round figure reached under a balloon-like creature standing on four stick legs. "Iggy's in the hay barn, and Thelma's in the house."

Iggy pointed at two square boxes on the paper and nodded. "Yup. That's the barn and that's the house."

"This is very nice, but I don't see you in the picture." Thelma felt bad that Freddie didn't think he belonged in the drawing.

"Miss West wants to see my family."

"You're one of us," Iggy said as he grabbed the pencil. "Here, let's draw you in the empty space at the top."

"You let Freddie draw his own picture." Thelma took the pencil from Iggy's hand and gave it back to Freddie. She watched closely as he drew a round featureless figure in the spot Iggy suggested.

"This is me."

Iggy grabbed the pencil, pinched it between finger and thumb and drew a curved line on the face of the small figure. "Here, Freddie. You gotta look happy."

As the smile appeared on the picture, it disappeared on their little brother.

CHAPTER THIRTEEN
A NEW TRACTOR
(Fall, 1940)

Thelma washed the supper dishes and stacked them on the drain board to dry while her brothers played whist at the table. Svez's radio scratched and whistled in the background, as he sat at the small desk and fiddled with the dials. A newscaster described Germany's invasion of Poland, and their bombing of London. He claimed the war in Europe did more for the United States economy than any of Roosevelt's New Deal programs. He reported the local news and finished with the price of feeder pigs. Svez clicked off the radio, and Thelma waited for his humph that signaled his dissatisfaction with events they had just heard. Her brothers' arguments about trump cards, stupid plays and good or bad luck filled the room. Her father slapped a folded copy of The Farm Journal against the palm of his hand, a gesture of satisfaction Thelma calculated, and his change in attitude confused her. He pulled a slip of paper from his shirt pocket and gazed at it. What were those notes about and why was he so secretive?

"Where's Arnie?" He rose from the desk, stretched his arms and bumped the single light bulb hanging from the ceiling by its cord. His shadow raced back and forth across the wall.

"In the barn, I suppose." George trumped Iggy's card and grinned. "What's up, Pa?"

Svez stuck the magazine back on the desk, glanced at the cards on the table and shook his head. He walked out the door.

"He's sure acting strange lately." George shuffled and started to deal. "Anyone know what's up?"

"When he goes off to consult with Arnie, something's gonna happen." Herman leaned back on his chair and peeked at Thelma out the corner of his eye.

She caught the sarcasm. Whenever she wanted to assert her authority over her brothers she insisted they consult with her. She sat next to him and tousled his hair as she often did with Freddie.

"Hey, cut that out."

She felt an oily substance on her hand and smelled hairdressing from the Watkins man. She wiped her hand on her apron and decided not to tease him about it.

Ralph asked, "Did you ever watch him try to get an opinion from Arnie?"

Thelma studied his dark sparkling eyes from across the table. *You're a good looking guy. Quit going to see Ida and get yourself a real girlfriend.*

"Arnie never really agrees with him." Ralph laid the ace of trump. "Pa just keeps talking 'til Arnie gets tired of shaking his head."

"If he's talking to Arnie 'bout it, Pa's already made up his mind." George threw his cards on the table face up, his signal that he wanted to quit." We can expect something to happen real soon. Remember all his figuring the time he bought that forty-acre piece from Matt Gerhard? Matt had to sell off some land 'cause his boy left him, and he couldn't handle all his acres alone."

"Yeah, he left his pa, just like that." Ralph snapped his fingers. "We ain't never going to leave Pa, or you neither, Thelma." His eyes met hers. "We boys been talking, and that's what we decided." He shoved George's cards back to him and pointed to his ace. "We're gonna finish this game."

"That's a nice thought, Ralph." She glanced at Iggy who usually reported their brothers' secret discussions, but the bewildered look on his face told her that this conversation had taken place without him.

George glared at Ralph, then faced Thelma. "How 'bout when Pa got us hooked up to electricity through the REA? He sat at that desk for hours and even attended neighborhood meetings to study that decision."

"He claimed he did it so Ma could get her electric ice box." Thelma chuckled and pointed to the Frigidaire.

The outside door slammed shut and all heads turned. The kitchen door opened. Freddie stood and gawked back at everyone.

"Why you all staring at me?"

George said, "Thought you might be Pa coming back in. We was talking about the time we got electricity. That was before you moved in with us."

"Huh?"

"Just something that happened before you were born." Thelma always referred to Freddie's birth rather than his moving in, and she wished her bothers wouldn't even hint that he didn't belong with their family.

"I'm eight. We had 'lectricity that long?"

"Yeah, Freddie." Ralph sighed and tossed his cards on top of George's. "That same year we got two kinds of electricity, the REA and you. Both lit up our lives real nice."

Thelma smiled and silently thanked Ralph with her eyes.

"That's silly. I can't light up nothing. Svez kicked me out of the barn 'cause he was discussing something with Arnie."

"That's what we was just talking 'bout. What do you 'spose is their secret?" George asking Freddie for his opinion pleased Thelma.

"I heard him say something 'bout a tractor. Are we gonna get one?"

Thelma was surprised that Freddie guessed what she had assumed for sometime but never told her brothers.

"Wow, it better be a John Deere." George jumped up. "They got lots of power and they make loud noises when they're working real hard. Chicka-chicka-chicka." George imitated the sound of a two-cylinder engine, grasped an imaginary steering wheel and drove around the kitchen table swinging his hips back and forth to the rhythm of the sound.

Thelma felt embarrassed by her brother's child-like reaction. "Don't get carried away, George. It probably won't happen anyway."

"Pa's talking to Arnie, 'bout it." He made two more trips around the table with his new John Deere.

****

Arnie felt sorry for Freddie when Svez told him to get out of the barn. Being shoved aside so important people could talk was not a new feeling for Arnie. What's so important that the kid ain't 'sposed to hear? He watched Freddie saunter toward the barn door, stop beside a cow and squirt milk at the cat lounging in the aisle. When it backed away and licked its fur, Freddie peppered it with corncobs. The tom jumped onto the heifer's back, stretched and continued cleaning his fur. The cow lay undisturbed on the fresh straw, her head stuck through the stanchion, and chewed her cud. Freddie opened the door, glanced back and gestured like he was about to throw one last cob. He walked out slamming the door behind him. Arnie enjoyed Freddie's stalling tactics.

"We got four grown boys to do the field work, so we don't really need one." Svez glanced at the floor, then at Arnie.

Arnie expected his brother to point out the bad parts of his idea first. He always did that, and Liz used to tell him that he'd make a poor poker player. Arnie, according to Liz, had the poker face that kept everyone guessing. Every time Arnie thought about Liz he felt sad. He took off his glove and tried to brush an imagined piece of chaff from his eye.

"But who knows how much longer they'll be with us?" Svez paused as two Bantam roosters squabbled over whole kernels of undigested corn in some cow dung.

Arnie shook his head. Svez, not the boys, would decide when its time for them to go on their own.

"George, Herman and Ralph already got their own cows and horses. All they need is farms to put them on. With them extra forty acres, we'd have trouble getting the plowing and planting done with just horses."

Arnie stared at his feet and waited, but Svez had ended his argument. He had to agree now, or Svez would buy the tractor without his consent. He waited until the two Bantams settled on the pipe that fed water to the cows and roosted side-by-side.

"Henry jus' got hisself one."

"By God, then we gotta get one, too." Svez looked over his shoulder like he expected someone to be listening and then repeated, "By God, let's do it!"

Arnie felt Liz's presence in their discussion, and Svez probably did, too. She would have scolded him for blasphemy and for trying to keep up with the relatives. Arnie felt like he let his sister-in-law down.

"I'll go see Victor Cunningham tomorrow." Svez shoved a clod of manure into the gutter with his shoe. "Sure wish Walt Cunningham still run the implement business. A fellow could deal with that guy."

Arnie spat, not from an excess of tobacco juice as he seldom did that, but from the idea of dealing with Cunningham or any one else in Bovine. He followed Svez out of the barn but stopped at the outdoor privy on his way to the house. Talk about dealing with town folk upset his stomach. He knew that Svez enjoyed jostling with them and making up funny stories to entertain neighbors and relatives. He also realized that they told just as many ugly stories about the hicks from the country. He felt it best for country folk and town folk to keep apart as much as possible.

The full moon shone through the crescent cutout on the door and he could barely make out the banner on the newspaper stuffed in a rack on the door, THE BOVINE JOURNAL. He remembered when it was called THE SKUNK HOLLOW JOURNAL. He had been a young man when the town folks changed the name of their town. He liked the old name better. He didn't have much use for their newspaper except for some of the silly gossip and maybe a few advertised specials at York's. He preferred to wipe himself with cobs.

****

Back in 1888, the duly elected representatives had completed applications, filed sworn statements with the county and state offices, and presented the articles of incorporation to the locals gathered at the community center. Melvin Trask, self appointed chairman, cleared his throat to call for the vote when a tall man, salt and pepper hair sleeked and fastened at a bunch in back, pants and shirt freshly pressed, rose and requested the floor.

Melvin said in a loud and official voice, "The Chair recognizes Walt Cunningham."

"Everyone recognizes Walt Cunningham," Hank Sturgis, local dairy farmer, whispered to fellow committee member, Albert Wentzel, Skunk Hollow's only blacksmith. "He's bin a pain in the ass ever since he brung his implement business here."

Albert whispered back, "If Cunningham's so damn smart, why don't he run for the council 'stead of laying in the weeds 'til we gits all the work done?"

"I feel that our new town deserves a better name than what we've been calling it since the time of Moses." Walt drew a large white handkerchief from his suit jacket and wiped his forehead. "Some day we'll have a post office, and *Skunk Hollow* will be postmarked on letters mailed to our out-of-town friends."

Hank Sturgis and Albert Wentzel faced each other and wondered who had such friends.

"My wife's already embarrassed to tell her family back home where we've established our business." A general murmur rose from the crowd. "Mind you, I'm not complaining about the people. It's just the name that, quite frankly, stinks."

Those who actually lived in Skunk Hollow or, by decree of the board of directors would live within the boundaries of their newly incorporated town, generally agreed with Cunningham, but he was a newcomer to the area and his house wasn't even within the proposed boundaries. Most farmers such as Hank, however, felt the name quite aptly described the missionary settlement near the banks of the Skunk River, and Father Alexis Busch, the young priest about to become permanent pastor of St. Alphonse Parish, never complained about it either.

"Do you want to make that into a motion?" asked Chairperson Trask, who recently returned from a visit to the State Capital where he observed lawmakers in action.

"Yes," Walt responded. "I move that we change the name of our town."

"That's half an idea, and a dumb one at that." Ben York, the owner of York's Mercantile, a grocery, furniture and clothing store across the street from Cunningham's Implement, stood and expressed his opinion of the suggestion and of the younger man who proposed it. "Ain't that right, Albert?" He hoped the old blacksmith, a fellow businessman, would agree.

"Yer jest pissed 'bout losin' that bet with Cunningham," Albert taunted back. Everyone at the meeting burst out laughing.

****

A year earlier, Hank Sturgis, Albert Wentzel and Melvin Trask sat at the picnic table behind the newly-constructed community center and rehashed what had become known as the York/Cunningham wager.

Melvin claimed Ben York's raspy voice challenged Cunningham to a daily cup of coffee all year at Bud and Emma's. Adding the piece of pie must have come from Walt, speculated Albert.

Hank, whose acreage next to the town had been swallowed up in bits and pieces by townsfolk for their new homes, said, "I heard big amounts of money was hollered back and forth. My wife was standing next to Ben's wife and Betsy heard Clara say she didn't know where Ben would get five hundred dollars if he lost."

"I tell ya, the coffee, the pie, and the money was dropped when the biddin' got nasty." Albert scraped away dark residue from under his fingernails with a pocketknife. "We won't never know 'cause Walt started whisperin' and writing on that little note pad he always carries with him." He blew and dark specks scattered across the table. "Ya know, the one where he uses to figure how he's goin' to swindle ya on a horse trade."

"They're never together at the café, so I knowed that part of the deal got canceled." Sturgis bit into a plug of tobacco, and a bulge appeared on his left cheek. "Walt wid never squelch on a deal." He poked his tongue through pursed lips, removed a flake of the tobacco and stared at it. "Once I traded him a spavined horse. He got mad, but he held to the deal." He wiped his hand on his pant leg.

"Ben ain't 'bout to renege neither." Albert switched his pocketknife to his other hand. "My guess is they called all the bets off, 'cept the one 'bout the Union Suit."

"That's how I reported it in *Scent of the Skunk*." Melvin Trask, publisher of *The Journal*, paged through the notebook that had become his trademark.

"Yeah, Betsy saved it." Hank glanced toward the opened page and Melvin slammed it shut. "She got every *Scent of the Skunk* ya ever writ. I kin still see Ben in his long johns, standin' at Cunningham's front door durin' Walt's open house. Every time a customer walked in, he bent over and lifted the flap."

"Yeah, but nobody got to see Ben's bare ass, just a sign that read GRAND OPENING." Melvin grinned. "I printed it for Walt at my shop."

****

Ben York continued standing, his face flush with anger at the put-down in the middle of a town meeting, and waited for the laughter to subside. He shook a finger at Albert. "I ain't got no hard feelings 'bout the wager." He glanced around the room and back toward Walt. "That's still a dumb motion," and sat down.

"Ben's right." Chairman Trask tapped the table, fisted the head of the gavel and pointed the handle toward Cunningham. "You gotta give us a new name to consider, if you intend to make that motion."

Walt considered *Cunningham Town*, but kept that idea to himself.

Hank rose, scanned the crowd and faced Walt. "If ya can't hanker to skunks, maybe some other animal, like a cow. We gots plenty of 'em 'round here." The crowd chuckled.

When someone shouted *Cow town*, Gavin Dowdy, full time harness maker and part time butcher, yelled *bull shit*.

Melvin Trask, soon to be a shoe-in mayor of the new town as well as publisher of the local newspaper and author of the weekly column, *Scent of the Skunk*, banged the gavel, and asked for other suggestions.

Walt rose and jabbed his finger toward the men laughing and slapping Gavin Dowdy on his back. "That vulgarity wasn't a suggestion, but an opinion of a stupid name." He sneered, "Cow Town."

"How about Cow Shit." Melvin Trask smirked as he searched the crowd for reactions, always on the alert for editorial material. "Cow Shit, Minnesota."

"*Cow Town* sounds okay to me. Farmers raise 'em, and I butcher 'em." Gavin Dowdy reminded those who might need his services at slaughter time.

"Just like a town in a dime novel." Ben York reminded everyone that he sold such books at his store.

Walt's face began to resemble a beet. "Cows around here are different."

"Like how?" Hank Sturgis defended the cattle he no longer raised since he made more money selling his land.

"Well, for one thing, they're dairy cows, not the kind you round up from the open range, brand and drive to the railhead." Walt didn't like the direction his suggestion had taken.

"How about *Holstein Town*? Them's the most common kind 'round here." Melvin grinned at the crowd. "And, what about the bull?" He prodded for more feature material. "The bull and the cow. That's what life's all about."

"Bovines," Walt exclaimed.

"Yeah, let's name the town after one of them bovine critters, whatever they are." Albert gave his view of the unusual animal. "That'd keep folks guessing 'bout it."

"Bovine's just a fancy name for cattle, and...." Walt started to explain that he was against the idea of a cow by any name.

"Bovine, Minnesota." Melvin Trask banged his gavel, and people began to leave.

The decision didn't become final until the next Thursday when he printed minutes of the community meeting in his first edition of the newly named *Bovine Journal*. He expected responses to his first feature, *Bullshit, Minnesota*, but only Walt sent a letter to the editor. He went back to calling his gossip column *Scent of the Skunk*.

****

The morning after their decision to buy a tractor, Svez climbed onto the seat of the "A" John Deere tractor parked on the street directly in front of Cunningham Implement. He felt Victor Cunningham had purposely ignored him when he inspected the smaller "B" model displayed inside the store where a potbelly stove used to sit. He knew Victor was just giving him time to build up interest. He pulled his watch from the bib pocket of his overalls and checked the dials. Two minutes, he decided, and Victor would be out there looking to sell him this tractor.

Victor stuck his head through the door and looked up and down the street.

Svez continued to finger the tractor's dials and switches in front of him.

"There you are." Victor walked up to the tractor and grabbed the tire as if he planned to shake Svez off the seat. "Thought you maybe snuck away without buying something. Can't let that happen."

Svez estimated the position of the sun and checked his watch, shook it briefly and held it up to his ear. He glanced down at Victor as if he had just noticed him.

"Whatcha think, Svez?"

"Huh?"

"Of the 'A' model."

"Too much for what I need. I got five boys and twice that many horses. 'Fraid they'd go soft on me if I got something like this."

Victor released the tire, clapped his hands once and started to back away.

"But, they'll be leaving me some day, and then where'll I get the help. A fella should get the fall plowing done before the snow flies." He let go of the steering wheel, slapped it once with both hands and climbed down. He walked back into the store, stood alongside the smaller tractor and leaned on one of its tires. Victor followed and grasped the wheel across from him.

"This is a good little tractor, but you really need the 'A' model to get your plowing done 'fore winter freeze-up." Ralph took a notepad and fountain pen from his shirt pocket and started writing. "Tell you what." He lifted his hand and waved the pen toward Svez, like he was thinking real serious or maybe blessing him with it. He focused back at his notes, scratched over some numbers and muttered just loud enough for Svez to hear, "No, that won't work." He repeated, "Tell you what." He put his note pad and pen back into his pocket. "We might get another "A" model next spring, but that won't help with this fall's plowing, will it?" He slapped the tire like it was a horse's backside.

Amused, Svez wondered if his next tactic would be to refuse to sell the machine. He reached into his shirt pocket and took out a small black book and a stub pencil peppered with teeth marks. He studied the perfectly formed numbers representing his current bank balance. Earlier that morning, he had watched Mildred's hands, her delicate fingers paging through ledgers and entering numbers in his bankbook, and he thought of Liz's strong hands. Often throughout the day, he visualized her performing routine tasks around the farm. Although he had never asked her to help in the barn, he knew her capable hands could have done any of the work around the farm. His mind returned to the balance in his bankbook, and he calculated that he had enough money to buy both tractors. He had no intention of doing so or letting on that he could. However, the extra funds did give him an idea.

"Why don't you jostle some more numbers and if the price ain't too high, I might be willing to deal on one of them new fangled milking machines, too." He purposely didn't say which tractor he decided to buy, and Victor's startled reaction pleased him.

Victor took out his notepad, started to ask, "Which one," and stopped. He quickly opened it and scribbled some numbers. "I'll knock fifty dollars off the price of the 'A' today if you agree to buy a milking machine." He paused and made eye contact with Svez. "Or any other machine you might need on your farm."

Svez considered the offer. He had already decided to buy the larger tractor when he read the article in *The Farm Journal* weeks ago, but he hesitated about the milking machine. Arnie would never use it. It might upset the cows. It could spoil the boys. He wished he hadn't mentioned it. He had to make up his mind quickly, if he wanted to get the deal on the tractor.

After he and Victor settled the details of the two-part transaction, Svez felt more confident about his decision. He had the tractor that he wanted and a good story to tell everyone about whittling down the price.

Victor followed Svez to his car and shook his hand a third time. "I see you're still driving that same Model 'A' Ford. At least you won't have a new name to remember."

Svez pretended he didn't understand.

"You know, a Model "A" car and a Model 'A' tractor.

"Oh, sure. I 'spose that's right." He forced back a smile. He had driven his sons' old car so as not to appear too prosperous.

Victor said, "How 'bout pie and coffee at Emma's? My treat."

"You mean Bud and Emma's?"

"Hadn't you noticed? Fred's folks been dead nearly twenty years, and he finally got around to repainting the sign." He put his hand on Svez's shoulder, aimed him in the direction of the café and pointed. "Actually, he just painted EMMA'S CAFE over the old writing. You still can see Bud's name if the sun hits it right. Now that selling booze is legal, he opened a real bar across the street. Named it *Buddy's Bar*. Wants folks to call him Buddy now, his middle name, I suppose." He put his hand in his pocket and jiggled what sounded like keys or loose change. "How about that pie?"

"'Fraid I won't have time for that." Svez thought about the pie Thelma had been making when he left home that morning. "After I get a bank draft for the things you sold me, I need to get home to lick my wounds."

The next day, Svez stood in the porch holding a cup of coffee and, through the clear crisp fall morning air, he heard an engine bellow as it worked its way up the hill near the schoolhouse. When it became quiet, he knew it reached the top. It barked just once, the driver probably shifted to a lower gear, and struggled against its own weight pushing down the hill. His John Deere tractor was on its way, and he watched for his family's reaction. Iggy and Freddie ran from the barn, and Thelma came out of the garden. They all stared at a huge green machine that seemed to float toward their driveway, only the noise and dust revealed the flatbed truck under it hidden from view by the thick hedge alongside the road. As it slowed, the brakes squealed and gravel splattered from under the huge wheels. When the dust caught up, it nearly hid the tractor. An arm stuck out from the cab and waved, as the truck jolted, turned into their yard and came to a complete stop with the engine continuing to lope like a wild animal after a chase.

"Pa did it," exclaimed Thelma.

Freddie climbed up on the truck and onto the tractor. Perched on the seat, he grabbed the steering wheel and pretended to drive.

Iggy peered between the slats of a wooden crate and yelled, "It's some kind of shiny machine, what else Pa bought."

Svez walked over to Thelma. "I'll have the boys put it in the summer kitchen. When winter comes they can put it in the basement." He enjoyed the curious look on his daughter's face. He knew the summer kitchen was cramped when she canned or prepared meals for thrashing crews, but he thought it belonged there.

"A milking machine in my summer kitchen?"

"Milking machine?" Svez felt pleased that Thelma had guessed wrong.

"Come on, Pa. You've been talking about a milking machine long before you went to see Cunningham."

"Didn't I say a milking machine would be no good, and didn't I say it would scare the cows?"

"You always say dumb things like that just to throw us off guard. Freddie and I learned that last Christmas, when you gave us the wrong clues about what you got us."

He was shocked that they had figured out his method to surprise them. "Well then, guess what it is."

"I don't care what it is. I don't want a piece of farm equipment in there. Put it in the machine shed where it belongs." She turned and stormed toward the house.

****

Later, when the boys were in the barn doing chores, Thelma went to see what Pa bought. When she opened the door, she saw a headless metal monster with four legs on wheels and a pair of rolling pins, its only arm pointing directly at her. She put her hands on her hips and stared. *I guess I could roll out pie dough with this contraption.*

"Well, what do you think of your new washing machine?" Her father stood behind her in the doorway.

"Oh, Pa. Thank you." She faced her father with the wringer sticking out between them. "So all the hush-hush these past few weeks was not just about the tractor. We all knew that was coming, and you knew that we knew. A washing machine. I saw one demonstrated at the county fair last year and never figured I'd ever have one." She pushed on the wringer. "Doesn't this move somehow?"

"Press this lever, and the arm will swing all the way 'round." He released the mechanism and it swung directly into Thelma's breasts.

"Oops. Good thing the machine weren't running. It woulda sucked you right in." He backed away from her. "Are you hurt?"

A favorite expression of George's popped into her head. "I'm not hurt, but I just about got my tit in a wringer."

Laughing, he reached to push it safely out of the way, and Thelma defensively folded her arms over her breasts. With the wringer no longer separating them, her father became quiet and his hands fumbled with the straps of his bib overalls, dropped to his side and finally found their way into his pockets.

"Thanks, Pa." Sensing that he felt uneasy, "For the washing machine, I mean." She touched his arm. "I better get back to the house." She turned and walked away.

CHAPTER FOURTEEN
AN AUTUMN MORNING
(1942)

Freddie thought about zebras when he saw the curved white stripes under the horse-drawn rake where the tines had protected the frost from the sun's penetrating rays. Liquid diamonds glisten on the rusted metal and created dark spots when they dripped onto the white ground. They reminded him of leopards from the jungle book that Miss West had given him. He glanced back at the footprints his bare feet made and imagined a bear had followed him to the barn. The sun had already melted the frost on the path to the woods where the cattle spent the night. Suddenly, he felt someone's eyes on him from the cupola on top of the barn but decided it was only the crow that caw-cawed and flew from its perch on the roof.

He jumped up and down to increase circulation in his feet and remembered the barn dance where Thelma taught him the bunny-hop. He whistled and Shep crawled out from under the corncrib and ran to him. Freddie warmed his fingers by raking them through his dog's soft shaggy hair, and together they pranced through greasy black muck down the cow-path. Even before they reached the woods by the pasture, the cows began responding to their morning routine. They slowly stood and, with udders and bladders full, headed single file down the path toward the barn. Their awakened bodies began to expel the residue of grass, reduced to cud, reduced to dung.

Freddie quieted an anxious Shep and allowed the cattle to pass. Instead of following them, he played hopscotch from one small pile of steamy dung to another reveling in the warmth and wetness of the recent droppings. He dug his toes into warm clusters of leaves that covered patches of ground where the animals had slept and awaited the rays of the low-lying sun to spread warmth throughout his body. He wore shoes at school but this was Saturday and he intended to go barefoot all day.

With the sun warming his back, he walked to the bank of the creek where the current had carved a hole deep enough to swim on hot summer days. Today might get that warm, but he doubted it as he shivered and stared down at his shadow on the smooth surface of the water. He needed to pee. One strap from his bib overalls hadn't been hooked when he dressed that morning and the other slid easily off his shoulder, his pants dropping to his ankles.

He aimed and watched the pee sparkle in the sunlight, arch and splash onto his shadow on the water. The ripples pleased him. Reaching down, he grabbed stones and tossed them at the ever-enlarging circles that etched across the surface of the water. Each stone made a new target for the next one. The sun's rays striking his bottom reminded him of his nakedness and he bent down, pulled both straps from his pants over his shoulders and hitched them to the brass buttons on the corners of the bib. He hurried back to the barn to continue his chores.

After Iggy dropped a forkful of silage in front of each cow, Freddie followed and added a mound of ground oats measured from a coffee can. When Freddie dumped the can in front of the cow Arnie was milking, Arnie got up, rubbed and patted the cow's neck and glared at him. Freddie stared back, and finally Arnie retreated to his milk-stool and massaged the cow's udder. Freddie had grown accustomed to Arnie's strange behavior, but this time he had glared longer and seemed angrier. Freddie had to force himself not to break eye contact first. He continued to distribute precise amounts of ground feed to each of Arnie's six cows and wondered what he had done to irritate him. He had been extra careful to do his job exactly as Arnie had demanded.

Freddie took a milk pitcher from its shelf and watched Herman pour steamy and frothy milk into a ten-gallon can that bobbed in the cooling tank. As the can filled, it settled to the bottom and the water covered everything but the lid. Cold water gushed into the tank through a pipe from the pump under the windmill. He knew the milk had to be cooled so it wouldn't spoil, but Thelma wanted warm milk for breakfast. Freddie held the pitcher with both hands, and Herman filled it with what was left in his pail. He walked to the two-part barn door, gazed toward the house through the top

116

half left open for ventilation and waited for Herman to unhook the bottom half to let him out. On the way across the yard, he again sensed someone watching him. He turned and saw Arnie framed in the half-open barn door. He ran the rest of the way to the house, milk spilling onto his hands.

****

From his perch inside the cupola on top of the barn, Arnie watched and waited. Some mornings Freddie was first to leave the house, but this morning he still lay sound asleep when Arnie peered into the boys' room. To avoid marking a path to the barn in the light dusting of snow, Arnie walked behind buildings, along the fence line and through the back door. The kid don't need to know a body was up in the cupola watching. Freddie burst out of the house, played with the dog and then headed down the path to the pasture. Arnie couldn't understand why it annoyed him. Still, he allowed himself to brood

He'd go barefoot to fetch Pubba's cows. The cold never bothered him. He'd warm his feet in cow shit when he got tired of making footprints on the frosty ground. When the snow came or it got real cold, Pubba let him wear shoes. He didn't need any special ones just for school like Freddie did. Least not after the fourth grade when he knew his math and could read good enough, and Pubba made him stay home. Mumma made him wear shoes to church on Sundays even in the summer.

He felt the cold wind pass through the vents, and he pulled his rawhide jacket tight around his neck. He needed to see Freddie and Shep replay more of his past life. He had a clear view of the pasture but couldn't see his house where Mumma prepared breakfast and waited for him to bring the fresh milk. After he and his dog got the cows headed in the right direction, Arnie watched himself jump from cow dropping to cow dropping and felt the warmth ooze between his toes. He felt the urge to pee as he stood along the bank of the creek. Pubba's farm didn't have a creek, but Arnie imagined it could have had one. He distinctly remembered a black and white dog. He wanted to relive more of his boyhood life, but a loud and stern voice interrupted his secret world.

"Arnie, are you up here?"

"I'm gettin' the cows." Why was Pubba mad?

"What?"

"Checking the vent." His confusion started to clear. "Hay's startin' to sweat and git hot."

117

"Let the boys do that. We're too old to be climbing these ladders."

"Boys don't know nuthin' 'bout hay getting hot 'nuf to burn down the barn."

"Stay there. I'll get them to help you down."

"I don't need no help." He looked through the vent again, but only saw Freddie, not himself when he was a boy, hitting the ground with a stick and walking back from the pasture with his dog, Shep.

He resented George and Herman when they climbed the ladder and helped him free his leg that had caught on the metal bracing. Down from the loft, Arnie started to milk his first cow, but his hands hurt and he couldn't squeeze the teats. While he rubbed the cow's neck to loosen the joints in his fingers, he locked eyes with Freddie who paused holding the empty can. The incident he witnessed in the pasture that morning flashed through his mind and he blamed Freddie for getting stuck in the cupola and making Vester mad at him. That kid needed more chores, and Arnie made up his mind to tell him after he finished milking. He sat back on his stool and continued to rub his hands on the cow's warm udder but his fingers wouldn't bend proper. He got up, walked to the door and watched Freddie head across the yard with the pitcher of milk. When he was that kid's age, his chores included feeding and milking the cows. After Freddie stopped near the house, turned and glared at him, he decided he had better talk to the boy right away. At the kitchen table, he faced Freddie but the instructions he had muttered to himself on the way to the house faded. He went up to his room and shoved his dresser in front of the door.

****

Svez didn't notice that Arnie had gone until he saw an empty milk can still floating in the cooling tank. "Arnie ain't milked his cows." George stopped picking pieces of dirt from the milk filter and glanced up. "Have you seen Arnie?"

"Ain't seen him." He slammed the funnel against the can to get the milk to continue flowing through.

"You don't suppose he went back up to the cupola again?"

"I doubt it. He was pretty shaky when me and Herman helped him down."

"You boys take care of his cows." He faced Herman and Ralph who had gathered near the cooler. "I'll check in the house."

"You want us should milk Arnie's cows?" Ralph grinned. "You sure he won't mind us messing with his girlfriends?"

"I don't think he'll even remember that he didn't do it." Svez checked a few hiding places and then left.

"He came in early, right after Freddie brought the milk this morning." Thelma filled his coffee cup. "When I asked if the boys are coming, he just grunted, like he does when he gets mad." She glanced toward Freddie who sulked at the table. "When Freddie asked if he could do anything for him, Arnie told him to mind his own business and went up to his room. Arnie never talked to him that way before."

"He had a bad morning." Svez splashed coffee into his saucer, sipped from it and set cup and saucer on the table. "I'll go upstairs and see what's bugging him."

"We heard him moving furniture around up there. I think he's blocked his door with his dresser again."

Svez pushed Arnie's door open an inch and asked, "What's up?"

After getting no answer, he used his shoulder to move the dresser far enough to squeeze in. Arnie lay on his back and stared at the ceiling. He still had on his buckskin jacket.

"Are you okay?"

"Nuthin's wrong. Just takin' a nap after chores."

"Thought you might be sick, or something." He sat on the side of the bed, and Arnie turned his head.

"Remember when you used to sit on my bed and tell me stories. You called me Vester?"

Arnie faced him. "I always call ya Vester."

"Only when we lived with Pubba. He wanted you to call me Svez, same as everyone else, but you just kept calling me Vester to piss him off. Remember?" He cuffed Arnie's shoulder. "Until we moved here."

"Pubba hated it when I called ya Vester. Liz didn't like it either, so I quit." He grinned. "For her."

"Want some breakfast?"

"Nah. Just a little nap. I got some pork hocks under my bed, if I get hungry. I'll be down at milkin' time." Svez squeezed out the door, "And ya kin tell that kid I don't want him messin' with my cows."

Svez returned to the kitchen where everyone had finished eating yet lingered at the table.

"How is he?" Thelma asked.

"Arnie's getting old and a little confused. Sometimes the past jumps forward and mixes with what's going on today. He'll be okay after he gets things sorted out."

"Is he still mad at me?" Freddie asked.

"He didn't say, but I doubt it." Svez lied. "He's just having a bad day."

"Should me and Herman keep milking his cows?" Ralph asked.

"Let's wait to see what he does."

Later that afternoon in the barn, Svez heard Arnie give Freddie instructions about the special way each of his cows liked to be milked.

Arnie's head jerked up and the tone in his voice became stern. "'Bout time Freddie starts doin' more work 'round here. I only got him doin' half my cows 'cause he still gotta go to school."

"Glad to hear you're starting to slow down a bit."

"He's doin' good, and I kin keep a eye on him."

"Okay. I'll tell Iggy to feed silage and ground oats. He won't mind 'cause he don't wanna do any milking."

Just as Svez suspected, before long Freddie milked all of Arnie's cows morning and afternoon with Arnie standing alongside, sometimes correcting him and sometimes muttering to the cow. Svez approved.

CHAPTER FIFTEEN
THE DRAFT OFFICE
(Winter, 1943)

"Daylight in the swamp." Svez's wake up call, raspy with the early morning phlegm, echoed through the stairwell and into the three upstairs bedrooms. With his faltering voice, he added, "It's five o'clock." He knew the boys would still be sleeping. Freddie, like Arnie, got up even before Thelma and prowled about the yard and barn. Even on the days Arnie wouldn't come out of his room, Freddie spent early mornings away from the house, and Svez worried he'd become a loner like Arnie.

Svez buttoned the work shirt he had slipped over his long johns during the night when the bedroom got cold, gathered his overalls and socks and went to the kitchen. He sat at the only chair left at the table; all the others faced the stove, their backs draped with steaming coats and caps, and shoes were spread open on the seats. Thelma was gonna spoil them boys.

"Morning, Pa." Thelma stood waiting, the spout of the gray speckled coffeepot pointing toward him.

He grunted and held out his cup. When he saw the fur-lined earflap dangle from the oven door, he knew Arnie was still in bed, probably wearing his buckskin jacket. He'd talk to him later.

The boys pranced into the kitchen, tossed their coats on the floor and sat in front of the stove where they finished dressing. Freddie wasn't with them. Bundled and braced for the January cold, they nodded, winked at Thelma and headed outside.

"Make sure that Freddie's in the barn," Svez called after them, then to Thelma, "Who knows where he and that crazy dog's been chasing this morning."

"He was gone when I got up. Had already stoked the fire. I imagine he's checking on Arnie's cows. Got really cold last night."

She tossed his coat over her shoulders. "Gotta get some meat from the smoke house." A gust of cold air burst across the room. "Guys left the darn storm-door open."

Alone, Svez contemplated his past life written on leathery hands clasped to the coffee mug for warmth. He manipulated his world with these tough hands for nearly seventy years, but he felt their grip faltering. He could feel Elizabeth's presence and wanted her arms around him again. He longed for the warmth of her body, to feel the gentle touch of her hand. He wanted Thelma to hug him like she did as a child but he knew she wouldn't do that, couldn't do it. Physical contact with his sons wasn't proper, and he hadn't held Freddie since he had grown too big to pick up and toss in the air. When he talked with Arnie, they might bump into each other if they leaned together on a fence post or a tractor tire to discuss a problem, but that didn't count. He wanted to hold, needed to be held.

He thought he heard Thelma stomp her feet to remove the snow from her shoes, and he braced for the blast of cold air when she'd open the kitchen door. But it didn't happen. An anxious moment peaked to a flash of near panic. Where had she gone? He felt the letters in his shirt pocket and shuddered.

"Thelma?" He got no response. His voice melted into a single "humph" when the door opened.

"I'm about as frozen as this pork roast." Thelma tossed what sounded like a rock on the table and threw his coat over a chair near the stove. "It'll take most of the day to thaw out."

"I 'spect it will." He responded but hadn't heard what she said. Why had he been so jumpy lately? No one's leaving him, least not yet. He removed the four letters from his shirt pocket and fingered them carefully. She set a basin of solid ice on the stove, and it made a sizzling noise. He stared at her.

"The boys left water in it last night after washing up." She stood behind him and peered over his shoulder. "What are you reading?"

"Draft notices." He stared blankly at them. He had been following the course of the war on the evening news. He barely knew about the Japanese and certainly didn't want the United States to fight the Germans. He thought about the names of some German ancestors that Liz had written in their family Bible. Harry Gross' prediction the previous day when he delivered the mail frightened him. He stuffed the letters into his pocket and downed the last of his warm coffee. "Tell the boys I went to Harrington when they get done with the chores. I'll be back 'round noon or so."

"What about breakfast?"

"Not hungry. I'll be back for lunch."

He walked to his pickup, got in, turned the key on and then off, climbed out and slammed the door. He felt Thelma watching him from the kitchen as he walked to the shed, used full choke to start the engine and backed out the Chevy. He shot a quick glance toward the house. "The boys kin pull the truck with the horses to get it started if they need it," he mumbled, as if she might be listening.

He stopped before turning onto the road to scrape the frost that collected from his breath on the windshield. The mailbox at the end of the driveway reminded him of his mission. He reached between the buttons on his coat and touched his shirt pocket. The letters were still there. He got out of the car, opened the mailbox and slammed it shut. "Too early." He checked the house again. No one heard him. "I'm worse than Arnie, talking to myself." Once out of sight of the farm, he rummaged through the glove box and found some stale cigarettes and matches left by one of the boys. He hated the taste of cigarettes but enjoyed watching the stream of smoke curl and spread as it climbed the windshield.

"Harry Gross, that asshole." A burst of smoke exploded from his lungs. He gasped, sucked some back in and coughed. Tears streamed down his cheeks as he opened the window and threw out the butt. For more than twenty years, Harry stuck the mail into the box at the end of the driveway, but yesterday he brought four letters to the barn. When Svez came in with a forkful of straw from the stack out back, he saw Harry, holding letters in one hand and pointing toward the cows with the other like he was counting them. By the end of Harry's route, every neighbor would know how many cows he milked. Harry jumped when Svez touched his shoulder. He held out the letters, but pulled them back when Svez reached for them.

"It's fer yer boys. From the gov'ment. Gotta deliver 'em direct."

Svez said nothing but continued to reach out until Harry finally let loose of his grip and dropped them into his hand. "Thanks. You could've left 'em in the box."

"Too 'portant for that. I gotta know gov'ment mail gits to the c'rect people." He glanced around the barn. "Is they here?"

"I'll take care of it." Svez watched the expression change on Harry's face.

"Watcha gwin to do wid all dem boys at home, Svez?" He dribbled a few drops of tobacco juice into the gutter. "The gov'mint's sure nuf gwin ta take a couple of dem fer da army, fer shure."

Svez tucked the letters into his back pocket, grabbed a pitchfork and scattered bedding between the cows. He waited until Harry left, and then he went to find Arnie.

By the time Svez got to Harrington, the car had warmed and he hesitated going inside the courthouse. He checked his watch. Nine o'clock. Would the draft office be open? How would he find it? He opened the letter addressed to Ignatius Rastner and chuckled. He envisioned Iggy in a uniform looking lost and forlorn. Iggy's expression turned to one of panic, and Svez became angry. He got out, slammed the car door and plodded up to the double brass doors at the top of the steps. The smell of oiled woodwork and sounds of clanking pipes and hissing radiators greeted him as he pulled open one of the doors and peered in. A sign attached to an easel had *SELECTIVE SERVICE* printed in bold letters over an arrow pointing to the left. The fancy name didn't fool him. The government wanted to put his boys in the army and make them fight on the other side of the ocean.

With her gray streaked hair rolled into a bun on the top of her head, Freda Hayes, according to the nameplate on the counter, reminded Svez of his maiden aunt who lived with his family when he was a teenager. When she glanced up and told him to come in, her eyes and smile melted his image of his demanding aunt. He removed his glasses and wiped the moisture onto his shirt that had bulged out the sides of his bib overalls. He placed them back on the end of his nose, pulled the letters from his shirt pocket and peered at the maiden aunt who had given him many birthday presents.

"Freda Hayes?" He inquired.

"Yes, I'm Freda."

"The Draft Board lady?" His mind cleared and his fear returned.

"Yes," she chuckled, "How may I help you?"

CHAPTER SIXTEEN
FRANK LORENZ II

Frank Lorenz II lounged in one of the large leather armchairs at St. Alphonse parish rectory. His shirtsleeves rolled up and his tie loosened, he slowly swirled the liqueur around the crystal snifter Father Shamus Reinhardt poured for him. He passed it twice in front of his nose and savored the sweet aroma before raising it to his lips. He reveled in its delicious bouquet as it washed over his tongue before he allowed himself to swallow it. He felt relaxed now that he was alone with his friend. After two hours of discussing church business at the parish board meeting, he decided to switch to a topic with which he had some expertise.

"Shamus, I'm afraid of what we're going to see when this war finally ends." His companion nodded his agreement even before Frank made his point. "I'm not thinking about the destruction in Europe and our boys returning home, many of them in wooden boxes."

"I see." Shamus pursed his lips and arched his eyebrows. Shaded light from a reading lamp, its brass arm extended over his rocking chair, accented the deep furrows across his forehead and the hollows in his cheeks.

"Although my father still presided as head of Bovine State Bank when the Great War ended, I got a first-hand lesson in post-war economics." He paused, swirled the remaining brandy in his snifter and glanced up to assess his listener's reaction. He was pleased that Shamus hadn't stifled a yawn since the board meeting ended.

"Yes, as a banker, I'm quite sure you did."

"Products that were in short supply during the war became available, and they sparked a buying flurry that didn't stop when personal bank accounts emptied. Even the farmers who kept their cash in buried cream cans came to my father for additional credit." Frank gulped his brandy and stared into the empty glass feeling he had somehow violated a sacred ritual. He set it on the end table, and, with a hand gripped to each arm of the chair, he pulled his body to the edge.

Father Reinhardt set down the empty glass he had been holding throughout most of the discussion and his rocking chair creaked forward.

Frank leaned toward the priest and spoke in a confidential tone, almost as if he were about to make his confession. "I'm not blaming my father for the condition of the bank's assets when I became president, but I inherited so many bad mortgages I almost became more farmer than banker. Why, they nearly ran Gloria and me out of town when we were forced to foreclose on some of those properties."

When his host stood and extended his hand, Frank realized that had given a false signal that he intended to leave. He accepted Shamus' hand, pushed against the arm of the chair and hoisted himself to his feet. He tilted his head back not to peer at his friend over the rim of his glasses. "Remind me to tell you some of the hostilities that Gloria and I had to endure back in those days."

"Indeed, a good topic for another time, but you and Gloria seem to have weathered that bad situation quite nicely."

When Shamus handed him his hat from the rack and held his coat for him, Frank felt slightly embarrassed and a little offended. He hadn't had a chance to explain how well he and Gloria had corrected the situation.

"I want to thank you for your patience tonight with Cunningham and York at the council meeting." Shamus patted Frank on the shoulder. "They're good men, but they don't often see things eye to eye." He shook Frank's hand again. "I'll have Stella write out a summary of the Board's decisions and get copies to each member."

"Thank you for listening to me ramble on and on with my problems." Frank decided on humility rather than indignation.

"Oh, you're welcome. Perhaps we can continue our discussion at dinner tomorrow night. I want to hear about your son's progress at Harvard. If I hadn't been called to the priesthood, I would liked to have gone there."

"Yes, it's a good university, and you'd have done well there. But, that conversation is for another time as well. I believe Gloria informed your sister we'll supply the dinner wine. It's of a special vintage imported from my family's winery in Spain." Shamus's eyes widened and Frank grinned. "I'll tell you more about it at dinner. Good night, Shamus."

At precisely 8:42 the next morning, Frank stood in his front doorway and faced his wife. "I may not be home at noon for lunch."

"Don't forget, we're having dinner tonight at the rectory with Shamus." Gloria picked a piece of lint from his double-breasted suit coat and touched the large silk knot lodged between two points of his starched shirt collar.

He scowled at her as he retrieved his pocket watch, briefly read the dials and the replaced it, careful to drape the chain evenly across his vest.

"I may be asked to carry the mortgage papers on some farms, so Tony and I will have to inspect the buildings first." He brushed the spot on his suit where his wife had located the offending thread or bit of lint and re-centered his tie. While he waited for Gloria to respond to his comment about lunch, he envisioned the picture they presented to their neighbors. Gloria wore the fur-trimmed dressing gown he had given her for their anniversary, and her hair was still perfectly shaped from her visit to the stylist yesterday. She slept on a silk pillowcase to minimize the damage done while tossing and turning in her sleep. He checked his watch again. He wanted his neighbors to see his impatience with his wife for delaying him. He dutifully pecked Gloria on the cheek and walked down the sidewalk without glancing back. He felt sure she waved as he headed toward the bank.

Although his wife's nonsense had cost him precious time, he refused to quicken his pace. He reflected on the interrupted conversation he had with Shamus Reinhardt the night before and rehearsed additional information to share that evening. Gloria would be with them so he wanted to avoid topics like economics. He didn't want to discuss such dull matters as the upcoming church picnic or changes in the liturgy. He focused on Shamus inquiring about his son and the interest he expressed in Frank's Spanish Ancestry. Perhaps Shamus didn't know the facts of his family, that he descended from the son of a Spanish nobleman who had arranged for his eldest son, Frank's grandfather, to marry into a German banking family.

"Three sons." Frank mouthed the words of his grandfather who came to America about the time of the Civil War. "A man needs three sons, at least." Frank punctuated the numbers with his index finger. "One to continue the family business, one to

127

serve in the military and one to serve God." He felt thankful that he had been his father's eldest son, the one marked to carry on the family's banking business.

Frank looked at his raised finger, lowered it and glanced around to see if anyone had been watching. He straightened his shoulders, tucked his thumbs into his vest pockets and pretended to whistle. He decided not to mention his grandfather's edict to Father Reinhardt since he and Gloria had only one son. This could lead to embarrassing speculations about their use of birth control, a topic to be avoided at the priest's dinner table.

Tray will replace me some day as president of Bovine State Bank, just as I followed in my father's footsteps. While mentally practicing his conversation for later that evening, Frank decided he would use his son's nickname rather than Frank III. *When my father realized he disliked my grandfather, but not necessarily the banking business, he decided to migrate west. Skunk Hollow, his sources were somewhat dated, a German-Catholic farming community in Minnesota had grown to the point where they needed a bank. Father presented his proposal to the family's financial backers, and Frank Lorenzo senior became Frank Lorenz I, owner and president of the Bovine State Bank.*

Pleased with the conversation he had scripted, he decided not to discuss Tray's progress at Harvard. He still fretted about the last letter Gloria received from him that included a bill for his tuition and a term paper he had written for his economics professor. Maybe in international affairs an expanded economy might work, but not in small town America. He refused to allow his son to drag the bank into the same trap that caught his father during the wildcat years after the Great War and the Depression that followed. He would insist on fiscal responsibility.

Frank Lorenz II entered the bank at 9:05, late and ill prepared for the day's order of business. He nodded a greeting to Mildred who stood behind the teller's window and flashed his eyes toward Tony who sat at his desk in the office visible from Frank's through a glass window.

"Is Rastner going to drive us to the farms he wants us to visit?" Tony followed him into his office.

Frank grimaced when he realized he had forgotten to bring his Pontiac to the bank.

"I suppose I could drive, if you'd like me to." Tony glanced down at his shoes.

Frank considered both options. He thought about being cramped with Tony and Svez in an old Ford or Chevy—he didn't know which since Svez never came to him for a car loan—that reeked of manure and chewing tobacco. He decided to accept Tony's offer.

"The bank will pay mileage, of course." He took off his hat and placed it on the shelf above the coat rack. "Gloria needed the Pontiac to run some errands for Father Reinhardt." That should explain why he hadn't driven that morning. Tony shrugged and went back to his office.

Frank removed his suit jacket, hung it neatly on a hanger and sat at his desk to study the abstracts Tony had prepared for him. He got up, took his coat from the hanger and put it back on. He mumbled, "A bit chilly in here," wanting to justify his indecision. He picked up the documents, put them in a neat pile and pretended to read the top one. He admitted to himself that he wasn't prepared to haggle with any of Bovine's businessmen that morning and was glad that his dealings were with a farmer. He knew what kind of information the yellowed and curled pages contained without reading them; land homesteaded in the mid 1800's by incapable immigrants, probably Eastern-European, he guessed from the spellings of their names, and then successfully farmed by a second generation of German immigrants who now dominated the county. The latest owners of these farms, mostly retired and living in recently built bungalows at the edge of town, offered contracts for deed with nominal down payments.

Frank didn't know Sylvester Rastner except from the rumors he heard, mostly from Mildred and some small-talk at Emma's Café. Rastner lived on a farm a few miles from Bovine with a motley array of family members. He paid his bills on time and had a fair amount of savings at the bank. It seemed out of character for a steadfast farmer like that to want to suddenly quadruple the size of his holdings. This was a clear-cut case of over-extension that he and Shamus had discussed. He would use this example tonight at dinner to support his post war production theory. Of course, he wouldn't divulge the farmer's name.

"Sylvester Rastner to see you, sir." Mildred peered through the partially open door. Frank noticed she didn't call him Svez. He also noticed that Sylvester wore dress- pants with a matching vest, not the usual Oshkosh overalls with his red and black handkerchief sticking out of his back pocket like an off-center tail. Mildred's face flushed as she accidentally backed into Svez who had followed her into Frank's office. Svez teetered and leaned forward. Mildred's hand shot up to her mouth and she lowered

129

her head. Frank stifled a smile at the image, a giant and a midget from a minstrel show peeking around the curtain at the audience.

"Thank you, Mildred. Come on in, Svez. Have a seat." Frank felt pleased that he had impulsively greeted this farmer informally. Using a man's nickname gave him the social advantage a banker needed with a client who may have more assets than he. "I've been studying the abstracts and the contracts for deed you brought last week. Each of the three farms look pretty good, especially the one that follows the river." He still hated calling it the Skunk River.

"That's what I thought, too, so I'll give that one to George. He's the oldest, and the better farmer. And he's marrying Otto Pluff's daughter come fall. She'll get him to put in an indoor privy and fix up the place. The barn needs some work, too."

"Oh, you're planning to have George buy the place." He paused to study the map in front of him, "The one in section two of Weimar Township?" Frank tried to make this more a question than an inflection of surprise. "Perhaps we should develop a credit report on George as well as you." Frank wished he hadn't mentioned the credit report, afraid he may have insulted Svez with this hitherto unspoken but necessary bank procedure.

"You know my credit's good, Mr. Lorenz. I'm going to put that farm in George's name, but I'll be co-signing the loan papers."

Thinking of his own father-son relationship, Frank asked, "Are you sure that's a good idea, Mr. Rastner?" In an effort to establish a more formal relationship between himself and his client, he leaned back on his chair and it rolled away from his desk. "Responsibility should go with the obligation." He pulled his chair forward, held the Rastner file in front of him and peered at his client over the top of his glasses.

"The other two farms are going to Herman and Ralph. They're of marrying age and it won't be long 'til they find wives to keep them in line." Svez paused. When Frank laid the papers back on his desk, he continued. "I'll be watching them real close."

"Yes, I'm sure you will." Frank strummed his fingers across Rastner's file and tried to reconcile his impression of Rastner boys with the overwhelming trust their father showed for them. Were they the wild ones that people always talked about? And, wasn't there one not quite right in the head? He decided to ask Mildred who would know all such rumors. He glanced through the window in his office door and saw her chatting with a customer. He reminded himself that he hated gossip and decided to trust his instincts.

"I'll need ten thousand dollars against my place and, with my savings here at the bank, I can swing the deal myself. You can come out to the farm if you like. Thelma's got the yard decorated right nice with those colorful lawn ornaments that Arnie and Freddie made. Arnie got laid up last winter and can hardly get his cows milked any more. He's taken to Freddie who can milk a cow pretty good now." He paused, pulled a handkerchief from his back pocket and wiped his forehead and the corners of his mouth.

Frank realized that instead of listening, he had been reconstructing Svez's family—the foundling child, the less than capable brother, spinster daughter, retarded son, and now three older sons each about to be given a farm.

Svez inhaled noisily. "If Freddie's Ma and Liz was still here they would be right proud of him."

Frank then remembered that Svez's wife had died about ten years ago. Mildred had gone to the funeral and told everyone at the bank how sad it was because of the baby. That must be the Freddie he referred to. He thought about Gloria. Would he be able to talk about her death so openly and casually? Could he even survive without her for a decade? He shuddered and then worried that Svez may interpret his reaction as a rejection to his proposal. He saw the dark eyes flash and realized that Svez hadn't even paused since he started talking about his family.

"Iggy and Freddie will stay on the farm with me." Svez looked at his hands folded in front of him. "Even if Freddie left, we could still get the work done with a bit of hired help." He paused and took a deep breath. "If you got the paper work ready, we can go out to look at the farms." He faced Frank and added, "If you want."

"That won't be necessary." Frank, startled by his own impulsiveness, smiled when he anticipated Tony's reaction to his decision. "We can settle the matter right here at my desk." Frank glanced through the window into Tony's office and saw Mildred hand him some blank forms. He went to the door and peered in. "Mildred, bring me a loan application. The one that doesn't require personal collateral." He watched the startled look on Tony's face and was tempted to tell her that Tony wouldn't need those mileage reimbursement forms.

"I 'spose you're wondering why my boys need to own farms all of a sudden. You see, I been to see this draft lady, Freda, and she told me...."

131

"I understand," Frank politely interrupted as many thoughts raced through his mind. He had assisted with farms changing hands within the family for as little as one dollar. He watched the fathers whose sons had been sent to war, and he understood their anger with those men who manipulated their property to avoid the draft. He knew this anger would turn to rage if any were returned home in coffins. "You've had enough losses in your life. I'm sure your boys will measure up to the responsibility of running their own farms quite well with you to guide them."

He also remembered his grandfather's words. *Three sons, at least. One to continue the family business, one to serve in the military and one to serve God.* This earthy man and his family would have to serve God and country in a different way.

CHAPTER SEVENTEEN
FARMS FOR EVERYONE
(Spring, 1944)

"What's with Pa lately?" Thelma asked Iggy as he sauntered into the kitchen. "He's sure acting strange.

"Like how?" Iggy grabbed the coffeepot, emptied it into his cup and peered into the spout. "Is that all there is?"

Thelma ignored his question and frowned as he loaded the dark-black liquid with sugar. "Like Pa letting you sneak back to the house when everyone else is getting ready for spring planting." She grabbed the sugar bowl from him before he turned his coffee into candy.

"Hey, I wasn't done."

"Yes, you were."

He emptied his cup with a single gulp. "Phooey." He sat down and stared at his hand still holding the cup. "I don't know what them guy's up to. Pa's just been pushing everybody but me. I don't mind. I got my own jobs to do."

"Like what?"

"Well, I gotta sweep the hay mow. All's that left on the floor is grass and weed seeds that'd make the cows sick. Chickens will eat that stuff. They mostly quit laying anyway."

"Then, why aren't you doing it?"

"Hay ain't ready to be cut. Pa ain't even planted the grain. They're still screening the oats seed."

"They've been doing that for two full days." Thelma felt she had been left out of an important decision. "What's Pa planning to do, rent more land? They never planted that much oats before. And why's Pa making them guys do it. That used to be our job, you, Freddie and me."

"I guess Freddie's helping 'em. I don't like to do that no more. It gets so dusty and it's hard work scooping grain. George and Herman and Ralph can do it if they're so dang interested. Besides, since Arnie got Freddie milking his cows, I got 'nother job I don't like."

"What's that?"

"Milking Pa's cows."

"What about the other guys?"

"They got their own cows. It ain't fair. They get to keep their share of the milk check."

Thelma knew this, but since she kept the financial records she also knew that Pa wouldn't let them spend any of the money. All the receipts from the Co-op went directly to the bank. "Well, you get your butt outside and get busy with something. I can't get anything done with you hanging around the house."

Iggy slurped some imaginary coffee from his cup and stood in the kitchen doorway like he couldn't decide where to go next.

"Go sweep the hay mow." She shoved him through the porch and onto the front step. She glanced toward the barn. "I watched you guys open the big door yesterday."

Iggy grinned. "I kin see the Collin's place from up there, at least the tops of their windmill and silo. Don't get to see Larry much any more since he got married and took over his Pa's farm. His folks moved to town, but his brother, Alfred, mostly lives with him."

"Mostly?"

"Sometimes he stays with his folks and sometimes with Larry."

Thelma heard the break in his voice and felt his sadness. "You still spend time with him, don't you?"

"If he's not too busy. Once in a while Alfred and me do things together."

She heard Iggy breathe through both his nose and mouth, and his head shook like when he became agitated. He sighed, turned and wandered across the yard. She stared into the gaping hole at the end of the barn and watched for him, but it was too dark to see inside. Opening the haymow door had become a spring ritual. Hinged at the bottom, it had to be raised and lowered with a team of horses attached to a rope strung along a track near the ceiling, through a series of pulleys and out the back of the barn. When the red door was half-lowered, Thelma imagined the barn was preparing to receive Holy Communion.

That night while Thelma cleared the supper table, her father coughed like he did when he wanted to say something important.

"I want you boys to stay a minute. I got something to discuss."
He glanced at Freddie. "You better stay 'cause this will concern
Arnie as well."

Freddie took Arnie's evening meals up to his room, and Thelma
knew that Freddie reported all family discussions to him. She
stood at the sink and listened to the conversation while she washed
the dishes.

"I went to the bank a while back and borrowed money to buy
three farms."

Thelma set down the kettle she had been scouring, dried her
hands on the dishtowel and returned to her place at the table.

Her father appeared startled, then said, "May as well join us
since this might affect you too."

You bet your life, this will affect me. She leaned over the back
of her chair.

"What farms?" Her brothers all asked at once.

"Where are they?"

"How are we going to handle three more farms?"

"Why now?"

While they peppered questions faster than their father could
answer them, Thelma went to the desk where she kept important
papers, drew out a township map and set it on the table. "Show us
where these farms are."

"I was just about to tell you to get that, but I wanted to explain
things first." He opened the book to a page with three areas circled
in pencil. "Here, here, and here."

All four boys stood and clustered behind their father stretching
their necks to see where he pointed. She didn't need to see the
exact locations. The three areas marked weren't very close
together. Her family was about to be spread all over the township.

"This one is George's, this one is Herman's and this one is
Ralph's." Svez sat back and folded his arms.

Iggy started to breathe noisily. "What about me?" He turned
toward Thelma. Suddenly, his eyes sparkled and he nodded his
head vigorously. "Yup! Yup! One for each of 'em. I get to stay
here with Pa and Arnie and Freddie." Panic seeped into his voice.
"Does Thelma stay with us?"

"Course, she stays here. The boys gotta find their own women
to help them run their farms. They're gonna pay me and the bank
back when they get on their feet."

"Who should tell Arnie?" Thelma asked. "These kinds of
things upset him."

"Arnie already knows. Me and him worked out the plan a while back." He walked to the desk, gathered some papers, and muttered, "Got things to do in the barn."

"Congratulations, you guys." Thelma waited for her father to leave and then stood behind George, Herman and Ralph who continued to stare at the book in front of them. Freddie pushed his chair from the table and went upstairs. Iggy walked to the sink and pumped water into his hand, gulped a mouthful and splashed some on his face.

"I guess we should have known this was bound to happen sooner or later." Thelma threw the dishtowel she had been holding to Iggy. "Did you guys know this was coming?"

"Pa just told us we'll be needing more seed this year." George went to the sink, pumped a glass full of water and downed it in one gulp. "We figured he wanted to sell some oats or rent more land."

Herman said, "I knew George would get his own farm one day 'cause this one ain't big enough to keep all of us busy."

"That's about to change." Ralph smiled. "We're all going to be busier than a grave digger, if Ida got the pox."

"This is serious business, you guys." She reached across the table and slammed the book of maps shut. "Have you any idea what it'll take to get three farms going all at one time?"

"Pa'll help us get started. But why the hell did he do this all of a sudden?" George slunk down in his chair. "He could've bought one farm each year just like each of us is one year apart." Herman and Ralph continued to stare at the cover of the book.

"That doesn't matter now." Thelma recalled that cold January morning when her father went to Harrington to take care of the draft notices. She wondered if he ever told the boys about them. She picked up the book, put it back in the drawer and returned to the table. "Sit down. We got some planning to do. We gotta stick together if we're gonna get the spring work done on time." She glared at Ralph. "I'm afraid we're going to be as busy as your grave digger and you may as well forget about Ida, too." She laughed and felt the tension relax. She spent the rest of the evening giving instructions and listening to her brothers' concerns.

That night she told her mother about the developments. "Why did he do this all at once, Mama? He doesn't understand how hard it'll be to feed the boys when they're spread so far apart. I need your help." The star twinkled its usual message, and Thelma felt somewhat relieved. She knew she had her mother's support.

CHAPTER EIGHTEEN
THE BROKEN BOTTLE
(Spring, 1945)

"So that's how they do it." Thelma glanced out the kitchen window and watched Alfred Collins stop his pickup in front of her yard, only this time he didn't expose himself. He placed something in the grass and glanced toward the opened hay-loft door and waved. She tolerated insults directed at her because she felt ashamed for seducing him. Getting back at her by supplying Iggy with whiskey wasn't playing fair. How often had he made a drop like the one she just witnessed?

Shortly after she ended their affair, Alfred stopped in front of her yard and stood alongside his pickup with his hand thrust through the slot in his pants. She had just come out of the chicken coop carrying a squawking rooster. Had he intended to pee? Couldn't he wait until he was back at his brother's farm? She accepted and even envied the way men relieved themselves whenever they felt the urge, but she expected them to at least face away from her like her brothers did. He waved with both arms, defiantly thrust his hips forward and sneered. He pursed his lips as if ready to kiss. She jammed the rooster's neck between two nails in the chopping block, lobbed off his head with one blow and squirted the blood in Alfred's direction. Damn! He had already driven away.

But, this time he didn't bother to taunt her. She glanced around the yard, but Iggy would most likely hide until she went back into the house. If he was in the hayloft as Alfred seemed to indicate, she would have time to destroy the whiskey before he could get to it. She walked out to the road, plopped down in the ditch near a small dark bottle partly covered with grass and felt she might cry. She wanted her brothers back home to protect her and Iggy, but they had their own farms with their own problems. Pa was usually gone to help them, Freddie was still at school during the day and Arnie stayed in his room most of the time. She felt abandoned.

Her life had been in turmoil the entire year since her father bought the additional farms. He said he did it to keep the boys out of the war, but it felt like the war had come to her family. Careful planning made their first spring planting possible, but everyone felt the pressure. The boys, excited about owning their own farms, didn't seem to mind the work even though it lasted from sunup to sunset, and they often slept on the floor of their newly acquired farmhouses. She had prepared all their meals and usually delivered them to the fields where they worked. She tried to wash their clothes every week, but sometimes the clean ones from the previous week still lay beside their beds.

"Mama, I can't keep up." She allowed her feelings to escape one starry night. "I feel like everything's wrong. We haven't had a full meal together for over a week, and that's just not right." She cupped her hands under her chin and put her elbows on the windowsill. "Arnie doesn't like things to be different from what he was used to, but he's getting feeble in his mind. I don't think he understands what's going on. When I brought clean clothes to his room, he asked, 'Why's them boys gone so much? They ain't pullin' their fair share of the work around here.' I didn't remind him that they no longer lived with us. Freddie does all of Arnie's work yet never misses a day of school. Next week, school will be out and Iggy'll have more help. Freddie's only thirteen, but he can almost replace a grown man. I don't think Iggy minds the extra work like I thought he would. The cows have mostly dried up and are in the pasture all day, so there aren't many chores. He just doesn't like to be out in the field alone. I take lunches to him every morning and afternoon, and I sit with him for a few minutes, but we're both too busy to talk much. At suppertime, Arnie's hiding and Pa's running between the farms, so Iggy, Freddie and I eat alone."

Thelma grabbed the whiskey bottle by its neck and wondered if drinking it would help her forget what happened last summer. Alfred did their chores while Pa, Iggy and Freddie helped with her brothers' first harvest. Alfred swatted the cows as they entered the barn. He appeared satisfied, as if he had caused them to perform that routine. She chuckled to herself yet secretly envied him. Just once, she wanted to have that feeling of control. She should never have taken those two beers from the refrigerator and followed the cows into the barn.

Alfred danced about as he slipped a strap around a heifer and attached the milk bucket under her belly. He held the coupler with the four pulsating cups draped like branches on the weeping willow tree down by the creek. By flopping them up and down, he created a rhythm of sucking noises that matched the electric vacuum pump racing and idling with each movement of his arm. She heard the *swoosh* and *smack* of each teat cup as he attached them one at a time. He glanced at her and grinned.

"There, that should do you, Elsie." He slapped the cow's backside. "You just keep chewing the cud, and I'll be back when you're empty."

"Thought you might be thirsty. I brought you a beer."

He took one of the bottles, snapped the cap loose on the door hinge, and a burst of foam drenched onto his hand. He gestured toward the second bottle.

"Actually, I brought you two beers, or maybe I should drink one."

"Have it." He licked some suds from his fingers and handed the opened bottle to her. He took the second one and repeated the process, but caught the foam with his mouth and let it drip off his chin.

Thelma used her apron to wipe the moisture from the bottle he had given her and, on an impulse, wiped his chest. He thrust his shoulders back and his hips forward in a sexual gesture.

She immediately dropped the hem of her apron and brushed it smooth. "You're worse than Iggy, spilling all over yourself."

He took another long swig, dribbled most of it and laughed.

She filled her mouth and squirted beer onto his chest, down to his navel and into the few strands of pubic hair exposed above his low-slung jeans. He shot some back at her. She set her bottle on the feed bin, removed her apron and wiped her face. She tossed it to him. When his eyes were covered, she grabbed her bottle, shook it vigorously with her thumb on the opening and waited until she had a clear shot. She let him have it directly in his face.

"Damn you."

When he stumbled to the cooling tank and dunked his head, she ran and hid deep in the barn.

He wiped his face and hung her apron near the door. He laughed, glanced toward the house and shook his fist. "Just wait. I'll get you, for that."

She climbed the ladder to the loft and waited for him to come up and throw down hay for the cattle. The beer and the sweet smell of dried clover made her giddy. She scrambled up the pile and slid back down, chaff clinging to her hair and falling down the front of her dress. She opened the buttons down to her belt, but before she could brush the hay from her bra, she heard Alfred climb the ladder. She held her dress closed and ducked into a recess in the mound of hay. He grabbed the pitchfork from the hook on the wall and, when he reached Thelma's hiding place, she jumped up.

"Hi." She had surprised him and decided to shock him. "I'll bet you're tired of all those cow's tits. Wanna see mine?" She flung her dress open, shrugged it back over her shoulders and reached to unsnap her bra.

Alfred gasped, and instead of accepting Thelma's offer, he held the pitchfork in front of him as if he wanted to hide behind it. He stammered, "You're naked."

"Ain't you been to see Ida yet?" Thelma was surprised at his apparent innocence.

"'Course I have. You just caught me off guard."

"Come here." She tucked her finger into the waistband of his jeans and pulled him close to her. He dropped to his knees, and the pitchfork teetered and fell on the floor behind him. She tipped him on his back, unbuttoned his pants and yanked them off by pulling them over his bare feet. When she saw that he wasn't wearing underwear, she realized their game had become serious. His naked body excited her, and she suddenly felt anger toward Ida who took advantage of so many young boys. She had to deprive Ida of her next victim, and she allowed her instincts to direct her moves. She stood and slowly finished undressing in front of him. When she leaned over him and cupped her hands over his genitals, he jerked back and covered his face.

"I, I'm afraid I just...." He began to sob.

"You're doing just fine." She wiped her hands on the loose hay. "When that happens a girl should be flattered." She felt naked. She was naked, but she knew there was no going back, or he might be too embarrassed to ever face her again. "Just lay there until you get your second wind."

She felt the wait interminable and desperately wished she hadn't attempted to salvage his ego with a second chance. She wished she had never brought him a beer in the first place. She listened to him breathe as he lay back with his eyes closed. His chest was as smooth as Freddie's, not all hairy like her brothers'. She ran her finger along the thin line of pubic hair that led to his groin and his erection returned. She accepted her responsibility. *I know I can do this.* She cupped his face in her hands and kissed him gently on the mouth.

Alfred came often to *do the chores* after that. With Freddie back at school and Iggy busy in the field, they could sneak into the haymow unnoticed. Pa said that he appreciated the Collin's boy offering to help around the farm. Almost immediately, Thelma lost the illusion of control, but the pattern had been established and she could no more break it than the cows could refuse to enter the barn.

"At least they have a pattern to their sex life," she complained to Alfred, who stopped to see her whenever he felt like it. "I can't do this anymore. You gotta find a girl friend your own age." He agreed but kept coming back. When she remained firm, he embarrassed her whenever he could.

Thelma never told her mother about this indiscretion. Her passion for this young man eroded like the rage she felt when her father violated her many years ago, and she wanted the aftermath of all her sexual experiences to disappear. Pain and embarrassment interrupted all her erotic fantasies, and she became pleased with her ability to overcome her sexual urges. She was sure Ma had forgiven her and Pa, but she didn't need to be told about Alfred. She felt determined it wouldn't happen again. She accepted responsibility for her actions, but questioned the roles of men and women in any relationship. She began to understand why Miss West and Mildred Bushman never married.

Thelma held the whiskey bottle against the sun and the world around her seemed dark and dreary. "We don't need this." She laid it down and selected a fist-size stone. After three attempts, the bottle broke and it lay with jagged points of glass still adhering to the label mimicking the teeth of some horrible yet fallen monster. But, it was not really dead, and she knew it.

****

Iggy spied Alfred's pickup as it passed over the hill toward his brother's farm. The dusty chore of sweeping put him in a foul mood. Here had been a private place where he could let his fantasies run wild, but now his erotic thoughts burst into fits of anger that he couldn't direct at anyone. He loved his sister and didn't want to lose Alfred as a friend, but they had invaded his private place. He struggled with these feelings and anticipated the escape that awaited him in the ditch alongside the road.

He knew what they did when they went to do the chores and it was too early for chores. He knew about their spot in the hayloft. They did what the dogs did, what the cows and chickens did, and Pa had that ugly word for it. When Babe let Rex do it to her, they stayed together a long time, even after they tried to go different directions. Roosters were always in a hurry. "As long as a dog and as often as a rooster," was what Pa told the guys when they got together and said dumb things. He wished they wouldn't talk that way. But, it wasn't like the dogs or the chickens; maybe like the cow and the bull except he imagined they faced each other.

From up in the hayloft he had seen the signal. Careful not to be discovered, he waited what seemed a very long time. When he approached the appointed spot along the road, Iggy forgot his resentment and started to breathe a little harder than normal, inhaling and exhaling noisily through mouth and nostrils, the passing air sounded like the last drops of soda pop sucked through a straw. The expression of pleasure etched on his face turned to one of panic that rushed throughout his entire body. He pressed clenched fists against his stomach and released his fingers as they slid over his body, past his genitals and down his legs. He dropped to his knees. He reached for the fragments of glass, and his nose flared as the aroma increased his cravings. Sobs and snorts emanated from his mouth and nose.

"How could he be so careless, so mean, so...Thelma!" The thought introduced both fear and anger to his already entangled maze of feelings. "I'm gonna make her sorry for this, gonna tell on her..." He realized that everyone already knew about Alfred doing the chores with Thelma, even though nobody talked about it. Now, she knew his secret. Would Pa and everyone else find out? He suspected they already knew.

CHAPTER NINETEEN
THE LAST GRADUATION
(Spring, 1946)

Although it was only Friday, Thelma laid Iggy and Freddie's Sunday clothes on their beds for them to change into after chores. She didn't need to remind them because they had been talking about Freddie's graduation party all week.

"Where's the baking soda?" Iggy yelled through the kitchen door.

Thelma peered into the porch and cringed when she saw him rubbing his teeth with the corner of a grimy towel. "You use a toothbrush for that."

"I don't got one." He scraped his teeth with a fingernail.

"I'm getting one for you. Just hold your horses." She grabbed a bottle of hair oil from the self above the kitchen sink and found the toothbrush stuck into a box of baking soda in the pantry. Back in the porch, she handed him the soda box and grimaced when she touched his hair. "You guys been having milk fights in the barn again?" Wiping her hands on the towel, she emptied the washbasin into the slop pail under the washstand and pumped clean water into it. "Stick your head in here." She pushed his shoulders closer to the basin and his head down into the water.

"Hey, that's cold," he protested.

"Ain't got time to heat it. This'll have to do." She rubbed a bar of lye soap on his head and dug her fingers down to his scalp. "Knew I shoulda given you a haircut before the party. At least they're clean. Now, stick your head under the pump." She gave the handle two rapid strokes and went to the kitchen to fetch a clean dishtowel. When she returned, Iggy faced her and squinted through strands of hair screened across his face.

"You got soap in my eyes."

"Quit whining." She handed him the towel. "Here, dry your hair."

He swooped his hand across his forehead, pressed his hair back flat and swiped over it with the towel. He began to brush his teeth, and foam embedded with flakes of tobacco dribbled from his mouth.

"Where's Freddie?" Thelma asked as she rubbed hair oil onto her hands and then into his hair.

"He's out by the pump-house," his words garbled through a mouthful of foam. "A sink ain't good 'nuff for the cleaning he's giving hisself." He spit, put his mouth under the spout and pumped. "Where's that sweet smelling stuff you bought off the Watkins man when he came through here last month. You know, that stuff to use after you've done shaving?" He began stropping his razor.

Thelma went to the kitchen and returned with the after-shave lotion. She watched him dunk a brush into the basin and vigorously stir lather inside a mug that stuck to the unpainted boards of the washstand.

She said, "I'm glad you're coming along to the party tonight. It wouldn't be fair to Freddie if I was the only one to show up." His quick yet smooth movements with the razor always impressed her, and she liked hearing the scratching sounds it made.

"Why ain't Pa goin?" Iggy wiped his face and dumped the foamy mess into the slop pail.

"Said he was too busy at the boys' farms to take the time." She pumped water into the basin, sloshed it and dumped it. "Here." She pointed to the pail under the sink. "Take this outside. It's about ready to run over." She thought about how handsome he had become as he hoisted the five-gallon pail and lugged it out the door. Even Ma would have approved of the way he wore his mustache. Thelma felt proud to be seen with her brother that evening.

Iggy returned and put the empty pail back under the sink. "The story in *The Journal* last Thursday said it's for all students of District Twelve, even those who didn't finish the eighth grade. We was her first class to graduate."

"*We were,* not, *we was,*" Thelma corrected. "We have to use good grammar when we talk to Miss West tonight, or she'll take our diplomas back."

"She can't do that, can she?" Iggy flashed his eyes toward Thelma and then back to the sink. "I ain't talked to her since we graduated."

"She's been teaching here a long time. Remember how we always called her our favorite teacher?"

144

"Yeah, like we had more than one." Iggy grinned, then shook his head. "It ain't right, shutting down her school."

"That just makes Freddie's graduation more special. When we graduated we didn't have a party at school." Thelma patted some stray hairs on the back of his head. "I have to finish getting ready."

Iggy wriggled out of his pants as he walked toward the kitchen, grabbed a sandwich from the stack on the table and headed upstairs.

Thelma picked up his dirty clothes and hung them on hooks along the wall. She studied the towel, shook it and draped it over the rack near the washstand. Back in the kitchen, she stared into the mirror above the sink. What would happen to Miss West? Would she go back East and move in with her father? Freddie said she often talked about him. He'd be old and might need special care. These thoughts made her feel empty and sad.

Freddie, shirtless and dripping wet, rushed in and announced, "I'll be ready in a minute. Where can I find the...?"

"Oh, my. You look like a drenched...." Thelma realized he did not resemble a drenched rat, the expression that fit her brothers with dripping wet hair. His auburn hair and round face made her think of a sunfish but, instead, called him, "a wet puppy."

Freddie smiled at the reference and repeated, "Where are the...?" still not finishing his question.

"The soda and the after-shave are by the sink where Iggy left them." She noticed the light shadow that sprouted under his nose had disappeared, and a pencil line of red pointed outward from one of his nostrils. She decided not to embarrass him by commenting about it and waited until he was dressed to compliment him on how nice he looked.

Thelma waited by the car, and when Freddie dashed toward the door to the back seat, she said, "No, you drive." She knew Freddie drove through fields but never on the county roads, and she wanted to be the first to grant him that honor. She enjoyed Iggy's expression of disapproval when he ran from the outhouse and gaped at Freddie behind the wheel. "You can sit next to him in case he needs help. I am quite content to sit in the back and let you guys be my chauffeurs."

With both of her brothers looking and smelling acceptable, she sat back and enjoyed the ride to the country school from which all three had graduated.

****

Sonja West sat at her desk in the empty classroom and stared at her prepared farewell speech to the community that she had served for the past twenty years. The School Board had recently elected to consolidate their rural one-room school into the public system in Bovine. Before they voted to disband their authority, they agreed that in all fairness she should be considered for a teaching job at the larger school. They instructed her to write her own recommendation and all five members signed it at their final meeting. However, she rejected the contract that followed, not because it required her to return to college during the next three summers to earn a special endorsement on her teaching certificate, but because students in the consolidated school were segregated into eight different grade levels. What would one teach at each grade level? How would older students review their math if they didn't help the younger ones? How could anyone make history and geography come alive with a new group of students every year? And, wouldn't it be boring to teach the same content over and over?

She had discussed these problems with her friend, Mildred, and concluded, "It must be progress, and I'm afraid I'm not willing to change."

The wives of the Board members planned a farewell party, and Sonja decided to use the opportunity to honor Frederick Tate, her only graduating student that year. Of all her past students, he was the most deserving of any special attention from the community. Also, she knew this would please Thelma who had expressed her concern about his avoidance of people outside their family. Sonja cherished Thelma's periodic visits to the school as much as it seemed to embarrass Frederick.

Sonja reached into the desk drawer for the unfinished letter to her father. She opened her fountain pen and suddenly felt confident of her answer to his request in his last communication.

I found what I came looking for, Dad, but now I don't know if I made any difference in the lives of these people. You warned me when I begged you to let me come to the Midwest, the land that Ole Rovaag and Ignatius Donnelly wrote about so eloquently. You said I might not like what I find here and would not be satisfied with what I could accomplish. You were right.

My career has run its course but, I am sorry, I can't come back to live with you. Thank you for the kind offer, but even without a career I belong here.

Twenty years ago, a six-year-old girl entered my classroom on the first day of school, my first day as well, dragging an older brother with her. I recall her exact words. "This is my brother, Iggy. He's a year older but Ma wouldn't let him come to school until I could go with him. Where do you want us to sit?" How could a little girl with

146

so much spirit not rise to great accomplishments in her life? At the expense of sounding cynical, I will tell you how her enthusiasm sputtered out. Life in this harsh culture did it to her.

I came here because I wanted to see the self-sufficient, self-reliant people you had called the salt of the earth. Such families do prosper here, but the independence of individuals often becomes squashed in the process, especially the girls. My male students become men, and they do whatever men have done for generations. The girls become women, often as young as thirteen or fourteen, and are required to do every chore the men choose not to do. I realize that I sound defensive, but the women out here get the short end of the stick. Pardon my local idiom. Many of my girls stopped attending because they were needed at home to help take care of families growing too quickly for their mothers to handle. Some of these girls were given total responsibly for siblings after their mothers died from childbirth or over work. However, the ultimate violation of common decency is the community condoning the marriage of a teenage girl to a widower because he needs help raising his children.

My six-year-old, now a twenty-six-year-old, will bring her youngest brother, Frederick, to his graduation party. He has developed into the most sensitive young man I have experienced in my entire career. I should be proud, but I am afraid for him. I may not have prepared him adequately for the male dominant environment in which he must live. Even his sister didn't reach his level of sensitivity during her time with me. However, she has the strength to survive. I fear the boy she worked so hard to nurture may not.

I may have failed to make any significant changes in their culture but, like Frederick's sister, I survived and I choose to remain among these people. They can be cruel and insensitive yet always painfully honest. They truly are the salt of the earth.

Sonja stared at the letter and thought about the issues she and her father avoided including what he had attempted with her shortly after her mother died. She shook off the memory and visualized the little girl who introduced her to her first teacher-student experience. In many ways, their lives had become similar. Each had either chosen or inherited a vocation that absorbed all their energy, and their experiences may leave them feeling empty. Although she had erased the term old maid from her lexicon, she heard it whispered about, and she knew Thelma felt the same harsh judgments from her family and friends. She remembered Thelma's intelligence and her spark of curiosity that Sonja wanted to help nurture through discussions of great books. If she could develop a relationship with this former student, she could also perform a role of mentor as well as a friend.

Her mind flashed to Mildred and back to Thelma. She placed the letter back into the drawer, intending to add more later.

In preparation for the student reunion, she had reviewed the names of all her past students listed in record books that she kept in her trunk of memories near her bed. She touched her mother's wedding ring, smelled the aroma from one of her father's pipes and read some old letters from a time when her prospects seemed much better. The 1945-46 record book still lay on her desk along with other items yet to be selected, catalogued and stored among all the other memorabilia from the previous years. There would be no next year, and she had to make many hard choices, not only about her possessions but also about her life in general. She felt prepared to greet by name any or all of the one hundred plus students who had attended her classes.

"Ignatius, Frederick, and Thelma." Sonja excused herself from the group of women gathered around her and met the trio at the door. "It's wonderful to see the three of you together. Congratulations, Frederick, on your graduation. I have something for you so don't leave before I have a chance to give it to you."

Freddie shrugged and walked to his seat in the back row.

She turned to Thelma and felt her face flush. "We need to get together for tea or coffee. It would be good for you to get away from all those bachelors at your place and come to see me in town."

"Thank you, Miss West. That would be real nice."

"Please call me Sonja, and I do want you to visit me, soon."

"You can still call me Ignatius," Iggy cut in. "That's okay with me." He started to nod and breathe loudly, and Thelma elbowed him in the ribs.

"I remember that you always used everyone's full name, but I never had a nickname. Just Thelma."

Sonja flinched at Thelma's comment, then chuckled. "Sometimes parents had actually forgotten their child's official name and had to look it up in their baptismal records. Father Busch used to insist their children have Latin ones, like Ignatius, and many families ignored these names as soon as they came home from the church."

"You called me Ignatius and I called you Miss West. I like it that way."

"You mean Egnutz." Larry Collins tip-toed from behind and cuffed Iggy on the shoulder.

"Iggy, to you, Mr. Collins." Thelma glared at him.

"We were just talking about names." Sonja smiled and held out her hand. "It's nice to see you again, Lawrence."

"Yeah, good to see you, Lawrence," Iggy snorted.

"You too, Egnutz." They faked hitting each other with their fists and edged their way out the door.

"Iggy…" Thelma shook her head and breathed though pursed lips. "I'm afraid Larry has whiskey in his pickup. It's Iggy's weakness, and I haven't been able to help him."

"Some things are out of our control, and we just have to accept what we can't change." Sonja sighed. "I guess you already know that. But, I am serious about you coming to visit me at my home in town when you find the time."

"Thank you Miss…Sonja. That would be real nice." Thelma glanced toward the back of the room. "Freddie's sitting alone. I better join him."

"And, I need to meet my other guests. Remember, come visit me soon." Sonja turned to a group of women gathered around the cloakroom, their husbands still lingering outside the door.

Although most of the women had changed their last names, Sonja remembered all their faces. Some, she hadn't seen since they were students and some had since enrolled their children in her class. The occasion afforded her the opportunity to act as hostess rather than guest of honor as the wives of the board members intended.

At her accustomed place in front of the room, Sonja retrieved a pointer from the chalk tray and tapped it on the desk to call the group to attention. Surveying the crowd, she saw them as students, now older but still looking to her for directions. She exercised her usual patience while the group shushed itself into attention. The men, attracted by the silence in the room, filtered in. She suddenly felt that she was a damper on this vibrant crowd and hesitated to interrupt until she saw Freddie sitting at his usual place in the back of the room, eyes fixed on her as if awaiting instructions in math or science.

"Ladies and gentleman." Sonja paused and gave the desk three more taps with her pointer. "I almost said boys and girls, out of habit."

There was a light laughter, and all her guests seemed focused on her as they had when they were children in that same room.

"This is a happy and a sad day for me as I know it is for many of you. The Board has acted in everyone's best interests by agreeing to consolidate our district. However, a little of each of our lives remains here in this room." She choked back a tear, realizing how much rather than how little of her life remained in the building and all it represented. "We need to remind ourselves that our memories are not here," she waved the pointer, "but in each and everyone's heart who spent many hours of their young lives here. I will always cherish our time together in this room. You have given me much joy."

She bobbed the pointer up and down as if she were counting her students or conducting an orchestra. To dwell any longer on this aspect of the requiem as she secretly called it might make her cry.

"I have the pleasure of presenting to you the last graduating class of one person. We've had smaller classes in the past." Another wave of polite laughter. "And we have had larger ones. When a single student has to represent the final graduating class of District Twelve, we can all be thankful that that person is Frederick Tate who, as you all know, is a member of the Sylvester Rastner family. Frederick tragically lost two mothers but, fortunately, has had wonderful care and nurturing from his cousin, Thelma. For as long as I have known him, Frederick has been mature and responsible beyond his age. He has been an involved learner and a helpful custodian to the care and maintenance of this building. He chopped the wood that you so thoughtfully dropped off for our heat in winter, and he arrived half an hour early every cold morning to start the fire. I'm sure he did his chores at home before he walked the mile to school each day to tend to his duties here. However, his most remarkable achievement, one that no one else in this room tonight or anyone who has ever attended this school can claim, Frederick has never been absent throughout his entire eight years of enrollment. It is for perfect attendance that I now present him with this certificate of achievement. Frederick, please come forward to receive your award." She paused and held the envelope in Freddie's direction.

****

Freddie felt his face get hot when he heard his name called. He felt anxious ever since Miss West greeted them at the door. Once in his regular seat, he expected to feel more comfortable but it didn't help. Everyone seemed to talk at once. That wasn't what this room was for. Everything had gotten out of control. He wondered what would happen to the school when there wasn't a teacher any more. He heard a neighbor bought the building to use it as a storage shed, and that didn't seem right. What bothered him most was the haunting light from gas lanterns that cast dark shadows mimicking Miss West's movements along the blackboard. Most farms had electricity, but no one bothered to hook it up to the school because classes were held during the day, not at night. And now with all these people who don't belong…. Why didn't his teacher do something? When she began to speak, he felt better, but he still didn't like all these strangers in his classroom.

Freddie's neighbor, Davie Smith, peeked at him from his seat between his parents and waved. Davie wasn't old enough to go to school but one time he ran away from home and joined the students in a game of *Red Rover* during recess. When Davie rammed into him, Freddie pretended to be knocked down. He wished he could run and fall down and wrestle with Davie like his brothers used to do with him.

When Freddie heard his name called and saw Miss West hold something toward him, he just stared at her. When she called him a second time, he rose from his seat and walked to the front of the room.

CHAPTER TWENTY
FREDDIE'S BICYCLE
(Spring 1947)

Thelma had been gathering eggs from nests scattered around the yard and was about to check the empty chicken coop to see if the boys had prepared it for baby chicks when she heard noises coming from the machine shed. What had broken and needed fixing? She peeked inside and saw Freddie standing over a workbench that was cluttered with gears, wheels and an iron frame.

"What on earth did you do to your bicycle?" She set down her basket and stood beside him with her hands on her hips.

"Just checking how it works. I didn't wreck nothing."

"Did Pa see what you did?"

"Think it would make him mad?"

"Maybe not, if you know how to put it back together." She picked up a sprocket and inspected it. "It was your graduation present, you know."

"Svez said it was for you and Iggy, too. I shoulda told you guys what I'm doing." He picked up the chain and draped it over the sprocket while she still held it.

"It's okay." She let loose and it dangled from the chain he held at both ends. She wiped her hands on her apron and stared at the dark smudge on the white cloth.

"You see, each link in the chain catches on a tooth, and when you pedal it drives the wheel."

"I can see that."

"I wanted to know why the wheel stops when you try to pedal backwards."

"Have you figured it out?"

"I think so. You see..."

"I don't think I need to know that just now." She pointed to the eggs showing through the wire mesh. "Eggs is what I understand, and I don't have to take one apart to know how it works."

"You gotta bust the shell open to cook something."

Thelma tousled his hair, and he didn't duck away. She returned to her kitchen where she cleaned the eggs and held them up to the sun to check for cracks and blood spots. The clear ones she put into the case to be sold the next time she went to town. She checked the afternoon sun and decided there was time enough to bake a cake. She cracked the rejected eggs into the bowl and thought about Freddie's dismantled bicycle. Maybe Pa was right. Two years it hung on the rafters in the garage, used but once or twice. She remembered the argument she had with him about buying it. She had waited until she had fresh baked goodies before she brought up the subject.

"How about getting Freddie a graduation present."

"Like what?" He flipped a steaming roll from the platter to his plate and lathered it with a chunk of butter stuck on the end of his fork.

"A bicycle." She refilled his cup with coffee and watched him slosh some into his saucer.

"A bicycle?" He tore a corner from the roll, tossed it into his mouth and sipped from the saucer. "I can't see spending money on anything unless it's got a practical use on the farm, or the house for that matter."

She poured herself some coffee and wondered what he considered an essential item for the house.

"I ain't never heard Freddie say he wanted a bicycle."

She held her cup with both hands and blew the steam across the top. She decided not to respond.

"He walked a mile to school and back every day for eight years. Never complained 'bout it."

She saved her prepared argument for when she sensed his resolve was weakening and stuck to the basic, "He just wants a bicycle."

"Hell, he can drive the pickup in the field and on the back roads whenever he needs to get someplace."

She remained silent.

"I'll talk to him."

"You know he won't admit a bicycle's important."

"Then how the hell do you know he wants one if he won't say so?"

154

"Yesterday, he said it would be nice to have a bicycle to go to town and be with some friends." She invented the friends part and realized it didn't fool him.

"If a bicycle would get Freddie to find friends to run with, I'd buy him one today." Their eyes met. "You know, Thelma, it won't bust him off the farm even for an afternoon."

She winced when he addressed her directly like he did with the boys when he was frustrated or angry, but he hadn't changed the subject like she expected him to. "Freddie never asks for anything. Even if he wasn't serious about a bicycle, I think you should get him one just because it's time to do something nice for him."

He shrugged, gave a slight tug on the bib of his overalls and began to push his chair away from the table. "I'll wait for a while to see how bad he wants one."

"Pa, I want the bicycle." A desperate move that she didn't expect to cinch the argument, but it would make him rethink his objections.

"Well, why didn't you say so right away?" He paused as if he needed to rethink the situation. "You can take the pickup, or the car for that matter, whenever you want. You do it every time you go to town to get the groceries."

She looked directly at him but gave no sign of agreeing.

"Tell you what." He glanced at the clock on the wall like he needed to be someplace. "I'll have Iggy take you to Harrington to get your license, and then you can come and go as you please."

Thelma smiled, not because of the offer but because he said please rather than need. She decided not to allow him off the hook.

"What I meant is that I want Freddie to have a bicycle, if he wants one. I think you owe it to him."

Thelma played her trump card, and from the expression on his face she realized it hit home. Nobody in the family ever owed anyone anything. Everyone just did what needed to be done, and satisfaction from completing a job was the only gratitude anyone expected, or got. After her brief conversation with Sonja at Freddie's graduation, she began to question her role in the family. She used a church word, epiphany, when she tried to explain the experience to mother that evening.

"We don't owe Freddie nothing and Freddie don't owe us nothing. He's one of us, one of the family, no different than you or Iggy or the boys."

His reaction startled her. "I don't mean that you really owe Freddie anything. That was just an expression."

"Henry don't think it's just an expression."

"He was just mad at dinner last Sunday because his other boys are about to leave him. He doesn't really believe that you're keeping Freddie just for a farm hand."

"He said folks is whispering 'bout it."

"If anyone's talking, he's the one doing it, and it isn't making him any points either, except maybe at Buddy's Bar. And, he's too cheap to pay bar prices for his booze, so he don't even go there much." She glanced at the door to the porch, fearful that Freddie might be within hearing. "Freddie felt real bad about what Henry said. He spent all that afternoon with Arnie in his room. Soon he'll be taking his meals up there too." She looked into the front room toward the stairs to their bedrooms. "I wish I knew what those two talk about so much."

"Iggy never had a bicycle. If I buy one for Freddie, it'll look like I'm favoring the boy."

"Then, for once, favor him." She felt Ma's voice reverberate in her demand and the silence that followed frightened her.

The next day Svez came back from town with the bright red Schwin in the back of his pickup.

She rolled her eyes toward the ceiling and whispered, "I got him to do it." She shoved a piece of wood into the firebox and slid the coffee pot over as he walked into the kitchen.

"I 'spose it could be useful around the yard." He grabbed his cup from the sink and sat at the table. "Go on out and help 'em learn to ride the darn thing. I'll wait here for the coffee to get hot."

She watched from the porch as Iggy held the bicycle upright and Freddie swung his leg over it. It reminded her of a small iron horse. He began to pedal, the bike moved and Iggy fell behind. Chickens scattered and Babe crawled out from under the corncrib. Iggy kept turning in circles to face Freddie as he made wide swings around them. Iggy took his turn, and after his third attempt, he wobbled forward, out the driveway and down the road, Babe barking and chasing close behind. A few minutes later, he pushed the bike back and Babe followed, the handlebars pointing toward the sky. He handed it to Freddie and yelled to Thelma that he had to talk to Larry Collins. He got into the pickup and drove off.

She went out to the yard and held the bike by its misshapen handles while Freddie ran to the tool shed and returned with an adjustable wrench. With the handlebars properly adjusted, she

156

hiked her skirts much like she did when she rode horses, and with Freddie and Babe running alongside, she pedaled out the yard, down the road, and returned still upright.

That was two years ago, and she and Iggy hadn't ridden it since. Freddie rode the bike off and on that summer to get the cows or run errands, but after that it stayed in the garage. She had avoided talking to her father about it. At least by taking it apart Freddie might learn something.

****

Freddie wished Thelma had stayed in the machine shed to help him. She could pull the chain across the sprocket wheel as he adjusted the arm attached to it. However, when he stuck it into the vise, he was able to figure out how it worked. He picked up each part and inspected it, matched it to another piece and observed how the two pieces operated together. He marveled at the precision of the tiny gears and the smoothness of the ball bearings. He figured out how the wheel kept going when the pedal stopped and why it braked when he tried to pedal backwards. As the rays from the low-lying sun became visible through the dusty air in the tool shed, He realized it was nearly time to start chores.

He reassembled the bicycle and lifted it into a wooden crate that held it in place with the rear wheel inches off the ground. He mounted the bicycle and began to pedal. After attaining the desired speed, he stopped, paused a few moments and then applied back-pressure. The wheel stopped. He turned the seat around and repeated the process facing backwards. He smiled to himself as he turned the seat back, removed the bicycle from the crate and rode it to the granary.

****

Svez watched Freddie ride his bicycle across the yard, and it both pleased and annoyed him. At least he finally took it from the garage where it sat all last summer. He had often wanted to point that out to Thelma but never found the right moment. Maybe she was right, or maybe Freddie just wasted an entire afternoon in the tool shed with the dang thing. He studied the sky reddened by the oversized sun as it began to sink below the horizon and decided that tomorrow the boys better get the seed-grain ready for planting.

The next morning, Svez delegated the day's activities over breakfast. "The oats needs to be fanned today. Next week we can start planting the west forty."

"Me and Iggy'll do it, Svez." Freddie called him by the only name his family ever heard him use. When Freddie was in the first grade, Miss West had sent a note home encouraging the family to have Freddie call him Dad or Pa. Svez felt it was the boy's decision to call him any name he chose, and he ignored her advice.

"Yup. Me and Freddie." Iggy, who usually avoided the difficult and dusty job of cleaning oats, nodded in agreement a bit too easily for Svez's notion.

"I better go too." Thelma gathered the plates and set them on the sink. "The dishes will wait."

"With that new hopper Freddie made last year, it's only a two-man job." Svez glanced at Freddie and noticed that the recognition seemed to please him. "One guy can feed the hopper and bag the cleaned oats, and one can turn the crank to the blower. They can change off if the guy cranking needs a break." He turned to face Thelma and then lowered his eyes. "The brooder house needs to be set up. Our new chicks will be ready at the Co-op later this week." He was conscious of how he delegated chores to Thelma. The boys he could tell directly what they had to do, but with his daughter he made the task sound like something that should be done, and she usually took the hint. He downed the last of his coffee and left the house, confident that the day's work-orders had been acknowledged.

He stepped outside the machine shed where he had cleaned and oiled the grain drill and listened for the humming of the fanning mill in the granary. Although cleaning oats was a job he gladly delegated to his boys, he liked to watch the golden grains flow into burlap bags, the chaff and weed residue blown away in the air chamber. Those seeds were the results of countless crops going back to the time Pubba came to America and had to borrow seed oats from a neighbor to begin his first crop. They would continue regenerating long after he was gone.

He checked the brooder house and noticed that Thelma hadn't set up the chick feeders and heat lamps. He reached down, grabbed a hand full of the fresh sand the boys had laid on the floor and inspected it. When the chicks got big enough, they would need it to help digest hard grain. He stepped outside, looked around the yard and counted about fifty hens scratching and pecking at the ground. They should supply enough eggs and meat throughout the summer if Babe kept the foxes away at night. When Shep or Podue were still alive, no foxes ever made their way into the yard.

He stared at the granary and felt something unusual about the humming noise from the fanning mill. "They ain't taken no break since they started," he muttered and went to investigate. As he approached, he heard laughter and shouts over the noise from the machine. When he opened the door, he could scarcely believe what he saw.

Thelma clapped her hands and cheered as Iggy giggled and ran from the hopper to the exit chute. It was like opening presents on Christmas morning. Svez began to laugh when he saw Freddie. He leaned forward and grabbed his knees to keep from falling over. Freddie showed his teeth as he sat backwards on his bicycle and vigorously peddled, but it went nowhere. The crank that should have been powering the fanning mill lay on the floor. In its place, Freddie had connected his bicycle through a series of pulleys and belts.

That night at the supper table Svez said, "The contraption Freddie rigged to the fanning mill worked good."

Freddie beamed.

CHAPTER TWENTY-ONE
THEN THERE WERE FOUR
(Spring, 1950)

While Thelma cleared the breakfast dishes from the table, she glanced out the kitchen window and saw her father get into his pickup. She wanted to tell him that the boys don't need his help to get the spring planting done. They've been doing good, able to pay him back on time for seven straight years. He reminded her that the Bible said seven good years would be followed by seven lean ones. He quoted only what suited him.

She checked again and saw him still sitting in his pickup. Suddenly, he hit the steering wheel with the palms of his hands, started the engine and drove onto the road, through the ditch and stopped back by the machine shed. She realized he was confused and suspected he would be back in for coffee. She would tell him that he was getting too old to run from farm to farm.

"Is there any coffee left?" Just as she expected, he walked into the kitchen and plopped down at the table.

"It's on the stove. Just gotta put a little fire under it, and it'll still be good." Thelma grabbed a small log from the wood box. "I'm glad you decided to stay home today."

"Ralph can do his field work without me."

She took two cups from the cupboard and placed them on the table. "I was about to suggest that same thing. Since he got married last fall, he hasn't asked for help from me either."

"That goes for George and Herman, too. They got their own lives and don't want me hanging 'round no more. Besides, Freddie and Iggy might need help right here at home. Later today when it warms up, they can start seeding oats if it didn't freeze too hard last night." He sat at the table and rubbed his eyes. "Any of them biscuits left?"

She reached into the breadbox and took out two sugar and cinnamon rolls. "Why don't you just take it easy this year? I hate to remind you that you'll be turning seventy five next summer?"

"That ain't old. Pubba was ninety 'fore he quit. Arnie's getting old, not me. Speaking of Arnie, have you seen him today?"

"I haven't heard or seen him all morning. Thought he must be out in the barn."

"Don't 'spose he'll go out there for a while, least not at milking time." He laughed. "Iggy teases him."

"Teases him?"

"I should make him stop, but he don't mean no harm. Last week, Arnie got there late, and Freddie was done milking. Iggy fibbed that Freddie hadn't showed up that morning. Arnie grumbled, grabbed a rusty pail and squeezed teats that had already been milked dry." He paused. "Remember when you thought I bought the milking machine, and it was really a washing machine?"

"Yeah, I remember. That was ten years and about a million loads of dirty clothes ago." She looked at the old man in front of her and tried to remember him from ten years earlier or even ten years before that, when Ma was still alive. "The boys got their milking machine, but I got my washing machine first." She felt a lump develop in her throat. "Thanks, Pa." Their eyes briefly met and she felt he was embarrassed. "Did you tell Arnie that Freddie already milked his cows or just sit back and laugh?"

"Oh, I weren't there when it happened. I heard 'bout it later. I guess Iggy asked Arnie if he forgot how to milk a cow. Then, he told him to go back to the house, and he would do it. Arnie stormed out and ain't been back at milking time since."

"It ain't right to tease an old man like that. Make Iggy stop doing it."

"Don't have to. Freddie made him quit that foolishness. Refused to talk to Iggy for days. Never knew Freddie could get that mad." He glanced toward the front room. "Better go upstairs to see if Arnie's okay." He picked up his cup. "Is that coffee hot yet?"

She approached the door to Arnie's room with dread, unsure if he was still inside. If he was hiding or in one of his moods, she knew he wouldn't answer when she knocked, yet she tapped lightly on the door.

"Arnie, are you in there?" She paused and listened. "I'm coming in to get your dirty clothes."

She expected the door to be blocked with his dresser or at least a chair but, to her surprise, it opened freely. She stared at an unmade bed surrounded by dirty clothes and dishes with dried-on food. She looked into an empty clothes hamper. His clean clothes she had laid on his bed last Monday were mixed in with his quilt and bed sheets. She collected three dirty plates, five coffee cups, one with blots of mold floating in a silvery gray liquid, and an assortment of silverware. When she looked under the bed, she startled a mouse nibbling on a crust of bread. She decided to come back later with a broom and dustpan.

Back in the kitchen, she put Arnie's dishes in the sink and checked a kettle of water she had been heating to do dishes. "He ain't in his room. Must be in the barn."

Iggy came in and walked over to the stove. Before she could stop him, he dumped coffee grounds into the boiling water. It frothed and bubbled over filling the room with a pungent odor. He jumped back, and Thelma grabbed the handle to move it away from the heat.

"Thought I told you never to put coffee in an open kettle. It'll spill over every time. Its gotta percolate in a coffeepot."

Iggy turned to Freddie who had followed him into the kitchen. "Thought that was what she had the water boiling for."

"Was Arnie in the barn when you left?" Thelma asked Freddie as she stared at the foamy gray mixture turning crispy on the stove.

"He weren't in the barn at all this morning unless he got there after me and Iggy went to the granary."

"I would have seen him if he left the house after you guys did." She used her apron to grab the kettle, lifted a dishtowel from its rack and strained out the coffee grounds as she filled each of their cups. "I was in the house all morning."

"He musta' got up during the night and went to the barn." Freddie sipped from his cup and set it back on the table. "I'll go find him."

"Check the chicken coop, too. I know he don't like it in there, but it's the only other place where he could stay warm all night." She thought about Arnie sleeping with the baby chicks or hiding in the calf pen while Freddie and Iggy did chores. Would she ever be able to get his clothes clean again?

"Oh, my gosh, his jacket." She jumped up. "I moved it when I looked for dirty dishes upstairs. His buckskin was still in his room. He went outside without it."

****

Freddie opened the door to the chicken coop and felt a blast of warm air as two hundred baby chicks huddled around the heat lamp and peeped loudly. He stooped to pick up a dead bird that had wandered too far from the heat and carried it to the barn. He tossed it to the large gray tomcat that met him at the door and searched between the cows, over the partition to the young stock pen and inside the cooling room. He went to the ladder that extended to the loft and hesitated, fearful that Arnie might have spent the night up there. Through the hay chute, he heard Babe whimper and remembered that she hadn't run to the barn with him and Rex that morning. He wasn't concerned because she probably spent the night with the neighbors' dogs.

"You might not be the papa this time, Rex," he had joked, "but, you ain't the jealous type." He whistled and Babe peered down at him. She refused to jump into his outstretched arms. He had often helped her climb into the loft where they would run and romp in the hay. "Why won't you come down, and how did you get up there?" He climbed the ladder and looked down at Svez and Iggy who had followed him into the barn and were staring up at him.

"I think I know where he is," he yelled to them and followed Babe to a corner where, huddled in a clump of hay, he saw Arnie. He grabbed and rubbed Arnie's hands while Babe licked Arnie's face. Freddie stammered, "I'm afraid he's dead." Arnie pulled his hand away and wiped the dog's saliva from his stubble. Freddie shouted, "He's alive."

Arnie grumbled, "Git that damn dog away from me."

"I think that damn dog kept you alive last night." Svez wheezed after climbing the ladder. He reached under Arnie's neck and raised his head. "We better get you to the house."

"I'm okay. Jus' make this damn dog stop slurpin' me."

Freddie helped Svez lift Arnie to his feet and held his arm as they walked to ladder. Iggy wrapped his arms around Babe to hold her back. Freddie climbed down first, and he heard Arnie swear when Svez and Iggy lowered him through the chute with the sling used to hoist hay into the loft.

When Arnie's feet touched the ground, he looked around and said, "What're the cows doin' in here?"

Iggy began to giggle and Svez said, "Cows belong in here. We're in the barn, Arnie."

Freddie glared at Iggy and asked Arnie, "Where did you think you were?"

Arnie looked at him like he was crazy. "'Course I'm in the barn. How'd they get in here so fast? I was just fetchin' 'em back from the pasture."

"Well they're in here now. They've been in here all night, and they've already been milked this morning," Svez told him.

Arnie faced Freddie and asked, "Is Pubba mad at me, Vester?"

Svez explained, "Those are the names he used to call our Pa and me when we was kids. He's just a little confused. Thinks you're me and I'm his pa."

"He calls me Vester quit a bit lately." Freddie looked at Arnie and felt like he had given away a secret. "But I don't mind."

Svez took Arnie's arm. "Let's go into the house. I think Mumma's got breakfast ready."

When they got to the kitchen, Freddie poured a cup of coffee and loaded it with cream and sugar while Iggy and Svez helped Arnie onto his chair.

"He was in the hay loft all night. Babe kept him warm, or he woulda froze to death." Freddie glanced toward Thelma as he held the cup to Arnie's mouth. Arnie pushed Freddie's arm, and some coffee spilled on is lap. He stared at it. He reached for the cup and emptied it with one long gulp. The cup dangled from his finger and his head plopped onto the table.

"Put some blankets on the couch. I don't think he should be left alone in his room for a while," Svez told Thelma. She nodded and left the kitchen.

Freddie and Svez helped Arnie get up off the chair, led him into the front room and laid him on the couch. When the rest of the family returned to the kitchen, Freddie stayed and sat on the floor close by. He listened to Arnie's breath. When he heard Thelma suggest that Svez call Father Reinhardt, he remembered what Arnie had told him about that.

"Maybe, when I'm dead but not before. Ya hear? Don't let them get that damn priest 'til I'm dead."

Freddie laughed when Arnie had said it, but it didn't seem funny now. He went into the kitchen. "Said there's no reason to call the priest." He made it sound like Arnie had just told him that. "He said not 'til he's dead."

"That sounds like Arnie." Thelma said.

"Well, he ain't dying just yet. He's tough as nails." Svez peered through the archway into the front room. "As a matter of fact, he's very much alive."

Freddie peeked around Svez and saw an empty couch. "He went up to his room."

"We gotta get the north forty seeded if we're gonna have a crop this summer." Svez pushed back his cup, his eyes locked on Freddie.

"Let's get going." Freddie grabbed Iggy's arm and dragged him from the table.

Later that afternoon, Freddie went back into the house to check on Arnie, and Iggy went to the barn to start the chores.

"How's Arnie?" Freddie asked when he saw Thelma in the porch washing her hands.

"He musta come down to get his lunch. I left it on the table right after you guys left. When I got done in the garden and came back into the house, his food was gone, plate and all." She wiped her hands. "He sure did give us a scare this morning."

"I thought he was dead up in the haymow." He stared at Thelma's hand as she poked a blister with a pin and dabbed it with the towel. When he glanced up, he saw that she was focused on him rather than her hand.

"You're worried about him, aren't you," she said.

"Guess so. He needs me to do things for him."

"What's he do for you?"

"Just lets me, I guess, do things." He looked at her. "He talks to me about what happened when he was eighteen, like me." He didn't want her to ask any more questions.

"Well, you better go and talk to him, then."

From the tone in her voice, he wondered if he had somehow hurt her feelings. "I gotta help Iggy with the chores." He walked to the door, stopped and turned. "Maybe I could take his supper up to him tonight.

You can take yours up there, too, if you like." For an instant he wanted her to hug him, and he felt embarrassed.

When he got to the barn, he heard Iggy grumbling in the silo and smelled the sour odor of fermented corn.

"We're 'bout out of silage." Iggy said as he peered through the small door near the floor.

"I think Svez will let the cows back in the pasture soon, maybe even tomorrow. The grass's greening up pretty good out there."

Iggy climbed out and jabbed his fork into the pile he had made.

Freddie went into the cooling room and grabbed the milk bucket, the lid with rubber-lined suction cups attached and the wrap-around strap to hold the bucket under the cow's belly. He hit the switch to vacuum pump and listened for the familiar and pleasant *whap, whap whap*. He decided to milk Arnie's cows first.

****

Arnie awoke and the dim evening light made him think it was morning. He felt hungry and reached under his bed, but his plate from supper was gone. He reached for his pants on the floor and realized he had slept in them. His dresser had been moved back and the door was partially open. He felt frustrated. On the chair beside his bed, he found his clean clothes where Thelma usually left them. It must be Monday. He shoved the dresser against the door, sat back on the bed and changed his shirt. He waited what seemed like a long time and then got up, moved the dresser and opened the door a bit so he could hear anyone in the hallway. He returned to bed and waited. Soon, the door squeezed open and Freddie appeared holding two plates of food.

"Come in and shut the door."

"Gotta get some coffee, too. Be right back." Freddie set one plate on Arnie's nightstand and one on the chair next to his bed.

Arnie sat up and waited until Freddie came back and knelt on the floor using the chair as his table. They ate but didn't talk, and when Arnie awoke early the next morning, he wondered where Vester went.

His door creaked open, he hadn't blocked it, and Freddie peeked in. He faked being asleep and breathed loudly so Freddie would hear and not rub his hand like he did in the haymow. When he heard Freddie go downstairs, he got out of bed and stood by his window. He watched the shadows slowly appear in the predawn light. Soon he saw Freddie skip across the yard, turn and run backward facing Arnie's window. Arnie chuckled when he saw him trip over Rex who had stopped, probably expecting Freddie to go the other way. He pulled his chair to the window and opened the curtain. He sat by the window all morning and slept most of the afternoon. That evening, when Freddie brought him his supper, Arnie told him to close the curtain and bring the chair back beside his bed.

After they ate, Freddie gathered the cups and plates. "Thelma said I gotta bring them right back."

But Freddie didn't come back. Arnie stood in front of his window, peered around the curtain and watched the shadows cast by the yard light. A cat stalked an invisible mouse, and a few hens pecked at the ground. He thought he saw a fox, but Rex or Babe wouldn't let one get that close without making a fuss. After he saw each member of the family wander to the outhouse and back, he knew they would soon be in bed. He could take his turn. He didn't like using the chamber pot.

"Are you still awake?" Freddie standing in his doorway startled him.

"Course I'm awake."

Freddie walked across the room and stood next to him as they both gazed out the window. "Svez said me and Iggy can build a little shelf outside your window so you can sit outside and watch us work during the day. Sort of like a balcony. Might make it a bit less boring up here."

"It'd fall down. You'd have to pull it off me with the horses."

"No, it'd have pillars in cement footings to hold it up. Me and Iggy helped Larry Collins build one just like it. His new wife wanted to sit out there and sun herself."

"Don't she get 'nuf sun weeding the garden?"

Freddie shrugged. "Svez said we can build one outside your window."

"I'd never use it."

"You might."

Arnie glared at Freddie. "Go on to bed." He waited for Freddie to leave and then crept downstairs, through the kitchen to the outhouse.

A few days later, Arnie heard a commotion near his window, and he realized Freddie was serious about the balcony. Iggy dug two post holes in the lawn next to the house and Freddie dragged the portable cement mixer from the tool shed. Early the next morning, Arnie watched the moon set between two posts planted outside his window. The next afternoon, Freddie stuck his head through the window and beckoned him to step out onto a small platform. On it sat a lawn chair Freddie had lugged up the ladder. Arnie went back to his bed and lay on top of the quilt. Each morning after that, he watched Freddie leave the house, and after a few days he decided to climb out the window. When Freddie turned and waved, he climbed back into his room. By the middle of summer, he sat on his balcony every day it wasn't raining and returned to his room only when it got too hot or he needed a nap.

One night, after everyone was in bed, Arnie crept downstairs and walked through the kitchen to the outhouse. The cold grass felt good on his bare feet, but they hurt when he stepped on the gravel between the house and the barn. He had to fetch the cows, and Pubba wouldn't let him wear shoes. He stopped under the yard light and brushed the small sharp stones off his feet in a small patch of grass. He heard Pubba yell at him, but his feet hurt too bad to run and hide.

"Arnie, what are you doing out here at this hour of the night?" Vester, not Pubba, stood at the gate, barefoot and in his nightshirt.

"Tell Pubba I need shoes to get the cows. I used to go barefoot, but I can't no more."

"Come back to the house."

He obeyed, grimacing as he walked back through the gravel.

"Are you done in there?" Svez pointed to the outhouse.

"I can't go. I tried, but I can't piss."

"I thought so. Remember when Pubba couldn't either and we had to help him with that little rubber hose?"

"I kin go now. Don't need no hose." He turned his back and in a few minutes said, "There. Now I gotta git to bed."

"I'll pick up one of them hoses from Doc tomorrow, and I'll help you use it when Iggy and Freddie are in the barn. You gotta start using the chamber pot in your room from now on, or you'll wander off some night and get lost."

The next morning, Arnie heard the door open just enough for Svez to shove the chamber pot through. He whispered as loud as he could, "I kin go in that thing. Don't need that hose."

When Svez came back into his room at noon, Arnie grimaced and asked, "Did ya get one of them things?"

"Yeah, and Doc showed me how to use it." Svez laughed. "Not on me. He had a rubber prick he keeps in a drawer."

Arnie sat on the edge of the bed and watched Svez thread the hose through his penis. He flopped back, closed his eyes and made believe he was Pubba and Vester was helping him pee. Soon he felt relief and wanted to sleep.

Arnie propped himself on his elbows and said, "Ya won't tell Freddie 'bout the hose."

"Nah, just that he has to empty the chamber pot. That's not a job for Thelma."

Arnie mumbled, "She hid my shoes," but then he saw them standing alongside his bed. He laid back down and closed his eyes.

****

Freddie brought Arnie his supper every evening, and ate with him as often as Thelma would let him. On warm nights, they stood on the balcony and watched the shadows disappear as the sun set, and then reappear when someone switched on the yard light. Freddie told him about his cows, about the condition of the crops and, if Arnie asked, about how Mumma and Pubba were feeling. He tried to change the subject whenever Arnie talked about dying, but Arnie often told him what to do when that happened.

When Freddie told him about one of his cows that had gotten sick, Arnie said, "Better ship that one 'fore she dies on us. I sure 'spected she'd last longer than me."

Not wanting Arnie to worry about the low milk production, Freddie lied by a hundred pounds when he reported it to him at the end of the month.

Arnie said, "That new feller at the Co-op can't get his weights right. Better tell 'em he over paid me."

One evening, after sitting and listening to Arnie's irregular breaths, Freddie assumed he was asleep for the night, and he stood up to leave. He felt Arnie's leathery hand grab his arm and heard him whisper, "Don't go."

"Okay. If you want me here." He sat back down and leaned close to Arnie's head. He felt Arnie's cold hand against his face, and he smelled his sour breath as he whispered instructions.

"Tell Thelma she gits the money I got in the bank in town. You git my cows and horses."

"Okay." Freddie didn't remind him that his horses had been sold a couple years ago. "Thank you."

"I wanna be buried next to Mumma and Pubba. You better call Father Busch. Mumma wants me to have a priest. Not until I'm gone." He squeezed Freddie's hand. "I gotta' be dead. Then Father Busch. Do you understand? Not till I'm gone."

"Okay, Arnie." Freddie felt his voice crack.

"Never did like him. Too holy." Blue lips curved slightly. "He thought he was St. Alphonse. But, he was jus' Father Busch."

Freddie became frightened. "I better get Thelma, so I don't forget anything."

"No, don't go. I got more to tell you." Arnie started to sit up but fell back. "Liz weren't your real Ma. You know that?

"I know that, Arnie."

"But she treated you real nice. She treated me nice, too. But she's gone. Me and you, we miss her. I miss Mumma. She was my real Ma."

Freddie began to cry, and Arnie pulled him closer. "Ya don't worry. Svez is a good guy. He'll keep you. He kept me. I'm his brother."

170

Freddie felt Arnie's breath wash over him and heard him gasp as he tried to inhale.

"He picked you to be his son. That makes him almost your real pa.

Freddie felt Arnie release his grasp but didn't move away because he wanted to hear Arnie breathe. Freddie felt lonelier than he ever had before. He envied Arnie for the memories he had of his mother when he was young. He began to understand the loneliness Arnie must have felt. He became frightened for Arnie and for himself. He knew Arnie was dying.

He walked to the window and stared out at the full harvest moon, the time when crops were gathered and stored for the animals that winter. He felt this would be Arnie's last harvest, and wondered about life after death. He hoped God would give Arnie a home where he felt he belonged.

The next morning, Freddie awoke when Thelma touched his shoulder as he sat on the floor and slumped on the edge of Arnie's bed. They didn't speak. He felt her arm around him as he stared at the lifeless form lying on the rumpled covers. Thelma straightened the sheet and covered Arnie's body up to his neck.

"He said Father Busch, but he meant Father Reinhardt. Maybe Svez should call him."

He watched a field mouse scamper through a hole in the wall. Probably had a nest in there for the winter.

CHAPTER TWENTY-TWO
THELMA VISITS MISS WEST

Thelma stood mute as the door opened and Miss West reached out to her with both arms and slowly let them drop to her side.

"Thelma. What a pleasant surprise. Come in."

"I had to bring the eggs to town." The explanation she had prepared for her unannounced visit sounded silly, like she was back in school making an excuse for something she shouldn't have done. She entered the small porch that opened directly into the living room, not the kitchen like most homes, and she became more flustered.

"Errands, of course. Please, let me take your coat."

She allowed her long gray-speckled coat to slide off her shoulders, but when she saw it draped over Miss West's laced sleeve and then slide between two other coats in the closet, she wished she had gone home right after grocery shopping. In the living room, a woman sat at one side of the couch holding a tiny china cup in one hand and a matching saucer in the other. Like her rustic coat sandwiched between two delicate and frilly garments, she felt out of place.

"Oh! I've come at a bad time. You've got company." Thelma reached back to grab her coat and felt her arm pushed away as the closet door shut.

"Yes, and all the more reason I am delighted you chose this exact time to stop by." She took Thelma's hand and led her into the living room. "I was just having tea with someone you know, Mildred Bushman, who works at the bank."

Thelma felt Miss West grip her arm as if to prevent her running away, something she wanted to do.

"Mildred, look who has come to join us for tea. One of my former students, Thelma Rastner." She directed Thelma to sit on the side of the couch opposite Mildred and clasped her hands together. "Please, sit down while I steep another pot." She walked toward the door in the back of the living room and turned. "Do you take cream or sugar?"

Scrunched toward the side of the couch opposite Mildred, Thelma remained quiet. She didn't know how she took her tea.

"Maybe you would prefer something other than tea," came the voice from the kitchen. "I can make some coffee."

Yes, coffee, Thelma thought. She said, "Tea is just fine. I take it black. I mean, without cream and sugar." She corrected herself and was embarrassed that she would be an imposition to her host.

Mildred's eyes followed Miss West to the kitchen and then back to Thelma. "Sonja's certainly happy to see you. My goodness, she never chatters like that." She set her cup and saucer on the coffee table in front of the couch. "Now, you and I have a chance to get acquainted. We talk briefly in the bank, but that doesn't really count."

"Yes, or no, that doesn't count, really."

"I was so sad to hear about your uncle passing away. It was a wonderful funeral, though. Mr. Lorenz was kind enough to allow me the time off to attend it."

Thelma remembered her brothers' comments about Mildred coming to Arnie's funeral. When Freddie complained that not many people came, George joked that Mildred Bushman showed up. Ralph said that you gotta die to make that old maid happy. Everyone except Freddie laughed, but now it embarrassed her and she felt her face get hot.

"Goodness, you must have been out in the cold. Your face is still quite flushed."

Thelma put her hands to her cheeks and scolded herself for enjoying Ralph's cruel comment. "Yeah," she straightened and put her hands on her lap. "Yes, it is quite cold. Mostly, just windy, though."

"I thought so. I was just telling Sonja how cozy it felt in here with the wind raging outside."

"Yes, it is. Cozy."

"I bet you miss your uncle very much. He lived with you and your family, did he not?"

"He'd been with us as long as I can remember. He was a quiet man, and I never felt close to him like Pa did." She wished she had said Dad. "Like Freddie did." She wished she had said my brother Freddie.

"I was never close to anyone in my family. I never knew my mother, at least not very well. She died when I was five. By the time my dad remarried a few years later, I was too set in my ways to accept another woman as my mother. I'm afraid we had a rather bad time of it for the next few years, especially when two new babies arrived, my half sisters. If Sonja hadn't invited me to join her here in Bovine, I would never have broken away by myself."

Thelma paid close attention as Mildred reached for her saucer, raised the cup to her lips and quietly sipped. She planned to imitate her when Miss West brought her tea, or coffee. She envied Mildred's close friendship with her old teacher and refused to dwell on the speculation her brothers made about them.

"I'm afraid I've bored you enough with the story of my childhood." She set the saucer back on the table and used both hands to replace the cup.

Thelma heard it clatter and saw Mildred's hand shake. Why would she be nervous in her friend's house? The silence that followed made her uncomfortable, and she was glad when Miss West reappeared with a cup of coffee and a plate of small cakes.

"Good. Here's Sonja with some treats for us." Mildred took one of the cakes, faced Thelma and smiled. "It's so wonderful to be a guest in this house."

Thelma accepted the coffee, refused a cake and wondered if Mildred was just a guest. Her brothers often joked about their relationship, but she never questioned if they lived together. Slowly, she allowed herself to relax and began to feel good about being with these two women.

Sonja reminded Thelma to use her first name, sat in the middle of the couch and inquired about Thelma's health, her family's health and the weather. She rose, walked to the bookshelf that covered nearly an entire wall and selected an anthology of Elizabeth Barrette Browning's poems and one with Shakespeare's sonnets.

"Remember these?" Sonja returned, one book in each hand. "You used to read to our two seventh grade girls from this one." She handed Thelma the book of poems and held the other on her lap as she sat back down. "You were so serious and became very angry when they giggled."

Thelma fingered the book but didn't open its cover. "I'm afraid I haven't had much time for reading with the farm work and all. I remember, you said books can take us places we could never actually go ourselves."

"Not only the places we may never go. They help us see ourselves, discover feelings that are often hidden and need to be induced by insightful authors." Sonja faced Thelma and then Mildred who nodded in apparent agreement.

"Exactly." Mildred leaned forward. "Like an emotional loss such as Thelma recently experienced with her uncle's departure."

"I think he was ready to go." Thelma slid forward on the couch, selected a cake from the tray and looked at Mildred. "He felt it was his time."

Mildred sat back and sighed, "I suppose life on the farm inures one to the concept of death."

"I'm not sure what that means, but on the farm we accept death as a natural part of life." Thelma decided to share a concern. "Freddie seems to miss Arnie more than the rest of our family does. Maybe he feels more of that inuring thing you mentioned."

Sonja beamed. "That's very perceptive of you, but—"

"Exactly." Mildred leaned forward and faced Thelma. "Freddie probably finds it hard to accept the loss of a family member. If I recall, he never knew his mother."

"Not his mother, or my mother, for that matter. Do you think this might effect how he deals with Arnie's death?"

Sonja interjected, "I'm afraid this conversation is taking a morbid turn. I'm sure Frederick just needs time to accept and grieve his loss. Let's not analyze him to his death. Goodness, his ears must be ringing."

"Maybe we could suggest a book for him to read, Sonja. Do you have anything to recommend that might help him?" Mildred slid back on the couch and put her hands on her lap.

"Yes, I do have something for him to read, but it hardly deals with death." She handed the second book to Thelma. "This book of Shakespeare's sonnets made me think of it." She glanced back toward the bookshelf. "I'll try to locate it and see that he gets it. Ignatius, too, might like to read it."

Thelma was shocked that Shakespeare made Sonja think of her brothers. "I'm afraid Iggy hasn't taken much to reading, except maybe some gossip in the paper." She felt she was speaking too fast and tried to slow down. "Freddie likes to read articles in the *Farm Journal*, especially those that deal with mechanical things."

Sonja rose and faced Thelma. "I have something for you as well, and I know exactly where it is. If you two will excuse me for a minute, I will be right back." She walked to a door opposite the couch, opened it and turned. "Better yet, come with me," she smiled, "I want to show you something of mine as well. Perhaps,

Mildred, you will steep some more tea and warm the coffee while I take Thelma down memory lane."

Thelma followed Sonja into her bedroom and watched her open a cedar chest and carefully lift some doilies wrapped in a blue ribbon, hold a man's pipe to her nose before setting it on the nightstand and sort through papers in a manila folder. She surveyed the rest of Sonja's bedroom. In church at Arnie's funeral, thoughts of Sonja's sleep habits distracted her. A white flannel gown with red stitching flowed over the back of a small chair that faced a mirror-backed chest of drawers suggested what she wore to bed. Despite the ugly jokes her brothers made directly about Mildred and implied about Sonja, she felt assured they didn't sleep together.

Sonja held up a sheet of paper and rose from beside the chest where she had been kneeling. "I found it, right where it should be." She pointed to the remaining contents "Here is my past life, exactly in the order it happened, at least up until our school closed. I'm afraid there hasn't been much worth adding to the collection since then. Anyway, this is what I found for you. You may keep it, if you wish."

Thelma recognized the carefully formed letters in pencil on lined tablet paper, an essay on Robert Frost's *A Road Not Taken*, written when she was in the eighth grade. Thelma accepted it and held it to her breast.

"You kept it all these years. I can't believe it."

"Perhaps you can keep it with your other cache of memories."

Thelma flushed. "I'm afraid I haven't saved many things, except some childhood toys and clothes." She thought about her mother. "I do have a quilt that my mother made for me that brings back memories." But the memories associated with the quilt were not pleasant, and in the bedroom of another woman whom she felt she could love, her emotions became conflicted. When Sonja opened her arms, Thelma hugged her and quickly backed away. "I shouldn't have done that."

"Of course you should be able to hug you favorite teacher."

"That's what Iggy says, as if he had any others."

"Well, let's you and your favorite teacher join Mildred for tea."

"And coffee."

Thelma read her essay on Robert Frost's poem aloud, and they shared some of the choices they had to make. She noticed each of them avoided the one they had in common, the decision not to marry. Thelma felt her mother dying deprived her of that choice, and probably Sonja and Mildred just never had the opportunity. What do they do with those empty and lonely feelings that happen usually at night? Her fantasies began to emerge, and she quickly denied her affair with Alfred Collins. It was not a road she had chosen, just a slight detour. When she tried to force it back into the black hole she had created for unwanted memories, there was no longer room for it. The resistance she constructed to contain her feelings, one building block at a time, failed, and a rush of emotions exploded into a single expletive.

"Pa!" Warm coffee spilled onto her lap.

"Oh dear. Is everything all right?" Sonja asked as Mildred got up from the couch and ran to the kitchen. "Are you hurt?"

"I'm afraid I spilled my coffee."

"Don't worry about that." Sonja took the towel from Mildred and began to wipe Thelma's dress.

Thelma felt like a child with a runny nose, and she wanted to cry.

"What about your father disturbed you so?"

"My father?"

"Yes, you said 'Pa' and, well, that was when your cup tipped over. Did you think something had happened to him?"

"I just remembered an errand I was supposed to do for him. I can still do it when I leave here. Maybe I should go now."

"Not until your emotions settle down, child. You are white as a ghost."

Thelma, her phantoms momentarily locked back in their black box, felt a warm summer rain of country school memories wash over her, and she said to her teacher, her friend, "I'm fine now. Thank you."

Mildred reached for the towel. "I had a premonition once that my father was in trouble, and it turned out quite bad. I believe sometimes people can communicate, I mean when they are about to…."

Thelma saw a look of disapproval on Sonja's face like someone had given her an incorrect answer, and she watched Mildred turn and disappear back into the kitchen.

"Pa, my father, is all right. Iggy and Freddie are home with him."

"Oh, tell us about your brothers. We started to talk about them but got caught up in our own selfish interests. How are Frederick and Ignatius?"

"Fine, I guess. They don't seem to complain too much, unless I feed them leftovers." She thought about preparing supper and got up from the couch. "I better get home."

Thelma accepted Sonja's hand. She felt soft skin against the rough surface of her fingers.

"I have something I want to share with Ignatius, but I don't know when I will get to see him. And, I definitely want to talk to Frederick to find out what his plans are for the future."

Thelma flinched. What could she possibly have to share with Iggy? And Freddie even having plans for his future never occurred to her. It probably never occurred to him either. Planning was something people did for a special occasion like Christmas, but not for the rest of one's life. She expected he would get a farm of his own some day whenever Pa sets his mind to it.

Mildred came back from the kitchen and stood between them. "I'm glad you joined us today, Thelma. Sometimes Sonja and I need a third person to listen to our ramblings."

"Yes, we would very much like…" Sonja paused and Thelma thought she looked embarrassed, "Please come and see me again."

Mildred followed them to the closet where Sonja retrieved Thelma's coat and helped her put it on. "Do your brothers still cut firewood? Like they did for Sonja's school?"

"Yes, we still heat the house and cook with wood."

"Mr. Lorenz has been looking for some well-seasoned red oak. Would they have some extra to sell to him?"

"I'll ask them when I get home."

"Good. Just leave word with Sonja if they're interested. Mr. Lorenz would certainly appreciate it."

"Thank you, Mildred. You're very kind." Then she turned to Sonja who stood in front of the door. "I'm sorry about the mess with the coffee. I don't know what came over me. I was so careless."

"Nonsense. It caused no problem. I hope it didn't hurt you in any way."

"The coffee wasn't hot, if that's what you mean. Just a little wet."

Sonja laughed and opened the door but didn't move from in front of it. "If Frederick and Ignatius have some to spare, I'd like to purchase a small amount of firewood for my cook stove. I must confess that I couldn't give it up even after I had those gas burners installed last year. Wood adds so much flavor to the food, and I like how warm it keeps my kitchen on cold mornings."

Thelma edged past, and faced her host as she slowly backed toward her car.

"I'll tell them when I get home."

"Perhaps, if you could entice Frederick and Ignatius, the three of you could come for dinner next Sunday. Then I could ask them myself."

Thelma stopped and took a step toward the house. "Sunday, for dinner. Yes, I, we would like that, very much"

"I hope they will be willing to spend an afternoon with us women."

"I'll ask them, tell them, as soon as I get home. We'll be here on Sunday." Overwhelmed by the invitation and anxious to bring her brothers to see their old teacher, Thelma wondered if she could make them come. She would have to call in all her favors with Iggy before he would agree. She was sure she could do it, but she didn't know if Sonja considered dinner a noon or an evening meal. Some people in town called dinner what her family called supper. "What time would you like us to come?" She found the solution.

"Would twelve o'clock be too early, considering church and chores on the farm?"

"Twelve o'clock would be just fine with us. We can go to the ten-thirty Mass and come right after that."

"Good." Sonja turned to Mildred who now stood by her side in the doorway. "If you're available next Sunday, I surely hope you will come too."

Thelma didn't hear her response, but she felt sure that Mildred would join her and her brothers for dinner at Sonja's next Sunday.

CHAPTER TWENTY-THREE
FREDDIE, IGGY AND MISS WEST

"Been to town?"

The harsh tone in her father's voice and the acrid odor of scorched coffee greeted Thelma as she walked into the kitchen. She nodded, set the groceries on the table in front of him and held a brown paper package in one hand and then in the other as she removed her coat. He leaned forward, peeked into the box and then flashed a quizzical expression, but he didn't ask what she had tucked under her arm. She smiled, turned and walked into the front room.

"Did you get the eggs dropped off at York's Mercantile?" he yelled after her.

"It's taken care of." She laid the package on the sofa and hung her coat in the closet Freddie had built for her. She pressed the sleeve to her face. The aroma that still lingered was proof that she had really visited her old teacher. By the time she returned to the kitchen, the groceries were out of the box and scattered across the table.

"Did I forget something?" She began shelving each item.

"Thought maybe you might have got me some ice cream." He handed her the can of salmon he had been holding up to the light like he was reading the label. "How come you're late?"

"Just takes time." She slipped the loop of her apron over her head and deftly tied the straps behind her back into a bow. "I had business to do in town."

He shoved his chair back from the table, leaned forward with his hands on his knees and pushed himself up. He walked out to the porch, turned and asked, "Supper at the regular time tonight?"

"Yeah, Pa. It'll be ready." Thelma felt slightly rebuked.

Later, tears ran down her cheeks as she diced onions onto sliced potatoes that simmered in a kettle on the stove next to a pan of sizzling pork sausage. She looked at the four plates she had set on one end of the large table and fumed that Iggy hadn't taken out the extra leaf as she'd asked. She listened for sounds of footsteps in the porch and water sloshing from the pump, but there wasn't any noisy bantering like in the old days. Soon, remnants of her family sauntered into the kitchen, sat at their places all scrunched down at one end of the table and looked straight ahead. She placed the single large bowl of spiced potatoes mixed with chunks of fried sausage on the exact spot where they seemed to be staring.

"Dig in." She went to the stove and paused to observe each of them help themselves to meat and potatoes, the only sounds were forks scratching across their plates. She returned with the coffeepot, filled her father's cup and paused behind Freddie and Iggy. They turned and held out their cups, confusion etched on their faces.

"You guys are invited out to dinner." She poured their coffee and waited for a response. They just shrugged. She sat down and stared across the table at them. "And it's not George, Herman or Ralph's place like you're thinking."

"Where?" Iggy jumped up and stood behind his chair.

"I can't tell you." His excitement pleased her. "Now, sit down and finish eating."

"When?" Freddie looked at her, and she saw sadness in his eyes.

"Next Sunday. That's all I'm gonna tell you for now."

"Svez, too?" Freddie asked.

"Nope, just us kids." Her child-like response embarrassed her, and she realized that her father might feel left out. He looked like he wasn't paying attention to the conversation, but she knew better. "We'll be going to ten-thirty Mass, and I'll have Pa's dinner ready before we leave." She expected he would be happy to skip church, and she wanted Freddie and Iggy to understand they would not be excused. "All you'll have to do is stick it in the oven."

"Don't worry 'bout me. I kin take care of myself. Probably go to George's place."

"That's a good idea. George would like that. Should I call to tell him?"

"I kin call him if I decide to go." He pushed his chair from the table. "'Didn't 'spect to be included in your invite. I wouldn't go anyway." He stood up. "I 'spose there ain't no dessert."

"We got some canned fruit in the cellar."

"I don't want none. Besides, there's something I gotta do in the barn."

"Need any help?" Freddie asked.

"Nah. Just stay and hear what Thelma got to say." He left the kitchen.

"Nothing more I'm gonna tell them, least not now," she called after him as the outside door slammed.

The suspense Thelma intended didn't seem to affect her brothers; Iggy liked surprises and Freddie trusted all her decisions, but she noticed that each morning her father lingered longer and longer in the kitchen after breakfast.

"Them boys can't get a damn thing done, all the time guessing where they're going Sunday."

She ignored his comment and wished he'd quit bothering her.

"I told them I'm gonna be gone, too."

"Where to, Pa?" She stopped peeling potatoes and looked at him, but he kept his head down.

"Said I'd tell them where I'm going when they tell me where they're going."

"Any of your daughters-in-law would be happy to have you join their families for dinner. Why don't you call one of the boys and get yourself an invite? Or if you want, I can call and ask for you."

"I told ya, I kin take care of it myself," he grumbled and emptied his cup with one gulp. "I gotta' check on my boys I still got at home. See if I can't get them to do something today." From the porch he yelled back, "Call George and tell 'em I'll be there for dinner on Sunday."

A few nights later at the supper table her father leaned toward her and whispered, "Have you told them yet?" as if the two of them had been keeping a secret from the kids.

She whispered back, "Their old teacher," and looked at Iggy, but he didn't seem to be paying attention. It was Friday, and he was no doubt figuring how to ask for some egg money to spend in town later that night.

"Miss West?" Svez blurted out.

Iggy shoved his hands under the table. "What's she want? I ain't done nuthin'."

Thelma remembered how he used to pinch himself to keep from peeing in his pants when Miss West leaned over his desk to help him with a lesson. One time during recess, she heard Larry Collins tell him what he should do to the teacher with his *thing*, and Iggy ran home instead of going back to class. Her plan to surprise him might have backfired.

"She wants us to come to dinner this Sunday after mass. That's the surprise I teased you about earlier this week. I went to visit her on Monday after I finished grocery shopping."

"What the devil did you see her for?" Svez demanded. "Ain't no one left to go to school, and she ain't even the district teacher no more."

"We talked briefly at Arnie's funeral, and she invited me to visit her. Monday, when I took the eggs to town, I decided to stop at her house." She paused, sat up straight and put her hands on her lap. "That's why I was late coming home. I had to stop back at York's to buy Iggy a new shirt, too." Svez stabbed a chunk of sausage with his fork, swished it around the potatoes and gravy on his plate, and stared at it. "We had a very nice time. Mildred Bushman was there, and we talked about books and other things."

"Mildred Bushman from the bank?" He shoved the sausage into his mouth, scraped it off the fork with his teeth and gazed into the tines.

"Yeah, Pa. Mildred was there, and we just talked." Thelma stood her ground, and she sensed her brothers staring at her.

"Mildred's a nice lady." He set his fork down and pushed his plate away. "She's always friendly when I see her at the bank."

She felt he was mellowing. "Yes, and so is Miss West." She hadn't expected his approval, yet she felt a kind of victory and turned her attention to her brothers. "Miss West wants to talk to both of you."

"I ain't gonna eat no dinner with a bunch of women, 'specially them kind of women."

She had anticipated Iggy's reluctance and tried to tweak his interest. "Miss West has something she wants you to have." She waited for a break in his resistance and added, "Bet Larry Collins never been in her house, or his rascal brother either." She felt herself blush and wished she hadn't included Alfred in the discussion. "By the way, aren't you going to town with Larry tonight? You'd better take a dollar out of the egg money. I don't want him to think that you don't have a little cash to spend when you guys go out."

"Yup. Yup. Just a dollar."

She knew that would excite him and hoped his enthusiasm would distract him from the idea of dinner at Sonja's. She decided to offer another incentive. "Miss West and Mildred are both interested in buying some firewood just like what Freddie used to bring to the school.

"I never brought the wood. I just chopped it sometimes and started the fire in the stove on cold mornings."

She had overlooked that detail. "Well, maybe you and Iggy can spare some of the wood you got out behind the shed. It looks like more than we can use in a year. I'm sure you guys wouldn't mind some extra spending money." Freddie nodded, and Iggy hadn't stopped nodding since she told him he could have a dollar.

"What about Svez? What's he gonna do Sunday?"

"Pa's going to George's for dinner." She had forgotten make the arrangements, and she struggled to remain composed as she headed to the telephone on the wall above the desk. "I'll call him right now." All week she had been busy with preparations for their visit, and worried about how well she could pull it off. What kind of an impression would Iggy make, especially with Mildred who might not be as tolerant as their old teacher? What did Sonja have for Iggy and would he graciously accept it even if he didn't want it? How would Freddie respond to her questions about what he planned to do, and should he even be bothered with that now? What about her own future?

"If he ain't available, call Ralph or Herman." Svez pushed back his chair and stood up.

She nodded, spun the crank on the side of the phone and held the receiver to her ear.

As he walked out to the porch, he added. "Thanks, Thelma."

When the operator asked what number she wished to call, she was unable to answer. She stared blankly at kitchen door, *Thanks, Thelma* echoing in her mind. Iggy flashed the dollar he had taken from the canister where she kept the egg money, and Freddie carried dishes to the sink. She recited George's number into the mouthpiece.

Saturday night, Thelma stared out her bedroom window and reviewed her checklist hoping her mother would approve and perhaps even remind her of some important detail she may have overlooked.

"Their clothes are washed, and I ironed Freddie's best shirt. Sure wish I had enough egg money to buy him a new one, but Iggy's more important. He's going to be sitting on an anthill in Sonja's living room as it is. Freddie will be, well, just Freddie." She touched her neck searching for strands of hair escaping the tight pin curls. "I wanted to cut Freddie's hair but he wouldn't let me. Sometimes he can be so stubborn." She felt herself drifting off to sleep.

When she awoke, she rushed to the storage closet that Freddie and Iggy had converted into a bathroom for her and shook her head as she glanced into the mirror. She splashed cold water from the basin onto her face and decided she would heat water for a sponge bath in the kitchen when the men were in the barn. She banged on Iggy's door and checked Arnie's old room in the off-chance that Freddie might still be in there. She stood in the kitchen not sure what to do next when Iggy, still in his underwear, came storming past her to the porch where she had hung his work clothes from the day before.

"Freddie n' me'll get the chores done quick," he announced to his father who sat at the table, both hands clasped to his empty cup.

Thelma waited until she heard the outer door slam. "I think I'll get myself ready before breakfast."

"I 'spose I'd better help the boys with the chores this morning." He set his cup on the table, glanced at Thelma as she pumped water into a kettle, and left. Since that long-past incident in her mother's bed, she demanded privacy when she dressed or undressed, and he respected it.

When she finished, she filled the basin in the porch with hot water and draped two pairs of clean underwear over the towel rack. Iggy rushed into the porch and began to undress.

"Put clean underwear on when you're done washing up. And, I mean all over not just your hands and face." She gathered his shirt and pants and tossed them down the cellar where she would wash them the next day. While she was taking sweet rolls out of the oven, he traipsed into the kitchen in his shorts and opened the trapdoor to the cellar. He grinned at her, grabbed two rolls from the pan and ran upstairs. Had he actually tossed his underwear down with the dirty wash?

"I got your Sunday pants and a new shirt laid out on your bed," she called after him as she carried more hot water out to the porch. Freddie stood at the sink in his shorts, his pants and shirt on the floor by his feet. "When you're done, throw your dirty clothes down the cellar."

"Okay," a tinge of confusion in his voice.

She felt pleased but realized her father would never follow that new rule. She wondered why he hadn't complained that she hadn't made any coffee. Was he mad and hiding? Through the window, she saw him walk toward the house, but instead of coming in he got into his pickup and drove out the driveway.

****

Freddie stepped out through Arnie's window onto the balcony. He watched Svez' pickup disappear in the dust. Sundays were just like weekdays except for when Thelma made everyone go to church. This was a church Sunday with dinner at Miss West's rather than dinner at home. He wondered what kind of meals she made. He remembered the lunches she brought with her to school, the small sandwich and the light colored drink she called tea that she drank hot when there was fire in the wood stove and cold when the room wasn't heated. He offered to light the fire one warm school day, and she told him she liked tea cold as well as hot. He thought she just didn't want the room to get too warm. Her sacrifice for the comfort of the students raised his level of admiration for her, especially when he thought of the times he drank cold coffee. He waited until Thelma called him the third time before he sauntered downstairs. She would be busy fussing with Iggy, and he didn't want to be treated that way.

****

Thelma sat in back of the Chevy and leaned forward to tell her brothers how to excuse themselves if they needed to use the bathroom even though she hadn't given them coffee that morning. She was sure Sonja had indoor plumbing, her bathroom probably off the kitchen.

"After church we better stop and use the toilet at Emma's Café." Although Iggy had spit out his chew of tobacco before he came into the house, she still smelled it on his breath. "We can buy some gum or something." Freddie seldom chewed tobacco, but he needed gum, too.

After an interminable time in church and a functional stop at Emma's, Thelma led Iggy and Freddie up the walk to Sonja's house. When she raised the small brass clapper and let it fall against a metal plate on the front door, Iggy giggled. She shushed him. The door opened, and Mildred Bushman greeted them.

"Sonja's in the kitchen so you'll have to put up with another guest to take your coats and make you comfortable."

Thelma allowed Mildred to help her with her coat and wondered why she made such a point of not living with Sonja. Was she hiding something?

"It's so nice to see you again, Thelma." Mildred took a hanger from the closet and fitted Thelma's coat over it.

"Thank you, Mildred." Thelma walked into the living room and turned to introduce her brothers, but they still stood on the front stoop fidgeting with the doorknocker. "Come on in, guys." They squeezed past Mildred and stood one on each side of her. "Mildred, I would like you to meet my brothers Freddie and Ig— Ignatius." She had hoped Sonja would greet them at the door and make the introductions.

"Nice to meet you in person. Sonja has spoken about you so often that I feel I already know each of you." She looked at Freddie and extended her hand. "I know Sonja called you Frederick. What shall I call you?"

"Freddie's okay." He grabbed her extended hand and shook it quite hard.

Thelma blushed. "I think Mildred wanted to take your coat." Freddie shrugged it off is shoulders and laid it across Mildred's arm. She hung it in the closet next to Thelma's.

"And Ignatius." Mildred didn't give Iggy the option of which name he preferred.

Nodding his head vigorously, Iggy responded, "Yup! Ignatius, That's right." He backed away when she reached for his coat.

Thelma saw fear in his eyes. She nodded her head at him and silently mouthed the words, "Give her your coat."

He looked desperate. He closed his eyes, wrapped his arms around Mildred in a full embrace. Mildred reeled back.

Thelma pulled Iggy in the opposite direction, helped him take off his coat and handed it to Mildred. Mildred held it at arm's length.

Sonja came from the kitchen. "Thelma, Frederick and Ignatius. Welcome to our little dinner party." She looked at Mildred. "If the closet is full you can put it in my bedroom." Mildred reached into the closet, shoved coats tight together and hung Iggy's coat against the wall. "There's not much room in my small closet." She looked at Thelma. "Living alone, one does not need much space."

Thelma feared Sonja might have guessed what she was thinking about her and Mildred.

"Come, have a seat in the drawing room where we can chat awhile before we eat." She touched Thelma's arm. "Here, you and I can sit on the divan."

Iggy looked confused, but smiled when they sat on the couch. Freddie wandered over to the bookshelf.

"Perhaps, Ignatius, you could help Mildred bring two chairs from the kitchen."

Thelma thought Iggy was going to cry. She was about to tell Freddie to get them when she saw Mildred, a chair under each arm, work her way through the doorway. Freddie walked toward her, took both of them and handed one to Iggy.

"I'll call when dinner is ready." Mildred backed into the kitchen.

"Set them across from us," Sonja pointed toward the coffee table, "and we can form a circle like we used to in school." She waited until the boys sat down." I don't have many guests so there's no need for a lot of furniture in this small room. I'm afraid we'll just have to make do." She glanced back toward the kitchen." Mildred came over after early mass to help prepare dinner. I don't know what I would do without her."

Thelma chided herself and wondered again if Sonja knew what she had been thinking?

Iggy kept his head down and folded and unfolded his arms. When asked if he wanted a glass of wine before dinner, he raised his hand as if he was still in school.

Thelma said, "Coffee when we eat will be just fine for all of us. Iggy lowered his hand and stuck it into his pocket.

"Since Mildred has graciously volunteered to finish making dinner, I can unlock the mystery gift I have for Ignatius." Sonja walked to her bookshelf. "My father lives in a suburb of Philadelphia, and he found this story about his old friend who spent many years in Minnesota." She drew out a magazine. "As you can see," she held it up, the cover facing Iggy, "his name was Ignatius, too."

Iggy gaped at his name in bright red letters with a picture of an old man under it. "Was he a saint? Ma said he was. Not a 'portant one like Saint Christopher who helped her find things." He reached for the magazine and held it for Thelma to see. "Remember Halloween night in church?" He chanted, "Ora probis, Ignatius," and giggled.

"Iggy used to imitate that Latin prayer sung by the priest during All Saint's Day. Ignatius is Iggy's patron saint." Thelma smiled at her brother as he thumbed through the magazine. "She often said that she shoulda named him after Saint Jude, the patron of lost causes."

"Ma was just joking when she said that 'bout me." He closed the magazine and laid it cover up on the coffee table.

"Of course she was. She never meant noth—anything by it." Thelma realized she had embarrassed him in front of his teacher. She considered apologizing.

Sonja interrupted. "Ignatius Donnelly wasn't a saint, but he was an honest man, an important man. He moved to Nininger City, a small town in Minnesota, and led an unsuccessful fight to keep it from being incorporated into the larger city across the river. He also failed to get the combined towns named Nininger City, and, alas, his favorite town is no longer on the map."

"What'd they call their new town?" Iggy glanced back at the magazine and then up at Sonja.

Thelma was surprised at his interest in such details.

"A name you probably heard of. Hastings, Minnesota."

Iggy shrugged his shoulders and shook his head.

Thelma watched him gape at Sonja, and it reminded her of story-telling time back in school. But, why did Miss West choose a two-time loser to be his hero?

"Yes, Ignatius Donnelly might have failed at a number of things, but he never gave up once he set a goal for himself."

Thelma blushed, convinced her teacher read her mind.

"He also believed in the story of Atlantis, the lost city and set out to prove it did exist."

"Did he prove it?" Freddie asked as he picked up the magazine from the coffee table. Iggy opened his mouth but didn't say anything.

Thelma felt a tinge of excitement. Sonja used to read the story of Atlantis to her class every Friday afternoon when the students got all their work done.

"No one ever proved it, at least not to my satisfaction, but Ignatius Donnelly came about as close as anyone. He wrote *Atlantis*. The mystery of a lost city has a certain fascination for children."

Iggy wiggled in his chair and touched his crotch. "Are you going to read it to us now?"

"No, I don't have the book any more."

Thelma asked, "Have you ever met the Ignatius that did all those things?"

"I'm afraid he died before I was born, yet he played no small part in my decision to come to Minnesota." She faced Iggy. "You might say Ignatius Donnelly made it possible for me to meet Ignatius Rastner."

"Your pa knew the man who wrote the book you used to read to us?" Iggy sat on the edge of his chair.

"Yes, that was a long time ago, and when my father found this magazine he sent it to me. Now I want to share it with the Ignatius that I know." She pointed to the magazine Freddie was reading. "It's yours to keep, Iggy."

Thelma gasped, and Iggy opened his mouth again.

"Yes, as you read in this article, Ignatius Donnelly's friends called him Iggy. I believe my dad referred to him as Iggy. Both are very nice and important names."

"Last Monday you told Mildred and me that Shakespeare reminded you to give Iggy this book. How could..."

"That was perhaps the darker side of Ignatius Donnelly. He conducted a study of all of Shakespeare's major plays to prove that somebody other than Shakespeare wrote them."

"That's dumb." Iggy took the magazine back from Freddie. "Why'd he let someone else write them?"

"Actually, Donnelly thought Shakespeare was just an actor or director who worked at the Globe Theatre, where the plays were produced."

"Who did write his plays, if Shakespeare didn't?" Freddie leaned forward on his chair.

"Roger Bacon, according to Donnelly."

"Bacon." Iggy giggled.

"Yes, Bacon was a real person, a nobleman, and Shakespeare was just a commoner."

"If Shakespeare was just a commoner, how come he dressed so fancy?" Thelma remembered the pictures of him from the book they looked at last Monday.

"I guess he was a fancy commoner, and that didn't mean he was illiterate. As a matter of fact, noblemen refused to write anything. They hired scribes to do it for them. That's why Roger Bacon might want to deny that he wrote plays and sonnets. His friends would have looked down at him."

"Did Ignatius know them guys?" Iggy's eyes opened wide.

"Gracious, no. Shakespeare and Bacon were dead at least three-hundred years when Donnelly lived." Iggy looked disappointed.

"Donnelly went to England to meet a distant relative of Roger Bacon who claimed to have proof that her ancestor wrote the plays. He found her in an insane asylum, but he took her research and wrote a book called *The Great Cryptogram*."

"Have you read that book?" Thelma was overwhelmed yet enthralled, not so much about the controversy of Shakespeare, but that she and her brothers would be involved in a discussion of this importance with their teacher.

"No, I'm afraid it would be frightfully boring. He counted all the words and even all the letters from each character's lines and tried to find some secret code that Roger Bacon put there for someone to discover years after his death. Besides, the book is hard to find since only a few collectors and fans of Bacon's theory have copies. He wrote other books, too. One or two of them are in the Harrington County Library."

Mildred came from the kitchen and stood behind them.

"Anyway, Thelma, that's how our conversation about Shakespeare made me think of Ignatius Donnelly, and he made me think of Iggy."

Iggy said, "You can call me Ignatius, I don't mind."

Mildred said, "Dinner is ready, whenever you are."

"Wonderful. After we've eaten, I want to talk about Freddie's plans for his future." She looked at Freddie and Iggy. "Please bring your chairs to the kitchen with you."

CHAPTER TWENTY-FOUR
TWO JOURNEYS

"Brrrrr." Thelma shivered as the door opened and a burst of cold air spread into the room. Iggy rushed through the porch and directly to the stove, lifted the lid from a kettle and bathed his face in the steam. Freddie followed, closing the kitchen door behind him. The animal residue embedded in their clothes gave off almost visible odors that blended with the smells of smoke from the fire, fresh baked bread and sizzling sausage.

"Get out of them potatoes. Soon as Pa gets in we can eat. What's he doing out there anyway?"

"I don't know." Iggy put the cover back and wiped his face with his sleeve. "Thought he was in the house with you."

"I saw him at the wood shed." Freddie turned back toward the door. "I'll get him."

"Yeah, you better." With one hand she reached down for the hem of her apron and grabbed a potholder hanging on the oven door with the other. "What's with him anyhow? He ain't said but two words since we got back from Sonja's on Sunday." She used the cover to hold back the potatoes, and a burst of steam erupted as she drained the water into the pan of hot sausage. The outside door slammed shut just as Freddie opened the kitchen door.

"Supper's ready, Svez." Freddie held the door for him.

Svez took off his coat and tossed it in the corner behind the stove. "Didn't need to wait for me." He glanced at the washbasin in the kitchen sink, then sat at his usual place at the table.

"What were you doing in the woodshed, Pa?" Thelma stirred the sausage and added a liquid paste of flour and water.

Svez grumbled, "We ain't gonna have 'enough wood for the winter. If it's cold like this already in October, we'll be cutting and burning green wood by spring."

She looked at Iggy and Freddie, but they stared at their plates and made no effort to explain the disappearance of a cord of firewood.

"The boys took some to town yesterday." She put her hands on her hips. "You knew they were doing it. You should have stopped them if you thought it weren't right."

"I guess a promise is a promise." He picked up his cup from the table and pointed it toward the coffeepot on the stove. "We'll probably get by."

"We put the cash in with the egg money." Thelma filled all the cups and then set the potatoes and sausage-in-gravy on the table.

She realized she had sassed him, and felt she should apologize, but she didn't feel sorry. His silence seemed to make everyone uncomfortable. Iggy squirmed in his chair, set down his fork and put his hand on his lap.

"Pa, I need to go to Hastings." He brought his hand back to the table, picked up his fork and jabbed it into the mound of potatoes and gravy. "Yup, I need to go to Hastings."

Svez lifted his gaze from the table and faced his son. "You mean the city of Hastings? Hastings, Minnesota?"

Iggy nodded. "Yeah, the city of Hastings, Minnesota."

Thelma was surprised that Iggy would talk about his recent daydream. After supper each night since Sonja had given him the magazine, he sat at the kitchen table and traced with his fingers line-by-line on each page of the article, and then on the branch-like roads on a Minnesota map between Bovine and Hastings. She decided to support his plan.

"It's about two hundred miles from here." She smiled at Iggy. "We'd have to stay overnight."

"I know where it is." Svez sounded insulted. "Me and Ted Collins went there to get some tractor parts, a while back. Shipped up the Mississippi from Moline, Illinois." He laughed. "Ted bought his Minneapolis-Moline tractor 'cause a Minnesota company made it, but then they moved to Moline. Parts got hard to come by." He picked chunks of sausage from the gravy with his fork. "Good thing we got a John Deere." He raised the fork, caught some gravy about to drip with his tongue, and stuffed it into his mouth.

Thelma shushed Iggy with her hand and waited until she was sure their father had finished his story about him and Ted Collins. "We can leave here early in the morning, maybe one day next week. If you don't think the Chevy's up for the drive, we could take the train, but then it'd take two days and two nights." Svez traced furrows in the gravy on his plate with the tines of his fork. "We can use the money from the wood to pay for the gas and a night at a hotel in Hastings. We'll pack a lunch so we won't have to eat at any restaurants, least not more than once or twice."

"Hold on! The whole idea is screwy." He swiped both sides of his fork across his tongue. "What in tarnation do you wanna do in Hastings?" He wiped his mouth with this sleeve.

Iggy sat straight and grabbed the edge of the table. "Miss West told me that Ignatius Donnelly lived there." He glanced at Thelma. "He's the guy who wrote the book she used to read to us." He paused and took a deep breath. "His house still stands and people come from all over just to see where he used to live, because he don't live there no more. I wanna go see his house and some guy there will tell me 'bout his life when he used to live there. He wrote 'bout Shakespeare, too, and some fellow named Bacon." He blushed but continued. "That's his real name and Ignatius is the real name of the man who lived there, when he wasn't in England talking to some broad in the crazy house."

Iggy looked down and his hand went back under the table. Freddie grabbed a piece of bread and wiped the gravy from his plate. Thelma glanced toward her father and saw his lips slowly curve into a smile.

"Me and Ted might've gone to see that house, if we knowed about it. Weren't much older'n you guys when we went there." He got up, walked to the stove and came back with the coffeepot. He filled his cup and set the pot on the table. "Take the Chevy. There's a couple extra tires in the shed. I'm sure you can't drive that distance without at least one flat." He looked at Freddie. "How about you? You wanna go, too? I can get the boys to come home to do chores for a day or two."

"No, I'll stay and do my own work. I can do Iggy's for a couple of days too."

Iggy grabbed the map from on the desk where he had left it, and he and Thelma stood on each side of their father pointing and talking at once.

****

The morning they planned to leave, Iggy became nervous and Thelma decided to drive even though she didn't have a license. When she backed the car out of the garage and waited for him to return from the outhouse, Freddie got in on the passenger side.

"You change your mind about going?"

"Nah, but I got an idea. When you get back let's me and you go to Harrington to get our driver's licenses. Then we don't have to keep on just the back roads."

"Good idea. Let's do it." She glanced toward the outhouse and saw Iggy stumble as he tried to untangle his suspenders.

"Soon as you get back, okay?" He got out of the car. "I gotta get the chores done."

Thelma handed Iggy the map as he slunk into the passenger seat. "I'll drive and you can give the directions once we get past Bovine."

After unfolding the map, he held it against the dashboard and traced his finger along the line drawn between Bovine and Hastings. He held it sideways, studied it briefly, and finally returned it to the dashboard upside down. "Now we're going in the right direction. South."

"I ain't changed directions, Iggy."

"Well, now the map says you're going the right way. Don't wanna go through Harrington."

"Are you sure? That sign says *Harrington ten miles.*"

Iggy turned the map like a steering wheel. "Nope, not Harrington. Better go the other way."

"I'm stopping so we can get our directions straight." She parked on a short drive that ended at a farmer's pasture. "Give me that map."

Iggy held tight to the map, turned it sideways and then upside down. She grabbed it, got out of the car and pressed it onto the hood. When she glanced up, she saw him wander toward the fence where a cow swished her tail and kicked at a large calf that tried to suck on her teats. Iggy pulled a plug of tobacco from his pocket and bit off a chew.

After locating the proper road, she walked toward the fence and heard Iggy mutter to the calf, "I think you better learn to eat grass." She stood beside him before he seemed to notice her. I think I know where we are." She folded the map and started to walk back to the car. "You can drive and I'll navigate for a while." A small trickle of discolored saliva appeared at the corner of his mouth. "If you're going to spit, do it now, not out window while we're driving."

Tracking his finger between his teeth and cheeks, he pulled out a brown wad, still recognizable as tobacco, and tossed it onto the ground. He opened the door, slid behind the wheel and flashed Thelma a grin, teeth speckled with brown flecks. "Which way, sister?"

"That way." She pointed. "If you see the morning sun off to your left, we're going in the right direction. Come noon we should be heading directly into the sun."

He nodded, rolled down the window and stuck out his elbow. "I would go even if you didn't wanna come along, even if Pa said no. I was going no matter what."

His firm conviction surprised her. "How'd you've gone, if Pa said no?"

"I could've' snuck off with Larry Collins. He could take his pickup and we woulda' gone together."

"Maybe you don't want me to go. I wish you would have said something."

"No, I want you to go." He pulled his arm back into the car and rolled up the window. "I don't really like Larry anymore."

Shocked by his sudden honesty, she asked, "Then, why do you still hang around with him?"

Iggy sounded perplexed. "I guess we're just friends. Ain't got no one else, 'cept Freddie, and he don't wanna go to dances and things."

"Larry always calls you 'Eggnutz' and gets you drunk all the time."

"Not all the time." He sounded defensive. "Sometimes I go to dances alone and hang out."

"And look at all the girls?" Thelma knew she was getting into dangerous territory, but she couldn't quell her curiosity about her brother's interest in girls. Maybe a girlfriend would make him happy. Suddenly, she remembered that they would be spending the night in the same hotel room. If she could keep him from drinking there shouldn't be any problem, she assured herself. Since Larry's younger brother stopped taunting Iggy with whiskey about the same time he stopped exposing himself to her, Iggy only got drunk when he went to town with Larry.

"Girls used to like Larry, but not me. He's married now, so he only wants to go to Buddy's Bar.

"When you go alone, do you ask the girls to dance?

"Nah, they don't wanna be with me." He squirmed in his seat and the car swerved.

Maybe if you'd be nicer to them they'd dance with you." She wanted him to stop hanging out in Buddy's Bar. "Girls like to be treated special."

"One time Larry's sister, Sally, asked me to dance."

"Well, did you?"

"I don't know how. Larry told her to get lost, anyway."

"Did you like it when she asked you?" Her voice sounded like she had asked him if he wanted a piece of candy.

"I guess so. Maybe if she asked me again I'd do it, but I don't go there much any more." He felt his shirt pocket where he kept his tobacco, but put his hand back on the steering wheel. "Maybe if I had a couple of drinks…"

Or, maybe you should ask her. The guy is supposed to do that." Thelma realized she was entering into an area where she did not want to venture.

"Do the guys ask you to dance? And things?"

She reflected on the weddings of friends and relatives and realized she only paired up with her brothers and a few of the older men. She felt Iggy deserved an honest answer. "I guess the guys don't often ask me to dance. And things." She glanced at the map she had been crunching in her hands, straightened it and pretended to check for directions.

Iggy turned his head and their eyes met. "What about Alfred?"

A ten-mile painful silence followed. Thelma still felt embarrassed about her affair with Alfred, but she learned to rely on pain and anger to combat her sexual urges. What defense did poor Iggy have against the desires he had for her? Years ago she stopped him from spying on her from the porch roof by plugging the peep hole with newspaper. When Larry got married and stopped dragging him along to Ida's, he'd sometimes wander into her room after he came home drunk. He'd beg to sleep with her, but he never argued when she told him to leave. The next morning he'd agree that the whiskey made him do that. She knew better and he probably did, too. She thought about how lonely each of them had become.

"Is Miss West your best friend?" Iggy broke the silence and Thelma's spirits soared. If she had friends like Sonja and Mildred, not having a man in her life would be okay. It was acceptable to talk to her brother about her friendships, but not to talk about the other part of her life, the part that was confusing and painful.

"Sonja and Mildred are fine ladies. I want to be just like them." Thelma surprised herself with this juvenile statement, but it probably made good sense to her brother.

"I wish I had good friends like that," Iggy confessed.

She felt like hugging him.

Once in Hastings, Iggy drove until Thelma glimpsed a building with HASTINGS HOTEL embedded into the stone above the door. He parked in back of the building, got out and grabbed the suitcase from the back seat. Thelma continued to sit on the passenger seat motioning him to open her door.

"That door works." He walked around the car and opened it for her. "It's the back one that sticks sometimes."

"I don't care. I just think the escort should open the door for his date."

He bowed. "Yes, of course, your high ass." They giggled like children.

"How may I help you?" asked the tall thin man behind the desk, his hair slicked back and a bow tie bouncing over his Adam's apple.

"We're here to see the Donnelly house," Iggy explained as Thelma filled out the registration form.

"Like off to see the wizard of Oz?" The desk clerk smirked. He held the card up to the light. "Hey, your name is Ignatius too. You don't see many people with that name anymore."

She had signed the register as Thelma and Ignatius Rastner, purposely leaving their relationship vague. "Are you and your wife interested in Ignatius Donnelly?"

"She's my sister. That's why she asked for two beds." He looked at Thelma and grinned. "How do we get to his house?"

Iggy's honesty made Thelma feel exposed, but then relieved. She felt a tinge of genuine pride in her brother, possibly for the first time in her life. She felt quite sure that sleeping in the same room wouldn't create any problems.

They followed the directions to Donnelly's abandoned house just before sunset. The front door hung open and loose from the top hinge creating the impression of an invitation, and the scattered empty beer bottles and paper bags suggested that many other visitors accepted the offer. The brick two-story building looked more like the high school in Harrington than any house people actually lived in. The front room had a huge fireplace. Off to the left were stairs twice the size of the ones back home. Two and even three people could walk up or down side-by-side. The steps were broken, and they didn't seem safe. They stood at the foot of the staircase and stared at their shadows cast larger than life ascending half way up the steps. The crack in the window split the beam of light giving each shadow a companion shadow.

199

Iggy's arm made exaggerated movements across the wall from side to side as he poked Thelma and pointed. They both laughed hysterically.

"No wonder Donnelly screwed up everything he did. Living in this house would make anyone nuts." Iggy's insight seemed to erase all the mystery about the man who had held such a spell on them. "Let's look in the kitchen to see where he kept the bacon."

"Maybe we can find lost Atlantis." She felt they were children again, laughing and peeking in all the cupboards.

"Keep looking," Iggy giggled, as he peered into a quaint broom closet. "Shakespeare's bound to be in here somewhere."

"To be or not to be. That is the question." Thelma recited the only line of Shakespeare she knew and proceeded to pry open a drawer in what appeared to be the pantry. "Iggy, look what I found." She showed him a ragged and stained newspaper with the headlines, ESTATE OF IGNATIUS DONNELLY, AUTHOR OF *ATLANTIS*, DONATES HOME TO CITY OF HASTINGS.

His lips moved but he didn't utter a sound. She knew he was reciting lines from the stories Miss West read to them.

"Do you think we…" He looked at Thelma.

She held the newspaper in one hand, grabbed his arm with the other and pulled him out of the building that looked like a schoolhouse. They were two students skipping class. Back at the hotel, Iggy bumped into a man at the check-in desk, knocking a briefcase from his grip.

"Oops." Iggy glanced at the papers scattered on the floor and continued toward their room.

"We're terribly sorry." Thelma helped the man gather his papers.

As she headed down the hall, she heard the desk clerk tell the man, "Said they was brother and sister. Newly weds, I suspect."

CHAPTER TWENTY-FIVE
THE LIBRARY

Thelma ducked into the lady's room a few doors down from the testing area and stared dumbly into the mirror. As she suspected, the hot sensations had created red blotches on her cheeks. She felt humiliated and embarrassed yet couldn't squelch a tinge of excitement.

"Hey, Matt."

Thelma gritted her teeth and squeezed her eyes shut as she recognized the voice from out in the hall.

"That dame from Hickville's out in her car, waiting on her check ride. And that ain't all she's waiting for."

She muttered, "The town's Bovine, not Hickville, you lecherous old goat." Anger blotted out all other emotions, even the sudden fear of being caught eavesdropping. She splashed cold water onto her face and then noticed the towel didn't loop through the dispenser but dangled into a puddle on the cement floor. From a roll of toilet paper in the single stall, she made three wraps around her hand and dabbed her face dry. She opened the top button on her dress, pressed the collar smooth and slung the strap to her purse over her shoulder. If the cop who kept touching her arm and shoulder while she tried to write still wanted to look down her dress, he'd have something to see, and then he could eat his heart out 'cause he won't ever touch any part of her again. She purposely stopped in front of the room where he sat at his desk and pretended she forgot something.

"Oh, there it is," she said loud enough for him to hear and removed her coat from one of the hooks along the wall opposite his office. Switching her purse from one side to the other, she slipped into it and raised the collar. She flapped it open, shook it free from her dress and let it settle back onto her shoulders. She fumbled with the buttons. When she was sure she had his attention, she said, "I'll tell my brother you're ready for him." She clutched her purse to her side, walked down the hall and through the exit to the parking lot.

Freddie jumped down from the car's fender and walked toward her. "How was it?" he asked as they met between car and police station.

"We both could have taken the written test at the same time. I'll tell you all about it later." She eyed the cop, probably Matt, scowling at her car as he kicked loose some dried mud from under the fender. "You better get inside while I show him," she gestured toward Matt with her head, "how well I can drive." She walked directly to the driver's side and settled behind the wheel.

Matt slid onto the passenger seat, placed his clipboard on his lap and tugged at the lapel of her coat. "Better take that off. It's not cold in here, and I may need to see your reflexes."

She remained sitting and slid her arms through the sleeves.

"Posture's important. You gotta be ready to hit the brakes at any moment." He tapped her leg with the back of his hand. "Full dresses like you got on can sometimes get in the way."

"If I can ride horses wearing one, I can drive a car."

"Good thought." He pinched a fold of material near the hem and slid it over her knee. "Make believe you're riding a horse."

She opened the door, got out and muttered, "I have to drive on cold days, too." She reached for her coat, put it on and slid back behind the wheel. "What do you want me to show you?" She glared at him. "About my driving."

When they returned to the parking lot, Matt said, "Well, I guess you passed. Come in and I'll write out a temporary license." Back in his office, he winked and nodded toward his partner as if he had succeeded at something.

She sat on the bench next to Freddie, the only other person in the waiting area. "Well?"

He shrugged, "Ain't took the test, yet."

She avoided eye contact with Matt when he faced her from behind the counter and waved a piece of paper. She waited until he set it down before she walked over and picked it up. She turned to Freddie.

"Good luck on your test."

She stopped in front of an office with the door open, tucked her temporary license into her purse and stared at the officer who sat behind his desk with a coffee cup in his hand.

"My brother's ready to take his written test now."

He set down his cup and stood. "I'll be right with him." He pointed to the chair opposite his desk. "Have a seat while you wait for him to finish. Would you like something to drink?"

"I'll wait in the car." Her coat flared as she turned and walked down the hall.

Within the hour, she saw Freddie burst out of the building, glance around the parking lot and walk to the car with a smug look on his face. He got into the passenger side and waved a sheet of paper in front of her.

"Well, how'd you do?"

"I passed." He folded the paper and put it in his wallet.

"I guessed that much." She wondered why she didn't get to keep her completed test. "I got one hundred percent on the written part." She waited but got no response. "Well, what score did you get?"

He shrugged. "Didn't do any written part. The guy who smelled like baked ham just asked me some questions 'bout rules for driving and then told me I passed."

"That was cloves." She fumed. Did the jerk with the sweet-smelling breath who humiliated her assume Freddie was illiterate?

"Huh?"

"He smelled like the cloves I use when I bake things. Almost made me sick." She pretended to stick her finger down her throat. "What was that paper you just waved in my face?"

"Told me it's my temporary license."

"You haven't taken the road test, yet."

"Don't have to do that part."

"How'd they know you can drive proper if they didn't test you?"

"Guess they just figured I knew how." He smiled. "When they asked me, I told them I'd been driving in fields and on back roads since I was thirteen."

She jammed her foot on the starter but applied too much choke, and the Chevy engine coughed a couple times, released a cloud of smoke and died. Her anger grew like the blue-gray exhaust behind her when she restarted the engine, and she slammed the transmission through all three of its gears on the way out of the parking lot.

Freddie broke the silence. "They joked a lot, mostly about kids from Bovine. Called it Hickville. Told them I didn't get to town much, and they just laughed. Said I should stick to the back roads." He sucked in his breath. "Don't need a license to do that."

"No written part?"

"Nope."

"No test drive, either?"

"Said I didn't need it."

"If you're that darn good, you better take over right now." The car swerved to the curb. She got out, stormed around to the passenger side and yanked open Freddie's door. "Move over."

"You don't have to be mad about it." Freddie grabbed the steering wheel and pulled himself to the driver's side. "How do we get to the library?" The car lunged forward and stopped. "Oops, I hit third gear by mistake." He restarted the engine.

"At least, you got the number right. It's on Third Street."

"I know it's on Third Street. I meant, how do we get to Third Street?"

"You'll have to find first gear before you can find any street." Thelma folded her arms and stared blankly ahead. She wished Pa had caught that guy peeking down her dress or the one who messed with her in the car. Even if they were cops, he would've busted their heads together.

"Do I turn on one of these streets named after presidents?"

"Washington." She smiled and blurted, "George." Her oldest brother would beat them one at a time. She pictured him drooling tobacco juice, possibly mixed with a few droplets of his own blood, and standing over two unconscious thugs. "Turn South on Washington Avenue just after Lincoln Avenue."

"They ain't in order."

"What?"

"Washington should come before Lincoln."

"It will when we head back. This way they're alphabetical." Pleased with her witty comment, she forgot about her anger. Freddie parked the car on the side of the street in front of a red brick building with ANDREW CARNEGIE etched in stone across the door and HARRINGTON COUNTY LIBRARY in black letters on the sign near the sidewalk. She slid from the passenger seat, brushed her coat with her hand and waited for Freddie. He opened his door into the path of an oncoming car. It swerved just in time to avoid hitting him. She heard the driver holler, *asshole*.

204

She yelled back, "No, just a couple of dumb farmers come to town to check out a book," and she grumbled, "with lots of pictures 'cause we don't read too well." Freddie stuck his hands into his pockets and pretended to whistle as he walked toward her. She tucked her arm under his. "Come on, Frederick, we're off to get a book for Iggy." Together, they strutted up the walk to the library door.

****

Doris Hopkins, student assistant at the library, glanced at the note taped to Mrs. Sorenson's office door, huffed and flung it into the wastebasket. She knew what had to be done without reading a detailed description of a routine task. She reached back into the basket and retrieved the note to see what excuse Mrs. Sorenson had for leaving the library early this time. Family emergency. Again. Doris sorted the books by their number, loaded them onto the portable cart and rolled it down to the history section.

"Damn." She snagged a fingernail on the biography of Julius Caesar. She glanced up and down the aisles, making sure that Mrs. Sorenson had left. "Double damn." She bit off the remains of a half-broken nail. She wanted to lay it on the librarian's desk with a note explaining that the Roman army attacked her, but decided on a better plan. She glanced around the room again. Assured no one was watching, she opened the book, found a chapter about Cleopatra and spit the jagged fingernail onto a picture of the Egyptian Queen. She wrote in the margin, *Here, Cleo, use this to scratch out Caesar's eyes.* She took a stick of gum from her pocket and shoved it into her mouth.

She glanced out the window and said aloud, "What do you know? Lock up the children, 'cause here comes Hicksville's marching band." She shoved Caesar and Cleopatra onto the shelf and pranced toward the door. "Featuring Woody on the washboard, Chester on the cream can and a host of trained goats." She pushed the door open. "Welcome to The Grand Ol' Opry."

"Thank you, young lady, but we just came to get a book. Won't have time to stay for any music."

Doris felt disappointed. The woman's accent wasn't as pronounced as she had expected, but she imagined the boy in bib overalls to have a stem of hay held between his teeth. She gestured for them to follow her to the checkout counter, placed her elbows on Mrs. Sorenson's writing tablet and settled her chin onto her hands, fingers laced together.

The woman leaned forward and whispered, "Where can we find a book written by Ignatius Donnelly?"

"You don't need to whisper here, only back in the reading area."

"Of course." The woman looked embarrassed and repeated, "Ignatius Donnelly," and nodded toward the boy.

Restraining a giggle at the ridiculous name for a country boy, Doris said, "Pleased to meet you, Ignatius. How may I help you?"

"Oh, no, my brother's name is Ignatius, back home. We call him Iggy."

"Good." The woman seemed to talk for the boy. Maybe, he ain't got a tongue. "I like the name Iggy better anyway, it's easier to say." She caught a glimpse of his blue eyes before he dodged behind his sister. "What book are you looking for, Iggy?"

"I'm afraid I confused you." The woman looked at Doris and then at the boy. "This is my brother, Freddie. My other brother's name is Iggy." She nodded as if Doris should understand. "Ignatius wrote the book we want to find."

"Your brother wrote a book?" Doris was impressed. Had she misjudged the brother and sister of an author just because they looked like farmers? She began to thumb through the card catalogue. "What's your brother's last name again?" She glanced back at the woman who was shaking her head. "Did you say, Donnelly?"

"No, our brother's last name is Rastner." The woman looked at Doris and spoke slowly. "The author of the book we are looking for is Donnelly, Ignatius Donnelly."

After an uncomfortable pause Doris said, "You have a brother named Ignatius. Do I have that right?"

"Yes, but we call him Iggy." The woman nodded.

Doris looked at the boy. "And, your name is Freddie." His ears turned red, and he clung tightly to the straps of his overalls.

"He's Freddie Tate." The woman touched the boy's shoulder and he grinned.

Doris sneered. "Not Donnelly?"

"No."

"Not that other name you mentioned either?"

"Yes, Rastner. No. Freddie Tate and Iggy Rastner are brothers even if they have different last names. I'm their sister, Thelma."

Unable to sort out the names, Doris lost interest and asked, "What title do you want?"

The woman looked confused and possibly embarrassed. "It's Miss, but I prefer just Thelma."

"I'm sorry, Just Thel-a-ma." Doris purposely added a third syllable. "I meant the title of the book you're looking for. The one by Ignatius Donnelly who, if I understand it, is no relative of the family."

Thelma huffed. "We don't know the title, but we were told your library has one of his books."

"It's a surprise for Iggy," Freddie said.

The boy had a tongue. "Your brother, Iggy?"

Freddie nodded

This matter cleared up, Doris searched the card catalogue, jotted some numbers on a slip of paper and walked to the stacks. She came back with a dull-colored hard cover book. "Do either of you have a library card?" She spoke directly to Freddie. He shook his head.

"Well, you need a card to check out a book." She put the book under the counter and watched his reaction.

"Can't we have it?"

She enjoyed the expression of disappointment etched on his face. After a brief pause, "All you gotta do is fill out an application. I just need one, so Freddie, you do it." She pursed her lips slightly and handed him a form.

He grabbed it and asked, "You got a pencil?"

She pointed one at him but didn't release her hold on it. His fingers slid off the end. "Here, try again." His knuckles turned white as he gripped it, and she let go like it was too hot to touch. "You'll need to return the book in two weeks." She placed it back on the counter, pulled a card from a pocket attached to the inside cover and scribbled *Freddie* on it. She glanced at Thelma, and let her eyebrows form the question.

Thelma answered, "Tate."

"Tate?"

"We've already been through that." Thelma pointed to the card. "Just write Freddie Tate"

"Okay." She printed *TATE* in large letters, jabbed a rubber marker onto an inkpad and stamped the date on the card and on a grid outlined on the first page. She pushed the book across the counter toward Freddie. "Your permanent library card will be ready when you return the book."

Freddie said, "Thank you," as he laid the form and pencil down, not taking his eyes off the counter. "I'll bring it back in two weeks." He grinned, "I have my driver's license now." He glanced up at her, but turned away when she made eye contact.

He reminded Doris of the puppy that Fritz made her return to the pound, and she felt her eyes moisten. She blinked and faced Thelma. "I'm sorry if I embarrassed you with my confusing questions." The gum in her mouth snapped. "I can be such a dolt at times."

Thelma grabbed Freddie's arm and said, "Escort me to the car, brother." She glanced back. "Good day, Miss."

"Goodbye, Miss Thelma. See you in two weeks, Freddie." She rushed to the window and watched them strut down the walk like some kind of royalty. Freddie opened the car door for his sister and then got in on the driver's side. Exhaust burst from the tail pipe, but the car didn't move. Freddie slapped the steering wheel, and Thelma covered her face with both hands. They were laughing.

Doris decided to tell Burt about Thelma and Freddie. She didn't care about the restraining order. That was her mother's idea, not hers.

CHAPTER TWENTY-SIX
FREDDIE'S FATHER

Thelma struggled to find a topic of conversation that would break the uncomfortable silence, but Svez, Iggy, Freddie and Henry just sat mute at the dinner table. When she wondered aloud where Henry's boys and her older brothers were eating their Thanksgiving dinner, Henry belched, and she thought he might have sneaked a chew of tobacco when she turned away. Svez pushed his chair back.

"Don't you guys run off just yet. I got a special treat for dessert." At the stove, she stirred the rice pudding and hoped Iggy would ask the question she made him memorize, but he just squirmed in his chair.

Maybe confronting Henry was a bad idea. Sonja had asked Freddie about his plans the Sunday they visited her, and he told her that was up to Svez and his Pa. Thelma seldom heard him even mention Henry, and he never referred to him as his father. Since then, she discussed Freddie's situation with Sonja twice when in town to do shopping. They agreed Freddie needed to know what would be expected of him in the future. She had instructed Iggy to ask Henry what he planned to do now that his boys had left home.

Her father reached for the bowl of pudding Thelma set on the table and asked, "What are Herbert and Clyde doing these days, Henry?"

He must have read her mind. She stood beside him and ladled pudding into each of their bowls. "Yeah, Uncle Henry. What's new with them?" She spoke her lines too fast, and her memorized response sounded awkward. Henry's eyes darted from her to the kitchen door, as if planning an escape route. He slapped his hands on the table, pushed himself up and walked out the door. Maybe he just went to the outhouse, but soon she heard a loud bang.

"Either Henry shot himself or he flooded the carburetor again." Svez raised a heaping spoon of pudding, blew across it and shoved it into his mouth.

She heard an engine rev and sounds of gravel hitting the side of the garage as the car sped out the driveway.

****

Henry woke the next morning with a headache and a pain in his stomach, and a fresh chew didn't make him feel better. He studied the remains of the tobacco plug in his hand. Indian Red, not Bull Durham. Had no use for Indian Red. It was Thelma's fault. If she hadn't made him throw out his last good chew before dinner, he wouldn't have this pain in his gut. Spoiled a damn fine meal. As good as either of his wives ever cooked for him, until each got sick and died. Food needed tobacco to start the digestion. If Arnie weren't dead, he could've begged a chew of Bull Durham like he used to when they went to the barn after dinner. Arnie never chewed Indian Red.

He propped himself on one arm and propelled a glob followed by a fine mist toward a rusty milk pail he kept near his bed. He blamed Thelma for his miscalculating the distance. He pressed both eyelids to stop the throbbing. Rot-gut whiskey. He rested his head back on his pillow and tried to remember all that happened after he left Svez's place.

Buddy's Bar seemed to be empty when he peered through the glass of the front door. Light from the neon beer sign flashed red then blue on Buddy's bald head as he snoozed on his rocking chair between a stack of empty beer cases and gallon jars of pickled chicken gizzards. Henry opened the door, careful to not ring the bell attached to the inside handle and crept to a stool across from the sleeping proprietor. He tapped a coin on a glass half full of stale beer. Buddy blinked.

"Henry, you old fart, how are you?" The rocker creaked as Buddy shifted his weight and stood up.

"Seventy-eight, and still cookin'." Henry flashed a toothless grin.

"I wanted to know how you're doing, not how old you were." Buddy drew a deep breath through the cigar stub glued to the corner of his mouth and the ash on the tip turned cherry red. He coughed

210

puffs of blue smoke. Leaning over the sink he rolled the stub between finger and thumb, the coals hissed as they dropped into the water, and he shoved loose bits of tobacco into his mouth pressing them against his cheek with his tongue. "What can I do you for?"

"I need some Bull Durham."

He grabbed a package the size of a deck of cards from the back bar and tossed it to Henry. "Indian Red's all I got left."

"Can't stomach that stuff." He was about to toss it back when Buddy reached under the bar and produced a bottle, its label rubbed unreadable from multiple use.

"Top shelf, my friend, and on the house."

Henry looked at the whiskey and then at the tobacco. He opened the wrapper and bit off a chew.

"Here's to seventy eight Goddamned-fuckin' years." Buddy poured his famous three-fingers-in-a-water-glass and slid it across the bar. He left the dark bottle with the tired label set in front of Henry.

Bad whiskey and bad tobacco. No wonder his head hurt when he lifted it from the pillow. His feet, covered with wool socks pulled over the leggings on his long johns, felt hot. He shoved the quilt aside and it fell onto the floor. Getting out of bed always presented problems, but this morning seemed worse than normal. He expected to find his shoes, open-laced and in the exact spot at the side of the bed where he stepped out of them, but yesterday he had worn his Sunday shoes. He considered wearing them to the barn, but they were low-cut and he didn't like manure oozing through his stockings. He walked to the kitchen and stepped into his work shoes, but when he stooped to tie the laces, pressure on his chest and stomach made breathing difficult. His heart raced, and he sat at the table until it settled down.

He lifted the lid on the kitchen stove and shoved crumpled newspapers into the firebox. When the flames surged he closed the lid and shoved the pan of leftover bacon and pot of day-old coffee over the warming iron surface. He felt pressure in his bladder and he lumbered back to the bedroom, what used to be the front room before he found it too difficult to climb the stairs, but the pail beside his bed was full. He lugged it out the back door and sloshed it over the bushes behind the house. He stood on the top step and urinated over the edge, wishing he could relieve the pressure in his head as well as his bladder.

Back in the kitchen, he inhaled the satisfying odors, warmed-over coffee and melting bacon grease. He tried to piece together the remnants of a recent conversation with his son. Herbert had come to borrow some tools, and as so often happened, they argued.

The words were still an open wound. "Pa, you're too damn old to run the farm by yourself. You best get yourself a place in town." Herbert gestured toward the barn. "Sell your cows. You ain't got but three left that's worth keeping." He paused and glared at his father. "You'd be a lot closer to church."

"Ya mean closer to the grave yard." Henry's raspy voice echoed in the empty kitchen twenty-four hours after the argument. "I ain't goin' to live in town, and you and Clyde is gonna help me stay right where I am." He slammed his fist on the table, but with the coffee and the meat ready, Henry buttered some stale corn bread and ate his breakfast. On the way to the barn he tracked though a blanket of fresh snow, his shoe laces making squiggly marks as he walked, and he decided to drive back to Svez's place after chores and talk to him about Freddie.

Later that morning, Henry parked in Svez's yard and waited for his brother-in-law to come out of the house or the barn. He wanted to deal face-to-face with Svez, but no one seemed to notice him drive into the yard. He half expected to see Arnie peer from the barn or from that stupid shelf outside his bedroom window. That old bachelor never did never take care of hisself. Never had a family of his own. Always relied on the charity of others.

Suddenly he felt a wave of loneliness. In half a dozen years he'd be as old as Arnie when he died. He needed to get his family back together or he might end up alone too. He figured he could run the farm by himself, but it would be nice to have all his boys help him. Herbert's suggestion about moving to town angered him. And Clyde hadn't been back to help but once all last year. They could both go to hell. He decided to give everything to Freddie. Together they could build back the herd, and he wouldn't need to rent out any of his land. They might even need some additional acreage from the neighbor's to support a large herd of milk cows. He still had good heifers, more than the three Herbert said, and Freddie got Arnie's herd. No reason why Svez should get all that milk.

Henry smiled as he developed this strategy—justice for his older sons who waited for him to die so they could pick his possessions apart like hungry vultures. He jumped when Freddie tapped on the car window.

"Are you looking for Svez?" Freddie asked through the glass.

He had come to make his deal with his brother-in-law, not to talk to Freddie. If he didn't answer, the boy might go away or maybe he'd run to get Svez from the barn. When Freddie just stood there and stared at him. Henry rolled down the window.

"I could use some help." He saw youth and strength in the young man's features, and his anger with Svez for stealing his son flared. Freddie opened the door and reached for him. "Help on my farm, I mean. I kin get out of the car myself, if I take a notion to." He pushed Freddie's arm back and held the steering wheel with both hands. He wanted to tell Freddie to come home where he belonged, but he couldn't say the words.

"Svez is in the barn." Freddie pointed. "Should I get him for you?"

Henry didn't look at Freddie but stared at a greasy jagged piece of metal on the seat next to him and tried to remember where it belonged.

"Is that the cam from your plow?"

Henry remembered that's what it was, but why did he put it in the car?

"Looks like the trip lever broke off. If you got it, I can weld it. I do that for Svez all the time."

I do that for Svez all the time. Henry's resentment peaked. He remembered the lever in the back seat, the cam in the front seat to remind him to get it welded the next time he went to town. Henry grabbed the lever and felt like going into the barn to show Svez that he was serious about taking Freddie back. He knew it was a foolish idea, and he handed it to Freddie who held it up to the light and inspected the break.

"Hand me the cam so I can see how they fit together."

Henry reached back, yanked it to the front seat and pushed it through the window.

"It'll only take a few minutes if you wanna wait."

Henry didn't decide to wait. He just sat there unable to move, as he watched Freddie walk away with a metal part in each hand. Lighting-like flashes emanated from the machine-shed window, and Henry felt terrified that Svez might see him and come over to talk. He had missed his opportunity, and he had no idea how to proceed next.

****

Freddie returned to the car, not surprised to see Henry still sitting there. He remembered Arnie and felt a surge of pity for this old man most people claimed was his pa. He never doubted it but never gave it much thought either. It certainly didn't bother him, until now. Freddie put the pieces of this unusual visit together much like he welded the pieces of metal together. Need help on the farm, was one piece to be fitted with a very unusual visit from a father/uncle who never just dropped in to get welding done.

When he was fifteen, he spent a week at Henry's farm. Henry was hospitalized and Svez told Freddie to help his boys with the chores. He drove the pickup on the back roads to Henry's farm and returned each evening. Herbert and Clyde, older brothers Freddie assumed, reluctantly alternated doing the evening chores. Freddie was not to leave until one or the other came to relieve him. They often came late and sometimes not at all, leaving Freddie alone all day at a place that terrified him. He went into Henry's empty house to eat the sandwich Thelma had made for him, but he preferred the familiar smells in the barn. The rest of the week he ate his lunches in the haymow.

That night as Freddie lay in Arnie's old bed, surrounded by many of Arnie's things, he felt an urge to slide the chest of drawers in front of the door. When Arnie lay dying, Freddie sat on the floor next to the bed wondering what was going through his mind. Freddie now felt he had the answer. Arnie never truly felt he belonged in the family, and he always feared he would be asked to leave. With the dresser in front of his door, Arnie believed he wouldn't be kicked out in the middle of the night. Freddie stood on the balcony outside Arnie's window and watched his breath, made visible from the yard light, but it couldn't penetrate the darkness he felt.

CHAPTER TWENTY-SEVEN
DORIS HOPKINS

Doris confided to her reflection in the bathroom mirror. "I'm gonna look like shit at school today." She applied her mother's eye shadow, her face powder and her rouge, but she still saw red eyes and swollen cheeks on the face staring back at her.

With both hands on the sink, she leaned forward and asked herself, "Why does Mom put up with that drunken bastard?" She felt a surge of fear and saw an expression of panic on her face before she realized the bedroom next door had become quiet. The wheezing and moaning accented with short gasps and snorts had stopped. Was Fritz awake? Would he suddenly appear in the doorway with his hand in his shorts like he had last week? He can't get in. Her mother had the lock fixed. Yesterday, he stood outside and yelled, "Goddamned locked door." If he had taken a notion to break it down, nothing could have stopped him. He made that point very clear before he stomped downstairs and out the back door, slamming it behind him. He'd probably blame her if he got arrested for indecent exposure because she wouldn't let him pee in the bathroom.

"Please God, make him dead." A single gasp for air, a deep cough and a gulp, probably phlegm from a night of smoking and drinking, and Doris realized her prayer hadn't been answered. At least he still slept. She had time to make herself presentable for school and her afternoon job at the library.

Her stomach retched from fear and anger, a sufficient excuse to stay home, but it only increased her resolve to go. When Fritz woke up, he'd probably blame everyone else for his problems or, worse yet, cry like a baby and beg forgiveness. At least he hadn't beat on her mother last night like he sometimes did. Doris would rather be beaten than listen to his sniveling; then she'd have the courage to kill him. She watched her lips curve into a smile. She'd get Burt to do it.

A tear tracked down her cheek, creating a path for the next one forming in the corner of her eye, and she decided not to hide behind the makeup. She turned the faucet on full blast, and with both hands washed away her efforts to cover her misery.

She pleaded quietly to her mother, "Next time he gets drunk with his war buddies, don't go after him. Let him sleep in the gutter." She knew her mother couldn't hear, wouldn't listen anyway. She was too busy trying to keep peace in the family, like last night when a loud crash downstairs had awakened Doris in the middle of the night.

"God damned kid with his roller skates." Fritz cursed her kid brother, Teddy.

"Hush, you'll wake the kids."

"Clara, your kids is gonna kill me, yet."

"Get up off the floor and go to bed."

Petrified that Fritz would beat on her mom, she ran to the stairs and peered from behind the banister. Sprawled on the floor, Fritz pushed a roller skate back and forth and made farting noises with his lips.

"Just like tanks back in Korea. They wrecked 'em, and I fixed 'em. Fixed 'em good, too. Ain't no tanks in Harrington needing fixing."

"For God's sake, get up. You aren't in the war anymore."

"Saved his life, once, but he got killed anyway."

"I don't want to hear about that, now. Please get up."

"Saved my buddy, your loving husband, but they shot him anyway." He continued to make obscene noises and push his make-believe tank back and forth.

Doris ran back to her bedroom and muffled a scream by biting her knuckles. It wasn't fair that her dad got killed, and that jerk lying on the floor downstairs survived. Did Dad really ask him to look out for his family, or did Fritz stumble on that idea to impress Mom? Surely, Dad wouldn't want his buddy to sleep with his wife. Teddy needed a father because he was still in junior high. Phooey! She and Teddy once had a father, and Fritz could never replace him.

When Fritz thumped up the stairs, urinated loudly in the bathroom and plopped onto her mother's bed, she put her hands over her ears and hid under the covers. She blotted out most of the sound, but the image of her mother crawling into bed with that monster disgusted her. Through the covers, she sensed light from the hallway flood into her room, and she felt her mother's presence, probably wanting to make cheap excuses for Fritz. Doris hated these mother-daughter discussions. She fought back sobs by holding her breath until the light disappeared and the door shut. Maybe they would talk in the morning.

Doris ruffled random strands of hair, half bleached and half grown back to brown, until it carelessly covered her forehead and partially masked the red around her eyes.

Nodding her approval to the mirror, Doris reminded herself, "Today's Wednesday." Her mother would be at The Hub Café for the noon rush. Maybe Fritz would still be out cold, and he could storm or cry all afternoon in an empty house.

She scanned her reflection one last time and made some adjustments to the scarf that covered the scar on her neck. "Let's go, kiddo." She bounded down the stairs, pecked a kiss on her mother's cheek and cruised out the door, avoiding the motherly bits of advice that she resented almost as much as her mother sharing a bed with the jerk who terrorized their lives. She glanced back and saw Teddy twirl around as their mother grabbed him at the door

"Don't you leave this house without having a decent breakfast, young man. Come back and eat like a civilized person."

"But, Mom, Doris won't wait for me." They disappeared back into the house.

Doris lit a cigarette, leaned against a tree in their front yard and waited for her brother who hadn't been quick enough to avoid their mother's morning ritual. He probably slowed to dig his finger into the peanut butter from the government-surplus tin, always open and always on the table. She knew he panicked when he had to walk past Burt Wilson's house alone, so she decided to give him as much time as it took to finish her cigarette. Just as she snuffed it out on the tree, he burst out the door, Mom yelling after him.

"You forgot to kiss your mother goodbye."

He caught up with her before she reached the Wilson house, gasped for air and asked, "What's your hurry?" He glanced toward Burt's front door. "We're just going to school."

Normally, she'd expect him to yell *wait for me*, but that might sound like he needed her for protection. Burt had accused him of spreading rumors and then called him a little wart and a sissy for tattling to his sister. Teddy refused to tell her what the rumors were. Everyone knew about the knife incident and the restraining order, but she wondered what other stories about them floated around junior high.

After they passed the Wilson house, Teddy asked, "How come you're not afraid of Burt?"

"Oh, he's just a big bully." She twisted open the wrapper from a piece of bubble-gum, licked it and shoved the gum into her mouth. "Don't pay any attention to him." She wadded the wrapper and tossed it at her brother.

He ducked. "Yeah, but he's a mean big bully."

"What are your snot-nosed friends saying 'bout me and Burt?"

"Nothing."

Burt wouldn't tell her what the rumors were about, either. The next time Teddy sneaked into her room to hide from Fritz, she'd force it out of him. Sharing their fear and anger when their stepfather went on a binge brought them closer together.

"He's just an ordinary big bully." Doris reduced her encounter with Burt to this simple conclusion and assured herself that he wouldn't dare hurt her again even after he'd been drinking with the guys. The judge who issued the restraining order said he'd go to jail the next time.

She reflected on the larger threat, the man who slept in the bedroom next to hers, and felt her neck and face get hot. Re-adjusting the scarf, she touched the scar and realized her mother couldn't help her. Mom couldn't even help herself.

After school, Doris decided to skip the shortcut through a few back yards on the way to the library. She needed time to think, and wanted an excuse to be late. For two full weeks, Burt had complied with the restraining order and avoided her at school. Did he even miss her? Did he blame her for calling the police? Her mother reported it as an assault with a knife and an attempted rape, and no one seemed to care that it was her knife. She didn't intend to use it, just show him what she would do if he kept getting drunk and messing with other girls. The knife nicked her when he tried to take it away. He didn't mean to hurt her, and the cut only required a couple of stitches.

She walked around front instead of entering through the back door as usual. A painted sign read HARRINGTON COUNTY LIBRARY but CARNEGIE LIBRARY had been carved in granite. Inside, an office door had DIRECTOR etched in frosted glass and MRS. SORENSON printed on poster board. She imagined Mr. Carnegie, back from the dead, knocking down the temporary sign outside his building and reclaiming his office.

"Where have you been? You knew I had a doctor's appointment this afternoon." Mrs. Sorenson, not Mr. Carnegie, greeted her as she walked in.

"Folks won't let me cut though their yards no more. Takes longer to get here."

"There's a stack of books that needs to be put back on the shelves. Please, try to get them exactly where they belong."

Doris nodded, pushed her tongue through her chewing gum and popped a small bubble. "I'll be careful." Mrs. Sorenson huffed, walked out the back door and slammed it shut. Doris wadded the gum in her mouth, pinched it between finger and thumb and stuck it under Mrs. Sorenson's chair. Rather than stoop or squat to reach the lower shelf behind the checkout counter, she sat frog-like on the floor and started replacing reference books. She heard someone wheeze much like Mrs. Sorenson sounded when she was nervous. She leaned forward, shifted her legs into a kneeling position and stood. She faced a tall, handsome man with black hair and mustache. His dark eyes darted as he jerked his head back, obviously startled by her sudden appearance. He wore a plaid shirt and bib overalls and wiped discolored saliva from the corner of his mouth with a red and black handkerchief. Doris faced an honest-to-goodness country bumpkin.

She brushed the dust from her pants and asked, "Can I help you?"

"I'm Iggy." He blushed and became quiet as if he forgot why he came to the library.

"Ignatius Donnelly?" Only bits and pieces of a previous conversation surfaced.

"No, Ignatius Rastner." He stood up straight and held a book in front of him. "Ignatius Donnelly wrote this book I gotta return for my brother, Freddie." His speech was heavily accented. "Said you might have a library card ready for him." He laid the book on the counter. "Guess it's overdue."

She felt his speech, manner of dress and barnyard odor somehow was in conflict with his deep-set brown eyes and sculpted facial features. "I'll have to check." She flipped through a box of index cards, selected one and matched it with the title of the book. Attached with a paper clip was Freddie Tate's library card. "Yes, we have it." She handed it to him. "Let's see, the fine comes to twenty cents."

Iggy pulled a few coins from his pocket, picked out two dimes and handed them to her. He continued to gaze at the remaining coins, as if counting them.

"There's no charge for Freddie's library card, if that's what you're thinking."

He put the money back into his pocket, stood straight like he was about to salute, and said, "'Spect I better get going. Pa's waiting at the hog market." He turned and walked out.

After Mrs. Sorenson returned and excused Doris for the evening, she walked home and yelled to Teddy who was playing stickball with some friends in the empty lot next door. "Hey, Teddy, get your butt in the house. Mom's at work and you gotta help make supper."

"I already ate a peanut butter sandwich. We're in the middle of a game. I'll be home in a little while."

Doris retreated to the house, leafed through the mail on the table and began making a grilled cheese sandwich.

Teddy came in and asked, "Can you make me one of them?"

"Thought you ate. Didn't you say you ate?"

"Just a peanut butter and crackers."

"Take this one. I couldn't eat it anyway."

"Thanks."

"I gotta' leave for a little bit. You okay if Fritz gets home before Mom?"

"Yeah, sure. Where you going?"

"Tell Mom I had to go back to the library."

"Okay." He blew over the melted cheese and touched it with his tongue. "Is that where you're really going?"

"Just never mind. You tell her the library, okay?"

"You're goin to Burt's house, aren't you." He held the sandwich with both hands and stared at it.

"Yeah, so what. I just want to tell him about this farmer who came to the library today, from Bovine out in country some place. Burt does a good imitation of how they talk. He can be so funny." She paused and said, "You don't like him, do you."

"He scares me all the time. And the kids say dumb things about you and him." He looked at her. "Are they true, Doris?"

"Like what?"

"Like he almost killed you with his knife. And did that other thing to you."

"What other thing?"

"You know."

"Everyone's making a bigger deal out of it than it really was. He didn't mean to hurt me, and he said he was sorry. He got real scared when Mom called the police. Guess we can still be friends."

"But all the kids say—"

"Those damned little brats. They don't know nothing that went on between me and Burt."

"Is anything going on between you and him?"

"You tell them that made up that story, I'll cut off their weenies if they aren't careful. Tell Mom I'm at the library."

CHAPTER TWENTY-EIGHT
MISS WEST AT THE LIBRARY

At the Harrington County Library, Sonja West waited with an armful of books while Mrs. Sorenson sat in her office, nose and eyes fixed on an open ledger. Sonja purposely scheduled her trip to the library late in the afternoon so Doris, a high school student, rather than the prig librarian would check out her books. But, Doris seemed to be absent. Mrs. Sorenson glanced toward the checkout counter and immediately returned her attention to the ledger on her desk. Sonja sorted her books into three stacks, one for herself, one for Mildred and one for Thelma, when she noticed something new had been added. A small silver bell on the counter glinted in the afternoon sunlight, and a sign taped next to it read *ring for service.* She reached for it but reconsidered. Mrs. Sorenson wanted to be summoned from her office. How petty.

She wandered over to a bulletin board and pretended to read the notices posted there, hoping Doris would appear from the back room or the basement. She and Mildred had laughed when Thelma told them about Freddie's encounter with the young girl, and she wanted to ask Doris if she remembered their visit. Freddie missed his chance to see her a second time because Iggy returned the book, a week overdue, according to Thelma.

She noticed the empty chair in the director's office and heard a file drawer close, but Mrs. Sorenson returned to her desk. She found the rudeness unbearable and remembered her father's opinion about *those kinds of people,* and his recent suggestion she move back East to live with him. The cultural opportunities available in Philadelphia tempted her, and she felt a tinge of guilt.

Thanks to his generosity, she had an education, a house, an income from a trust fund he established, and, compared to Thelma's situation, she had her freedom. Was there a subtle message in his invitation to return home? His home, not hers? She belonged with the people she nurtured as children, like Thelma, and friends like Mildred. Cherished memories of her teaching experiences were best preserved near the rural district where she spent her career.

She returned to the checkout counter, looked into the director's office and intoned, "Hello?" Mrs. Sorenson didn't respond.

She picked up *David Copperfield,* and thumbed through it. Mildred had suggested Thelma would enjoy reading it, but Sonja felt it might be too difficult for her. Besides, Freddie wasn't an orphan if that was Mildred's intention.

She decided not to wait. She opened one of the books she had selected, removed the card from the pocket glued to the inside cover and placed it on the counter. She took her fountain pen from her purse and, with the flourish of her best Palmer-method signature, added her name to the list of other names, each carefully printed and perfectly fitted between the lines. She did likewise with the rest of the books. As she dabbed the rubber stamp on the ink pad and prepared to apply the date to the little square next to her name already circled from the swirl of the S of her first name, she felt Mrs. Sorenson's cold fingers pluck the stamp from her hand.

"I'll do that." She glared at the stack of cards that Sonja had signed. "If you had rung the bell, I would have known you were ready to check out." She skipped one line below Sonja's signature and stamped the date. With the pencil attached to a chain probably borrowed from a light fixture, she carefully printed *Miss West* on the adjacent line. On one card, Sonja's signature filled the last line leaving no room for the correction. She placed the card aside and said, "I see it's already full. Doris will have to prepare a new one if she ever comes back."

Sonja felt vindicated for the insult she endured and decided to pursue polite conversation. "Where is that charming young girl who sometimes helps you?" The disgust evident in Mrs. Sorenson's expression switched to anger and then eroded into a kind of pseudo empathy.

"Doris hasn't showed up this past week." Anger returned. "Not a call or a notice of any kind." She shook her head. "Totally irresponsible behavior." A mild reconciliation, "but, what can one expect from someone who lives in that part of town?"

Sonja collected her books and placed them in a cloth bag she carried for that purpose.

"Now, I can tell you that I do miss her, with all these books needing shelving." She touched Miss West's gloved hand and immediately pulled back. "But, the truth is…" she glanced around the room as if the truth needed to be kept a secret between them. "The truth is, I think Doris is in serious trouble."

"What kind of trouble could that nice young girl get into?" Sonja felt solicitous.

"Oh, there is more to her than meets the eye." Mrs. Sorenson's eyes rolled, darted toward the empty aisles between rows of books and locked briefly on Sonja.

Exasperated with the librarian's theatrics, Sonja decided to forego the details of Doris' problem. "From what I've observed, that young lady has resources to help her through any troubled times." She slung the strap to her book-bag over her shoulder and clutched her purse. "Is there anything you or I might do to help Doris with her problems, whatever they may be?"

"I'm afraid Doris' problems are her own doing, and I'm quite sure she would shun any of our noble attempts to help her, Miss West."

Although piqued by her emphasis on *Miss*, a not-too-subtle message that one needed children of one's own to qualify, Sonja said, "I'm not so sure about that. Sometimes we adults can be very helpful just by listening to our young people."

"Oh, I've offered to help this young lady all right. You'd be surprised at her stubbornness. She as much as told me to mind my own business when I asked what was bothering her. I am in a good position to help, having raised my two girls. I expected Doris to confide in me like they did. But, what can one expect? She gets no direction from home. Her stepfather can't keep a steady job, and her mother's just a waitress at the Hub Café. Doris roams the streets at night with a very tough crowd."

Sonja stood in disbelief as Mrs. Sorenson paused from her tirade and again glanced between two rows of books, obviously in preparation for the juiciest bit of gossip.

"Now Doris has this boyfriend. His name is Burt Wilson…"

Sonja turned, and her book-bag made a wide arc. "I will return these books within the two week period." She started walking toward the door.

Mrs. Sorenson followed her. "You asked about Doris, and I felt it my place to inform you of all I know. I'm sorry if you've misinterpreted my intentions. I have a great deal of affection and concern for this girl, and I felt that sharing the details of her behavior with another caring adult would help her."

Sonja opened the door. "I'm sure your good intentions and unique association with her will help her make the right decisions. Good day, Mrs. Sorenson."

CHAPTER TWENTY-NINE
DORIS AT THE HOSPITAL

When Doris heard the door to her room open, she pretended to be asleep. She sensed someone standing over her. Probably a doctor who came to read her chart hanging from a chain across the foot of the bed, or that woman with the starched white hat on her head and *Nurse Otto* printed on a name-tag pinned to her uniform. She thought her charade had been exposed when she felt warm and minty breath near her face. *Nurse Otto*, like *Nurse* was her first name. She peeked and saw white shoes, white stockings, white gown and white cap disappear through the door, except for the brown hair that escaped around her neck, a perfect ghost.

Doris decided she'd never be a nurse, or a librarian. She might consider being a teacher like the one from Bovine, although she faked sleep the entire time Miss West sat beside her bed. Who told her she could come and why did she bring flowers like it was a funeral? Did that bitch, Sorenson, send that hick-town schoolteacher to get some juicy gossip about her? Probably not. Sorenson don't like that teacher lady from Bovine. Called her a lesbian once. When Doris asked what that meant, she made believe it was a kind of religion.

"I'm afraid I misspoke." The dreaded voice echoed in Doris' head. "I believe she's a Catholic. Everyone's Catholic in Bovine."

Dumb bitch. They were in a library and Doris looked up the definition of lesbian.

With her disgusting need to be totally accurate, Sorenson had continued her train of thought. "No, she can't be Catholic. She came from that town just outside Philadelphia, the one with a cult religion, Byrn Anthen."

Doris located the Philadelphia suburb on the atlas and wondered why anyone would leave that exotic place to live in Minnesota.

And why had Miss West wanted to see her in the hospital? The gentle tapping on her door might have been her mother, but she had already snuck in before visiting hours, before her shift at the café. She closed her eyes and hoped Burt would appear when she opened them. He'd never knock that lightly, or even at all. She recognized Miss West's whispered voice like in the library and smelled the flowers she set on the cart alongside her bed. Doris kept her eyes shut until she finally went away.

The door swung open, and this time no one knocked first. A young girl dressed in a white gown with red stripes strolled into the room carrying a tray of upside-down bowls hiding Doris' supper, probably fish from the smell.

The girl said, "My name is Beth."

Doris looked at her but didn't answer. Maybe it would be okay to be that kind of nurse. At least, they don't smell like medicine.

"Your name is Doris." Beth set the tray on a bedside cart next to the bouquet of flowers. "It's on the chart."

"I know."

"You know that your name is Doris, or that it's on the chart?"

"Stupid." But Doris couldn't keep from laughing. Soon both girls started to giggle. She grimaced and wrapped her arms around herself.

"I'm sorry. I just thought it was funny." Beth took a deep breath and tapped her mouth with her fingers. "Do your ribs hurt when you laugh?" She squeezed her lips together, but another burst of laughter escaped through her nose.

"Does your nose hurt when you laugh like that?" Doris continued to laugh and hugged herself tighter.

Beth asked, "Was it bad, the accident, I mean?"

"The car's totaled, but it was an old one anyway. Burt, the guy who was driving, didn't get hurt. Just me."

"Is he your boyfriend?"

Doris nodded.

"Why doesn't he come to see you?"

Doris didn't respond.

"Were you guys really running away?"

"I guess we were, sort of."

As Beth shoved the cart toward the bed, the platform with the dinner-tray shook, and the vase with flowers teetered.

228

"Be careful." Doris grabbed the vase just as it was about to fall. "I got enough things hurting the way it is." She smelled the flowers while Beth uncovered her food.

"Sorry." Beth took the flowers and set them on the nightstand. "Was she your teacher?"

"Who?"

"The woman who brought the flowers."

"Miss West?" Doris picked at the fish, but decided not to taste it.

"Yeah. My cousin lived on a farm and had her for a teacher, long time ago. He really liked her."

"No, she don't even teach no more. She just comes to the library where I work."

"You work in the library?" Beth sounded surprised.

"You work in the hospital?" And they both burst out laughing again.

Later that night in the quiet of her room Doris blurted out, "Mom told her. Miss West talked to Mom at the café." Doris covered her mouth with her hand and held her breath. Did the ghost nurse hear? She reflexively closed her eyes as she heard the door open.

She recognized Nurse Otto's subdued voice. "Did you need something? I checked earlier and thought you were asleep."

Doris didn't answer.

Nurse Otto left the door slightly ajar. A sliver of light crept in, widened as it tracked across the floor to the back wall and projected shadows of people passing in the hallway. Why did she always whisper, like it was a morgue or something? She remembered her father's wake. Everyone in the room talked real quiet. Everyone, except Daddy, and he didn't care how loud or soft they talked. She plopped her head on the pillow and laughed, then cried. As a rush of breath bypassed her vocal cords, she let out a nearly silent yell and expected the door to swing open, but it didn't. In the library, most people whispered but not Sorenson. She always talked out loud, except when she had some gossip to spread; then she talked real soft, like she shared some secret.

Doris started counting to one hundred, a diversion that sometimes worked when unpleasant thoughts kept her awake at night. She felt the stillness of the hospital room with its high ceilings, drab green walls and sparse furnishings made faintly visible by the light from the hallway. The etched glass in her only window, source of light during the day, became a diffused mirror at night.

She whispered, "Mrs. Sorenson" when she saw her image scattered into a thousand parts, erasing much of her chin and exaggerating her pursed lips. Her mouth curved into a smile and she began to laugh. The similarity of her image with Mrs. Sorenson disappeared, but not her memories of the evil things the librarian had said about Miss West.

"That teacher thinks she's so important." Doris remembered the twist of Sorenson's mouth that always indicated more trash-talk would follow. "Just because she's from out East. And exactly why did she leave the Philadelphia area? And what about that bank lady who followed her?"

"You think they're lovers?" Doris compared the relationship of these two ladies with hers and Burt's and shuddered. But they probably didn't hurt each other.

Mrs. Sorenson said, "Pshaw. What do you know about such matters? Whose been filling your head with nonsense? Should have their mouths washed out with soap." She had stiffened her entire body into a gesture Doris recognized as one of disgust.

Doris imagined what it would have been like in a one-room school with Miss West as her teacher. She wondered if Freddie, the boy she met in the library, went to Miss West's school. She felt sorry that she and Burt made fun of how he looked and talked. She no longer needed to count to one hundred. The vision of Miss West, salt and pepper hair rolled into a donut, reading glasses dangling a chain around her neck and pointer in her hand, surrounded by country kids, pleased Doris. She wanted to go back to grade school, sit next to Freddie and become part of Miss West's class. She remembered the clock in her grandparent's house. Each hour small wooden creatures marched out of a tiny schoolhouse, the leader struck a bell announcing the hour and they all scampered back in. Doris slept soundly.

CHAPTER THIRTY
A CHILD OF THE NIGHT
(Spring, 1951)

Sonja West sat on her couch and reminisced with Mildred Bushman about her various living arrangements since they moved to Bovine, when they heard a tap, tap, tap barely audible above the steady rhythm of sleet ticking outside the window. She paused, more curious than frightened, and glanced toward the door.

"Now, who could that be at this hour?"

"Please, Sonja, don't open it. It's probably just someone whose car skidded off the road."

"If that's the case, we need to see what we can do for them."

"They can get help at the cafe."

Sonja rose and went to investigate. "No one should have to walk anywhere in this weather. Maybe they're hurt."

"I better go into the kitchen."

"Nonsense." Sonja put her ear close to the door. "Stay right where you are. It's probably just the wind slapping some branches against the house." She touched the dead bolt, but didn't unlock it. "Besides, you're my guest, and we don't have to explain anything to anyone."

Sonja shared Mildred's concern about her neighbors' perceptions of their relationship, but there was a perfectly good reason why Mildred temporarily moved in with her. They had laughed together at the notice in the local news section of Bovine's weekly newspaper, *Cunningham Family and Renter Forced out of Home.* The article that followed explained that the Cunninghams had moved to a suite of rooms at Harrington Hotel while their entire home was being remodeled including the mother-in-law apartment Victor installed for his mother before she passed away.

After a detailed description of the hardships borne by Mrs. Cunningham and the community's anticipation of the open house soon to be announced, it mentioned that their renter, Mildred Bushman, stayed with a friend.

Sonja shrugged and returned to the couch. "We shared a small apartment the summer we first located here, and no one made a big deal of it. It's perfectly natural for friends to live together."

"We were still a curiosity back then, before the gossip mill starting grinding out it vile accusations."

"Insinuations, Mildred. No one ever actually accused us of anything unnatural, or indecent."

"Well, they would have if the school board hadn't forced you to move in with parents of your students." Mildred reached for her saucer, stared down into the empty cup and rose from the couch. "Shall I steep two cups?"

Sonja shook her head and watched her friend turn and walk toward the kitchen. She glanced about the room. She loved her house, and having Mildred this close felt wonderful. What would she have done without her friend's support these last few years since her teaching career ended? And, of course, the financial trust her father established that made living here possible. She chuckled quietly. And Sylvester Rastner many years earlier.

The Graff family was the first and only one Sonja had to endure before the school board abandoned its live-in rule. Ernestine and Oliver Graff had seven children and a maiden aunt with whom Sonja shared a room. She walked to school early each morning to light the fire in the wood stove and cherished the quiet time before the students arrived. After much discussion, the school board consented to her keeping a car, but she was only allowed to use it on weekends when she could shop and visit friends in town. During the week, Oliver kept it in his machine shed. In winter, if her Ford wouldn't start or if the roads were impassable, she was marooned in their house. She couldn't escape to her classroom on Saturdays because heating the school when the children weren't there was considered a waste of firewood. Of course, they expected her to accompany them to church every Sunday.

Mildred returned, paused in front of the couch and said, "You look, shall we say, contemplative."

Mildred's comment jarred Sonja back to the present. "I was just thinking about my father and Thelma's father."

"What an unlikely pair." Mildred sat back on the couch and breathed in the steam rising from her cup. "What on earth could they have in common?"

"Well, Dad sent me money to buy this place, and Mr. Rastner convinced the school board to allow teachers to reside in town. I think his wife, Elizabeth, wanted me to stay with her family the next school term, and he didn't. Ignatius needed special help with his studies, and Thelma demonstrated a remarkable intelligence. They were going into the second grade. Their three older boys went to school once in a while just to create mischief."

Mildred took a sip and then spoke through the rising steam. "Have you ever regretted not living with Thelma, when she was a child, I mean?"

"In a way, yes." She wanted to quell the tinge of jealousy she sensed in Mildred's reaction, but a sensory memory of fresh furniture polish mingled with the summer's dust brought her first two students into focus. A six-year-old Thelma introduced her older brother like she was his parent. Her mind locked on that schoolhouse scene and she couldn't break her stare.

Mildred said, "Sonja West. If you don't share that reminiscence with me immediately, I will never speak to you again."

Sonja chuckled at an incongruous thought. "Sylvester Rastner explained women's emancipation to the school board."

"He did what?"

"He didn't exactly use that term. He said, 'After all, this is the 20's. Women vote and have other rights, too.' Ernestine Graff sat on pins and needles, because she had requested my services for an additional year. She jabbed her poor husband in the ribs, and he jumped up but couldn't manage to say anything." Sonja gestured with her elbow. "Ernestine poked him in the thigh and he almost toppled over."

"Good thing he wasn't facing her." Mildred blushed.

"Mildred, you're nasty." She touched her friend's arm and some tea splashed onto Mildred's saucer. "Finally, Mr. Graff looked at Sylvester and said, 'like what rights?' and sat down. Ernestine began chewing on his ear like Brer Rabbit in the cabbage patch."

"What did Sylvester say?"

"Nothing. Apparently, he couldn't think of any other rights women should have either." Mildred laughed, but her eyes darted toward the door when the tapping sound resumed.

"Gracious, someone is out there." Sonja pulled her bathrobe closed, walked to the door and asked, "Who's there?"

She glanced back at Mildred who held her shawl tight around her neck covering the top button of her pajamas and sat rigid with teacup and saucer in her free hand. Sonja opened the door, and in the mist made visible from the light in the foyer, she recognized Doris from the library.

"Come in, child. Have you been standing out in the cold all this time? You must be positively frozen."

"I thought you weren't home, and then I guessed I had the wrong house. That creep at that old run-down café maybe told me wrong. I checked next door, and some crabby guy assured me this was your house."

"Your teeth are chattering. Take off that wet jacket and come in where it's warm."

"I'm sorry to barge in on you like this." She pressed the palms of her hands on her cheeks, then unbuttoned her coat and handed it to Sonja.

"Nonsense. It's wonderful to see you again. A surprise, but wonderful, all the same." She turned to Mildred who stood, knees pressed against an arm of the couch. "Mildred, this is Doris, who used to work at the library." She hung the girl's coat in the closet. "Doris, this is my friend, Mildred." Doris' eyes fixed on Mildred, and Sonja wondered what the girl might be thinking. Had Mrs. Sorenson filled her head with slanderous stories about the spinster who checked out books for her old-maid friend? Would a street-wise kid like Doris even care? Will Mildred be able to tolerate this run-a-way in her house?

"Come, my young friend and my…" she gestured to both ends of the couch, "my vintage friend. Let's make ourselves comfortable." Mildred frowned, sat and looked away. "Can I get you some tea, or possibly warm milk?"

Shaking, Doris sat scrunched at the opposite end of the couch from Mildred and folded her arms. "I 'spose you're wondering why I came here."

"Yes, but only when you're ready to tell us." Sonja postponed the milk and sat between them. After a brief pause, she said, "You can start by telling us how you got to Bovine on such a cold and wet night."

"I walked, until an old guy in a beat up pickup stopped." She rubbed her hands together. "He said the heater didn't work too good. Actually, it didn't work at all."

Sonja chuckled, and Doris seemed to relax.

"You probably already guessed. I was running away."

"What made you decide to come here?" Mildred adjusted her shawl and took a sip of tea. "Don't you have friends you could stay with?"

234

"Give Doris a chance to explain, Mildred." Sonja held her gaze on the young girl.

"Miss West came to see me last winter when I was in the hospital." Doris turned toward Mildred and folded her arms. "Thought I could pay her a visit back."

"Indeed, I did." Sonja put her hand on Doris' arm and turned toward Mildred. "Mrs. Sorenson claimed Doris hadn't been to work for a while," she glanced back, "and your mother told me about the accident." Sonja felt Doris recoil slightly, and it made her feel defensive. "I was concerned about you. We had talked quite often at the library, and I just wanted to cheer you up. I didn't mean to intrude."

"I don't mean to intrude either, but I got no other place to go." She held a jagged fingernail to her mouth, but didn't chew on it.

Sonja brushed a tuft of hair from the girl's forehead and handed her a handkerchief for the tear that streaked down her cheek. "Please go on. Tell us what happened."

"My friend Burt and me got into this accident."

"Goodness, that was months ago when you got hurt. I understand you were in that young man's car when it crashed into the ditch. That certainly wasn't your fault." She took back her handkerchief and tucked it into her sleeve. "I meant, what happened today that made you want to run away?"

"It didn't happen just today. I never went back to work after the accident. When I got out of the hospital, Mom insisted I quit my job and come right home after school every day. Mrs. Sorenson would probably have fired me anyway. Fritz, my step dad, put me on a strict curfew." She glanced toward Mildred and quickly back. "The truth is, that night with Burt, I was running away, too. Since we had already violated a court order, I asked him to take me far away from Harrington. He wouldn't have been driving if... I guess it wasn't such a good idea. I know that now, but I wasn't thinking too good at the time."

"It wasn't right to encourage him to take his dad's car, but he has to take responsibility for what he did," Sonja assured her.

"Well, his dad and my step dad blamed me for Burt hauling me off to God knows where. That's what Fritz called it." She glanced at Mildred. "He's the man my mother married after my real father died." She unfolded her arms and raised both hands in a gesture of giving up. "Maybe God knew where we were going, but I sure didn't, or don't."

"Well, where did this Burt fellow think he was supposed to take you?" Mildred seemed curious. "After all, he must have had some destination in mind?"

"Burt just does things for me, ever since..." Doris looked at her hands. "Well, we'd gotten into trouble once before, and he kind of got blamed for it."

"What kind of trouble?" Mildred leaned forward.

"I got scratched a little," she touched the faded scar on her neck, "and he got blamed." She quickly added, "He didn't mean to hurt me, but the judge put a restraining order on him. After the car accident, his dad grounded him, and he still might face charges because he took the car without permission," she laced her fingers and looked at them, "and some money. I didn't know about the money, but he probably did that for me, too. I didn't think about much of anything, like gas and food." Her eyes met Mildred's. "He told the police that we were going to Florida, but I don't remember that part of the plan. He had a cousin who went there one time, and I think that's why he thought of Florida."

"You didn't say which you preferred, tea or warm milk. What can I get you?"

"Milk would be nice." She drew a deep breath, sighed and looked around the room.

Sonja walked toward the kitchen, turned and said, "After you've settled down and had some milk, you need to call your mother and tell her where you are. She's probably worried half to death."

"Mom might be, but Fritz sure don't give a damn. Maybe, I'll call her tomorrow before she goes to work."

"No, immediately after you've had some milk." Sonja went into the kitchen, and when she returned she saw Doris standing beside her bookshelf.

"Where'd you get all these books? I never seen this many books, other than at the library, of course. Have you read all of them?"

Sonja nodded and handed her the glass. "Since I retired from teaching, I have a lot of extra time. My father sends me all his books after he's done reading them."

"My dad, my real dad that is, used to read to me at bed time when I was a kid. Fritz hates books, and Mom's too busy with her jobs and all." She gulped half of the milk and wiped her mouth with the back of her hand. "I could read in my room at night, but I just can't seem to concentrate lately. I can't even keep passing grades at school any more." She looked at the floor. "That's why I decided to drop out."

"I'm sorry to hear that, but, there are more practical matters at the moment. You, or I, must call your parents right away to let them know that you're safe."

"I'll talk to Mom, but not Fritz. He was so drunk he won't remember that I left, or why." She drank the rest of the milk. "He came home from the bar, and got on my case about my eating habits." She wiped her mouth a second time and handed back the empty glass. "Said I ate like a slob."

"He was drunk, and he told you that?" Mildred rose from the couch and approached Doris and Sonja. "Goodness, what were you doing that upset him?"

"Me 'an Teddy, he's my kid brother, licked peanut butter off our fingers while we listened to *The Lone Ranger* on the radio. I know that wasn't lady-like, but we were just goofing around." She looked up at Sonja. "I guess you can call, but don't tell them where I am."

Sonja felt Doris had withheld details about the real reason she ran away from Fritz, and she repressed a memory of an incident with her father when she was Doris' age. She decided not to question Doris further.

"I'll talk to your mother and tell her that you're safe at my place." She walked toward the kitchen and looked back, "You will be staying with Mildred and me tonight. Tomorrow, when we're alert, we'll decide what we should do." Doris and Mildred sat back on the couch.

When Sonja returned, she said, "It's all set. Your mother agrees you can stay here for now and…" She thought Doris had gone until she saw Mildred's eyes flash from hers to the girl's head resting on her lap. Mildred had either guided it, or it had found its way there on its own accord. Doris was sound asleep, and all expressions of fear, anger and cynicism had blended into one of peaceful repose.

"I thought she fainted when she fell on me like this." Mildred seemed more concerned than disgusted. "But, I think she just fell asleep."

"I'm afraid your bed for the night has been usurped by our young guest." With all the propriety she could muster, "If it is all right with you, you can share mine tonight."

Without answering, Mildred retrieved the pillow, sheets and blanket from the closet and spread them on the couch while Sonja directed a sleepy Doris to the bathroom. Mildred carted her teacup and Doris' empty glass to the kitchen. They retreated into Sonja's bedroom and stood looking into the front room until Doris returned, crawled under the sheets and let out a deep sigh.

When Mildred tiptoed toward the bathroom, Sonja whispered, "Leave the light on and the door open so Doris won't be frightened in a strange dark house." Sonja sat at her dresser and stared into the mirror. A flood of memories washed over her; that summer thirty years ago when Mildred accompanied her to Bovine, she with a teaching contract and Mildred with no immediate job prospect crammed into a small apartment. So much had happened since then. She saw Mildred's reflection as she walked into the room.

"I'm ready. Which side should I take?"

"You decide." She watched Mildred remove her slippers, cover her head with her sleeping cap and gracefully slide under the covers. "I'll be right back."

When Sonja returned, she folded back her half the covers, sat on the edge of the bed and lowered her head to the pillow. As she pulled the sheet to her chin, she realized they were lying on the same sides as when they shared a bed many years ago.

In the cover of darkness *good nights* were exchanged and, after an extended silence, Sonja admitted, "I need to be held."

CHAPTER THIRTY-ONE
DORIS' NEW HOME

Thelma scratched *tea* from the list she had prepared immediately after Sonja called, and she inspected the rest of items on the kitchen table: *flowered table cloth, fresh baked bread, butter, grape and strawberry jams, molasses cookies, milk, coffee, cream and sugar*. Maybe add raspberry sauce. If they don't want butter or jam, they could dunk their bread, one of Freddie's favorite treats. She pushed away thoughts of Freddie and couldn't imagine Sonja dunking bread. Butter and jam would have to do.

From her to-do list she checked off: *scrub kitchen floor, wash hair, wipe sink and stove, put out clean towels and toss dirty ones into basement*. Sonja and her surprise visitor will just have to understand how little time she had to make the house and herself presentable.

The porch! They were due to arrive anytime, and she had forgotten the dirtiest room in the house. She looked in horror at the wash basin and the slop-pail, both full of grimy water covered with an oily film. Dirty towels lay crumpled and strewn across the mud-tracked floor. Few coats, shoes and boots remained since the men needed to dress warm for their work in the field that day, but the smell of manure still hung heavy in the air. Maybe her guests could come through the back door into the front room. It had been sealed for the winter, but after Christmas she made Freddie open it and drag the tree out that way. She felt her chest heave and tears run down her cheeks.

She bit her fist and muttered, "I cannot cry. Keep busy. Don't think about him now."

Methodically, she dumped the slop pail on the shrubs alongside the house, emptied the basin into the pail, and rinsed it with cold water from the tap. She wiped everything dry with the soiled towel and hid it behind the curtain that masked the toilet and shower. Freddie had installed them. Last night after grumbling to her mother about Freddie's misfortune, she cried herself to sleep and, all morning, she kept busy to avoid thinking about him. Until now. She sat on the top lid of the toilet and allowed herself an unrestrained cry. She thought about the day she took him to school, and Sonja told her she needed time to grieve the death of her mother. Now, with Freddie gone, she felt that same grief even though he wasn't dead.

Back in the kitchen, she dried her eyes with her apron and checked her personal appearance in the mirror above the sink. She looked pale except for the red around her eyes. Pinching her cheeks, she decided to buy some rouge from York's drug counter next time she went to town. Her hair looked rained-on and sun-dried. She picked up the comb that lay beside the sink where her father left it, but seeing knots of his gray fuzz between the teeth, decided not to use it. She put it in the cabinet behind the mirror with his razor and shaving mug. *Why can't he shave in the porch like the boys?* She attempted to fluff her hair with both hands and remembered the soufflé she attempted years ago from a recipe in a magazine. George had told her it looked like cow-shit after the chickens picked it clean. She felt a chill run down her back as she heard a car slow and then turn into the driveway. Why couldn't she go to Sonja's house to meet her young friend? And should she call her Sonja or Miss West in front of this person?

She greeted them at the door. "I see you had no trouble finding the place." Embarrassed by her silly comment, Thelma blushed, inadvertently adding the color she failed to acquire in front of the mirror.

"Hello, Thelma. I always knew you lived just down the road from the school, but I never drove out this way. I see you have a beautiful farm."

"Thank you, Sonja." The name came to her naturally. "Now, please, come into my not-so-beautiful house."

They stood in the porch. "Thelma, I would like you to meet Doris Hopkins. Doris, this is Thelma Rastner."

"Hi." Doris flipped her hair out of her eyes and looked around the room.

"I remember you." Thelma waited for Doris to face her. "From the library. You helped Freddie and me find a book last fall, the day we got our driver's license."

240

"I told Miss West that we met, but I didn't think you'd remember me." She peered into the kitchen. "Did Iggy like the book?"

"Yes, very much." She wondered why Doris would remember such a detail.

"I was glad when I heard we was coming out here to visit."

Thelma glanced toward Sonja and then back at the girl. "Let's go into the kitchen. I have a small lunch set out." From habit she wiped her hands on the apron, the one she planned to take off before her guests arrived.

"Look at Thelma's table." Sonja touched Doris' arm. "Why don't you sit here at the end."

"Pa sits there." Thelma spoke without thinking. "But, he and Iggy are gone. Please, have a seat."

"Okay. Like I'm the queen."

"Yeah, something like that." Thelma attempted to bow and everyone laughed. She paused, then sat next to Doris.

Sonja remained standing. "Circumstances brought Doris to me but, with Mildred staying, my little house is quite cramped." Her eyes moved from Doris to Thelma. "She needs a place to stay for a while." She sat at the end of the table opposite Doris and became quiet.

"I already feel like she belongs here, and she can stay forever if she wants to." God had sent this girl to make up for Freddie. The house had felt quite empty with just her, Pa and Iggy, and this vibrant young girl could change all that.

Thelma paid scant attention to Sonja as she added details of Doris' situation. She watched Doris touch the jars of jam and sniff at the bread. When Thelma cut thick slices from the loaf, Doris held one close to her nose and sighed.

"You can have both butter and jam. If you'd like to dunk your bread, I have raspberry sauce in the refrigerator or, maybe, a bowl of thick cream with sugar. Iggy always likes that."

"I love raspberries." Doris' eyes lit up.

"Yes, me too, please." Sonja reached for a slice of bread. "When I was a child my father and I dunked bread, much to the annoyance of my mother. I would love to try it again, especially in raspberry sauce and maybe a little of that thick cream you mentioned."

As Thelma went to the refrigerator to get the raspberries and cream that she had earlier decided against, she asked, "Is it all right with Doris' folks if she stays with us?"

"They don't…" Doris glanced at Sonja, paused, and fixed her eyes on the slice of bread in her hands. She tore it in half.

"Mrs. Knox agreed to the arrangement for now, but she wants Doris to go back to school soon."

"Mrs. Knox?"

"Doris' mother is remarried and has a different last name. I'm afraid Doris lost her father when she was still in grade school."

"Fritz ain't my real father." She flinched. "I mean, Fritz isn't my real father."

"Doris, do you want to stay here?" Thelma felt Doris' eyes fix on hers.

"Oh! Yes." The *oh* an expression of surprise, the *yes* one of conviction.

That evening, Thelma intercepted Iggy at the porch and handed him a clean shirt. "Be sure to wash up good before you come in for supper. We got company."

He hung his coat on a hook and pulled off his boots. "Pa's still plowing. Might be a little late for supper." He unbuttoned his shirt and the top half of his long johns. "Was that Miss West's car I saw when I came in from the field?"

"Yes, and she brought one of her friends to stay with us for a while. Come in and meet her when you're done."

He stripped to the waist and repeated her instructions. "I better wash up real good."

Thelma allowed time for him to make himself presentable, but not so much that he'd changed his mind and escaped back to the barn. "Come with me, Doris. I want you to meet my brother, Iggy." She walked into the porch, and Doris stopped in the doorway. When Thelma pulled Iggy closer and prepared to introduce him, she noticed both of them smile as their eyes met. She felt foolish that she worried they wouldn't like each other.

"Doris, this is my brother, Iggy." Her grip tightened on his arm. "This is Doris, Iggy. She came with Miss West today, and she'll be staying with us for a while." She hoped mentioning Sonja would ease the tension she expected, but his arm felt relaxed.

"When you said Miss West's friend I 'spected maybe, Mildred." He shook off Thelma's hand. "But you're from the library."

"Yeah, and you scared me half to death the day you returned your book." She stepped into the porch. "You caught me sprawled out on the floor like some kind of hooker." She looked at Thelma. "Oops, sorry."

"Iggy and I know what a hooker is. I'm sure Iggy didn't feel that way."

"I was scared." He grimaced. "That sure was a spooky place, just like the Donnelley house me and Thelma saw." He kicked his work-shirt under the sink. "I was just washing up for supper. I get real dirty in the field." He looked at Doris, but she seemed to be fascinated at something behind him. "That was sure a good book. It's my favorite." He turned his head in the directions she was staring. "About Ignatius Donnelley. My real name is Ignatius too." He put his hand on the pump next to the sink. "But everyone calls me Iggy."

"What is that? The red thing with an arm on one side and a dog's snout on the other?"

"That's a water pump, but we hardly never use it no more. Pa put a 'lectric one in the basement, and the water comes out this faucet." He turned the handle and water splashed into an empty grimy basin. "We keep the old one just for emergencies. We gotta toilet that flushes, too. Me 'n Freddie installed it." He looked at Thelma. "Well, I helped Freddie."

As Iggy pushed the curtain aside exposing the solitary fixture with lid in the upright position, Thelma grimaced and said, "This bathroom's for the men so they don't traipse through the house. You and I use the one upstairs." Although he must have removed his chew before he came into the porch, she noticed brown specks in darkened saliva when he grinned. She was sure Doris noticed them.

He pulled the curtain all the way back and said, "We got a shower. Actually, it ain't a real good shower. Pa ain't put in a hot water heater yet. Before church on Sunday Pa and I use it anyway."

Seeing Doris' startled look, Thelma said, "Upstairs there's a bathtub. We have to heat water in the kitchen and lug it up there, but we don't have to take cold showers."

"I think I need to use that bathroom now." Doris looked slightly pale. "Did you say it was upstairs?"

"Yes, it's just off my bedroom, where we put your luggage this afternoon." Thelma had wondered how someone who just ran away would have so much stuff, then realized a trip to her parent's home was the errand Sonja needed to make before they came to the farm. "Take your time and relax on my bed before Pa gets home. I'll call you when supper's ready."

Thelma walked to the sink, sloshed the water in the basin and dumped it. She watched it swirl around as it drained into the slop-pail below. Iggy looked over her shoulder into the mirror and patted his wet hair. "What do you think of her?"

"She sure is pretty."

"I mean about her staying with us for a while?" She folded her arms, anxious for his answer.

"After that time in the library, I never 'spected to see her again." He grabbed his shaving mug and brush from the shelf, added water and whipped the cake-soap at the bottom into lather. "Is she staying long?" As he raked the brush through three day's growth, black stubble peeked through white foam.

"Just until she gets things right with her parents." She patted down his collar. "I think I'll fix up Arnie's room for her."

"That's Freddie's room."

"And Doris' room, for a little while."

****

When Doris came downstairs, she saw an old man sitting on the chair that had been hers earlier. She shook his huge, rough but warm hand when Thelma introduced them, and said, "Pleased to meet you, Sir."

Iggy laughed and said, "Everybody calls Pa 'Svez'. His real name is Sylvester." Iggy blushed and suddenly became quiet.

Doris wondered if mentioning his father's name embarrassed Iggy, and became concerned about what she should call him, if anything. She refused to call Fritz dad, and usually just said "hey, you" because she knew it made him mad.

She felt relieved when Thelma said, "Why don't you call him 'Pa' like Iggy and I do?"

"Yeah, just call me Pa." Svez smiled, "Or Grandpa if you like."

"Thank you," and after some hesitation, she added, "Pa. And thank you, Thelma and Iggy, for letting me stay here."

Pa said, "Let's eat."

Thelma said, "Iggy, say grace."

Thelma's order surprised Doris, and she immediately shoved her hands on to her lap under the table.

Iggy looked at Thelma, clapped his hands together and said, "Grace." Thelma and Iggy laughed, Pa stabbed his fork into a pork hock smothered with sauerkraut and Doris breathed a sigh of relief.

Between each mouthful and sometimes while chewing her food, Doris told stories about some of her teachers at school. She enjoyed making everyone laugh. After supper she offered to help with the dishes while Pa and Iggy went back to the barn.

"Well, Doris, what do you think? Will you be comfortable living here with Pa, Iggy and me?"

"Where does your other brother live, the one who came to the library with you? Freddie."

"I'm afraid Freddie had to move back with his real dad." Doris saw Thelma wipe her eyes as she walked to the stove and came back with dirty pots and pans. Confused, she remained silent until Thelma said, "We've got an extra bedroom for you, but maybe you should sleep in my room tonight. Tomorrow, we can get your room ready."

"Thank you. I would like that."

Doris slept very little. All night she heard strange house noises and was glad Thelma had offered to share her bed. She pretended to be sleeping in the morning when Thelma quietly slipped out from under the covers and got dressed in the dark. She rolled to Thelma's side of the bed, wrapped the quilt tight around her and slept soundly until the sun shone in on her face.

After getting dressed for the day, she walked into the room Thelma said would be hers. It appeared to be empty, but when she looked out the window she saw Iggy standing on a roof of some sort. He gazed toward a field behind the barn where a green tractor belched black smoke and chugged across the horizon. She was about to leave unnoticed when he spoke but didn't turn her way.

"That's last year's corn Pa's plowing under. It never got big enough to make silage." He turned and looked at her.

To her relief, there was no sign of tobacco juice nor did he display any of the mannerisms that bothered her. He just looked sad.

"Cows need more'n just hay."

"Did the cows die?"

He ducked and stepped back into the room. "No, they just didn't give much milk. They gotta eat silage."

"What stuff is that?"

"Chopped up corn, stalks, cobs and all."

" Does that makes you sad?"

"No, but this room does. It used to be Freddie's room."

"I know. Thelma told me. It was your uncle's room, too. Does that make you sad?"

"No, he's dead. He died…" Iggy stopped in mid sentence.

"Did he die in this room?" Doris feared she went too far with her questions when she saw his face tighten and his breathing increased. But, he didn't make those little movements with his head that annoyed her.

"I think he died in the hay mow."

Doris suspected Iggy tried to shelter her from a harsh truth, and it pleased her.

"Freddie's dog was with him." He rubbed his eyes then gazed out the window. "Freddie used to sit out there at night and do his thinking. He was a good thinker." He gestured toward the window. "Me and Freddie built this balcony. If the house caught fire, Arnie could climb out there and jump." He shook his head. "Arnie was too old to jump."

Doris stepped through the window and stood on the balcony. The sun felt warm on her face, but the air was cold. She came back into the room and shivered.

"There's no lock, but Arnie used to push furniture in front of the door when he didn't want anyone to come in. Pa said a lock wasn't safe in case he died or something." His eyes avoided hers. "But he died in the hay mow."

Thelma appeared behind Iggy and put her hand on his shoulder. "So, this is where you guys are. I been waiting breakfast on you." She smiled and came into the room.

"Let's get some bright paint and make it cheerful in here. You can sleep with me a few more nights while the paint dries." She looked at Doris. "If you bring some of your old throw-away clothes, we can make a quilt like the ones Ma made for Iggy and me."

CHAPTER THIRTY-TWO
PART OF THE FAMILY

Svez stood barefoot on the cold grass, wet with the early morning dew and waited for his bladder to release. He blamed the indoor plumbing. Didn't seem right for a man to piss inside his house, but even outside on cool spring mornings he couldn't relieve the pressure. A lock on Arnie's door? His irritation extended beyond his immediate problem. That girl had been with them one week and already she wanted to change things. What was she afraid of? Arnie slept in that room thirty years without a lock. Freddie didn't even close the door when he slept there.

He suddenly felt self-conscious standing in his long johns, and he turned away from the house. *Modesty*, Thelma explained when she told him and Iggy they couldn't walk around the house in their underwear anymore. Some of Miss West's fancy words just plain don't belong on the farm, but he agreed to be more careful. His stream started but immediately stopped. Damn. He looked toward the field behind the barn where rows of limp and broken cornstalks had endured the winter, waiting to be plowed under in preparation for spring planting. Laid to rest in the ground. Sometimes, he too, wished for that.

A yellowish light swept over him, and the dew glistened on the tender shoots of green peeking through the gray winter mat. He turned and through the window saw Thelma walk into the kitchen. He quit trying to urinate, but didn't button-up and go back into the house. She had said Iggy might wander into Doris' room some night, but who did she really worry about? Memories of a cold morning just like this one many years ago seeped into his consciousness—the day after Elizabeth's funeral—but guilt, not grief, washed over him like a bucket of cold water. A shiver began at his feet, moved to his groin and up his back.

The dam in his bladder burst, and he didn't even bother to turn away from the house. He relished in his relief as he studied the stars slowly retreating from the twilight. Soon, he'd need the rubber hose just like Arnie. But, who'd help him use it? He shook off the last few drops, shoved his penis back inside his Union Suit and headed toward the house.

"I'll just do it to myself when the time comes," he muttered, as he trudged through the kitchen, stopped in the front room and turned to face Thelma.

"Do what, Pa?" Sparks shot up as she stoked the coals in the stove.

"Can't see why Doris needs to lock herself up at night."

"You're cheerful this morning." She covered the flames with the iron lid and slid the coffeepot over it. Her voice followed him into his bedroom. "Coffee will be ready in a minute."

He came back into the kitchen fastening the straps to his overalls. "I'll be back for coffee later," and he headed out the door. He stooped to ruffle Babe's neck as she nuzzled up to him. "You miss him, too, don't you?" He checked her ears for ticks. "And Arnie." He let her follow him as far as the barn but made her stay outside. Through the top half of the door, he pointed toward the pasture. "When the cows stay out all night, you'll get to fetch them."

He collected the hoses and suction cups from the hooks where they had been hung to dry and fastened them to the canister, but he waited for Iggy to strap the contraption to the cows and attach it to their teats. Never could quite get the hang of it. He looked at the row of empty stanchions where Arnie's, then Freddie's herd once stood. A wave of sadness passed through him just as Iggy burst into the barn.

"Thelma forgot to wake me." Iggy stopped and stared at the milk bucket, assembled and ready for use. "I kin do it."

"What's with the lock on Arnie's door?" He waited until Iggy tossed the strap around a heifer and attached the suction cups. "Thelma said she's gotta have one." Milk pulsed through the hose into the bucket.

"Guess she's afraid I might stumble into her room and scare her some night." Iggy stood and patted the animal's rump. "I wouldn't do that."

"Course you wouldn't." He walked toward the door. "I better go tell them they can have their lock."

248

The coffee simmered on the stove, but Thelma wasn't in the kitchen. Svez poured a cupful and took it with him upstairs where he found her in Arnie's room. He never got used to calling it Freddie's room, and now they wanted him to call it Doris' room.

Thelma whispered, "We need to be quiet, so we don't wake Doris."

He tried to hide his disgust, but she must have sensed it.

"She's still adjusting to the strange house. Been sleeping with me all week, but now she's ready for her own room. Iggy painted it real nice, and I made some curtains."

He never thought of his house as being strange and wondered what adjustment anyone would need. "She knows she's welcome. I told her so the first night she came here." He remembered his reason for coming back to the house. "Is that why we need to put a lock on her door?"

"When Iggy felt sad, he used to sleep in Freddie's bed. Some night he might wake up and forget this is Doris' room. I don't want him to accidentally walk in on her."

"I don't think he'd do that, unless he was drunk." He followed her gaze to his feet. "Oops, I didn't mean to drag cow shit into Freddie's, ah, Doris' room."

"Don't worry. We're going to give the room a good cleaning today."

As he stared at his shoes and the flakes of dried manure scattered around them, he felt awkward, like he didn't belong there. He looked up at his daughter and said, "You don't think that I would ever…"

"Pa, you needn't beat yourself up for something in the past, long forgot. No, I don't want the lock on the door because of you. Doris has been hurt and she just needs to feel safe. She knows it's all in her imagination. She told me so."

"Well, if it makes her happy, better buy one when you take the eggs to town. Iggy can help you install it. If they're playing Bovine Bingo out behind Cunningham's, she might get a kick outta watching for a while."

"That game's disgusting."

"Why?" He never heard his daughter express such an opinion. "It's just some harmless gambling. Never hurts the cow. That's what she'd do in the pasture, 'cept if she shits on someone's lucky number he wins a few dollars."

"Sonja said it's cruel to treat a poor dumb animal that way, making her stand in the cold with those men jeering and cursing

her. Even an animal should have some privacy when nature calls."
She shook her head. "Honestly, men can be so crude."

He left the room thinking she sounded like her old teacher.
Back in the kitchen, he emptied his cup into the sink and refilled
from the pot still steaming on the stove. He sat at the table and
wondered what happened to the hose that he used when Arnie had
his problem.

****

The next morning, noises from someone pounding interrupted
Doris' nightmare and became a part of it. Stark naked, Fritz fisted
his erection with one hand, held a broken lock in the other and
stood besides the door hanging loose from its hinges. She tried to
scream, maybe did scream, as the intruder disappeared and the
door repaired itself. She sat up, pulled the covers to her chin and
looked around. She recognized Thelma's voice from somewhere
outside the room.

"Quiet, Iggy. You'll wake her up."

"I can't pound quiet. The hammer's 'sposed to make noise."

Thelma's voice continued whisper-like as if she was reading
someone to sleep.

He responded, "Yup, Yup. Just like you read in them
'structions. When I turned the key that little thing came right out.
That's what locks the door."

Doris thought about Iggy's strange mannerisms as she snuggled
under Thelma's quilt. She didn't worry about him coming into
her room when she slept, and Pa seemed too old to even come
upstairs. But, Thelma had insisted they put a lock on her door.
Maybe she shouldn't have told her about Fritz' habit of busting
into her private space. He mostly just embarrassed Doris and made
her mad. Except for that night she ran away to Miss West's house.
She had been real scared that time.

The warm bed felt wonderful, but she wanted to be with her
new friends who were so concerned about her comfort and security.
Swinging her feet out from under the covers and onto the cold
floor, she gasped.

"See, all that pounding woke her up."

"Told you, I can't hammer quiet. What's she sleep so late for
anyhow?"

Doris pranced across the cold floor to the closet-turned-
bathroom, and sat on the icy toilet seat. She'd get used to living
on a farm, maybe even let Iggy show her the cows like he promised.

Nothing could smell worse than the coats that hung in the porch after the men wore them in the barn, except maybe their overshoes. Thelma wouldn't even allow them in the house. Said he stood in the manure when he cleaned the gutter. *Shit* had yet to become common usage for her, but she enjoyed hearing it used quite different from the way she had in conversation with her friends. The men always scraped the bottom of their shoes on a piece of metal sticking out of the ground near the porch creating a small pile of that stuff. In the porch, they washed their hands and face with cold water from a chipped basin. The pail under the sink, usually full and spilling onto the floor, and the dirty towel hanging from a hook on the wall were disgusting to look at, but she didn't have to use them. She shuddered when Thelma told her about the slop pail they used to keep under the kitchen sink for table scraps and coffee grounds to feed to the pigs. Except for that, she could get used to everything else.

Doris dressed quickly and went to the room being prepared for her.

"Mornin' Miss Doris. We got a new lock for your door, and only Thelma has the extra key."

Doris half-expected him to lift his cap and bow, but he just smiled at her. She wished he wouldn't get so flustered every time they were together.

Thelma explained. "We got two keys, just in case of an emergency."

"Emergency?" Doris couldn't imagine anything urgent out here in the country.

"In case you get sick and faint, or something." Thelma sounded defensive.

"And in case of fire." Iggy gurgled and pointed toward the window. "You could climb out there and jump from the roof me and Freddie built." He swallowed and cleared the saliva at the corners of his mouth with his tongue. "If Thelma couldn't find the key fast enough."

"The lock is just fine, but not necessary. Of course, I want Thelma to have an extra one. If there is a fire, or if I decide to elope, I could use Arnie's balcony." Thelma and Iggy grinned. She envisioned Romeo below but Burt's image invaded her fantasy. She half-chuckled and half gasped. "I mean, if I ever get a boyfriend who'd actually want to marry me."

CHAPTER THIRTY-THREE
SYLVESTER'S LAMENT
(Summer, 1951)

Svez stood by the kitchen table and stared into the sugar bowl. Iggy had emptied it into his cup, gulped the remaining coffee and ran out the door, his only goodbye, "Doris 'n Thelma's already left with the car." The screen door and then the pickup door slammed shut, and Svez listened as the truck coughed, sputtered and rattled out the driveway.

He didn't like sugar or cream, but today his coffee tasted bitter. His family had begged him to join them at the Independence-Day celebration in town, but he wanted to tend to his cornfield. The stalks, already knee-high-by-the-fourth-of-July, had been stripped and trampled by a hailstorm early that morning and he needed to plow under the damaged crop. *A fitting way for a man to spend his seventy-sixth birthday.* His cynicism made him shudder.

With familiar measured steps, he walked to the pantry where Thelma kept her supplies, and he pulled open the flour bin by mistake. He touched and tasted it to be sure. He was about to open another, when a photograph of his parents on the wall caught his attention. His mother sat wearing a long dishwater colored dress that squeezed her waist and made her breasts appear large. His father stood to the left of her, one hand on her shoulder and the other holding his hat in front of him. Pubba, the name Svez and his brothers had given him, had insisted his wife always be at his right side whether sitting at the table, walking down the street or having their picture taken. Svez felt his emotions well up. He gently removed the picture from the wall, wiped some flour dust from the glass and carried it to his bedroom where he propped it up on his dresser. He sat on the bed, still unmade since Thelma had been in too much of a hurry to run off to town that morning, and he wondered why she moved the picture from the front room. He spent a rare moment thinking of his parents. Pubba claimed his youngest son's arrival on the one-hundredth birthday of his newly adopted country was a good omen. God had given him good neighbors, good weather for his first crop and a child long after his wife was considered too old to bear children. Sylvester, the name sounded American to his German immigrant parents, would be the son to care for them in their old age.

Svez had fulfilled his duty to his parents and kept a promise made to Mumma that he would look after his brother, Arnie. Why did he feel so sad? So empty? He remembered the sugar, and on the way back through the front room he saw the picture that replaced his parent's wedding picture. In it, Freddie stood next to his bicycle contraption, a broad smile across his face.

He decided to skip coffee and start to plow instead. He needed to bury the shattered rows of corn stalks that looked like ranks of wounded and fallen soldiers after their battle with the hailstones. He couldn't stand to see these defeated warriors left to mock the remaining growing season, nor did he feel like celebrating with his family. He became mesmerized as the plow rolled the black soil into long shiny tubes from one end of the field to the other. At row's end, he automatically tripped the lever to engage the cam that hoisted the triple row of curved steel blades, and he released it for the return round. He recalled how Freddie had studied this mechanism and then welded together the pieces broken by hidden rocks. Svez buried row after row of just corn, no longer defeated soldiers, and his mind drifted back to his parents and what they had asked of him. He never complained about his responsibility to care for the generation before him or the one that followed, and he seldom regretted any decisions he had to make. That is, until last winter.

He thought about the young girl that he allowed Thelma to bring into their family, just when he was suffering his greatest loss since the death of his wife nearly two decades earlier. One orphan had come into his life to ease his grief then, and now another sort of orphan entered his small world to ease the loss of the first one. He understood that what happened to Freddie wasn't his fault, but he felt responsible. The decision hadn't been his to make. Freddie, by blood, belonged to Henry. Why was Thelma blaming him? Why did he blame himself?

He remembered that dreary January morning when he and Henry stood beside his horse though. Henry's words, "I come to git my boy," and his own grief and anger visible on shards of broken ice encrusted with green moss came back to plague him. He couldn't recall the rest of their conversation, if there had been any, but he knew he had to give up Freddie to his real father. Svez wasn't surprised because Henry had hinted at it many times, and, according to Iggy, Freddie guessed it might happen after Henry's unusual visit a few days earlier. Svez's twisted reflection on the ice held his gaze until he heard Freddie approach.

"Get your things. You gotta go with Henry." He didn't say, "…with your pa." He didn't say "…with your uncle," as Henry was sometimes called. He didn't tell him what things to get. He had loaned Freddie to help with Henry's chores before, but Freddie seemed to understand this time it was forever. For nineteen years, Svez felt comfortable that Freddie slept safely in his house. Since then, fear for Freddie's welfare kept Svez awake at nights.

Did Freddie miss Thelma and Iggy as much as they obviously missed him? Did he miss the man he always called Svez? At this thought, he chuckled. Since the night Liz died, he had secretly taught Freddie to call him by his first name, and everyone wondered why Freddie didn't call him Pa. Every time he heard Freddie use his name, he heard Liz's voice. Now Freddie was gone, and, no doubt, he blamed Svez for being sent away.

He shook off the sadness of all his losses and got back to the business of turning the wet earth to black silver.

CHAPTER THIRTY-FOUR
FREDDIE'S AWAKENING
(Summer, 1952)

The tall grass gently fell back, and the sharp staccato sound from Henry's two-cylinder John Deere created a sensory filter that obliterated most of Freddie's conscious thoughts. He cherished the monotony of fieldwork because it helped block the painful memories that plagued him. But, the pleasant odors released from sweet clover and grass as the sickle bar sliced a swath penetrated the spot in his memory he struggled to keep empty. Thoughts of Thelma and Iggy and Svez rushed in as tears streamed down his cheeks.

He replayed the scene he had watched from the machine shed between Svez and Henry when they stood at the horse trough and decided his future. He still felt the shock of being told to leave without even a chance to say good-bye to Iggy and Thelma until the following Sunday when Henry let him come back to get the rest of his things. Thelma cried while he packed his clothes, but Iggy just sat on Arnie's balcony and wouldn't talk to him. Iggy even refused to walk down to the car and hug him or shake his hand or anything. But, Freddie felt most betrayed by Svez who let this happen.

Get your things. You gotta go with Henry. These words haunted him and echoed through the noises surrounding him on the tractor, in the barn and in bed at night when the wind struck the sides of the house. Even the windmill screeched each syllable like an owl until he climbed up and greased the bearings. Henry chewed him out for that because he needed those noises to predict rain.

Come back to visit us. Like Freddie was only a guest, a nephew invited to Sunday dinner. And Svez's voice was all scratchy and cracking, like he didn't really mean it. The heat radiating off the tractor's engine made Henry's house and barn appear to quiver off in the distance, and Freddie felt the sun directly overhead. One more trip around the field and he'd return for lunch. Before Henry left for Herbert's farm that morning, he told Freddie to mow on the south forty 'til noon and then rake what he had cut yesterday. He didn't say, but Freddie knew Herbert would come to help him load the hay tomorrow. That meant a return favor at Herbert's farm, probably the next day. When they worked together, Herbert seldom talked to him but constantly swore at Henry. Freddie felt most of their arguments were about him.

Back at the house, he chewed and quickly swallowed the dried slices of summer-sausage to avoid the sharp taste of the spiced meat. He didn't put them into a sandwich because the bread smelled stale, and the green specks around the crust made him feel sick. He walked through the front room where Henry slept and slid back the curtain across the archway to his bed in what used to be a dining room. None of the rooms upstairs had been used since the boys moved out, and Henry sealed off the stairway to save heat in the winter.

The colorful quilt lay crumpled on his bed, and it reminded him of Thelma who had told him it was a gift from her and Ma. He wished he could remember Liz and liked to hear Thelma talk as if she was still alive. Every Thanksgiving, Thelma would set an extra plate for her and make Svez say a prayer before they ate. He looked at the picture of Liz that Thelma had reproduced, one for each family member. Svez kept the original on the dresser in his bedroom. Freddie didn't have a picture of his birth mother, and if Henry had one, it wasn't displayed any place in the house. He sat on the quilt, but the mattress under it didn't feel like it belonged to him.

He wanted his old bed, but Thelma said they should keep it in his room for when he came to stay overnight. He only visited on Sundays and hadn't stayed even once since he moved in January, half a year ago. Now, a girl slept there. He decided to take a short nap on Thelma's quilt, but memories of his past life began to haunt him, and he needed the monotony of driving the tractor back and forth on the field.

When the teeth of the side-rake rustled yesterday's cuttings into windrows, the sweet aroma of hay drying in the warm breeze attacked his senses. His anger, cloaked in sadness, surfaced and triggered an idea that he had been trying to squelch since last week when he spent Independence Day with Thelma, Iggy and Doris. If she ran away, why couldn't he?

What about a job like her friend had at Harrington Manufacturing? Maybe Freddie could make enough money to pay someone to take his place on Henry's farm. He thought about the cows that Arnie had given him. They were supposed to be the seeds of a herd to take with him to his own farm, like George and Herman and Ralph. But, they just got mixed in with Henry's, and Freddie never knew what happened to his share of the milk check. He was used to asking Thelma for spending money, so that part didn't seem different. Most of the time he had no need for any.

His mind strayed back to Doris and his mixed feelings toward her since their time spent together that day. He seldom saw her at any of Thelma's dinners because she went back to her ma's home in Harrington most weekends.

The day Thelma introduced her, Doris asked after they finished eating, "Wanna come up to my room, your old room, I guess, and see what we did to it? Iggy painted the walls, and Thelma made curtains." She giggled, "Pa made Iggy put a lock on the door to keep out the bogey man."

"It weren't my room. It was Arnie's room. I just slept there for a while after he died." He told her he didn't want to see it. He resented the casual way she referred to his family, letting him know she now belonged with them.

However, since he spent that day with her, he started to feel different. Herbert had agreed to do his chores that afternoon, and Henry gave him a dollar to spend. Freddie took the farm pickup to town where he met with Thelma, Iggy and Doris.

When Larry Collins stopped to say hello, Iggy said, "Oops, I gotta go." He faced Freddie. "Why don't you come back home sometime. We can hang out together. The perch are starting to bite."

Freddie craved for their time together on the bank of the creek, but Iggy walked away with his buddy before they had a chance to share some of the memories.

Thelma said, "Pa's not coming to town today. Said he gotta plow under the corn that got beat down by the hail." Her eyes followed Iggy and Larry to the beer stand until they blended into the crowd. "How'd Henry's corn survive the storm?"

"He ain't hardly planted any corn, mostly hay. His cows don't give much milk anyway. They're kind of old." Freddie didn't want to talk about crops or cattle. He wanted to tell Thelma that he missed her, but it didn't feel right to mention that in front of Doris. He probably wouldn't have told her anyway.

Doris said, "Iggy showed me some of the contraptions you built on the farm. I really like the bicycle that doesn't go any place." Freddie tried to smile. "You should get a job at Harrington Manufacturing. Burt, a boy who was in my grade at school, started working there and gets a dollar an hour. He only took shop in high school and didn't finish any of the projects his teacher assigned."

"I never went to high school," Freddie admitted.

"High school's dumb. I quit my senior year, and I'm glad I did. I don't need high school for what I want to do."

"What do you plan to do, now that you mention it?" Thelma glanced toward the beer stand and then faced Doris.

"Oh, I don't know. Stay with you guys, until Pa gets tired of me and kicks me out."

He wanted to say Svez wasn't her pa, but he just glared at her instead.

"We'll never ask you to leave." Thelma turned from Doris to Freddie. "She's one of us now." Doris smiled and Freddie frowned. Facing Doris again, "What would you like to do when you get older?"

"I don't know. Maybe get a job, get married and have tons of kids. But, I suppose I better find a husband first."

"Ain't you gonna marry that guy you see on weekends?" Maybe if she got hitched and moved away, he could get Arnie's room back, at least on Sundays.

"Who, Burt? He ain't a real boyfriend."

Freddie wondered what a real boyfriend, or real girlfriend, was.

"Let's go to Emma's and have some ice cream." Doris grabbed Thelma's hand and reached toward Freddie. "Iggy and his friend, too, if we can find them."

Freddie resented Doris for pushing people around, yet he also felt strangely excited by it as he followed them through the crowd.

"I work there as a waitress every morning." She turned back toward Freddie and kept walking. "Iggy gives me a ride when he takes the milk to town, and I always find a way home after the noon rush. At least, I ain't had to walk home yet."

Freddie didn't want to go to Emma's. He didn't want ice cream. He didn't want to be with Thelma and Doris. At the café, people stood in line, but Doris walked to an empty booth, stacked the dirty dishes onto a tray and gestured for Thelma and Freddie to sit. Davie Smith, the neighbor kid who worked at Emma's as a busboy, protested that someone had been waiting to sit there. Doris just handed him the tray and slapped him on the butt. He stuck his finger into a glass half filled with water and snapped a spatter onto her face. She gave him the finger.

Doris and Thelma chatted, and Freddie watched Davie clear tables. The little kid who used to sneak onto the school grounds at recess to play had a job that earned him money. Freddie envied him.

"Freddie looks bored," Doris said to Thelma as she jabbed his arm. "Let's go back and find Iggy and his friend."

Larry Collins stood at the bar, planks across wooden sawhorses, drinking beer with some buddies. "Iggy? Ain't seen him. Guess he staggered off toward his pickup."

Thelma looked at Freddie. "We better find him and get him home. I made him bring the pickup so he could go back early to do chores. Doris and I came with the car and planned to stay for the fireworks."

"I'll drive his pickup back. Maybe I can do his chores tonight." Freddie wanted to be close to Iggy. He wanted to hide in Svez's barn.

"We better leave, too. I don't want Iggy to be home alone when he's this drunk." She turned to Doris. "You can use my car to bring Freddie back to town after he finishes the chores."

When they got to the farm, Freddie was glad Svez wasn't there. He didn't want to talk to him, and he certainly didn't want to hear Doris call him Pa.

While driving Freddie back to town, Doris asked, "Do you still have to do the chores tonight at that place where you're living?"

"I don't live there. I'm just staying there for the time being. One of Henry's boys is doing the chores." He wondered what kind of favor Herbert would expect of him in return.

"I got the day off, too," she giggled. "My job at the café is kind of a joke. As a matter of fact, I ain't got any responsibility worth mentioning. I was in real trouble until Miss West helped me find Thelma, and," her face now serious, "your family. They're real nice."

Freddie had clasped his hands to his knees, and she put her hand on top of his.

"You're real nice, too." He slid his hands free, and she returned hers to the steering wheel.

Her touch excited him or agitated him, he couldn't decide which. They drove the rest of the way in silence, but when Doris stopped at Henry's pickup, she said, "Since neither of us has to be any place special, why don't we hang out for a while? The sun's down and pretty soon it'll be dark enough."

Freddie said, "I gotta get home."

Doris grabbed his arm. "Hurry, the fireworks are about to begin."

CHAPTER THIRTY-FIVE
FREDDIE AND DORIS
(Spring, 1953)

Freddie created pleasurable fantasies throughout the fall harvest, but they became jumbled and finally haunted him after his long winter isolation. By spring, his hopes to see Doris more often and his plans to get a job in Harrington fizzled like the fireworks on that night when the thunderstorm struck. On a grassy field behind the church, Freddie and Doris had huddled under the horse-blanket they found in the back of Henry's pickup and waited until the drizzle became a downpour. When word came that the fireworks had been cancelled, they held the blanket over their heads and ran back to Thelma's car. Freddie continued to hold it as Doris got in, and then he tossed it into the back of the truck parked alongside. He stood in the rain and looked at her through the partially opened window.

"Sure got wet in a hurry." He raised the collar of his shirt and pulled it tight around his neck.

"No shit, Shakespeare." She lifted a sleeve to her nose. "Shit is what this smells like, too. Don't you ever wash that thing?"

"I guess it's getting a pretty good washing now."

"Well, don't just stand out in the rain." She rolled up the window.

Through the glass, he saw her point toward the passenger door. He ran around, pulled it open and, in the light from the dome, he saw the bare flesh of her stomach as she used the hem of her blouse to wipe away dark stains from under her eyes.

"Take off your shirt or you'll get Thelma's seat all wet."

Freddie obeyed before he realized he would be sitting next to a girl practically naked. The rain felt cool on his bare back.

"I'd take mine off too, but a girl ain't supposed to do that. Guys are just plain luckier than gals. Well, are you going to just stand there?"

He got in and laid the shirt over his knees letting it drip onto the floor. He looked away, but felt her stare at him for a long time.

"You ever been kissed by a girl."

"No." He blushed.

"Aw, come on. Someone must have kissed you at one of them barn dances I hear so much about.

Thelma used to kiss me, 'til I started school. Wouldn't let her, after that."

"That don't count because she was your sister, almost your mother." She kept eye contact until he became embarrassed and looked down. "You want me to kiss you?" She put her hands on the steering wheel and leaned back. "Not like boyfriend-girlfriend. Maybe just like you was kissed before you got too big."

Drops of water trickled down his neck and forehead. He wanted to wipe them away, but he couldn't get his hands to move.

She pointed to his shirt. "Give me that." She didn't wait but grabbed it, wrung it onto the floor and wiped his face. She put her hand on his chest as she leaned close and touched her lips to his.

"I better go." He leaned back against the door and stared at her.

"You liked it. I know you did." She pursed her lips and peered at him through spread fingers as she moved her hand back and forth in front of her face. "I can tell."

"I guess so." The dome light reflected in her eyes and appeared to go on and off between the intervals.

"Then, kiss me back." She straightened and faced the windshield. "This time, open your mouth a little. Just enough for me to put my tongue through, if I decide I want to. I won't say I will. Only if I get a notion."

"Maybe I don't want to," he lied. He felt naked, back in a tub of warm water, and Thelma was washing him all over except *down there*. When he started school, Thelma made him wash that part. He remembered her kiss, not on his lips like he told Doris, but on his neck, and he felt Thelma's face touching him from ear to shoulder, the area that felt white hot at the moment. He wanted Doris to put her face there.

"Chicken." With both her hands on the steering wheel, she flung her head back and made squawking noises that sounded like a pullet laying her first egg.

He laughed and responded with a rooster crow.

264

"That's good." She faced him and leaned against the door, one foot on the floor with the other tucked under her leg. She closed her eyes. "I'm back in my bed, your bed actually, and that damn rooster just woke me up. Now, what should we do?"

On impulse, he swung forward and lost his balance. He fell against her with his open hand cupping one of her breasts.

"No, boys don't get to touch girls there." She smiled. "At least not right away."

His hand pressed tighter as he pushed himself back. "I didn't mean…"

"Try it again. I'm gonna close my eyes, so you only do what I told you." She placed one hand on his knee and one on his shoulder.

He leaned forward and kissed her with his mouth slightly open.

"There, wasn't that nice?"

"I couldn't feel your tongue."

"Didn't do it that time. "I wanted to, but it gotta be the right moment for that." She shivered, pulled back her arms and held them against her breasts.

Freddie had no intention of touching them again and wondered why she protected herself that way.

That *right moment* became the pivotal point in his fantasy into the following winter. He never dared imagine what might have happened after that touch, although sometimes in sleep and to his embarrassment, his body completed the thought for him. He was thankful it hadn't happened when they were together in the car.

His resentment of her for taking his place at Svez's evaporated, and each Sunday when he went there for dinner he hoped to see her. He hated the boy who took her away most Saturdays and returned her to her job at Emma's Café on Monday mornings. When spring fieldwork began, Henry kept him busy seven days a week and reminded him that he had spent every Sunday all winter with Thelma and Iggy, as well as Christmas. It was time he stayed home for a change.

One Sunday afternoon, after Henry accidentally backed his tractor into a stone wall, he swore loudly, and told Freddie to take the broken hitch to Svez's place to weld it. Freddie removed the part that was left on the tractor and said a job that big needed to be taken to Wentzel's Blacksmith Shop in town. After cursing Svez and his welder, Henry agreed.

Early Monday morning, Freddie dropped off the broken parts at Wentzel's, parked in the alley across from Emma's Café and waited. Soon a car double-parked near the front entrance. He saw Doris lean over, kiss the guy behind the wheel and then jump out the passenger door. The car sped away, its tires squealing. She glanced toward Henry's car and rushed into the café. He had taken the car because she would recognize Henry's pickup, but he still worried that she might have seen him. He was startled by a voice in his ear, and a face inches away. Davie Smith peered at him through the open window.

"Kind of sweet on her, are you, Freddie?"

"No, I just..."

"You know she has Burt's class ring." Davie opened the top buttons on his shirt, shook it loose nearly to his waist and raised the collar. "Wears it around her neck on a chain and lets it dangle so the guys know she's not available. Maybe they'd be less interested if she just kept her blouse closed"

"...just had to get something welded."

"At Emma's?"

"Waiting for it. Thought I'd get a cup of coffee."

"Come on in. I'm gonna smoke one and have a coke before I stock the coolers."

"Changed my mind. I gotta go."

Embarrassed and angry, yet he had seen Doris' boyfriend. Dark hair with sideburns and a black leather jacket even in summer. And she kissed him. He detested and envied him. Why wasn't he working at his dollar-an-hour job at Harrington Manufacturing?

The next Sunday, Henry relented and allowed him to have dinner at Thelma's. Would Doris be there? Did she see him spying on her? Would he ask her about the guy? On the way to Svez's place, he counted his heartbeats as they pulsed through his eardrums. When he got out of the pickup, chickens, geese, and a nanny goat scattered as Babe slowly crawled out from under the corncrib and whimpered when Freddie didn't stop to greet her. He didn't go the barn to look for Iggy, but ran to the house, stopped at the kitchen door and saw Thelma, not Doris, getting dinner ready.

"Hi, Freddie." Thelma wiped her hands on her apron and reached out as she rushed to him. He blushed when she put her hands on his cheeks, pulled his head down and touched his hair with her lips. Had Doris told her about their kiss? He wished he hadn't used the hair oil he found in Henry's cupboard.

"A goat?" Freddie never said hi or any other greeting when he visited. "Is Iggy milking goats now?"

"Might as well. The heifers all but dried up." She wiped her mouth with her apron. "Doris brought the nanny a couple of weeks ago. Fritz, her step dad, won it from a raffle at the Blue Bull Bar and couldn't keep her in town." She returned to the stove. "I wish promoters would think ahead when they come up with these big ideas."

"Is she here?" He tried to hide his anxiety, but Thelma's eyes said she understood. She always did.

"You'd like to see her, wouldn't you."

"I guess so."

"She's got a fellow, you know." She turned to face him, but he just stood in the doorway.

"Saw him drop her off at Emma's." He didn't wait for Thelma to ask her next question. He turned and walked out.

Freddie sat quietly as he ate with his family, and only gave a brief account when Svez asked about Henry's crops. His sadness peaked when Iggy talked about the Fourth-of-July celebration coming up in a few weeks. Thelma told Freddie to encourage Henry to come with him to dinner soon, but Freddie knew he would never ask him to do that. He didn't want Henry here, and today he didn't want to be here either.

A car drove into the yard and Iggy ran to the door. "It's Miss West and Doris." He hurried back to his place at the table. As Thelma rose to greet them, Doris, hands covering her face, ran through the kitchen and stomped upstairs.

"We're sorry to interrupt your dinner." Sonja glanced toward Thelma and then the rest of the family. "Hello, everyone."

Freddie felt like he was at the movies. Thelma pointed to Arnie's, now Doris' chair and Miss West sat down. Thelma returned to the table and everyone seemed to just stare at each other. Svez got up, mumbled something and shuffled outside. Iggy put his hands in his pockets and looked down at his plate. Thelma and Miss West talked, but all Freddie heard was, "He hit her and she's got a black eye." When they left the table and headed upstairs, Iggy got up and sulked out of the kitchen, his hands deep in his pockets. Freddie stared straight ahead and felt his face grow hot. The kiss that had taunted his memory since that morning in front of Emma's was replaced by a fist that sprung from a black leather sleeve and slammed into her face. He felt his fist smashing into the guy's nose. He walked to the stairway and stared up toward Doris' room where he heard loud sobs over soothing voices. He wasn't wanted up there, and it wasn't his business to beat up the guy who attacked her. He pushed that part of his anger from his consciousness.

He walked outside and watched Babe pull herself out from under Henry's pickup, her brown eyes looking sad. He nuzzled the fur around her neck, whispered "Goodbye, old girl," and kicked the nanny away from the pickup. He looked back at the window above Arnie's balcony, got into his pickup and drove off.

CHAPTER THIRTY-SIX
FREDDIE AND DORIS
(Winter, 1953)

"Let's go upstairs." Doris paused briefly in Henry's kitchen, looked around and walked directly to the boarded-up door in the front room.

"Henry got it closed off. Don't want nobody up there." Despite his and Thelma's efforts to make Henry's house presentable for her visit, Freddie sensed that the place he had lived in the past two years disgusted her.

"He don't live here now, and you can do anything you want to. It'll be yours some day, won't it?"

"He still wants to come home, but the doctors won't let him."

"He ain't gonna get better, even Thelma said so. Now get a hammer and let's go upstairs."

Freddie went to the machine shed, the only place on the farm where he felt comfortable because Henry had allowed him to make improvements and buy equipment like the welder and assorted tools. Also, Henry called it Freddie's shed and hardly ever walked in when Freddie worked there. The barn and the house remained exactly as Henry kept them, even six months after he had been confined to the nursing home following his stroke. At Thelma's Thanksgiving dinner, Doris expressed an interest in visiting Freddie at his house if he would pick her up at her Mom's the following Monday. Freddie reluctantly agreed, and the next day Thelma arrived with cleaning materials just after Freddie finished his morning chores. They met at the front door.

"I would have done this years ago, if Henry hadn't refused my help." Her hair fell loose as she removed Iggy's cap and mopped her forehead with it. They tossed out the slop pails, removed a wagon-load of trash, moved Henry's bed from the living room to the wood shed, and swept and scrubbed all three downstairs rooms. By the time Freddie picked up Doris at her mother's home Monday morning, he was exhausted.

When he returned with the hammer, the curtain that separated his bedroom from the front room had been pulled back and Doris stood next to his bed.

"Ain't this supposed to be the dining room, or something? But, where's the furniture?" She sat on his bed, bounced a few times and then reclined on her side, her head propped with her arm. She raked her fingers across his quilt.

"Henry never had much company, so we always ate in the kitchen and slept in these two rooms. Ain't never seen no other furniture, just the beds and dressers." He wanted her out of his room. "I got the hammer." When he raised it to show her, she jumped off the bed and ran as if frightened of him. He stood still and kept staring at the spot on the bed where she had lain. Then he glanced at the raised hammer in his hand.

"Come on. Let's do some snooping." She stood by the stairway door, shaped her mouth into a pout and stamped her feet.

Freddie pulled the spikes that had already split the woodwork, opened the door and coughed when a gray cloud burst through. He blinked to wash the dust from his eyes and saw a wedge of Doris' stomach as she pulled up the tails of the man's shirt she wore to cover her mouth. She edged past him and ran up the steps.

"Come on up. You can breathe up here, sort of."

The upstairs was a repeat of the ground floor except for a short hallway that connected a large room directly over the kitchen with the two smaller ones over the living and dining areas. Cobwebs filled the corners of drab green walls, blisters and cracks appeared on the varnished woodwork and shreds of ceiling wallpaper drooped. Except for the missing bed, the larger room looked like someone's dirty and messy bedroom with clothes, personal possessions and boxes scattered about. The smaller rooms contained furniture that belonged in a living room and a dining room.

"I knew it. It's all here." Doris clapped her hands. "Let's get Thelma and Iggy to help us put this house back together like it used to be." She walked over to a picture of a woman and a man in front of a church. "Is this your mom and dad?"

"Looks like Henry." He wanted to say Dad or Pa but those names just didn't fit. "She's Clyde and Herbert's ma."

"You know why I called, don't you?" She blew the dust from the picture and set it on the dresser.

"You said you wanted to see Henry's house." He glanced at her and then back at the picture. "Or, maybe just needed a ride back from Harrington."

"You idiot, I wanted to see you." She moved between him and the picture. "You're seldom at Thelma's anymore and you never come to Emma's."

"Been busy here since Henry's stroke." And keeping Clyde and Herbert from stealing all Henry's things, but he didn't want to tell her that part.

"Thelma said you got your hands full, so I figured, if I wanted to see you..." She paused, looked straight into his eyes and kissed him.

Freddie felt the pressure of her mouth pressed tight against his. Her tongue slipped between his lips and ran back and forth across his teeth. He remembered that he was supposed to open his mouth, and he relaxed his jaw. Her tongue entered and it felt like the tip of a warm soft lollipop. He closed his lips around it. She swished it around and slowly slid it back past his teeth and around his gums. With her mouth open she put her face against his neck and sucked gently.

"I felt your tongue." Freddie stammered.

"That ain't all you felt, I can tell." She smiled at him and walked from room to room humming, occasionally making a comment about where some piece of furniture belonged.

Freddie realized she felt his erection, and he hoped she didn't know what else had happened. "I gotta put the hammer away. You can stay up here, if you want to."

When he came back into the house, the stairway door had been closed and the shirt Doris had been wearing lay on the floor, its arms pointing toward his bedroom. From beneath the closed curtain protruded legs from a pair of jeans, a bra draped over one and panties across the other. He wanted to run away but his legs felt weak.

"Well, are you going to accept the invitation or not?" Doris called from his bedroom.

He poked his head around the curtain and saw her, covered to her waist with his quilt, cradling her breasts with her arms. She unfolded her arms, reached behind her head and grabbed the spokes on the headboard.

"If you want to see the rest of me, you gotta come here and take off my cover."

He reached for his quilt but forgot to let go of the curtain. The rod struck him in back of his neck and the curtain covered him as he fell on top of Doris.

"Oh, no. Not with your clothes on and certainly not wearing that stupid sheet." She sat up, untangled the curtain and pulled his shirt over his head without opening any buttons.

When he stood and clasped his arms across his bare chest, Doris opened his pants and pulled it over his hips. They fell to his feet and he stumbled when he tried to kick them off over his shoes. He fell back onto the bed and scrambled to cover himself with his quilt.

"Honestly." Doris huffed. She got up, removed his shoes and pants and crawled back under the covers. "But, you gotta take off your own underwear."

His heart pounding, he obeyed and waited for her to tell him what to do next.

"If you're afraid, we can just lay here together. I don't mind." She paused. "Is that what you want?"

Freddie felt it was more than he wanted. "I guess so."

"Okay." She pulled on the hairs around his nipples and brushed over the tips softly.

Soon Freddie decided he wanted much more.

CHAPTER THIRITY SEVEN
DORIS' DAY
(Spring, 1954)

As Doris stared out the window into the night sky filled with stars, she thought about Thelma's story of her mother becoming one of them many years ago. Even though Thelma admitted it was a young girl's silly idea, Doris sensed that she still believed it. How wonderful to have a mother who appeared every night to listen to her daughter's problems. Even on overcast nights, the thought of her being just behind the clouds would be comforting. Doris felt her mother was farther away from her than if she were a star in the sky, and she certainly never listened to any of her problems.

When she introduced Freddie, Doris hoped to get her mother's approval, but all she said was that he seemed nice, until Fritz gave his opinion. After that Mom didn't call Freddie a clodhopper like Fritz did, but she obviously disapproved of their relationship. She hadn't liked Burt either, but that was just as well. Burt would never have been a good husband like Freddie. And if Mom and Fritz didn't like him, it would be their problem.

She selected a particularly bright star and decided it was Thelma's mother. Tonight the star could be her mother, too, sort of on loan like a book at the Carnegie Library. An image of Mrs. Sorenson appeared and Doris had to squeeze her eyes shut and concentrate on the picture of Liz she had seen on Thelma's dresser. Did the star know she hated the library woman? Did she know about Burt?

She pulled her quilt over her head, and the star said *look at me*.

Doris obeyed. Had Freddie ever felt frightened and hid under the covers in this same bed? Had he ever needed either of his mothers to help him like Thelma, and now she, did? That didn't matter, even if Thelma or Freddie or Iggy or even Svez was talking to Liz's star at that exact same moment.

"I don't care," she muttered. "I need you more than Thelma or anyone else. I'm going to marry your son, and I'm afraid. I don't know why."

Twinkle, twinkle little star. How I wonder what you are. Up above the sky so high, like a God dam light bulb. Doris gritted her teeth and pressed the palms of her hands over her ears, but Fritz's ugly laugh at his hideous nursery rhyme wouldn't stop.

Go on, said the star. *Tell me about Fritz.*

Does your farm boy know about Burt? Fritz stole the star's voice. *Or how about when you showed yourself to me and got me all harded up?*

"I never did that with you! I mean flirted with Fritz or let him see me naked. I was afraid of him when I lived there, and now I hate him." She blinked and the star disappeared behind closed eyelids. She could hide from Thelma's mother if she felt a need to. "His eyes used to follow me around, and one time he walked into the bathroom when I was showering. I screamed, but he just stared at me. If my mother hadn't been in the kitchen, I am sure he wouldn't have left me alone that time." She lifted the quilt over her face until the ugly secret crept back into its hiding place. "Once, I even wet my pants rather than go to the bathroom when I was alone in the house with him." She muffled her sobs with her fist, but continued to stare at the North Star. "He knew about me and Burt. Said that he wanted his turn. He threatened to tell Freddie. He was drunk when he said it, but I knew he would do it if—"

"Doris. Are you all right?" Thelma's thin voice was followed by a slight knock. "Can I come in?"

Did Thelma's mother tell her that Doris was stealing her star? "Yes, come in."

"Should I get my key?"

"Oh, shit." She jumped out of bed and ran to the door. "I'm sorry, I musta locked it by mistake." When she saw Thelma in her nightgown and her hair in rollers, she remembered that she and Freddie were to be married the next day. She burst into tears and put her arms around Thelma.

"You were talking in your sleep." Thelma took Doris by her hand and led her back to bed. "Who do you think you were talking to?" Thelma spread Doris' quilt over her and sat on the edge of the bed.

"The stars, I guess. Maybe even to your mother." She surprised herself with her honesty. She suddenly realized that she didn't need Liz's star, she had Thelma. If anyone had been her mother figure, it was her, since that first day in her kitchen three years ago. Yet she couldn't share the ugly secrets with Freddie's sister, not if she was to become her sister-in-law the next day.

"I did some bad things with Burt, and Freddie doesn't know about them." Doris, disbelieving what she had just said, glanced from the star to Thelma and saw no scorn or judgment from either mother. She closed her eyes and blurted out, "I did it with Fritz, too." No response. She peered into the eyes staring back at her and felt Thelma's expression of shock and anger. She wished she hadn't told her secret and then was glad that she had.

"Move over." Thelma gently touched Doris' arm.

Thelma's response to her hideous truth surprised Doris, and she couldn't move.

"Please, I'm cold, and we need to talk."

Doris moved to the side of the bed. Thelma slid under the covers, and daughters of the same star hugged and comforted each other.

****

Thelma shared her deepest secret and confirmed their sisterhood.

CHAPTER THIRTY-EIGHT
MILDRED'S PARTY
(Fall, 1955)

A French twist or a flip? Maybe for the uppity women in town, but not her. Thelma became impatient with the young hairdresser who chewed gum while she encouraged her to try exotic hairstyles.

"It's long enough so I can cut and shape it to anything you like."

When Thelma explained that she wanted her hair set into pin curls, Suzie, her name printed on her uniform, stood behind her, snapped her gum and pulled a strand of Thelma's hair to its maximum length. "It's a bit long for pin curls. Maybe rollers." She gathered a second strand, compared it to the one in her other hand and shook her head.

From the annoyed expression on Suzie's face as it appeared in the mirror, Thelma thought she was checking for lice.

"Who in the world cut this last time?"

"They're not even," Thelma admitted, but avoided the question. She had cut her own hair as well as Pa's and Iggy's. She wanted to shake her head in fake disbelief, but Suzie held tight to the two ribbons of hair like the reins on a horse.

"Has to be pin curls." Suzie cocked her head like a robin. "After I even it out, it'll be too short for rollers."

Thelma watched her thumb nail grow white as she gripped the copy of *Life Magazine* displaying a picture of President Eisenhower on the cover.

"Anyhow, let's wash it first, and we can decide then."

"I already washed them…" An old inner voice gently chided her, and she made the correction. "It. I washed it this morning."

But, Suzie had disappeared. Thelma glanced right and left before she located her standing at a sink near the back of the room.

"This way." Suzie snapped her gum and waved a towel with both hands as if Thelma was supposed to charge like a bull. "Over here, so we can get on with it."

No one had washed and set her hair since long before her mother died, but Sonja had recommended she have it done for Mildred's party. She walked to the sink and stood confused, not sure how to straddle the small bench in front of it. Suzie huffed, grabbed Thelma's magazine and slapped it onto a shelf. She turned Thelma away from the sink by pulling on one shoulder, pushed her down onto the chair and tilted her head back.

Soon, the warm spray of water from a showerhead on a flexible hose, and Suzie's fingers raking the soft lather into her hair helped Thelma relax. Suddenly, she panicked that one of the women from Bovine might walk in and recognize her. She felt a shiver pass through her body.

"Is the water too cold?"

Without waiting for an answer, Suzie bumped the lever with her elbow, and Thelma felt a surge of increased warmth on her neck. She relaxed again. She was glad she had driven to Harrington where no one knew her. The woman in Bovine who did hair in her home was a terrible gossip. She felt her confidence increase and decided if someone she knew walked in, she would just say hi and talk about Mildred's party. She actually hoped Mrs. Lorenz had an appointment here so she could tell her how nice it was that the bank honored Mildred for her thirty years with them. But, when she sat back at Suzie's workstation and looked at her drenched image in the mirror, she didn't want anyone to see her.

"Do many of your customers come from Bovine?" Thelma watched large clumps of her hair land on the silky apron and tumble onto the floor. Her fear of being seen peaked.

"Merry has a couple of regulars from there. I think one of them is a spinster teacher, but I don't know her name." She pulled two short horn-like spikes of hair on each side of Thelma's head, her eyes rotated between them and she nodded approvingly.

Thelma thought of the carpenters who had built their machine shed when she saw Suzie load one side of her mouth with bobby pins. She glanced at the combs, clippers and scissors on the worktable, half expecting to find a hammer.

Suzie spoke through the side of her mouth free of bobby pins. "If you ask me, getting all primped-up won't do her any good.

She's an old maid and won't ever find a man anyway. She comes in once a week with an armful of books." The back of Suzie's head appeared in the mirror as she leaned forward and peered into Thelma's face. "Doesn't that hick-town have a library?"

Undaunted by Suzie's insensitivity, Thelma sat and watched her form small circles with her hair and lock them in place. Being an old maid in the company of such ladies as Sonja and Mildred was an honor, even in a hick town, and a young hairdresser who flashed an engagement ring couldn't intimidate her. She hoped Sonja would appear for Merry to perform her magic, but she and Suzie were the only two people in the shop. Sonja would have to wait like everyone else to see her new look.

On the drive back to Bovine, Thelma thought about the party that evening and the Lorenz home where it would take place. Before Freddie moved away, she and Iggy used to drag Freddie and Svez to Bovine to view the decorated houses during Christmas season. The Lorenz home was the most elaborate.

"A damned waste of electricity," was her father's usual reaction. "Your Ma used to put one candle in the window."

"And that looked real nice. We still do it, but the candle is a light bulb now. I'm sure Ma would approve."

"Wow! Just look at all them lights." She smiled as she remembered Iggy's fascination and his curiosity. "Wonder what it looks like inside."

It was October, and there would be no Christmas lights, but she'd have a chance to see the house decorated for a party. When Iggy dropped the mail on the table and rewarded himself with a piece of cherry pie, she opened the flowered envelope addressed to her and read Gloria's hand written invitation.

"Mildred came to us at the summer solstice when she was just a child of twenty-four." Thelma wondered if Mildred's retirement at some future date would, by necessity, coincide with the winter solstice. "It's rude to tell everyone how old someone is. A woman's age is personal."

"Yup. Quite rude." Iggy switched the dripping pie to his other hand and licked his fingers.

Thelma pointed to the cupboard. He flashed a toothy grin back, grabbed a plate and laid what was left of his pie on it. When he went to get a fork, Thelma delicately plucked one cherry and, half kissing it, placed it between her teeth and caressed it with her tongue. She puckered her lips and shot it into her brother's face.

"Hey! That was mine." He picked the cherry off the floor, held it against the tines with his thumb and slung it back at her.

Using the plate like a shovel, he scooped the remaining piece into his mouth. When Thelma made a grab at it, she was rewarded with a fine spray of cherry and tobacco juice. She hugged her brother, went to the sink and peeked into the mirror. She saw measles, and laughed.

All the way back to the farm from the hairdresser, Thelma kept the car windows closed so the wind wouldn't disturb what felt like a wig made of fine wire on her head. The goo in her hair made it feel grimy, but Suzie said that was the new look. She breathed a sigh of relief when she walked into the house and saw Doris sitting at the kitchen table.

"Is Freddie here, too?"

"We're not talking just now, but don't worry. He'll come around." Doris stood, placed her hand on Thelma's shoulder and twirled her.

"How do I look?"

"Just like a movie star. Close your eyes half way and stick your chin out a bit." Doris modeled and Thelma imitated her. "Yeah, like that. You'd look just like Rita Hayworth if that little bitch hadn't cut your hair so short."

Later that afternoon as Thelma was about to leave for the party, she glanced one last time into the mirror, turned toward Doris and said, "Thanks for the help with my makeup, and for trying to make me feel good about it." She took Doris' smile to be her acceptance.

Iggy stood alongside the car Thelma bought with some of the money Arnie left her. He held a can of polish in one hand and a rag in the other. "When my sister hob-nobs with the hotsie-totsies, she's going in a shiny car. I tried to spit-shine it but this Simonize works better." He flashed stained teeth but no fresh chew. "Unless, you'd like me to take you in my truck." Since their father put the farm in their names, he considered the pickup his.

"If my nerves don't settle down, I might just accept your offer, especially with you as my chauffeur."

"I'll take you in your Plymouth," He said hopefully.

"Sorry, but only on Sundays when you're wearing good clothes. I'm trying to keep my car from smelling like the farm." She realized she had offended him and tried to explain. "It's stuck on the clothes we wear."

"You never used to worry 'bout how we stink. You just made us change clothes because of the cow shit and dirt."

"We smell just fine. Farms have," she struggled to find the right word, "a country odor, like the smell of new mown hay. It's just that people in town trained their noses different, and they only like to sniff at other city people."

280

"They all wear perfume like you got on?"

"Yeah, something like that. It's just that we farmers need two different smells. One for home and one for town." She wanted to include two different sets of manners too, but he might consider that an additional insult.

"I like the farm smell better." He pulled a plug of tobacco from the bib of his overalls and bit off a chunk. "Have fun at your city party."

"Sorry, Iggy, but we do smell like the farm." She watched him walk toward the barn and added quietly, "It's good and honest, but I don't want to take it to town with me." She took a quick glance at her city hairdo and made-up face in the rear view mirror and left the farm, odor and all, behind.

At Sonja's house, Thelma ducked into the bathroom, took a quick check in the mirror and said, "Now, I'm ready to meet the leading citizens of Bovine."

"Not quite yet. Your rouge is a little..."

"A little too dark? I know. Doris fixed me up today. Not the hair. I had that done in Harrington, but she did my nails and plucked my eyebrows and helped me with my face. I guess, I'm not used to wearing makeup." Remembering her conversation with Iggy, she asked, "Is my perfume too strong. It's from Doris, too."

"Your scent is just fine, and I love your dress. It's new, isn't it?" Sonja produced a tissue and applied it to the rogue. Thelma remembered having her nose wiped in the first grade half a lifetime ago.

"Yes, Doris helped me pick it out."

"Well, it certainly is your color. There." The tissue disappeared as mysteriously as it appeared. "I think we are ready to face the social set."

Thelma followed Sonja into the Lorenz home and waited to be introduced to Gloria who greeted them at the door.

"Miss West, how good of you to come." Sonja accepted the outstretched hand. "Miss Rastner, welcome to our home." She talked on into the dinning room. "We never formally met, of course, but I see you in church often, and we don't stand on formalities in this house."

The chandelier, the place settings on a mahogany table, the foods with names seldom pronounced in Bovine said something quite different to Thelma. With Sonja at her side, she was ready to ignore her vulnerability and barge right in.

"I've been excited about this party ever since I got your invitation, and I want to thank you for that." Thelma recited her rehearsed line quite naturally.

"You were near the top of list of people to invite, after my husband's bank associates, of course. It wouldn't be proper to have Mildred's party without Miss West and you."

Thelma had received her hand written note long after Sonja received an invitation printed on flowered paper. She had her two friends to thank rather than her hostess.

"Miss West, I believe you know everyone here." Her eyes darted toward the front door. "If you will guide Miss Rastner through the crowd..."

Thelma followed Gloria's glance and saw Mr. Lorenz shake hands with Father Reinhardt in the foyer. Stella Reinhardt stood close by, hands clasped together almost as if she were praying. Gloria whisked her hair and sashayed toward them.

"Let's go," Sonja said, as she took Thelma's arm and led her to an elegant lady who stared vacantly into the crowd. "Good afternoon, Mrs. York. Nice to see you again."

"My husband just went to get us something to drink," replied the nervous lady.

Sonja moved slightly to intercept Alice York's view of her retreating husband. "I would like you to meet my friend, Thelma Rastner."

Thelma glanced toward the back of a short, stout and balding man and then at Mrs. York.

Mrs. York turned her head from her husband's path to Thelma and stared at her as if she were trying to remember something. She smiled and nodded. "Yes," an answer to an unasked question. "I read in the paper that you and your husband, Ignatius, bought the family farm. Sylvester must be very proud of you two."

"Iggy's my brother. I'm afraid no one would want to marry him, or me for that matter."

Alice York gasped, and Sonja said, "Thelma, Mildred and I are what you call old maids, but we're quite content with our stations in life."

"Thank goodness, here comes my husband with our drinks. If you will excuse me." Mrs. Bernard York headed in the direction of the bar with no sign of Mr. Bernard York.

"Well, Miss Rastner," Sonja teased, "are you ready for our next societal challenge? Gloria seems to have separated Father Reinhardt from his guardian, and she's steaming this way." Stella, her head making an abrupt twist to the right and left, aimed her body in the direction of Sonja and Thelma.

"Hello, Miss Reinhardt. It looks like someone stole you brother." Sonja greeted her. "Would you like a glass of champagne?"

"Yes." She looked suspiciously around the room. "The men must have their time together, and I wasn't welcome in that group." She looked conspiratorially at Sonja. "And, yes to the champagne."

As they headed to the bar, Sonja said, "You know Thelma Rastner. She can be so shy she blends in with the carpet." Stella glanced at the carpet as if making a comparison, the bold Spanish print with the colors Doris selected for Thelma's debut.

"Yes. I do." She reached to shake Thelma's hand. "Hello Thelma. We must attend different services on Sunday, because I hardly ever see you." Somewhere between the carpet and Thelma's face, Stella's expression brightened. "I knew your mother quite well. She was a strong Christian lady. You remind me a great deal of her."

"Thank you, Miss Reinhardt. Mama died some twenty years ago. Pa and Iggy and I still miss her."

"Those men should be thankful to have Thelma to take care of them."

"Amen to that." Stella lifted her glass. "They say God takes care of those who can't take care of themselves." She downed her drink. "Where are the women in that equation?"

After refilling and clicking their glasses, Sonja said, "Let's proceed to the inner sanctum and find the lady of the hour. Care to join us, Miss Reinhardt?"

"Yes, thank you, Miss West. I want to see who is monopolizing my brother. He can be so," she made a circle with her lips, "so manipulated," lips rounded tighter, "by those who take advantage of his good nature."

Sonja gestured toward Thelma and said, "I know someone like that." She faced Stella. "She's just too good and certain people take advantage of her."

Blushing from Sonja's comment, Thelma felt a flash of heat on her face and wondered what additional color it added to her rouge and lipstick, but she didn't care. Together with Sonja and Stella, she pushed forward to greet Mildred who had a startled expression on her face as Father Reinhardt approached her.

"My goodness, Miss Bushman." Shamus Reinhardt's voice boomed a bit loud. "You've been a part of St. Alphonse parish nearly as long as my sister, Stella."

He put his hands up in a gesture of surprise, and Thelma wondered if he intended to hug Mildred, shake her hand or bless her. She remembered a much younger priest who came into her mother's bedroom to anoint her body and bless her family. She began to feel sad.

"Thank you, Father." Mildred blushed. "I mean, yes, I have been here a long time." She turned to Sonja, who with Thelma and Stella, circled the two of them. "Miss West and I moved to Bovine at the same time, isn't that right, Sonja."

"Miss West. Miss Rastner." He bowed slightly and Thelma noticed his thinning and graying hair. "It's nice to see you again." He faced his sister. "Stella, you must invite these ladies to the rectory for dinner some evening."

"Yes, brother dear." She curtseyed and, teetering, put her hand on Thelma's shoulder to get her balance as her brother turned away.

"Excuse me, ladies." He pointed toward the door. "I must say hello to…"

Stella flinched and followed it with a smile. "Of course, Shamus. But don't get into trouble." She blushed, smiled sheepishly and faced her three companions as each began to laugh.

"Men always get into trouble when they go off on their own." Thelma surprised herself with her confidence. "If you want trouble, you should have four older brothers."

Mildred said, "I'm afraid Sonja and I have no experience with that. We have no brothers, and all the other men in our lives keep at a safe distance."

"Yes, I'm afraid we are considered quite untouchable." Sonja placed her hand on the small of Mildred's back as if to prove otherwise. Mildred smiled.

Thelma worried about being caught staring, and she felt a thrill when Sonja reached and touched her in the same way.

"Certainly not more untouchable than the sister of a priest." Stella placed her empty Champaign glass on the table and patted the back of Thelma's arm. "Even the women in town refer to me as the priest's house keeper. Most of them don't even know my name." She slurred her words slightly.

Sonja said, "I understand perfectly, Stella."

Stella peered over her shoulder as if Sonja had addressed someone behind her. She took a deep breath. "See what I mean? I don't even know my own name."

Mildred said, "To think I was so nervous about this party tonight that I didn't want to leave my bathroom. Thank you Stella, Sonja and Thelma, for making me comfortable at my own party. Together, the four of us can take on the rest of Bovine's elite."

CHAPTER THRITY-NINE
THE QUARREL

"Where's Thelma?" Doris burst into the kitchen and stopped short when she saw Iggy holding his shotgun up to the light and peering through the barrel. She had been uncomfortable with guns since the time Fritz got drunk and described in detail how her father had been killed.

"She's at Mildred's party." He placed the gun on his lap and wiped it with a rag. "What's up?"

"Thought she'd be back by now. I gotta talk to her." With her eyes fixed on him, she backed toward the front room, turned and glanced around. "Pa home?"

"Nope. He's at George's. Ain't coming back tonight." He slid his chair back, got up and walked out into the porch. "Where's Freddie?"

"At Henry's I suppose." She hadn't gotten used to calling it her home. "You know, that pigsty we live in."

"Henry weren't much of a housekeeper, I guess." Iggy sulked back to the table and stared at the shotgun. "He's still coming to hunt pheasants with me tomorrow, ain't he?"

"He'll be here. Maybe even tonight, to get me, but I'm gonna sleep in Arnie's room." After their many arguments about ownership, she and Freddie agreed to call it Arnie's room. She turned, walked toward the stairs and yelled over her shoulder. "And, he can't go up there. I won't open the door. Thelma can use her key if she wants to talk." She stormed upstairs and stared at Arnie's bed stripped of sheets and blankets. She wanted to go into Thelma's room and hide under her quilt, but that door had no lock. She plopped onto the bare mattress and burst into tears.

The part about helping Thelma get dolled up for Mildred's party was true, but she hadn't gone along to the party like she told Freddie. Instead, she went to her mother's house in Harrington. Burt had been released from jail, and he and Fritz made the arrangements for him to meet with Doris. Fritz promised to get her mother out of the house for a movie and dinner. It felt good to be with her old boyfriend, and when he kissed her, she nearly floated away. She convinced herself that they stopped before she heard Henry's old pickup with the bad muffler out in the driveway. Instead of following Freddie home with their car like she agreed, she turned onto a side road and drove to Thelma's. He could cool off alone at Henry's, or if he guessed where she went, come to Thelma's and try to take her back.

The air in Arnie's room was stifling and she opened the window. She slipped out onto the balcony and laid on her stomach, her chin propped on her arms. She heard the familiar broken muffler before she saw the headlights turn into the yard. He couldn't talk her into going home with him, she convinced herself. She crouched low and, within a circle of light from the bulb on top the pole, she watched Freddie get out of the truck and walk toward the porch.

Beyond her line of vision she heard Freddie tell Iggy, "Doris ran away from me," and she imagined Iggy standing in the doorway, his head shaking. Ever since they married and moved in together, that tone in his voice and his sad and hopeless expression, disgusted her. She laughed at her earlier fear that he might come upstairs and break down the door.

"She went back to that guy who used to beat her up."

Iggy began to make those annoying noises as he breathed, and she visualized him staring at his feet. He mumbled, "Thelma," but the door closed and she couldn't hear any more of their conversation. She thought about sneaking down the stairs to listen to what he was telling Iggy, but she worried she might start to feel sorry for him again. Each time she wanted to leave him, those feelings kept her locked in the relationship she no longer wanted.

She heard the porch door slam shut and saw Freddie re-enter the circle of light and head toward his truck. She panicked that he might have seen her when he glanced up, and was thankful she had left Arnie's room dark. She watched him crouch next to Babe, then sit on the sagging tailgate with his face buried in his hands. He wandered off toward the outhouse that Svez and Iggy sometimes used. She searched for movement in the shadows cast by the yard light. A few chickens scratched in the dirt and Babe sniffed the tires on Henry's truck. A car drove past the drive, turned around and disappeared behind the hedge alongside the road.

Disgusted, she climbed back through the window, not wanting to watch Freddie sulk around the yard. She heard a loud thud and then Freddie screaming for help. She ran to the window and saw Iggy rush out of the house, saw the flash before she heard the shotgun blast. By the time she ran down the stairs and out to the yard, the car had sped away. The outhouse was tipped, its door against the ground. Iggy continued to aim the gun toward the road, and Freddie peered out through one of the holes in the bench and sobbed quietly.

Doris and Iggy rolled the small building on its side so Freddie could crawl out through the door. She expected anger but, when a beam of light from Thelma's car washed over them as she turned into the yard, Doris saw only sadness etched in his face. It frightened her. She took him by the hand and guided him to the passenger seat in their car.

"I'll bring him back for the truck tomorrow," Doris said, when Iggy finished telling Thelma the events of the evening within a single breath. "You guys can go hunting if you're still wanting to."

"Is Freddie okay?" Thelma glanced toward the car where Freddie sat and stared through the windshield. "I better go talk to him."

"He mostly was upset, even before those jerks from town had their fun at his expense."

"You know who did it?" Thelma glanced at Freddie and then back at Doris.

"Maybe. Guys usually brag 'bout doing this kind of stuff at Emma's. The kid who does dishes after school might know. I'll ask him."

"Freddie told me he got into a fight with Burt." Iggy's breathing had slowed to near normal. "Think that guy mighta done it?"

"No, Burt's my old boyfriend, and Freddie's still a little jealous. He lives in Florida. Only comes to visit my step dad sometimes." She hadn't believed Burt when he threatened to run away to Florida. Maybe he would, now that Freddie punched him in the face, and he realized he couldn't even defend himself without going back to jail.

"Doris, are you and Freddie having problems?"

Suddenly, Thelma didn't seem like the mother who would understand, and Doris was glad she hadn't had a chance to tell her

287

what happened earlier that evening. Had Doris' marrying Freddie somehow changed her?

"I think he's just scared of being a daddy." Doris glanced at Freddie still sitting in the car. Maybe her pregnancy would restore her relationship with these people. She had been frightened when her second period failed, and that must be why she did something stupid like run to her old boyfriend.

"That's wonderful news, Doris." Thelma hugged her, and Iggy's breathing became louder.

"I got to 'gratulate him." Iggy turned, but Doris grabbed his arm and stopped him.

"Please don't. At least not now." She had to think fast. "We agreed not to tell anyone until I was sure." Tomorrow when she brought him back to get the truck, they could officially announce it. And, maybe if she told Freddie that she was pregnant, he would stop sulking. "I think me and Freddie better go home now." She hugged Thelma again, kissed Iggy on the cheek and left with the father of her unborn child. On the way home she reflected on the short time she spent with Burt and was glad that he had been in jail when she got pregnant.

CHAPTER FORTY
AN EXCHANGE OF LIVES
(Fall, 1956)

After four silos had been filled that fall, Svez got sick. The doctor said he had pneumonia, and he spent the entire winter in bed, his only complaint his necessary use of the bedside commode.

When Doris told him that Davie, the kid who worked with her at Emma's Café, was with the group who tipped over his outhouse, he said, "No, Davie wouldn't do that." He stared at the ceiling. "It don't matter," and he felt his mind slipping.

A boy about five years old had come out of the Smith's house and stared at the trailer that had just landed there. Svez got down from his tractor and walked back to where the kid was standing.

"What's your name?"

"Davie." His finger found its way into his nose.

"Were you trying to steal my trailer?"

Davie shook his head and his hand followed.

"Well, I 'spose you weren't trying to steal it." After backing his tractor, Svez examined the pin that let loose and shook his head. He jammed it back in place, looked at the boy and winked. He climbed onto the tractor, turned to Davie and yelled, "Climb aboard, and I'll give you a free ride."

Davie wiped his hand on his pants, walked to the trailer and touched one of the tires.

"Not back there. I don't wanna lose you and the trailer. Up here, with me on the tractor seat."

Svez hoisted him up to his lap, and Davie grabbed onto the steering wheel. Together, they drove the tractor a short distance down the road, into the ditch, through the field and back to the Smith's front yard.

"Tell your Ma you got a ride from Svez Rastner."

Davie jumped down and ran into the house.

Svez heard Doris tiptoe out of his bedroom. He smiled.

He saw a cloud of dust above the hedge alongside the road, and soon Iggy appeared, running into the yard and up to the barn.

"The car...the car rolled over...on the curve....right by the Smith house." *Iggy bent forward, put his hands on his knees and panted. In the pickup on the way to the overturned car, Iggy sat between Svez and Freddie and explained, "I climbed out the top door."*

"The top door?" *Freddie asked.*

"Yeah, the door faced up. I had to climb out like it was a trap door. It weren't easy without no ladder." *He smiled. "The Smith boy watched me."*

"What'd he say?" *Svez remembered the kid.*

"Nuthing. He just looked at me. But when I waved, he flapped both his arms like he wanted to fly."

The car lay on the soft grass of Smith's lawn. They weren't farmers, just some strangers who bought the abandoned buildings on what was once a neighboring farm. Davie stood by the front tire of the car that was inches off the ground, and he pushed on it like it was a small merry-go-round.

Svez said, "Fetch the grease gun from the back of the pickup. Now we can reach all the joints without crawling under the car."

Iggy giggled and went to the pickup but came back with a chain. They rolled the car back onto its tires and towed it home.

Sves grimaced from pain in his bladder. He thought he heard his voice call Thelma.

They sat on the front lawn and waited for Thelma to finish making supper. Svez had hired Davie to drive the horses from the thrashing machine to the granary. George teased Davie about going to see Ida, and Davie admitted he was sweet on a girl in his freshman class. Ralph and Herman joined in the teasing, and Iggy laughed so hard he had to run to the outhouse. Davie asked why they still kept the outhouse when they had indoor plumbing. George said it was for emergencies, pointed toward Iggy and laughed.

Svez told Iggy to burn the old outhouse and fill the hole with gravel and black dirt. The grass will be bit greener at that spot. But Iggy wasn't standing next to his bed like he had thought. Svez shook his head and closed his eyes.

He had let Davie drink beer, and that made him talk silly. Thought Thelma and Iggy kept Arnie's body in the attic—said the kids at school told him.

290

"We better go in." Svez raised his head and sniffed at the air. "I think Thelma's got supper ready."

Davie lifted the beer bottle to his mouth, gulped it empty and said, "Most people call me David now that I'm in high school."

"But I ain't most people." Svez squeezed Davie's knee. "You're still the Davie who tried to steal my trailer."

Svez dozed but soon awoke with extreme pressure in his bladder. He pushed his legs out from under the covers and sat on the edge of his bed. When he lifted the lid from the chamber pot, a snake-like coil slipped over his thumb. He dropped the cover and stared at the strange item that dangled around his wrist as he raised his arm and tried to shake his hand free. When the shock of it passed, he recognized the small coil of hose draped through his fingers. Thelma understood his problem. He remembered how he had worked it through Arnie's penis, and now he discovered how it felt when he did it to himself. Sharp pain and total relief. He slept soundly the rest of the night and woke with a vague memory of Elizabeth holding her hand on his forehead. He wondered why she had called him Pa. When he sat up and reached for the commode, he again felt the hose coiled on top of the lid. He hid it under his bed in case he would need it later.

Days were filled with memories, and each night these memories became real. Whenever he felt his bladder was full, he found the hose replaced on the chamber pot cover, and after each use he put it back under his bed. His family was his only contact with the outside world, and he appreciated their attention, but was quite content reliving the highs and lows of the past. He felt closer to the people who were gone than any still alive, except for Doris. He had other grandchildren, but her baby would be special, and he made a firm commitment to live long enough to meet him. He decided not to be disappointed if it was a girl. Sometimes Doris stayed overnight and slept in her old room, and one time she fell asleep lying on his quilt next to him. He stayed awake all that night listening to her breathe and watched her belly rise and fall. She would make everything all right for Freddie.

When Elizabeth came into his bedroom carrying her baby, he said, "Of course you can keep him." He blinked and Doris told him she had a boy. He told the baby to call him Svez.

One night, when his breathing became especially difficult and his thoughts kept vanishing and then reappearing in strange places, only the pressure in his bladder remained constant. Suddenly, he felt a jolt of pain in his penis and then relief. Thelma had made his journey more bearable, even pleasant, as he heard her whisper into his ear.

"Goodbye, Pa."

He thought she had kissed his cheek, and then his lips. He smiled, muttered "Little Freddie" and allowed himself to drift toward sleep.

****

Thelma kissed her father on his cheek and then on his lips. She tossed the hose into the chamber pot and carried it outside where the cool spring air made her eyes water. When she came back, she straightened his quilt and rearranged his arms and hands. She sat on the bed next to him and stared at her reflection in the window until the sun came up and she could no longer see the sadness on her face. When Doris wandered into the bedroom with her baby, Thelma placed him on the covers next to Pa. Then she went upstairs to wake Iggy.

After the funeral, Thelma held Doris' baby and sent her out to bring Iggy and Freddie in from the barn where she knew they had been hiding from Father Reinhardt. After Stella left, Sonja and Mildred were the only remaining guests so it was safe for them to come back. When she glanced out the window, she saw Stella still sitting in the car and Father Reinhardt near the barn with his arms around Iggy and Freddie. Doris trudged back toward the house. She heard the car leave the yard, and soon Doris, Freddie and Iggy were sitting around the kitchen table with Sonja and Mildred, the remaining important adults in her life. She stood, rocked the baby in her arms and decided she wouldn't feel bad until everyone went home. Then she cried.

Two weeks passed since the funeral, almost a month since Doris had her baby, and yet Doris and Freddie hadn't decided on a name or set a date for his baptism. Thelma pleaded with her mother's star to protect the baby from harm until his wayward parents committed him to the church and to God. She was tempted to perform an emergency baptism like the nuns had told her about in catechism class the next time Doris and the baby came to visit.

"Have you and Freddie decided on a name?" Thelma tried to make her question sound casual as she and Doris sat at the kitchen table and sipped coffee. "I don't think the priest will baptize him Baby Boy Tate." Thelma laughed but stopped when she saw the serious look on Doris' face.

"My baby's not a Catholic, is he?" The child began to fuss and Doris rocked him.

"He's not any faith until he's properly baptized." Thelma was surprised by Doris' lack of understanding and her apparent broken promise to take instructions in the Catholic faith so Father Reinhardt could bless their marriage. But, she decided first things first. "Your baby needs a name, two names actually, and one of them must be a saint's name. What have you and Freddie decided?"

"Sylvester?" Doris sounded hesitant.

"That's no name for a baby." Thelma thought about her father and reconsidered. "Maybe, it would be a nice middle name. He wouldn't have to use it if he didn't like it." She guessed at their second choice. "And, not Freddie, either, like Pa suggested. Don't want everyone to call him Junior, even when he gets to be a grown man."

"Teddy, after my brother?"

Theodore Sylvester Tate." Thelma chuckled. "That'd be a handle to hang a hat on, Pa woulda said." She glared at Doris. "You and Freddie haven't even discussed a name, have you."

"Freddie said I should pick one, and I haven't gotten 'round to it." She opened her blouse and held the baby's mouth to her breast. "I guess Father Reinhardt talked to Freddie about it at Pa's funeral."

"Well, have two names ready by Sunday after ten-thirty mass." Thelma stood. "I'm going to call Father Reinhardt right now." She walked to the desk and reached where the wall-phone used to hang, said, "Shit," and picked up the receiver from the desk-phone. She covered the mouthpiece with her hand and looked at Doris. "Teddy Sylvester would be nice names."

Doris nodded, and with two fingers guided her nipple into her baby's mouth.

"Of course, the child cannot be excluded from the sacraments," Father Reinhardt explained, "especially baptism, because of their parent's situation."

She felt relieved and promised the priest, "Freddie will be back in good graces very soon, Father. Soon as Doris converts." Thelma glanced at Doris who tapped her fingers on the table while the baby sucked. "Iggy and I will be the child's Godparents, and we will see to his spiritual life." She thought about Iggy's hesitation to make his Easter duty, confession and communion. "I will send Iggy to you shortly. Doris, too. For instructions." She put her hand over the mouthpiece and drew in a deep breath.

"One thing at a time, Thelma. If Iggy isn't in a state of Grace..." He paused. "I mean if he hasn't been to the sacraments in over a year, I'll be available to hear his confession after Saturday evening devotions. If Doris isn't sure of her conversion just yet, I can arrange for a mixed marriage. That way Freddie can continue to receive the sacraments. All she needs to do is agree to bring the child up as a Catholic and, with you and Iggy as Godparents…" He paused again.

Thelma exhaled and felt lightheaded.

"Thelma?"

"Yes, Father." She glanced back at the kitchen table and saw Doris button her blouse, wave good-bye and walk out the door.

"Bring the child to me after ten-thirty Mass."

"Yes, Father. Thank you." She dropped the receiver and ran to the porch. "Iggy and I will be over on Sunday morning." Not sure if Doris heard, she leaned against the open door and stared at the starless afternoon sky.

Iggy agreed to confession on Saturday night and returned home whistling as he walked into the kitchen. "That weren't so bad."

"What kind of penance did Father Reinhardt give?" Thelma tried not to sound too interested.

"Weren't none."

"What do you mean? Did you go to confession?"

"Yeah, I went." He smiled. "Told the priest I don't do penance, least not those prayers he used to make me say. He just told me I gotta set a good example for some young boy who may need special help with his religion. I'm gonna do that for Teddy." He cocked his head to one side and frowned. "Maybe for his daddy, too."

CHAPTER FORTY-ONE:
THELMA'S NEW LIFE
(Fall, 1959)

"Sonja?" Thelma peered through the open front door and saw Sonja on her couch, dabbing her eyes with the corner of her handkerchief.

"Please, come in." Sonja rose and gestured with her free hand.

Thelma entered the parlor and gazed at the loose papers on the coffee table in an attempt to avert attention from Sonja's repressed sobs. She waited for her to dry her eyes and tuck her handkerchief into her sleeve. She continued the conversation Sonja had stated on the telephone that morning.

"Maybe, your father isn't as critical as he made it sound. Pa lingered an entire winter after he became ill."

"Thank you for coming." She approached Thelma and squeezed her hand. "Dad's quite a bit older and never was physically strong like your father." She touched Thelma's face with her other hand." I'm afraid, I haven't the strength you had in a similar situation."

"I didn't really have to do much. Father Reinhardt…" Thelma pressed her friend's moist hand tight against her cheek and realized she hadn't felt Sonja touch this intimately since she had hurt herself on the playground. The reversal of roles embarrassed her.

Sonja raised her head. "You were with him the entire time, but I'm stuck here and he's dying." She sobbed and retrieved her handkerchief.

"You are going to see him, aren't you?" Thelma glanced at the train schedule sitting on the coffee table, and saw the receiver from the phone lying beside it. "Come, let's sit." She led Sonja to the couch, placed her arm around her and covertly replaced the receiver.

"I want to go, but I'm afraid to go alone." She put her hands on her lap, again clutching and twisting her handkerchief.

"Mildred will go with you. I'm sure Mr. Lorenz will give her the time off."

"I can't ask her to relive all those horrible memories she left behind when she joined me here in Bovine."

"But, she always talked about Philadelphia like it was her home."

"It was, but she had such terrible conflicts with her step mother that her father demanded she leave his house when she graduated from high school. She kept her vow never to go back, even after her father died and his wife was left with the family heirlooms." She looked at Thelma. "Will you go with me?"

Many times, Thelma had imagined traveling with her old teacher to distant and romantic places, but, confronted with the opportunity, she became frightened. What about Iggy, Freddie, Doris? And Teddy? Could she leave them? She smiled. She knew Iggy would take Teddy to church on Sunday, and maybe drag Freddie along. Doris was a bigger problem, but she decided to would wait until Teddy's first communion the next spring, and then put pressure on Doris to complete her religious instructions.

"Does that smile mean you will go with me?"

"I just thought of my reasons for not going, and they seemed small." She leaned back and stared at the coffee table. "Yes, I'll go."

"I talked to him this morning, just before I called you, and his nurse had to repeat everything he said." She reached for the train schedule and stood up. "How soon can you get away?"

"Iggy can take us to the train station tomorrow, if you can get tickets that soon." Immediately, she thought about what needed to be done, starting with getting Sonja to eat something.

"Oh, I didn't expect to leave that soon. Don't you need more time…"

"Time is all I have left of my life, and I can't think of a better way to spend it than with you, especially if you need me."

"Are you sure you want to do this? It probably feels like a frightening adventure."

"I'm scared to death, but you'll be there to help me."

"I'm afraid you will be helping me. I'm the student now. But, I am ready when you are, Teacher." Sonja smiled

Thelma went into Sonja's kitchen to prepare lunch for her friend.

****

While Iggy drove them to the station, Thelma gave him last minute instructions. "Doris will stop by each afternoon after she picks up Teddy from school. She'll make you supper and set out food for your breakfast. For lunch you'll be on your own, or you can stop at Emma's after you take the milk to the Coop."

"I'll be okay." He glanced toward the side window as if looking for cars in the mirror.

"Listen to me, Iggy." He stared straight ahead. "I'll be back in about two weeks." Had she just suggested that Sonja's father would die in that amount of time? Their return tickets were undated.

"I know. It's just that..." His breathing became louder and faster.

"You just told me that you'd be okay, and I'm taking your word on it."

They rode in silence until they got to the station and Iggy asked, "Where do I park?"

Sonja pulled herself forward and pointed between Iggy and Thelma. "Over there, just in front of the station, where those boys wearing blue caps are stacking luggage. If we tip them, they will take our bags, too."

"Tip them? You want I should run them over?"

"Oh, no. I meant give them some money."

Iggy's laughter convinced Thelma that he had accepted her leaving him.

Sonja opened her purse and took out a small pouch of change. "I believe they expect a quarter each. She showed the two boys their tickets as Iggy opened the trunk and set the bags on the wooden platform. She followed the boys with quarters held between her thumb and finger. Thelma and Iggy followed, but stopped when Sonja paid the boys and entered the passenger car.

"You're in charge of things back home, Iggy. If Doris brings Teddy along when she makes you dinner watch him so he don't climb up on the windmill." She reached to hug him but he backed away. "Come here, brother." She pulled him close and kissed him on the lips. "I love you." She took a seat next to Sonja and looked out the window. Iggy hadn't moved, but stood there with his hands in his pockets. She thought maybe she shouldn't have kissed him, but she didn't care. She just felt like doing it, and she knew he loved her even though he couldn't say the words.

Sonja talked almost non-stop in the passenger car as they sat side by side, and during their meals in the dining car. That evening, Thelma stood by their sleeping compartments and waited while Sonja used the bathroom. She was embarrassed when Sonja returned wearing pajamas and robe.

"You may as well get ready, too. There's only one bathroom and soon there'll be a waiting line." She set her traveling case on the lower bunk. "If you don't mind, I'd like to be on the bottom."

Thelma stared at her.

"Unless, you are bothered by heights. It would be quite a tumble if you fell out of bed." She smiled.

"Top bunk is fine with me." She picked up the book bag Sonja had lent her for her toilet items and walked down the corridor to the bathroom.

That night, Thelma lay on the top bunk and listened to the clack-clack of the steel wheels passing from one section of track to the next, but the rhythm didn't induce sleep. She thought about the few nights she had slept with Doris and how it felt to have someone in bed with her, especially on the eve of Doris' wedding when she cried on Thelma's shoulder and then snuggled even after she fell asleep. Thelma couldn't sleep that night either. She thought about Sonja, the woman whom she had loved since first grade, and wished she could comfort her like she had done for Doris. She completed the image in her mind and soon found slumber.

When they arrived at the Philadelphia station, Sonja requested a taxi, and they drove past many streets to what seemed like another part of that same city, but was called Bryn Anthen, where Sonja's father lived. At Sonja's old home, they found her father attended by a nurse and a man dressed in black with red trim that Sonja introduced as Bishop Smith. He looked relieved when he saw Sonja as if now he could allow her father to die. Since Mr. West did pass away within twenty-four hours, Thelma felt Bishop Smith had kept him alive until his daughter could be with him.

Sonja didn't cry when he died, nor did she kiss him as Thelma had done with her father. Instead, she spoke briefly to Bishop Smith who had maintained his vigil at the dying man's side, and took Thelma to the cathedral where they prayed. Thelma wondered why there were no kneelers under the pews, and if God could hear her prayers from such a strange church. She would talk to Ma about that when she got back home.

298

That night, as Thelma lay beside Sonja in Mr. West's bed, Sonja said, "I loved him, but I couldn't stay in the same house with him after Mother died." She paused and stared at the ceiling as if Thelma weren't there. "He grabbed and kissed me, here on this bed, in a way no father should kiss his daughter." She turned on to her side, away from Thelma. "I was sixteen years old, and I knew I had to leave as soon as I graduated." She sobbed lightly. "He said he was sorry, and that I reminded him of my mother. All that next year I could feel his wet mouth against mine every time he looked at me." She sat up and wrapped her arms around her knees. "I think he wanted me gone, too. He agreed to send me to Teacher's College in Minnesota and gave me the life my meager wages never could have."

Thelma sat up next to Sonja, knees clutched, and felt a tear wash over her cheek. She wiped it away with the back of her hand and then placed her arm around Sonja's shoulder.

"I understand."

The next day they returned to the church at noon and waited until the doors swung open and men wearing black suits wheeled a plain black box down the aisle and up to a small altar. Soon, individuals and then groups of people stopped to greet Sonja and Thelma as they passed toward the unopened coffin, then retreated to the pews with no kneelers. Bishop Smith appeared behind a desk-like shelf, described the accomplishments of his life-long friend and asked people in the church to tell everyone what they remembered of Mr. West. People spoke, the congregation sang beautiful songs in harmony, and the process was repeated every couple of hours as more people arrived and some left.

The stained glass windows surrounding the congregation had glowed in the noonday sun, each brightening as the sun passed, and all dulled as the sun set. The congregation sang three cheerful songs that Thelma had never heard, even on Saturday Night Hit Parade she and Iggy watched on their new black-and-white television.

When dusk turned to night, the men in back suits lifted the coffin and carried it to the cemetery a few blocks away. Everyone followed holding lighted candles. At the gravesite, Bishop Smith took a small silver shovel from under his cassock and handed it to Sonja who tossed a shovel full dirt onto the lowered coffin. She handed it back to Bishop Smith who gave it to each mourner in turn, starting with Thelma. Thelma thought this symbolic action, as Sonja later explained, was crude and she didn't like to think of her father lying under the ground. That night they again slept in Mr. West's bed and Sonja cried. Thelma comforted her.

The following two weeks, Sonja and Thelma sorted through a lifetime of possessions, attended two plays and an opera, visited the church daily, ate at a French restaurant and traveled on busses with arms that attached electrical wires suspended over the road. The times Sonja spent with attorneys and real estate agents, Thelma wandered through a park near the West home that seemed nearly as large as her farm.

With an additional suitcase filled with heirlooms that Sonja insisted Thelma accept as gifts, the remainder of her father's affects to be shipped separately, Sonja and Thelma began their train ride home. This time, Thelma talked non-stop about all that she had seen and heard as they sat side-by-side and in the dining car. That night, after dressing for bed, they slept together, arms wrapped around each other, on the lower bunk.

CHAPTER FORTY-TWO
NEAR THE END

The fawn no longer had its adolescent stripes and was barely visible behind a screen of yellowed and twisted stalks, but the doe had emerged from the cornfield, tensed and nose aimed into the wind. Crouched behind a cluster of sumac, Freddie felt calm and confident as he held a bead on the larger animal with Iggy's twelve-gauge shotgun. The fawn sprinted off and the doe's forelegs buckled as Freddie pulled the trigger. Her rear hooves threw clods of dirt into the air as she struggled forward, but her effort only pushed her nose through the weeds and grass near the fence-line. Freddie thought about his family, and he became frightened and angry. Doris and Teddy hadn't come home last night, Thelma and Miss West were still in Philadelphia, and Iggy lied to him. His whole world seemed topsy-turvy. Why would Iggy lie about Doris spending the night at the farm? He looked toward the barn, expecting the shot would bring Iggy back.

Earlier that week, Iggy had told Freddie about doe with her fawn and asked him to bag her when hunting season opened. Iggy couldn't stand to kill anything other than rabbits or birds. As soon as Freddie was old enough to handle a shotgun, Svez delegated that task to him, and Arnie provided the rules for killing. *Ya can't be mad at the animal, and it gotta be his c'rect time to die.*

When Freddie arrived that Sunday morning, Iggy ran from the barn, shotgun under his arm and led Freddie to the field where he'd last sighted the deer.

"Doris and Teddy still here?" Drooping cobs slapped against Freddie's legs as he followed the deer tracks between the rows of corn, and Iggy followed close behind.

"Weren't ever here this morning." Iggy stopped and crossed to the next row where Freddie could hardly see him.

"I mean last night. Did they stay over last night?"

"They ain't here." Iggy reached across and pushed his gun toward Freddie. "Take it. I gotta go." He turned, put his hands in his pockets, and walked away. "Be right back."

The doe snorted and bled and kicked. Freddie leaned the gun against a fence post and took the knife from his belt. He slid the blade through the soft flesh under her neck. Although the slug had burst her skull, her heart would continue to beat until all her blood was drained. He stared at the quivering body and at the steam rising from the wound in her head. Then he sliced through her underside. With a final shudder, she belched out her intestines. They slid from her body and flattened the twisted cornstalks already stained red with her blood.

Freddie grimaced as he signed himself and looked skyward. Had his anger violated Arnie's rule about killing?

"You got her." Iggy panted as he ran toward Freddie, one of the straps on his overalls left undone. He stared at the carcass, and with a look of fear in his eyes, he turned and faced Freddie.

"Yeah." Freddie leered back at him. "Why'd you lie to me?" He wiped his knife on his pant leg and sheathed it. "I know they stayed here last night. Might still be up in Arnie's room, and you got their car hid some place." He felt the hardened leather that contained his knife. "Why the hell did you have to lie 'bout it?"

Iggy took a plug of tobacco from his bib pocket and tore off a large piece with his teeth. He gagged and spit it onto the ground. He stared down, avoiding Freddie's glare.

"They must be here, because they weren't at her Ma's. Miss West ain't home, so they can't be there."

"Maybe they was." Iggy held the remaining tobacco as if frightened by it. "I can't remember."

"Are they still here?"

"I was in the barn 'til you drove up. Ain't seen them this morning." He put the plug back into his pocket. "Maybe they went to church."

"Are they gone?"

"Must be." Iggy continued to stare at the dead animal and the mess spread between its legs. "You want I should tell the butcher to make it into sausage?"

"Do what you want, but use your deer tag it if you plan to take it to town. I'm saving mine for the buck that's been eating Henry's corn. I'll take your shotgun for a day or two."

302

Freddie walked back to the house but hesitated at the porch door. Instead of going in, he walked around to Arnie's balcony and stared up at the window. Were they still up there, hiding? With his hand on the barrel of the shotgun, he stooped and grabbed a handful of acorns, tossed them and listened as they showered against the window and onto the floor under it. He thought he heard his son's voice but decided it was his imagination. He continued around the house as if it was a large wild animal, and he was stalking it. He stopped near the spot where the outhouse used to stand. Doris probably lied about Davie Smith tipping it over just 'cause they had worked together and teased a lot. *Worked together and teased a lot.* The thought developed into an image of them having sex in the storeroom. Why not? If what Fritz told him last night was true that he and Burt used to take turns... *All lies!* He kicked Thelma's lawn ornaments into the tall dry grass infested with thistles where he stomped them into the soft earth.

Holding the gun in front of him, he burst through the kitchen, ran up the stairs and stopped to listen at Iggy's bedroom door. He opened it and peered in. He stared at the single bed in the middle of the large room and thought about the time when all the boys slept there. When Freddie got too big for the crib in Thelma's room he got to sleep with Iggy. The quilt lay neatly folded as if Iggy hadn't recently slept there.

In the next room that had at different times belonged to Arnie, himself and finally Doris, he saw covers spilled half onto the floor, and Iggy's Sunday clothes lay scattered about the room. He refused to let his mind dwell on what might have happened there. But, what Fritz had told him made the unthinkable possible. All the other guys and now Iggy, too? After frantically looking for signs that Doris slept with him and finding none, he leaned the gun against the dresser, slumped onto the bed and lowered his head into his hands across his knees. He wept.

He felt Doris in the room with him, and he wanted her to cup her hands around his head and pull it to her breasts. He wanted to feel Teddy's tiny arms on his waist and small head on his lap. Suddenly, he realized he hadn't been dreaming.

"Where have you been all night?" He stood and shook loose from his wife and son. "I was scared that..." He couldn't admit to her or to himself what really frightened him. She hadn't come home with Teddy after his kindergarten class. When he had gone to fetch her at her mother's where she sometimes went after an argument, she wasn't there. But, Fritz was. Her stepfather's insults still rang in his ears. *What's the matter, plough boy, can't you keep tabs on your woman?* Although he sounded drunk, what he told Freddie about Doris and Burt might be true, but her sleeping with own stepfather had to be a lie. Or, was it?

"I was in no mood to fight with you last night, so me and Teddy came here instead of going home." She glanced around the room. "We slept in Thelma's bed last night. I needed to talk to Ma."

"Ma?" He looked at Iggy's crumpled nightshirt half covered with his quilt. "Why didn't he sleep in his own room?" A wave of shame made his whole body shudder.

"How would I know? Guess he just wanted to sleep in Arnie's old bed while Thelma's gone."

"Why would he do that?"

"Maybe he needed to talk to Arnie."

"Talk to Arnie?" Confusion overwhelmed him.

She put her hands on her hips and spit out the words, "You can't believe that Iggy 'n me..." She turned and stomped toward the door.

Freddie yelled "No," jumped up and grabbed Teddy's arm as he held the gun and began to teeter. "That's Daddy's. You're too little." He took it from Teddy, ejected two slugs into his hand and put them into his pocket. "Let's get outta here."

Doris leered at him, picked up Teddy who ran from his father and headed down stairs.

Freddie followed with the gun. "Maybe we could have lunch at Emma's or something."

Doris got into the passenger side of the pickup, hoisted Teddy to her lap and slammed the door. She rolled down the window and yelled to Freddie who walked toward them, the stock of his shotgun nearly dragging on the ground.

"Well, are we going to have lunch or not?"

Freddie wrapped an old blanket around the gun and tossed it into the back of his pickup. He opened the door on the driver's side but didn't get in. "Where's the car?"

"Iggy took it to his neighbor's place."

Freddie felt confused, and then a wave of anger swept over him.

"It weren't his fault. I told him to hide it."

"Why'd you get him to do that?"

"Just didn't want you to find me, I guess." She appeared offended. "Well, are we gonna have lunch or not?"

He glanced at her and then toward the tractor coming from the field with the deer draped over the bucket in front. He felt he should tell Iggy he was sorry, but got into the pickup and drove off instead.

When they got to the café it was busy, and the last booth was the only one available, which suited Freddie just fine. He was surprised to see Davie Smith tending the bar and grill because he had gone off to college about the time Doris got pregnant and had to quit. *Was that just a coincidence?* The two of them in the storeroom flashed across his mind, and he chided himself for his lack of trust.

"Ain't he gonna take our order? We was here before some of them guys." Freddie directed his frustration at what he considered bad service. "Is he avoiding us?"

"He's just busy. Maybe I should help."

"No." Freddie slapped the table. "You stay here." He felt people stare at him. "That's his job. You ain't worked here for a long time, and you ain't gonna start now."

"You know, Davie's one of the guys who tipped the outhouse," she mumbled as she ran a bobby pin through a tuft of her hair.

"You just made that up to get me mad at him." He gazed at her and then at his son. "I knew Davie when he was Teddy's age. He'd never do that to me." He smiled at the memory. "Used to sneak to school at recess 'cause we didn't have any kindergarten back then." He wished he hadn't smiled because he was still angry with Doris, and now with Davie. "Fritz told me a bunch of stuff 'bout you and him."

"Fritz." Doris slid the sugar bowl out of Teddy's reach. "He don't even know Davie."

"I mean that other guy. The one whose nose I busted."

"We settled that before Teddy was born. Why are you digging up that old dirt? And, when did you talk to Fritz?"

"Last night, when I couldn't find you. Your mom weren't home." He felt her glare as he stared at his hands. "Fritz was there."

"What lies did he tell about me this time?"

"Weren't lies." Freddie peered at her without raising his head. "He swore everything was true."

"You know he's out to get me." She held a napkin to her mouth and wiped Teddy's fingers with it. "Don't you believe a thing he told you."

Freddie slid from the booth and stood up. "I'm gonna tell that kid to get his ass over here right now."

He felt something sharp against his leg and realized he hadn't taken the gutting knife out of the sheath on his belt. Other hunters, wearing bright orange jump suits, gathered around booths and tables and discussed the kill they intended before the day was out. Freddie disliked killing animals and hated those who did it for sport or bragged about it later. He felt violated when strangers flooded the woods throughout the county during the day and proudly displayed their trophies on the fenders and luggage racks of their vehicles on their way back to the city.

He walked out to his pickup, pulled the knife from its sheath and examined it. A brown hair from the deer had crusted with black blood near the handle. He picked it off and rolled it between his thumb and index finger until it formed a round wad that fit under his fingernail. He tossed the knife onto the front seat, stalked back into the café and called to Davie behind the bar.

"'Bout time you took my order, ain't it?"

"You haven't been here but a minute. I saw you just now walk through that door."

"That was me. What about them?"

"Who?"

Freddie pointed to corner of the room where Teddy peeked over the high-back booth, then ducked out of sight.

"I didn't know anyone was sitting back there. I'm really busy with all these hunters, and I'm stuck here alone."

"Kin I bum a pinch?" Freddie pointed to the circle outlined in David's shirt pocket.

"Sure. It's Copenhagen." He handed Freddie the round tin of snuff, and said, "I'm trying to quit smoking."

Freddie tapped the tin cover with his knuckle, opened it and took a two-finger pinch. He deposited the bloody hairball from under his fingernail deep into the remaining contents of the can. He closed the lid, handed it back to David and pointed to the small head that appeared and disappeared over the back of the far booth.

"My boy, Teddy. He's 'bout as old as you were when you snuck over to the country school at recess time. Born 'bout the time you went off to that college." He placed his fingers between his lip and his teeth but didn't let loose of the snuff. He put his hand down by his side and brushed it onto his pants.

"I'm leaving again. This time tomorrow, I'll be in Chicago." He looked toward the far booth where a woman's hands now bounced Freddie's son up and down. "How about letting Doris help 'til I get caught up?"

"How 'bout taking our order, and getting us some food." He walked toward his booth but turned and yelled, "I know it was you." People standing nearby stopped talking and faced him. "That night in Svez's yard. It was you." Heads appeared above the backs of booths. "I ain't done nuthin' to deserve that." He hammered his fist onto a tabletop and splattered the half-filled beverage glasses. "'Specially in front of my wife, Iggy, and Thelma." He pointed toward the door. "You go on to your fancy job in Chicago, and don't come back. You hear?" For a moment he wished he hadn't taken his knife back to the truck.

Doris stood and scooped Teddy from the booth. She stepped between Freddie and David who had grabbed an empty Coke bottle and leaned across the bar.

"Lost my appetite." She grabbed his arm and pulled him toward the door. "Let's get outta here."

Freddie broke her grip and beckoned David forward with hand gestures.

Doris stopped at the door, walked back to Freddie and touched his face. "Please, let's go."

Freddie backed to the door while he glared at David, turned and walked to his pickup. He slid behind the wheel, started the engine and then jumped back out. He yanked at the blanket covering the shotgun, and it rolled toward him. He picked up the gun, shoved it into the cab next to Teddy who scrambled onto his mother's lap and jammed the transmission into low gear.

"Gotta keep it handy, in case I spot that buck that's been eating my corn."

That night, Freddie lay in bed and listened to the sounds of the farm, a harmony of animals blended into the singsong background of the whirring windmill. Something seemed wrong. He reached over and found Doris' place in his bed empty and cold. Earlier that night when Teddy had fussed, she said it was probably a nightmare. She slid out from under the covers and wrapped her robe around her naked body. She hadn't come back. He threw off the covers, slipped bare feet into his shoes and went down the stairs and out the door. He unbuttoned the front of his long johns and flapped the moist wool to release the sweat that suddenly developed. He shivered from the cold that spread throughout his body, and he created circles in the frost on the ground as he urinated. The whitened metal on the windmill tower glistened from the light of the half moon, and his eyes followed the missing vane in the fan as it rotated, its cadence interrupted. He located the broken piece, half on and half over the edge of the platform. He wanted to climb the tower and make it sound proper.

Still holding his penis, he wanted to finish what Doris had started and he rejected earlier in bed, but he knew it was fruitless.

He blamed the cold air as his genitals retracted, and he defiantly flung off the top half of his long johns, kicked off his shoes and stepped out of the bottom half. He wandered to the ladder and took the first step when he heard Doris' voice.

"What're you doing out here naked in the cold?"

He pondered, then stepped down and walked back to the house, his underwear still heaped beside the markings he had made on the ground. Back in bed, Doris warmed and enlivened his body and they consummated their frustration, their confusion, their anger.

As the sun peeked through their bedroom window, Freddie thought about the events of the previous day and remembered the buck that would be breakfasting on his corn. He dressed and went outside to retrieve his shoes, then hung his underwear on a rung of the tower ladder for the sun to thaw and dry. He walked to the pickup and grabbed the shotgun. The metal felt cold but not wet. He loaded two twelve-gauge slugs although he seldom needed more than one, and then he took the last two shells from the box and shoved them into the pocket of his overalls.

The first shell exploded the buck's front leg and the second severed its neck but caused no damage to the twelve-point rack on its head. Doris and Teddy waved as they drove past on their way to Teddy's kindergarten. He stood by the carcass and waved, still holding the gun.

He completed his chores, gutted the deer and greased the machinery to pick the corn not already eaten by the blackbirds and wild animals. He decided to confront Doris 'bout Fritz and Burt taking turns with her. He brooded at the kitchen table and waited, but she was late. Shouldn't take that long to drop off a kid at school and come back home. He slammed his fist on the table. Davie! Why did he run away 'bout the time Doris got pregnant? And when he saw Teddy yesterday, he got a notion to run away again. Freddie fought back a thought too hideous to consider. But when he closed his eyes, he saw his son's face, Davie's face. He heard a car door slam and gritted his teeth. When he opened his eyes, Doris stood in the doorway chewing on a pop sickle stick.

"Don't take all day to get the kid to school," he growled, and stared at the fingers of his hands laced tightly together.

"I just stopped to talk to some friends at Emma's." Doris took off her coat, hung it on a hook and spit the splintered wood into the trashcan. "You needn't get so bent out of shape about it."

"Who'd you see there?"

"Well, if you gotta know, I stopped to apologize to Davie for the way you treated him yesterday."

"He's 'sposed to be gone and you're 'sposed to be home."

"Me and Teddy saw him walk into the café so we stopped to talk. Said he needed to buy cigarettes because Copenhagen snuff made him sick."

"I did that to him."

"Huh?"

"I made him sick."

"You made him mad, that's what you did."

"You got Teddy to school late."

"Yeah. His teacher was mad 'bout it, too." She smirked. "I just blamed his coming late on his daddy."

Freddie jumped up and ran for his gun.

CHAPTER FORTY-THREE
IGGY EMERGES

The phone rang at the rectory while Father Reinhardt was praying over his evening meal, and Stella excused herself to answer it. When she returned with the terrible news her face was as white as a ghost. Had Jesus' last supper been interrupted, perhaps there would be no Eucharist for Shamus to take to those who strayed, and even that probably wouldn't save Freddie Tate's tortured soul. As he drove to Freddie's farm, Shamus clasped his hand to his breast pocket to feel the comfort of the paten that held the sacred host. Perhaps a miracle would allow Freddie a final breath for confession, absolution and a morsel of the Body of Christ to take with him to eternity. Shamus had accepted the theology of final impenitence as the only unforgivable sin but, until tonight, he had never been confronted with a probable example. Suicide needn't be an unrepented sin, or possibly not a sin at all under certain circumstances. He couldn't think of anything that would excuse Freddie from the consequences of what he had done. God would sort through his motives and hopefully find some redemption. He drove into the Tate yard and greeted the sheriff who leaned over the hood of his car filling out reports.

"That was quick. Seems like I just called you." The sheriff removed his sunglasses and gazed around as if bewildered by the darkening sky. "We're waiting for the coroner to sign the death certificate." He beckoned toward a black hearse under an oak tree, the driver slouched down in the seat. "I'm sorry I couldn't make the bodies more presentable for you. Freddie is in the barn and Doris is in the house."

Shamus thanked him and hurried to the barn, unconcerned about the physical mess that awaited him. He knew what a shotgun could do to a body but, throughout his entire vocation, he hadn't been called upon to deal with a possibly damned soul. Had he eaten his supper, it would have left him when he saw Freddie's body. He mentally reconstructed the part of Freddie's face that was missing and whispered an act of contrition into an undamaged ear. He anointed the body with holy oil. What had brought Freddie to such a level of desperation? Loss of faith? Of hope? Or, was it anger? He left the barn feeling God may have forgiven Freddie, not because of any prayer he said over the corpse but because of Divine Grace. He knew he had to bury his body outside the gates of the cemetery alongside the graves of two other suicides that occurred when Father Busch was pastor at St. Alphonse. How could he convince Thelma that Freddie had been forgiven if he couldn't lie alongside his mother? Or her mother? And, what if Thelma and Miss West couldn't get back in time for the funeral? He would delay it as long as possible.

He walked to the house prepared for the probable carnage that he would find, but felt lighter of spirit. He had baptized Doris a few weeks back and started instructions in the Catholic faith so she could take communion with her son when he was old enough to receive. She told him that she wanted her conversion to be a gift to Freddie, hoping it would restore his trust in her commitment to their marriage. Shamus helped her with her examination-of-conscience in preparation for her first confession, and was assured all her indiscretions were long past. He saved her soul from damnation with absolution, but how could he have protected her from the insane act of a jealous husband? He felt the anger toward Freddie that eluded him when he anointed his body.

Doris was covered to her neck, saving Shamus the horror of what lay under the sheet. He imagined an expression of repose on her face and recited the act of contrition while he stared at closed eyelids. He took a wafer from the paten, held it to her lips and said, "The Body of Christ." He then placed it on his tongue and repeated the incantation. Swallowing, he whispered in her ear, "That was your first Holy Communion." The gift she hoped would surprise Freddie could now be presented to God with a plea for his salvation. God will certainly listen to her humble supplication. With a heavy heart, he completed his priestly function and returned to the sheriff who sat on the seat of the open patrol car door with his feet on the running board, smoking his pipe.

"Completed your rituals, Father?" The Sheriff's pipe gurgled and the coals reflected on the stubble under his nose.

312

Shamus felt dazed. "Yes, they're in God's hands now." The sheriff nodded and grinned, the stem of his pipe clenched alongside a missing tooth. Smoke drifted through the gap. Shamus returned to his car wondering what luck Stella and Mildred had with finding a ride to break the news to Iggy. Stella told him that, although Sonja and Thelma were out of town, he needn't worry. Shamus never doubted his sister's ingenuity. They agreed to meet at the Rastner farm when he finished. He drove a mile down the road to the neighbor who had found the bodies and called the sheriff. They had picked up Teddy at school and taken him to their home, not telling him about his parent's deaths. Shamus was sure Teddy suspected something serious had happened because of the change in routine, and he prepared to break the news to him. He approached Teddy who was playing with the neighbor children under their yard light.

"Do you know who I am?" He worried his black cassock would frighten the boy.

"Yeah?" Teddy kept his head down but didn't back away.

"Would you like to go with me to see Uncle Iggy?"

"Iggy?" Teddy looked bewildered.

"Will you go with me?"

"Yeah." Teddy climbed over Shamus' lap, gazed through the open window and waved to the children who stopped playing, their heads following as Teddy and Shamus sped out the driveway.

****

Frank Lorenz squinted at the oncoming headlights and remembered the concern his wife, Gloria, had about his driving when his nerves were frayed. He barely knew Freddie Tate but, when he hung up the receiver after talking to Mildred, everyone at the dinner table agreed that his face had turned as white as a sheet. He didn't feel that he should ask Victor Cunningham, his dinner guest, to drive, and he wanted to do this favor for Mildred. He drove past the driveway to the rectory, stopped and backed up. He reversed the car and faced Victor. "I almost forgot to pick up Stella. Shamus is busy with the bod—Freddie and his wife." He flashed the headlights on high beam and cast Stella's shadow against the front door as she closed and locked it.

"Thank you for getting here so quickly," she said as she opened a rear door and slid to the middle of the seat.

Frank kept a white-knuckle grip on the steering wheel, nodded and backed out into the street.

"Oh, not that way." Stella pulled herself forward and placed her head between Frank and Victor. "We have to pick up Mildred at Sonja's house. She'd never forgive us, let alone be able to explain to Thelma why she wasn't along to tell Iggy about his brother's death.

Frank backed the Pontiac into the driveway and headed out in the opposite direction, hitting curbs on both sides of the road. He stopped in front of Sonja West's house.

"I'll have to get her." Stella reached for the armrest, pulled herself to the door and pushed it open. "Mildred won't let anyone else into Sonja's house while she's gone." She clutched her knees and slowly dropped her feet to the ground. She stood, brushed the back of her coat and walked to Sonja's front door.

During the drive to Iggy's place, Mildred alternately thanked Frank for the favor and apologized for the intrusion. Three times, she explained that Sonja was gone and that she hesitated to take her car and would never drive after dark.

"That's perfectly all right. Two ladies have no business driving these back roads alone at night." Frank slowed the Pontiac to a near stop, as he opened the window to see the intersection more clearly.

****

Iggy was encouraging a newborn calf to suckle when light flashed through the opened top half of the barn door. He went to investigate, and saw a large car, headlights extinguished, parked under the yard light. Obviously, someone was lost and needed directions. Both rear car-doors swung open, and two women emerged. The driver's door opened and, in the interior light, he saw two men remain seated. As the women approached, he recognized Mildred Bushman and Stella Reinhardt. Neither had been to the farm since Pa's funeral. He felt the air leave his lungs and, as he tried to suck it back, his tongue blocked his throat. Thelma and Miss West musta been killed in a train wreck. The barn radio said nothing about it, but that was the news they came to tell him.

"Let's go into the house where we can talk." Stella spoke first.

"We kin talk in the barn." His voice opened his throat and a gust of air rushed in. "Gettin' killed might not sound so bad in the barn." His words, spoken between sobs, again depleted his air, and he inhaled in short bursts.

314

"You heard?" Mildred sounded surprised.

"I just know." He reached for his tobacco, changed his mind and dropped his hands to his side. The calf stumbled up to him and began sucking on his thumb. He knelt and put his arms around the animal's neck. "Are they dead?"

"Yes." Stella extended her arms but didn't touch him. "Freddie didn't mean to do it."

"Freddie?" Iggy stood, and stared blankly at Stella and then at Mildred.

"And Doris." Mildred's head drooped, but her eyes continued to meet his.

He felt his stomach about to erupt. "I gotta go." He ran to the far end of the barn, climbed the ladder all the way to the cupola and yelled at the top of his lungs. Crows nesting in the vents fluttered their wings and flew away. Two bats swooped above the mounds of hay in the loft. Tears burst from the corner of his eyes, but he didn't move to wipe them away. He was confused about who died and how, but he didn't want to come down to find out. He peered through the vents at the car with four figures standing around it.

Why wouldn't they go away?

A second car entered the driveway, and he saw Father Reinhardt get out, walk around the car and let a small boy out the passenger side. When he recognized Teddy, he knew Freddie and Doris were dead. Another orphan in the family, and this time it was up to him to welcome the child. He crawled down the ladder, walked out the barn and held out his arms to catch Teddy who ran toward him. With tears streaming down his cheek, Teddy wrapped himself around Iggy's neck. Iggy watched the intruders, their shadows growing longer as they walked toward him.

"How'd they die?"

"It was an accident."

Iggy recognized Mr. Lorenz from the bank. "It weren't no accident." Iggy held Teddy tight. "He shot hisself, didn't he. I let him take my shotgun. He wanted to kill a deer, but he killed hisself instead." He squeezed his eyes shut. "And her, too?"

"I'm afraid so." Father Reinhardt reached for the child, but Iggy turned his back to him. "I gotta tell Thelma. And Miss West." He turned to face the group. "How can I tell them something that terrible?" He rocked Teddy back and forth. "They'll be back tomorrow. I gotta get them at the depot."

"We'll go with you, if you like."

Iggy recognized Victor Cunningham. "No. I gotta be the one to tell them."

"We can take care of Teddy while you're gone." Father Reinhardt again reached to take the boy.

"No." Teddy crawled higher onto Iggy's shoulder and nearly toppled him as he shied from the priest. "I stay with Iggy."

"He's right. We gotta do this together." He pulled Teddy free from his grasp and held him away. "You're my Godchild. You and me gotta do this." He turned to the group clustered in front of him. "You guys can go home now. Me and Teddy want to feel bad by ourselves."

Frank walked back to his car and got in. Victor opened the back door and held Mildred's arm as she dropped to the seat. He sat next to Frank, took off his specs and wiped his eyes. The car seemed to drift to the road. A red light flashed through a cloud of exhaust as the car turned and headed toward town.

Still holding Teddy, Iggy stood outside the circle of light from the single bulb atop the pole. He waited for Father Reinhardt to utter a prayer and sign a blessing before he joined his sister at the car. They drove away. Iggy carried Teddy to the barn where the calf had poked its head between slats in the cow pen as it tried to reach its mother. He set Teddy in the manger and hoisted the calf into the birthing pen. The cow, still lying in the blood-soaked straw, licked her calf while it knelt and nosed her teats. Iggy sat alongside Teddy until he was sure the boy was asleep. Then he carried him into the house. Iggy lay next to Teddy in Thelma's bed and stared out the window at the stars.

1995

"Thelma?" I stood in the porch, peered into the kitchen through an opened door and announced, "It's David Smith." Without answering or making eye contact, she remained seated and gestured for me to enter. I hesitated, wondering if this visit was a good idea. "Thank you for seeing me on such short notice."

She pointed to the chair to her right, got up and lumbered to the counter near the sink where Mr. Coffee gurgled and dripped into its glass decanter. Cupboards covered the wall where a door used to open to a pantry. Electricity had replaced wood for cooking, and the spout from a faucet that arched over a white porcelain sink had replaced the pump, water pail and dipper. A table that accommodated ten people now seated only four.

"Your kitchen certainly looks different from the last time I was here."

Watery gray eyes followed her hands as she set saucer and then cup in front of me. "I don't remember you ever being in our house." She sat, held her cup, half full and probably cold, with both hands.

"When I was in high school, your father hired me at harvest time and invited me to stay for supper." Embarrassed that a neighbor less than a mile away would set foot in their house only once, I tried to sound casual. "As a matter of fact, you told me to sit here on Arnie's chair." I patted the arm of the unusual chair and noticed its counterpart across the table where Svez used to sit. "I joked that his ghost might still be in his room upstairs."

"You said his body." Her voice sounded cold.

"Pardon."

"You said we kept his body upstairs in his room. Said the kids at school laughed about it."

My face flushed and I wished myself back at Emma's or, better yet, safely in Chicago.

"You still teaching school?" Her eyes met mine for the first time.

I shook my head. Why would she remember or even know about that short period in my life?

"I used to have a good friend who was a teacher." Her voice wavered. "She gave up her career when they closed our country school."

"Miss West." Her name came to me instantly. "She was never my teacher, but I used to sneak away from my yard and join the kids during recess." A private memory flashed, and I saw Freddie's face as he reached up to me. "Freddie…" I couldn't complete the thought, or at least I was unable to share it with Thelma. I didn't have to.

"Yes, Freddie went to her school. So did Iggy and I. She taught there a long time."

A moan too metallic to be human or animal pierced the silence and interrupted our separate memories. My loss of composure must have been obvious.

"The breeze just shifted." She glanced across the table toward the opened door. "The windmill needs greasing, but Iggy can't climb up there any more."

Until that moment, I hadn't realized what else seemed strange when I drove into their yard; the cacophony of animals bustling about. My eyes followed her gaze and locked onto the whirring blades on top of the metal tower near the barn. Like an animal awakened perhaps from a dream, it repositioned itself and fell back into the quiet of sleep.

"Why did he do it, Thelma?"

Her eyes glossed like she, too, had awakened from a dream. "Maybe he loved her too much." A tear glistened as it followed a crease down her cheek, but she made no move to dab it.

"I'm sorry. I have no right to pry into a matter that sensitive."

"You're right." She blinked back a second tear. "It's none of your business." She inhaled audibly and her voice became animated. "I haven't seen you or talked to you since you went away to college, except one time at your mother's funeral. I didn't know what to say, so I paid my respects and left. I know what it's like to loose parents, and Freddie."

"I'm sorry I haven't kept in touch." Although I was sincere, I felt a tinge of sarcasm in my voice. I sat straight in my chair and faced her. "Part of me is still here, and the rest of me wants to come back to find what was left behind." I paused, then lowered my head. "I barely knew Freddie. I was hoping you would tell me more about him."

"You going to write another one of your books? About him this time?" She glared. "About Iggy and me?"

"You read my novels?"

"Reading is mostly what I've done since Sonja died."

"But, you asked about my teaching."

"I wanted to gauge the size of your ego."

"Did I pass?"

"Loneliness is the test of one's character. We both understand that."

"And Freddie?" He was reaching toward me across time and space.

"He wasn't lonely. He was a loner. There is a difference."

I nodded as if I understood the distinction, curbed my curiosity and respected the pause that followed.

"Teddy was born a few weeks before Pa died, so he got to see Freddie's son. He had a big funeral."

"Your father?" The multiple tracks of her memory were hard to follow.

"Yes. Freddie's funeral was small because he couldn't be buried in a Catholic cemetery." She shook her head, and the deep grooves on her face accented what looked like a smile. "Pa really liked you when you were a kid. Thought your parents were uppity, but you made him laugh." The lines reversed, and I felt her anger emerge. "Why did you do it, with those kids that night?"

Shocked, I paused and took a deep breath. "I was just a kid who wanted to entertain everyone, sometimes going too far."

"At first, Pa refused to believe you were with the boys who tipped our outhouse. He had Iggy burn it where it lay, and he told us to forget it." She turned toward a picture on the wall of Freddie and Doris. Her voice sounded distant. "I forgave you, too."

"And Freddie?" I felt like a small boy asking if a friend liked him.

"Freddie had bigger problems."

"Like Doris?"

She changed the subject. "We didn't have Pa's wake at home. He wanted to be laid out in our front room rather than some old funeral parlor where nobody lives. Only dead people. When Ma died, we took turns sitting up with her all night." She stood, walked to the door and gazed outside the house. "People just don't do that any more."

"I'd better go." Had my interest in Freddie been a selfish effort to gather material for my next protagonist? Perhaps, Thelma understood my true motive better than I, and it shamed me. She followed me half way to my car.

"Stop here tomorrow morning and talk to Iggy." Her tone more a command than an invitation. "He's at Freddie's place today."

I stared back at her. "Freddie's place?"

"Before Henry died, he kept his word and left him the farm. Doris never took to a rural lifestyle, but Freddie had it whipped into a first class dairy operation before…" She brushed strands of white hair from her eyes. "Freddie's son, we call him Theo, and his wife live there." She wandered to the area where the outhouse once stood and tugged at some thistles that grew in a patch of grass, darker green than the rest of the lawn.

The next day Thelma met me at the door, touched my elbow and led me to Arnie's chair. Iggy remained seated at the head of the table and began a conversation that he probably rehearsed before I arrived.

"Freddie was a born farmer. Next to Arnie he was the best darn farmer there ever was." Iggy's eyes glistened. "Many's the time I watched him talk to an animal, and I'll be darned if that creature didn't understand what he said." When our eyes met, he slouched back, and his gaze dropped to his coffee cup.

I told him about the schoolyard incident where Freddie treated me so kindly. He responded by nodding his head as he inhaled in rapid bursts.

"Animals and kids. Those were Freddie's soft spots." His head continued to nod as if for emphasis. "He mostly kept quiet around grown ups." He glanced toward his sister and qualified his description of their brother. "Except around us family. And Doris."

"You should have seen him when he first met Doris at the library." Thelma flashed a grin with a hint of titillation. "She teased him mercilessly. He tugged on his cap with both hands until it nearly pulled in half."

I felt a slight thrill reminiscent from my pubescence when this saucy teenager flirted with me at Emma's. She accused me of kissing girls and doing other things with them I had yet to fantasize let alone accomplish. An image of Doris as wife and mother preventing a fight between Freddie and me erased all sensual thoughts.

Iggy cut back in. "Remember how disappointed he was when Pa told me to return the book." He pointed toward the barn. "He climbed that tower and didn't come down 'til after dark."

I glanced at the windmill through the doorway and half expected it to squawk in support of their anecdote.

"Up on the ledge." Iggy indicated with his hand held above his head. "You gotta be careful 'cause one of them vanes might knock you off." He lowered his arm and his eyes followed. "It's a long way down." He held his hand near the floor and his face peered up at me. "Freddie went up there when he wanted to be alone." He sat straight in his chair, and I recognized Svez. "Said it made him feel good to see everything all at once." He faced Thelma. "I had to bring him down when he was just a kid."

Thelma said, "He had another place where he would sit at night and think." Her gaze moved from me to Iggy. "The balcony you and Freddie built for Arnie."

"Yeah, the roof with no porch under it." His voice became solemn. "Arnie died," he made the sign of the cross, "and Freddie went to live with his pa." He brightened and placed both hands on the table. "Doris came to stay with me, Pa and Thelma."

"Doris and I worked together at Emma's," I lowered my eyes, "until I left for college." My need to insert myself into their story embarrassed me.

"We didn't even know they was courtin'." Iggy blushed and picked at a callous on one of his fingers.

Thelma touched her brother's wrist. "Freddie stopped at the cafe every time he visited with Henry at the nursing home."

Iggy pulled his hands back and tucked them behind the bib of his overalls. "Henry was Freddie's real pa. Had a stroke and he couldn't live at the farm no more."

Thelma nodded. "Weekends that we thought she was with her mom in Harrington, she actually stayed with Freddie. He lived alone in Henry's house. Freddie was smitten with her, and I think she learned to love him." She shook her head and blinked. "But, they weren't meant for each other."

"Henry died." Iggy freed one hand and signed himself a second time. "After his funeral, Freddie and Doris got hitched. Not by Father Reinhardt, but some judge in the courthouse." He shook his head. "Didn't know they could do that." He blushed. "Thought she might be pregnant 'cause they did it so secret-like. But, she wasn't."

"Doris wasn't cut-out to be a farmer's wife. They realized that but tried to make the best of it." Thelma gazed off into the distance. "She and Teddy sometimes ran away for a few days."

"Where did they go?"

"Occasionally, she stayed here with Iggy and me, sometimes at her mom's place or with Miss West. She and Sonja became quite close friends." Thelma swallowed, stood and walked toward the front room.

Iggy's gaze followed her. "Miss West died a couple of years back. She was very old."

Thelma turned and said, "Iggy, why don't you get the magazine Sonja gave you. It's upstairs in the store room." Without any hesitation, Iggy left the room. She slunk back into her chair, took a long breath and produced what must have been a well-kept secret from somewhere deep inside. "Doris wasn't always faithful to Freddie. She had a brief encounter with an old boy friend just before they got married. We all knew it, and Freddie accepted her anyway. But, her stepfather kept needling Freddie about it, even claiming that the relationship hadn't ended." Thelma blushed. "I think he might have molested her, too."

I refrained from asking any of the thousand questions racing about in my mind, not wanting to break her train of thought. Her eyes glazed, but she didn't share any of her memories with me.

Iggy came back and laid a dog-eared magazine on the table. I read the name across the cover. *Ignatius Donnelly*. His bright, dark eyes aimed back at me. "Your real name is Ignatius, isn't it?"

Iggy nodded, but his head moved slowly forward and back until it gradually stilled. "Miss West used to call me that. She called Freddie, Frederick." He furled his brow as if he had just discovered something. "Thelma got no other name, just Thelma."

Just Thelma. Perhaps that was how her family considered her. Maybe that's how she thought of herself, but I began to realize how much she had accomplished. She nurtured four generations of her family, and forced me to question my motives.

When I drove back to town, I realized I had learned none of the details of Freddie's death. It had become less important than the fact that he had lived and made a mark on his world. Nights in Chicago reminded me how much clearer the stars shone back in Minnesota. I remembered the childhood game *Star Light, Star Bright, I Hope To See the Ghost Tonight*. Those ghosts no longer plagued me.

I called Thelma to thank her and Iggy for their time, and she asked me to tell Freddie's story. I returned to Bovine with a series of questions and a tape recorder. Her only concern was that I might be influenced by gossip about Sonja or, worse yet, not include her at all. Obviously, she assumed I would treat Freddie fairly. I assured her Sonja West's character would be left unscathed. When I hinted that it would be more her story than Freddie's, she smiled.

"And about Pa?" She paused. "Guess I'll have to wait to read your book."

When I sent her a copy of the completed manuscript, she returned the cover page with a hand written note scratched across it. *This isn't exactly how it all happened, but it could have.*

BIOGRAPHY

After a teaching career in suburbia, Roger Storkamp developed a nostalgia for the rural Minnesota setting of his childhood and adolescent years. *Away to college* was his excuse to escape as a young man and *back to his origins* is an effort to endear himself to the people who helped mold his personality. The characters and their roles in his fictional Minnesota setting were created from the attitudes, values and foibles he has learned to cherish and respect.

Storkamp holds a Master of Arts degree from the University of Wisconsin and did post graduate work at Pepperdine University in California, Nova University in Florida, Fordham University in New York, and the University of Texas, El Paso. He taught high school English and education courses at United States International University in San Diego. He earned a Doctor of Arts degree from East Coast University in Florida.

Roger and his wife Laurie currently reside in Las Vegas, Nevada.